continued . . .

"With the imaginative magic, deadly creatures, and alien landscapes as varied and well-written as before, *Fortress Frontier* massively benefits from this new main character stepping into the spotlight. Bookbinder is quite sympathetic as an administrator who is suddenly torn from his family and thrust into a seemingly impossible situation where he must step up as both a leader and a soldier if he's to survive."   —Examiner.com

"There are some truly surprising twists and turns . . . If you enjoyed Myke Cole's debut, you should love this sequel."
—Tor.com

"This generation's *The Forever War* . . . Myke Cole is the most exciting SFF author to come along since Joe Abercrombie."
—*Neth Space*

"The action is again pretty much nonstop, the narrative is tense, energetic, and above all *convincing*."   —*SFBook Reviews*

"There is not a dull moment to be found within the pages of *Shadow Ops: Fortress Frontier*. Action-packed, smart, and entertaining."   —*Pat's Fantasy Hotlist*

PRAISE FOR

SHADOW OPS: CONTROL POINT

"A great book."
—Patrick Rothfuss, *New York Times* bestselling author of
The Wise Man's Fear

"Hands down, the best military fantasy I've ever read."
—Ann Aguirre, *USA Today* bestselling author of
Perdition

"Fast-paced and thrilling from start to finish, *Control Point* is military fantasy like you've never seen it before. Cole's wartime experience really shows in the gritty reality of army life and in the exploration of patriotism as the protagonist wrestles with the line between the law and what he sees as right."
—Peter V. Brett, international bestselling author of
The Daylight War

SHADOW OPS:
BREACH ZONE

MYKE COLE

ACE BOOKS, NEW YORK

THE BERKLEY PUBLISHING GROUP
Published by the Penguin Group
Penguin Group (USA) LLC
375 Hudson Street, New York, New York 10014

USA • Canada • UK • Ireland • Australia • New Zealand • India • South Africa • China

penguin.com

A Penguin Random House Company

SHADOW OPS: BREACH ZONE

An Ace Book / published by arrangement with the author

Ace Books are published by The Berkley Publishing Group.
ACE and the "A" design are trademarks of Penguin Group (USA) LLC.

For information, address: The Berkley Publishing Group,
a division of Penguin Group (USA) LLC,
375 Hudson Street, New York, New York 10014.

ISBN: 978-0-425-25637-4

PUBLISHING HISTORY
Ace mass-market edition / February 2014

PRINTED IN THE UNITED STATES OF AMERICA

10 9 8 7 6 5 4 3 2 1

Cover art by Michael Komarck.
Cover design by Annette Fiore DeFex.
Interior text design by Laura K. Corless.
Map by Priscilla Spencer.
SOC coat of arms by Paul Jacobsen / Tactical Graphic Design.
Crest and icon artwork by Paul Jacobsen—Tactical-Graphic-Design.com.

For Gotham, whose shadows gave me a hero, a crucible, and, at long last, a home.

ACKNOWLEDGMENTS

There is no "i" in "team." There's no "i" in "Myke," either. The team in this case is vast beyond counting and includes my family and friends, the tireless and dedicated staff at Ace, Headline, and JABberwocky, and the revelers of the movable feast we know as the Drinklings. It also includes the artists—some friends, some strangers—who daily give me something to fight for: John Scalzi, Chuck Wendig, Howard Tayler, Neil Gaiman, Molly Crabapple, Joe Hill, and countless others. When I think about dying for my country, you are the country I'd die for. China Miéville as well, revolutionary, intellectual, the most inspirational man I've never met. Thanks also to the New York City Police Department, the thin blue line I am so intensely proud to be a part of. Thanks also to the men and women of US Coast Guard Station New York, the most dedicated band of people I've ever had the privilege to serve alongside. You daily wade through trials that would make lesser people throw up their hands; you stoically accept a task where success is invisible and failure unforgettable, a shining example of the person I hope to be. Thanks also to Andrew and Megan Liptak, Major General Richard Schneider, Lieutenant Colonel Brett Cox, and the Corps of Cadets at Norwich University. Looking at your serried ranks, I know the future of our military is in good hands.

Thanks to my beta readers not thanked in previous volumes, Mark Lawrence and Justin Landon, brilliant and busy people who carved out time to help a friend in need. Thanks also to fandom, the congoers and bloggers and social-media allies who shore me up with humor, admonition, and relentless pedantry. My tribe, miles deep and eternal.

And Pete, as always. You're probably sick of the constant gratitude, but you'll have to deal. What's owed is owed, and life's too short and uncertain to leave the important things unsaid. Thanks.

NOTE

A glossary of military acronyms and vocabulary, as well as a brief guide to magical schools, can be found at the back of this book.

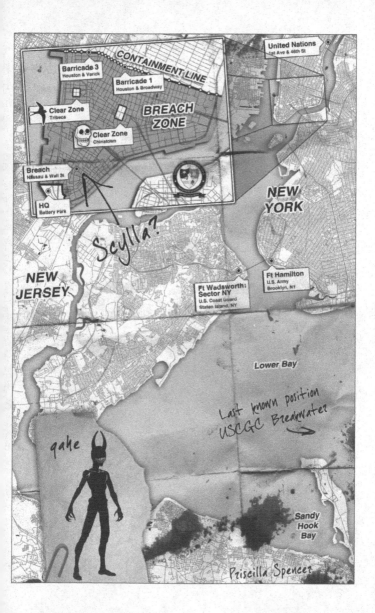

CHAPTER 1
IT'S GOOD TO BE HOME

My predecessor's involvement in the Shadow Coven and FOB Frontier scandals has shaken the public's faith in honest government, and rightly so. But this is no time to point fingers. Former President Walsh will have his day in court, and like all of you, I am looking forward to seeing the truth come out. Today is a day for looking ahead, for starting down the road to restoring the people's faith in their government, in matters of arcane security in particular. Today, I recommit myself to enforcing the provisions of the McGauer-Linden Act with total certainty, severity, and transparency.

—Vice President Howard Porter
On his inauguration as president
following the impeachment of President Walsh

Swift eased up the hood of his sweatshirt and kept his head down. The crowds in the Financial District were thick at lunchtime, hundreds of people with eyes on the pavement, on their way to grab cigarettes or food, or to run errands in the few precious minutes they had before heading back to their desks, the richest slaves in the world.

Swift sighed internally. He'd never been comfortable among the corporate wage serfs who made up most of the city, but a big crowd was best. It was easy to get lost in the throng, one more data point in a stream, nothing to draw the eye.

He felt his magical current thrumming. The scar of his ruined tattoo itched on his chest, an old reminder of older fights. He'd won them all and somehow still lost. His girlfriend, his baby were still gone, the man who'd killed them still alive.

He'd had Harlequin dead to rights, had looked down the barrel of a gun straight into his old enemy's eyes.

The moment had hovered, time frozen as Swift faced a pair of choices, each resulting in very different people. He'd let Harlequin go, watched him walk away, still breathing, and hoped the person he'd chosen to be was the better one. Even all this time later, he still wasn't sure.

He moved through the crowd, keeping his elbows in, not wanting to draw attention to himself by shoving anyone out of the way. At last, South Ferry Terminal hove into view, the water of the bay sparkling beyond.

Oscar Britton had wanted him to stay in the Source, to build a new life in the goblin village. Swift had insisted Britton send him back. The Supernatural Operations Corps had taken everything from him—his life, his love. They wouldn't take his home.

He'd found the broken remnants of the Houston Street Gang, the band of magic-using revolutionaries deemed criminals for their refusal to submit to government control. Criminals or no, they'd bloodied the government's nose for years until the SOC had replaced their beloved leader, Big Bear, with a monster. The deception caught them completely unawares, and the SOC had broken their spine, scattered them to the winds.

The survivors spent the intervening months hiding in the homes of sympathizers, trying to rebuild what they'd lost when Big Bear had turned out to be . . . someone else. Months of jumping at shadows, of desperately hoping the SOC had bigger fish to fry.

But Swift found time to come down to the water every day, to give himself a few minutes to look out over the glassy surface, to feel the breeze slide over his ears, whispering in his hair. Sometimes, he imagined it was his girlfriend Shai, speaking to him from beyond the grave.

Of course, it wasn't all fun and games. Swift allowed himself a quick glance around to make sure no one was watching, then headed back toward the posts that ringed the entrance to the South Ferry subway station.

He saw the can beside the third post, only got close enough to confirm it. Beer. Britton would be coming tomorrow. No can meant no visit. A soda can meant they'd been found out and had better run.

Swift made a mental note to tell the others. Britton promised that the moment would be coming when they could finally step out of the shadows, live free and open, but each time he visited, the answer was always the same: Be patient, wait. Things were taking time.

Most of the gang worshipped Britton, they would have waited until Judgment Day if he asked. But Swift was one of a growing number who were getting tired of waiting, and he still wasn't sure that Britton could be trusted. If Britton didn't . . .

Screaming reached him from uptown. It sounded like a lot of people. The crowd raised their heads, began moving north, bunching together, trying to see what the trouble was.

Swift cursed and went with them. He wasn't going to risk being the only person on the waterfront for the cops around the ferry terminal to grow suspicious of. Besides, curiosity was getting the better of him. He'd allow himself to go as far as Bowling Green, then disappear into the station once he'd gotten a look at what was going on. The tall buildings rose around him as he moved north, gray-white façades ornate with decorative stonework evoking Gothic cathedrals and European palaces. He glanced at the suit of the man in front of him, the fabric so fine that it nearly glowed. Such unimaginable wealth. So far beyond his reach. Not because he was lazy, not because he was stupid. Because he was Latent. Because he wouldn't knuckle his forehead and kill at the government's bidding. *I never had a chance, Shai. Just like you. I'm sorry.*

The crowd moved up past the entrance to the subway, and Swift went with them, driven more by curiosity than anything else, walking up Broadway until the crowd slowed to a stop as they turned onto Wall Street.

A shout echoed through the corridor formed by the buildings, followed by a sound like overripe fruit being smashed against stone.

The crowd stopped and began to surge backward, the people around him shouting. Swift fought to hold himself upright as they jostled against him, carrying him backward. He stumbled once, almost went down, was held up by the tight packing of the bodies around him.

It would be so easy to use his Aeromancy, to Bind his magic and rise above the panicked mob. But he couldn't risk it. To be discovered now would be to undo everything he'd fought for since he'd escaped the Suitability Assessment Section. He Drew his magic anyway, kept it ready, just in case. It rushed to him, rising in his own gut, buoyed by the panicked crowd. He could feel his heart racing and struggled to calm it. Limbic Dampener would have made the process easier, but only the SOC had access to the expensive drug. He'd fought against the SOC during his long tenure in the SASS, but he had learned this much from them: Skill beats will. Panic helped no one in a crisis. He centered himself, kept his cool, felt his magical tide recede to a low throb, still present and ready.

The crowd broke, parting to either side, streaming into the alleys, leaving the street clear before him.

The street ahead was dominated by a shimmering curtain of air, large as a cathedral door, bending and wriggling like a heat mirage. Another crowd of people stood frozen around it, staring in disbelief as the shimmering patch blackened at the edges. The black faded to green, and the curtain peeled wider, smoking as if a hole were rotting through the very air.

The stink reached Swift even where he stood, making him gag as the curtain rotted wider, and the first creatures stepped through and out onto the street. They were small, brown humanoids, no bigger than large children. Their ears were pointed, their noses long and hooked. They mostly clutched swords and spears, but a few brandished guns. The crowd finally broke, running as the goblins came on and on, an endless flood of them, many riding wolves the size of small ponies. One of them hefted a spear and threw it at one of the fleeing traders. It caught the man in the shoulder and sent him to his knees, screaming, as blood began to spread across his white shirt.

Goblins.

Swift knew he should run, but his body refused to obey, frozen in disbelief at what he was seeing. He stood rooted to the spot as the first sorcerers emerged, their skins white with the chalky paint the goblins used to mark their magic users. One of these spit something in its own language and gestured at the people fleeing up the steps. A fireball shot from its hand

and slammed into them, sending a woman flying, her gray suit-skirt crisping to ash as she tumbled through the air.

The crowd shrieked and pelted back into the building.

The goblins poured out of the portal until they filled the entire street and began to pile up the steps of Federal Hall. Here and there, standards bobbed, poles topped with the giant skull of a bird, striped red and orange. One of the goblins climbed up to stand astride the pedestal beneath the bronze statue of George Washington. It was slightly bigger than the rest, its face dotted with white, a long, leather cape around its neck sewn with shining bronze discs. It brandished a spear at its fellows, shouting.

The throng of goblins began to shift left and right across the street, clearing a path to either side of the curtain, leaving the cobblestones bare save for streaked blood and the bodies of those traders who hadn't gotten out of the way in time. A goblin walked among them, stabbing down with a spear wherever one of them twitched or cried out.

At last, one of the wolfriders raised a horn to its lips and sounded a long, low note. It was answered by a shriek from inside the gate. The sound cut through the crowd, they surged with even greater fervor, running frantically. The first of them reached Swift, and he stepped out of their path, numb with horror.

Then the first new creatures came through.

They towered twelve feet in the air, their skins liquid black and cut only by a slash of white smile, showing dagger teeth. Their humanoid bodies were topped with long horns, their hands dragging longer claws. They flashed through the gate, moving across the street in discrete blinks, one second in one place, another in the next. They lit among the stragglers streaming around the building, cutting them down with great sweeps of their clawed hands. The goblins drew back from them, shivering at the cold they exuded.

Gahe, the Mountain Gods of the Apache. Relentless, vicious monsters that froze with a touch or killed with a swipe of their dagger claws.

Swift's eyes widened as a woman stepped through the curtain, the giant black creatures parting respectfully around her.

She wore a suit of black leather armor, edges crudely stitched with strings of hanging beads, dotted with white patterns much like the skin of the goblins around her. Her own skin was milk pale, her black hair cut in a severe bob, almost jutting to points along her jawbone. Her eyes were wide, dark, and hauntingly beautiful. She surveyed the scene, the corner of her mouth quirked in satisfaction. A shimmering pulse passed through the air from her head to one of the huge black creatures surrounding her. It nodded, more pulses passed, and they began to fan out into the street, now eerily quiet.

She nodded back at the monster, then turned to the curtain behind her, extending her hands. The air pulsed and the curtain's edges began to rot once more, faster now, fading from green to purple to black in rapid succession, tearing ever wider, until the ragged hole in the air stretched beyond the edges of the buildings, easily admitting more of the slick black monsters, horned heads tossing, dagger smiles grinning, fanning out into the charnel-house corridor that had once been Wall Street. Training or no training, the panic won out then, and Swift was airborne, streaking through the sky back to his safe house.

Because he knew that woman. Because he knew what she could do.

What she would do.

She could have had a roc carry her the forty stories up. One of the goblin Aeromancers would have been happy to oblige. But this was a homecoming, and Scylla wanted to walk in the front door, just like old times.

For the most part, it was. Naeem, the doorman, showed no sign of recognizing her as she strode in, one of the tall *Gahe* beside her, a small cluster of goblins coming behind. He backed up behind the counter, mouth agape, eyes dinner-plate wide.

The building was just as she remembered it, wide-beamed hardwood floors and cast-iron sconces giving the lobby a stately splendor that served as a reminder: This wasn't a building for everyone. Only the greatest of the great lived here. The ceiling was hand-painted in rococo style, pompous and over-blown, replete with gold leaf. Fortunately, this was one of the few buildings in the city with ceilings so high that even a *Gahe*'s horns wouldn't scrape them.

"Hello, Naeem," Scylla said, "any mail for me?"

Naeem blinked, recognition dawning on his face. "You're . . . You're dead."

Scylla laughed. "Yes, well. Rumors of my demise have been greatly exaggerated."

He snatched up a phone, punched three digits, held it to his ear for a moment before pulling it away and looking at it.

"I think you'll find the lines tied up, old friend," Scylla said. She looked at her feet. He had been an old friend, after a fashion. It was all gone now. Ruined. She shrugged off the emotion. The die was cast. It was no time to go soft. "I'm heading up."

Naeem shrank behind the counter, uselessly punching those same three digits over and over.

She headed to the elevator bank. A single car occupied the end closest to the counter. It only serviced one floor: the penthouse, where Scylla had lived before magic changed everything. She pressed the single, stainless-steel button.

The doors didn't open.

She turned slowly toward him. The goblins surrounded the counter. One slapped a javelin down on the reflective surface and struggled to scramble up the smooth front with little success. Scylla guessed it might have been comical under other circumstances, but Naeem only stared at the javelin, face slack with horror. The creature finally rolled up on one elbow and mantled up onto the counter. It snatched up the weapon, jabbing it at the doorman's throat. Naeem screamed and backed into the corner, pleading in his native Urdu.

This wasn't the time for sentiment. She was a war leader now. But Naeem had served her faithfully all the years she'd lived here. He'd delivered her packages, taken her messages, made sure to send her holiday greetings for occasions counter to his own faith. He had, in his way, cared for her. He didn't deserve to be harmed.

But she hadn't won the goblin Defender tribes to her banner by promising mercy. They wanted revenge on humanity, and they would have it. She knew no single life was worth losing the loyalty of half her army.

She had to sacrifice a few for the good of many. She need only allow it until victory was secured, then she would turn her cheek, give the good cop control. She thought briefly of Mao's axiom: *The people are the sea, and the insurgent is the fish. So long as the sea is hospitable to the fish, you will never catch them all.* First she would hurt them, then she would win them.

The *Gahe* came to stand at her side, watching impassively. She suppressed a shiver. The things were damn cold. It thought-pulsed to her, pictures forming in her mind. The *Gahe* could speak to anyone with their thought-pictures. It was a useful trait, and had made it possible to communicate with the goblin tribes, to give them the words of inspiration needed to bring them to her banner. Revenge against the humans for FOB Frontier, that hated outpost in the Source that had brought such misery. Scylla had destroyed its perimeter, opened it wide for their plunder. Now she could complete their revenge. More importantly, she promised that with their help she could bend the humans to submission, ensure they never again set foot on goblin lands.

Even now, the creatures poured through the breach between the planes, eager to vent their rage. Too long had they been helpless in the face of humanity's superior technology and magical might. Now they would show the people who had built a military outpost in their backyard the other end of the spear.

The breach was one of two in New York, rotted out of thin spots between the planes. The *Gahe* could sense them but only pass through singly when some lucky shift in the planar fabric permitted it.

But they could show Scylla where the thin spots were, and her rotting magic Bound easily to anything.

The *Gahe* flashed another picture in her mind. The second breach, opened out in the water off Manhattan's tip. The other half of a pincer, closing around New York's tender throat. She nodded, and the *Gahe* changed the subject to the third breach, in Mescalero, showing her an image of the dust-choked pass between red cliffs even now filling up with goblins, *Gahe* marching at their head. Few humans lived out in that wasteland, the least populated corner of a sparsely popu-lated reservation. Those few ran out to the *Gahe*, grinning like fools, shouting greetings and wordless whoops of joy. The Apache Selfers, who worshipped the *Gahe* as their "Mountain Gods."

The *Gahe* thought-pulsed the image again. The single Mescalero breach wasn't enough. It pulsed images of the six thin spots it had shown her across the reservation grounds.

It didn't care about New York beyond the chance to visit violence on the humans who had shunted its children, as it thought of the Apache, into desert prisons. Once, the Apache had ruled the mountains as far as they could see. The white eyes had stolen everything from them: their families, their lives, their land. And now they would do the same in the Source.

Scylla smiled at the irony; she'd always thought it was humanity who would be influenced by the strangeness of the Source, but the influence ran both ways. To the Apache, FOB Frontier was another Fort Sill, an enemy encampment in the midst of an indigenous homeland, and the *Gahe* saw it that way, too.

It wanted to be in Mescalero. All the *Gahe* did. But that wasn't the deal. Scylla would rot the other thin spots open in Mescalero only after she was paid.

Her price was New York.

The goblin reached with the javelin, pricking Naeem's neck. His eyes ranged over the creature's shoulder, finding hers, pleading.

In spite of herself, Scylla hissed loudly, and the goblin froze, looking up at her. She motioned sharply and it stepped back, leaving Naeem gasping, a small bead of blood working its way down to stain his collar. The creature's eyes narrowed, and she saw the dawning sense of betrayal. Revenge denied, a promise broken.

She knew it was a tactical error, a softness she couldn't afford if she was to win this. She told herself that when Latent-kind took its rightful place at the helm of the world, they would still have to live alongside humans like Naeem. There was no need to antagonize them needlessly. Let her begin showing mercy now.

But she saw the anger in the goblin's eyes and knew the right of it.

Naeem fumbled frantically under the counter, and the elevator door chimed and opened.

"Thank you, Naeem," she said, then turned and entered the elevator.

"Wait here," she said to the goblins. They hungered for revenge, but they were terrified of her magic, and she'd shown her willingness to use it when she wasn't obeyed. It would hold them, and do double duty in cementing her position at the head of this army. If she was to lead, she had to be obeyed.

The *Gahe* joined her as the doors slid shut, and the elevator sped skyward. It was precisely as she remembered it, save that the new owner had removed the end table she'd kept in the elevator car, along with the apple-shaped dish her sister had given her as a college-graduation gift. She'd used it to store change and keys for years.

The elevator rose quickly enough to put butterflies in her stomach though much of that could be anger, or satisfaction. Outside, her army was spreading through the streets of New York, beginning to make good on the debt she owed this government, this country—justice delayed but not denied. Her apartment was only one small sliver of that, and perhaps the least important, but it would feel so good to make this right.

And make it right, she would. The invasion was one small indulgence, the bite of chocolate cake before launching the new exercise routine. She gambled to win, not just for herself, but for all people, Latent and human alike. When the dust cleared, Latent people would be free to use their powers as they saw fit, and humans would understand their place in the genetic order, no longer tying themselves in knots to hang on to power they'd long since lost the right to hold. With magic decriminalized, there would be no more need to fight one another. Many had died to bring her to this point, but their numbers paled compared to how many she would save. The new order would be just. The new order would be peaceful. The new order would be free.

At last, the doors chimed again and slid open on the past.

She didn't recognize the place. A man stood in the broad kitchen that connected to the open living room. He'd repainted, stark white covering the soft colors she'd preferred. The appliances had been replaced, a central stove with hood put in. Whoever this man was, he liked to cook. He was slim, gray-haired, good-looking in a distinguished way, in his late fifties. He wore slacks and an expensive-looking button-down shirt. She was sure she knew him from somewhere, but with his face contorted by fear, it was hard to say from where. He stared openmouthed as she walked in, the *Gahe* moving off into a corner.

Scylla was familiar with many types of fear. Some froze and screamed, as Naeem had. Some resorted to anger. This man was one of the latter. "Who the fuc . . ." he began, his face purpling.

"I'm the owner of this unit," she said, "and I don't remember selling it to you. So, the real question is, who the fuck are you?"

She let her eyes roam the living-room walls, scanning across a painted family portrait, some expensive-looking Asian tapestries, stopping at a number of corporate plaques. She paused as she read the name, then looked at the corporate logo.

Rage curdled in her stomach, souring all thoughts of freedom and justice, leaving only the sick bile of revenge. "Tom Hicks. Entertech's pride and joy. Why am I not surprised?"

Recognition dawned across the man's face. Angry fear gave way to another kind, sick and weak. Hicks's knees buckled, and he sagged against the expensive, granite countertop, staying upright only by an act of supreme will. The *Gahe* turned to the ceiling-high windows, tracing one long claw across the surface, leaving trails of dirty hoarfrost. Scylla had owned the entire floor, but she favored the south-facing glass wall that overlooked the cobblestone plaza where the famous statue of a bronze bull stood. The *Gahe* looked out over it, watching as her army spread across the street below.

"Look," Hicks said. "They told me you were dead. I had no idea that . . . I'll just leave. You can have the place back. I'm happy to make arrangements to get it put back into your . . ."

"Oh, please," Scylla said. "I don't care about the apartment. I'm here to free you. To free everyone. Things are about to change, and I'm going to need your help."

This would be the tricky part. The man would have to be made to listen to reason, to understand his place in the new order. Her first convert. "Limbic Dampener is going to play an important role here. I'll need someone to interface with Entertech, someone they trust to . . ."

Hicks launched himself over the counter, thudded to the tile behind, and stood, gun in hand.

The *Gahe* stutter-flashed across the floor, moving in short, teleporting hops to his side, seizing his arm. He cried out at its freezing touch, shivering, teeth chattering. He fired, the round vanishing into the creature's torso as if it had been swallowed. The *Gahe* didn't so much as flinch.

Scylla swallowed her shock, bit down on the rush of adrenaline. Disappointing. Humans never learned. It was bad enough that they tried to make her a slave, but they were so addicted to power that they'd rather die than yield one ounce of it. They'd take the carrot eventually, but first they'd need plenty of stick.

"From the moment I Manifested, I swore I'd find a way to do some good with this," she said as he pulled against the monster's grip, lips turning blue, crystals of ice forming on his arm, his gasps misting the freezing envelope of air around the *Gahe*. "You took that from me. At first I was angry, I thought I'd been robbed. But now I understand that you were just prepping me for the bigger show. This way will be much faster. I'm sorry you won't get to see it."

She leaned forward as his shivering grew more violent, close enough to feel the cold nip at her nose. "I'm not a monster, you know. Someone has to make the tough choice. Someone has to break the eggs to make the omelet. You'll never change on your own."

But he didn't hear her. He slumped to the floor, his frozen arm snapping off in the *Gahe*'s grip. She Bound her magic into his chest cavity, liquefying his heart and lungs. No sense in being petty. She'd made her point.

She turned back to the *Gahe*, then twirled briefly, taking in the space she once called her "deluxe apartment in the sky." It pained her to see this strange man's imprint on it, his furniture, his artwork. The place even smelled of his cologne.

She went to the window, watching as a troop of goblins raced down the street, spear tips trailing shredded clothing, the spoils of raided shops. One of them dragged a mannequin behind it by a single plastic leg.

Yes, the landscape had changed.

But it was good to be home.

CHAPTER II
SECOND CHANCE

The "goblins," as the army calls them, are a highly diverse species, adapting to their environment. The Three-Foots tribe trades with the Po-na-tu-ree, an aquatic subspecies of goblin. Usually furs or cattle horns acquired in raids are exchanged for fish and aquatic mammals. The sea has molded the Ponaturi; they are as comfortable under the water as above it. Their physical forms are much more varied than their land-bound cousins. Some look more like fish or octopus than goblin. They are crusted with barnacles and kelp, but they still hold the same basic beliefs as all goblins, and are united with them in their fervent hatred of humanity and the devastation our presence in the Source has wrought.

—Simon Truelove
A Sojourn Among the Mattab On Sorrah

The press conference drew to a close, and Lieutenant Colonel Jan Thorsson sweated beneath the makeup. The heat from the stage lights made his feet feel like they were burning inside his reflective, artificial leather shoes. The discomfort was a distant thing, an awareness that had no power to affect him. The Dampener helped, but most of his sangfroid was born of long experience. As special advisor to the Reawakening Commission, he was a man well used to television appearances.

His actions at FOB Frontier had betrayed his commander in chief but saved the lives of thousands, making him a pariah in the government and a hero to the public. That public acclaim had drummed the president he betrayed out of office and

forced the new one to promote him and keep him in front of
the cameras. Thorsson knew that President Porter thought him
a traitor, but keeping the hero of FOB Frontier around as a
spokesman helped lend the new administration legitimacy.

The assembled reporters shouted a flood of questions. Words
ran together, amplified by the tight confines of the pressroom.
Thorsson steadied himself behind the podium, remembering
his public-affairs training. *Back straight. Don't fidget. No ver-
bal pauses. Look serious, but not like you've got a stick up
your ass.*

"I'll answer that," he said, pointing to a reporter in the front
row, a young man in a button-down plaid shirt about two sizes
too small, jeans cuffed deliberately high, showing paisley socks.

Thorsson's gesture quelled the sea of questions. The assembled reporters sat down as a single body.

"The Porter administration has no intention of abandoning
the policies of the Walsh administration," Thorsson said.
"President Walsh's violation of the McGauer-Linden Act and
his trafficking in Probe magic does not invalidate the need for
systems to remain in place to protect the American people
from the dangers of unrestricted magic use. What happened at
FOB Frontier was the exception that proves the rule."

Thorsson had been an exception himself. When Walsh had
abandoned the FOB, leaving thousands of Americans to die to
keep his secret, Thorsson broke ranks and freed the political
prisoner Oscar Britton, the nation's worst enemy and the only
man with the power to bring everyone home alive. But excep-
tions had to prove the rule. If they became the rule, the machine
broke down. Everything unraveled.

He quelled the latest surge of questions with a wave of his
hand. "Please . . . Please. Settle down. Let me put it this way:
If you find out that a public official has been embezzling money,
that's not an argument to legalize embezzlement. It's an argument to prosecute the wrongdoer and revisit how we can better
protect our funds. It's the same case here. No further questions."

Further questions followed him as he left the podium for
the door between two flagpoles, one bearing the Stars and
Stripes and the other the emblem of the Supernatural Operations
Corps. On the latter, the eye in the pyramid was surrounded

by symbols of the four elements representing legal magical schools: Pyromancy, Hydromancy, Aeromancy, and Terramancy. The red cross above symbolized Physiomancy. The logo read: OUR GIFTS, FOR OUR NATION.

The young reporter intercepted him as he turned the doorknob. "Sir!"

Thorsson sighed. "Give me some space, huh? You've got your quote."

The reporter shoved a digital recorder under Thorsson's nose. "How do *you* feel about the administration's recommitment to the law?"

Thorsson pushed the recorder down. "Get that out of my face. I told you question time was over." He shot a dangerous glare over the reporter's shoulder at another man who was considering joining the ad hoc questioning, and the man thought better of it.

The reporter wasn't fazed. He switched off the recorder and pocketed it. "Fine. Off the record, just tell me."

"Off the record is the same as on the record," Thorsson said. "I'm a military officer below flag grade. My job isn't to set policy. My job isn't to interpret policy. My job isn't even to have an opinion. My job is to carry out the will of my civilian masters, who are ultimately elected by you. How I feel about this, about anything, is irrelevant."

The reporter leaned in closer, lowering his voice. "But . . . I mean, FOB Frontier, man. You rubbed the president's face in it. You saved all those people, he got the boot, and you got promoted. You're the motherfucking Harlequin. That's got to feel amazing."

Thorsson bridled at the man's use of his call sign, the radio names that kept Sorcerers apart from the rest of the world.

Being the motherfucking Harlequin didn't feel amazing. It felt exhausting, isolating.

"I did what I felt was right to save the lives of those people," Harlequin said.

"And to free Latent people."

"Latent people are already free. They have certain responsibilities that others don't, but that comes with having certain powers that others don't. FOB Frontier was never a political statement. I was saving lives. That's it."

The reporter gave him a knowing nod. "Well, I'll say it, if you won't. You're a fucking hero. Porter's going to have to change his tune soon enough."

Harlequin felt blood rush to his cheeks. His magical tide surged. He opened his mouth to answer, but the reporter began to back away. "I got it! I got it! You don't have to say anything. I just wanted to say thanks for your service."

The reporter nodded as if they were both in on the same inside joke, and Harlequin felt exhaustion swamp him. No matter what he said, the reactions were the same. If he wouldn't be the hero they wanted, they'd just make him that way regardless. He shook his head, went through the door, and shut it behind him, closing his eyes in the air-conditioned space beyond, feeling a modicum of serenity return as the door lock clicked behind him, shutting out the maelstrom of buzzing voices.

He breathed for a moment, calming himself, trying to keep his mind in the present. It wandered too readily to the past nowadays, and that was a dark path. There were decisions back there, decisions that had saved some lives but also cost some. Decisions that couldn't be changed.

He looked up at the TV monitor mounted to the wall. They'd be rebroadcasting the highlights from the press conference. Hopefully, he'd come off better than he thought he had.

But instead, the screen showed a breaking news clip, Oscar Britton holding court, another guerrilla press conference of his own, held in some deserted field. Britton would stay only long enough to make his point, then go back to the Source long before anyone could get close enough to apprehend him. Not that the SOC would ever do that on camera. After FOB Frontier, Britton was a bigger public hero than Harlequin.

"All right!" Britton shouted. "Shut the hell up if you want me to talk."

Britton's time on the run had made him leaner, harder-looking. He still kept his head shaved so close it shone in the sun. He still looked like he could bend cold iron with his bare hands. Beside him stood Therese Del Aqua, the Physiomancer who had escaped with him and returned to help save the people who'd held her prisoner. Her long brown hair hung nearly to her waist now, ragged, in need of a cut. It did little to diminish her fierce beauty.

The buzz subsided, and Britton had to lean back as a half dozen microphones were thrust in his face. "I've heard that President Porter has recommitted himself to the misguided principles of the McGauer-Linden Act. He doesn't get it, and if you support him, neither do you. Latent people are still people. We are citizens of this country, and we have the same rights as everyone else.

"The problem is a government that traffics in the same practices it prohibits. The problem is a law that makes it illegal for a class of people to simply exist. The people who are so hard over keeping Latent people second-class citizens are the same people who were willing to let thirty thousand people die to keep a secret.

"Well, I'm done with secrets. This law needs to change, and it needs to change now. You hear me Porter? I'm talking to you. A fancy suit and an office you weren't even elected to doesn't give you the right to put your boot on my neck. The only crime I ever committed was to Manifest a power I never asked for.

"The government uses a drug called Limbic Dampener to help the SOC control the emotional center of the brain, which conducts magic. If it were freely distributed, we wouldn't need a damn McGauer-Linden Act. Nobody would go nova. Nobody would ever have to go Selfer. It's expensive, but so is the cost of enforcing the current laws. And it doesn't have to be so expensive. The price is kept high, so Entertech and its subsidiaries can profit off the drug. The distribution is kept controlled, so the SOC can have a monopoly on magical power. You want to do some investigative reporting? Investigate that."

Therese moved up and jostled Britton aside, looking into the camera. "He's right. I may not be a Probe, but I'm a criminal, too. And for what? Let me show you something." She pointed, and the camera swung to cover a boom-mic operator, a young man in his early twenties with a thin scrabble of beard and much thicker glasses.

She moved toward him, and he dropped the boom, backing up, raising his hands. "Sir," she said. "It's all right, I'm not going to hurt you. Let me do this."

The cameraman and one of the reporters began yelling at the boom operator to let her, and he acquiesced reluctantly, closing his eyes and leaning away as she placed her hands over his face. A moment later, she pulled her hand back, taking his glasses. The boom operator stood blinking, a smile spreading across his face.

"How's your vision?" she asked.

He blinked, blushing. "Perfect. It's perfect."

She tossed his glasses over her shoulder and turned back to the camera. "He won't be needing these anymore. That's my great crime? A gun owner can shoot people, but they're still allowed to own guns. Sure, I *can* use my magic to hurt people, but I *don't*. We have free will, and with Limbic Dampener, we'd have control, too."

Britton overrode the chorus of questions. "I beg you to look past your fear. Latent people want the same things you do. Running them into the ground isn't going to make them less likely to harm you. It's only going to make them more likely to see you as an enemy. Let us live among you. As equals. Distribute the drug. Change. The. Law."

Harlequin stared. It was all true, but that didn't mean it would help. Harlequin had been in front of TV cameras non-stop since Britton had first escaped. Rants like that would frighten as many people as it convinced. In his heart, he wished Britton well. *You do it your way, and I'll do it my way. Let's see who changes the world first.*

He closed his eyes, gave himself another minute of peace.

The door at the far end of the room opened, closed. "Hey, Jan."

Harlequin opened his eyes to see the familiar face of Lieutenant Colonel Rick Allen, call sign Crucible.

He felt the smile spread across his face. "Holy crap, Rick. What the hell are you doing here?"

He gave Crucible a brief hug, then stepped back, still shaking his hand, grinning. "I haven't seen you in forever!"

He could see the urgency in Crucible's face. The Pyromancer was deeply worried about something, but histrionics had never been his style, and Harlequin knew he'd get to whatever it was in his own time.

Crucible forced a broad smile. "I see you all the time, Hollywood! You're on TV every other day! Hell, I'm getting sick of your ugly mug."

Harlequin's smile vanished. "Don't call me that."

"Whoa." Crucible's forced smile didn't falter. "What? Ugly

mug? I'm just kidding. You're a very attractive man. If I weren't happily married, I'd jump your bones right here."

"Hollywood. That's what everyone calls me now. I'm fucking sick of it. They think I like being on TV."

"No shame in liking it. You're good at it, and you're helping. Slinging lightning isn't the only thing Army Sorcerers do."

"What am I helping, Rick? Tell me how this helps anything."

Crucible was quiet for a moment. "Sorry, Jan. I really was just kidding about the Hollywood thing."

"I know," Harlequin said. "What's going on? This isn't a social call."

Crucible creased his mouth into a thin line and took a deep breath.

"How are you doing?" he finally asked.

"I'm okay," Harlequin said. "I'm sorry to be so pissy. I'm just getting tired of being a poster boy for a revolution I don't want. I did what I had to do to save the FOB, but I don't want the whole system to come down. Magic still needs to be controlled. Let Oscar Britton carry that torch . . . wherever the hell he is."

Crucible waved a hand. "Nobody is going to mess with him now. He's way too popular. If you think you're a folk hero . . . That guy is . . ."

"Hollywood," Harlequin finished for him. "Rick. You're practically crawling out of your own skin. What's the problem?"

Crucible reached into his pocket and pulled out his smartphone. "There's trouble in New York City. They want you to head out there and lock it down."

"What kind of trouble?" Harlequin worked to keep the excitement out of his voice.

Crucible held up his smartphone. "A cop took this on Wall Street this morning." He thumbed through some photographs before settling on a video clip stopped on the frozen image of the cobblestone street that ran past Federal Hall, the giant columns rising out of the broad stone steps like some giant's gap-toothed smile. The street was crowded with people, mostly in suits and ties, lacking the cameras and maps that would have marked them as tourists. Lunchtime then, the bankers, analysts, and computer geeks who made the country's financial system run heading out for a bite or a cigarette.

Harlequin took the phone from Crucible, hovered his thumb over the PLAY button.

"When you say 'they' want me to lock it down . . ." Harlequin began.

"'They' is actually 'he,'" Crucible said. "President Porter. He asked for you personally."

"It's got to be a hell of a thing to make that happen."

"It is." Crucible gestured at the phone.

Harlequin pushed PLAY. The video was slightly grainy, the digital zoom making the colors run together, the gray and white of the stone and asphalt blending. But it wasn't so fuzzy that Harlequin couldn't make out the shimmering curtain, the ranks of monsters marching through it.

Harlequin showed no reaction, and Crucible watched him, arms folded, until the video finally stopped, leaving the image frozen on a woman, arms spread, smiling up at the widening gate. Around her, tall ebony shapes spread out, white cuts for mouths grinning along with her.

Harlequin lowered the phone. "That's her, isn't it?"

The picture was too distorted to make out her face, but he recognized her anyway.

Harlequin searched Crucible's face for an accusation, found none. Relief mingled with guilt. If she was involved with anything, he was to blame. *No. Oscar Britton is to blame. If it went your way, she'd still be rotting in the hole and FOB Frontier would still be standing.*

"It's her," Crucible said. "We ran the image through facial-recognition software just to be double sure."

"Jesus," Harlequin said, resisting Crucible's attempt to retrieve his phone, his eyes returning to the picture.

Crucible nodded. "It's not just *Gahe*. There are goblins. Rocs. Giants. Everything we faced at FOB Frontier."

"What do they want me for?"

"The president is declaring this to be a national-security incident. He wants you as his incident commander on scene. You'll be back in New York, just like old times," Crucible said, "except I won't be there, and you'll be commanding the defense instead of liaising with the NYPD."

Harlequin finally let the phone go. "So, in other words, nothing like old times."

"They know who that is, Jan. You . . . know her. You've fought the *Gahe* before. You want out of this pasture they've put you in? You want to show them you're a team player? This is your chance."

Harlequin thought of the slim shape between the *Gahe* and felt his stomach do somersaults. She was easily the most dangerous Selfer in the world, the woman who'd single-handedly slaughtered hundreds and left FOB Frontier bared to its enemies. She called herself Scylla.

Once, he'd known her by another name.

INTERLUDE I
PARIAH

I feel bad for them, I do. I feel bad for people with infectious dis-
eases. I feel bad for people whose mental illness inclines them
toward violence. I am not blind to how tough that is on them and
their families. But if you think for a second that means I'm going
to let them hurt anyone else, you're out of your mind. We don't
quarantine in an epidemic because we think it's fun. We do it to
protect the larger population. It's no different for Selfers. I raised
my right hand and swore to protect the people who elected me to
office, and God as my witness, I'm going to do it.

—Senator John McGauer
Debating the McGauer-Linden Act on the Senate floor

SIX YEARS EARLIER

"I've got it," Lieutenant Jan Thorsson said.

Sergeant Ward looked doubtful, but he waved to the NYPD
cops crouching behind the cruiser. "Stay put!"

He turned back to Thorsson. The flames had singed Ward's
moustache. The black, crisped hair stank. Thorsson could only
imagine how bad it must be for Ward.

"You sure?" Ward sounded relieved. He didn't want to go
in there, and Thorsson doubted he would do any good even if
he did.

Thorsson nodded. "You've got the other exit covered?"

Ward nodded. "We see her . . ."

Thorsson nodded to the building in front of them, consti-
tuting the L-shaped corridor that trapped the Selfer inside.

"You shoot her. She's either coming out with me, or she's not coming out."

Ward's expression went pinched. "Harlequin, she's got kids."

Ward referred to him by his SOC call sign, yet another layer of distance between non-Latents and the SOC. He'd gotten the call sign during his favorite assignment, training navy pilots to combat Aeromancers. They gave him his call sign when he left, a parting gift and a tongue-in-cheek reference to his "clowning" them in the air.

Harlequin stabbed an angry finger at the building, drew a line from it down to the row of fire trucks and ambulances pulled up outside. EMTs were still running gurneys out, working on the victims strapped to them as they went. "How many kids are in that building?"

They were always mothers. Or confused. Or kids. Or a pillar of the community. There was always a reason why they ran, why they couldn't be bothered to do the right thing, turn themselves in and comply with the McGauer-Linden Act. Harlequin knew that this Bronx housing project had been part of Ward's beat for his entire career. He knew the Selfer, like he knew everyone else on the block. That bone-deep knowledge, that familiarity made Ward a great cop. But it also made him waver.

Harlequin recalled the words of his Stormcraft instructor at Quantico. *We're sheepdogs, Lieutenant. The problem is, we smell just like the wolves we guard against. The sheep can't tell the difference.*

He refused to think of people as sheep, but he understood the motivation to frame it in those terms.

It was much easier to put down a wolf than kill a human being.

When Harlequin came up Latent, he'd been frightened. He'd seen the path of his old life stop short, known the society that Ward enjoyed, the easy conversation with the man who owned the corner bodega, the Sundays coaching the neighborhood basketball team in the summers, the sense of belonging somewhere, would all be lost to him.

But he'd swallowed it. Because he had to. Distasteful as it was, his instructor's metaphor worked here. A Latent person had to decide if they were going to be a sheepdog who protected the flock or a wolf who devoured it. He'd made his choice, and he had no sympathy for those who chose otherwise. Ward, for all his law-enforcement training, couldn't make the hard call.

Harlequin made a fist, let the magic curl over it, felt the lightning sizzle between the tensed knuckles.

Thus always to wolves.

He stepped around the side of the burning building. A ground-level window burst, hot air buffeting him from inside. He summoned a wind to force it back, his anger growing with each step. Ward said the housing project contained fifteen hundred apartments. It cost the city millions. It was the place desperate people had called home for over fifty years.

And now it was gone because a scared old lady couldn't be bothered to make a simple phone call. To ask for help. To follow clear rules.

Harlequin hoped she resisted. *Give me an excuse.*

She crouched by the trash bins, on all fours. Her housedress smoldered, melted to her flabby torso, the pink floral print still visible in patches. Her hair smoked. She shambled on her knuckles, thick thighs quivering. Her eyes glowered, reflecting the firelight as if they glowed from within. She didn't appear in pain despite the burned dress, which meant she was moderating the temperature around her. She had better control than he'd thought.

Which made her all the more responsible. Ward said she'd told neighbors months ago that she feared she was possessed by the devil. How long had she known she was Latent? Every hour made the crime worse.

Ward said he was unsure of her English. Harlequin shouted in what little Spanish he'd picked up since being assigned here. *"Pare! SOC!"*

She pawed toward him, growling.

"Quieto! No se mueva!"

She roared and coughed a gout of flame, white hot and billowing, like the breath of a dragon out of myth. Dramatic, undisciplined.

Harlequin didn't bother to Suppress her. He conjured a wind that blew the flames back in her face. She squinted, rocking back on her haunches and throwing up her arms at the unexpected reversal, her demon's roar becoming a cry of surprise.

"That's enough." Harlequin gave up on the Spanish. "Quit fucking around. I'm taking you in."

That meant a Suppressed convoy to Quantico after the NYPD finished booking her. The richest city in the country had long lobbied for its own Suppression/Detention facility, and Harlequin was pleased the SOC had crushed that particular idea's head before it could breed. Magic was a federal issue. This might be the Bronx, but Selfers like this risked the safety of the entire nation.

She recovered enough to stand. A big-framed woman even without the obesity, Harlequin had to admit she looked like a towering demon, huge and flame-wreathed. But he was unimpressed. For all her power, she lacked discipline.

He reached her in five long strides, blowing off another burst of stylized fire-breathing. It was close enough to singe him this time, his uniform crisping and shrinking as the heat washed over him. He called up his magical current and Bound it across hers.

The flames winked out as her magic rolled back. She shrieked, covering herself as if he had left her naked. Then she screamed, reaching for him.

She was old, but she was a big woman, and Harlequin was in no mood. He ducked her clumsy swipe and punched her hard in the gut. He grabbed her wrist as she doubled over, forcing it around and stepping behind her, immobilizing her elbow and torquing the limb down until she cried out.

"Stop resisting me!" he shouted. "We're going to walk back out to the parking lot, nice and easy. Right foot first. If you continue to resist, I'm just going to yank on this arm, and I swear, it's going to hurt. If you comply, I'll bring you back to your buddy Sergeant Ward. Now, let's move. Do it now!"

She whimpered but moved as he pressed his forearm into the flab over her shoulder blades. She reeked of brimstone, dried sweat, and unwashed clothing. He felt her current pulsing against his own, seeking to break through. She was strong, he'd give her that, but nowhere near strong enough to throw off Suppression.

They rounded the corner of the building, Harlequin leaning far to see around the Selfer's bulk. Ward was stepping slowly around the open door of his cruiser, pistol pointed at the ground. "She okay?" he called.

I'm fine, thanks for asking, Harlequin thought. "She's fine! She just . . ."

The big woman twisted hard in his grip, her free arm wrenching so high it must have pulled her muscles. She dug a rusting corkscrew into Harlequin's chest, dragging it down, ripping through his uniform, tearing a line of agony across his chest.

He shouted, yanked on her arm, pivoting his body to spin her, put her on the ground. Her huge weight overbalanced and she pitched forward, escaping his grasp, head rebounding off one of the metal posts that held the chains screening the parking lot from the housing-complex grounds. Blood sprayed from her mouth, misting Harlequin's face. Her eyes rolled up in her head, and he felt her current go slack as she collapsed across his leg, pinning him. He felt her pulse, watched her chest. She'd taken a nasty knock on the head, but she was alive.

He looked down at his own chest, blood welling up to soak his shirt, mixing with hers. "Jesus," he said as Ward helped move her off him. He sent lightning crackling across his wound as soon as Ward let him go. It was an old wives' tale that immediate electrical cauterization of a wound could keep disease out, but Aeromancers all did it anyway.

He brushed a fragment of the woman's tooth off his shirt as Ward stared at her. "Jesus, Lieutenant. You didn't have to bash her head like that."

"I didn't do it on purpose," Harlequin growled. "She weighs like three hundred pounds, and she was fucking trying to dig out my heart with a . . ." He looked around for the corkscrew. It had vanished somewhere in the grass. The dancing shadows of the firelight made it impossible to see anything.

"Well, we got it now," Ward said. "We'll book her."

"I'm coming with you. I need to keep her under Suppression." Harlequin bent to help Ward lift the woman.

"She's out cold, Lieutenant," Ward said. "Help me get her a few more feet to the ambulance, and I'll make sure they sedate her so she doesn't wake up."

Harlequin shook his head. "If she comes to for any reason, it's going to be my ass. I'm coming with you."

"You've got a Suppressor at the liaison office. We'll take her straight there!" Ward argued.

NYPD had the command for this op, and Ward radioed in the results as they got her closer to the line of ambulances clustered among the fire trucks in the parking lot, their spinning lights adding to the glow from the police cruisers, making Harlequin squint. The seeds of a ferocious headache began to blossom behind his eyes. His chest burned as the Bound electricity did its slow work, the stink of his own flesh making him angrier.

The big woman sagged between them, limp hair covering her face, burned dress smoking. Her mouth hung open, blood drooling from one corner. The EMTs were busy, and Ward had to shout to get the attention of two of them. They raced over with a wheeled gurney, then stopped short, eyes fixed on Harlequin. For a moment, he saw himself as they must see him: streaked with grime and gore, his uniform covered in soot and blood. Small runnels of lightning still danced across the cut on his chest, as if they needed a reminder of who he was and what he did.

They stared, refusing to come forward.

"Come on!" Ward said, then cursed, dragging the woman closer to them. "She needs help."

The first of the press were arriving. Harlequin could see them over the EMTs' shoulders, setting up tripods, turning on lights, readying boom microphones. He knew he looked like a monster. The Selfer didn't look much better, but he was the one both Latent and conscious enough to be interviewed.

Harlequin looked at the EMTs, then at the line of firemen who'd stopped their work to stare at him.

He could feel their fear, their revulsion, as clearly as a magical current.

Sheep, seeing the sheepdog, but smelling the wolf. The press would be no different.

Maybe his instructor was right.

He fought down his anger and turned back to Ward. "Sedate her. Get her to the Suppressor stat."

Ward looked up at him, surprised, and nodded gratefully.

He kicked off and flew north. SOC policy was not to engage in overt displays of magic unless absolutely necessary. It frightened people, reminded them that powers beyond their

control were present in their midst. But right now, Harlequin
didn't care. He needed to be away from the burning building,
from the accusation in the stare of the people struggling to haul
order out of that chaos. Maybe a few hours from now, they'd
remember that he'd been the man who'd gone around that corner, who'd risked himself to take the Selfer down. Maybe
they'd remember and be grateful that there were people like
him out there to do it.

But probably not.

He let the wind rush over him, chilling his skin and washing the stink of smoke and blood away. He set down in Fort
Tryon Park, silent and dark at this late hour. The high ground
overlooked the city, giving him the silent remove he needed to
master his anger. He'd let Ward take the woman. He'd displayed magic openly. He'd gone airborne without filing a flight
plan. He was breaking regs left and right. *It's getting to you,
the isolation, the pariah status. Get it together.*

Harlequin pulled out his cell phone. It rang twice before
picking up on the other end. "SOC. Crucible." Crucible was
the call sign of Harlequin's supervisor, Major Rick Allen. The
two were old friends and didn't stand on formality.

"It's Jan."

"It's also late. What's up?"

"I just got a takedown and had to leave her under sedation
with the NYPD. They're taking her straight to the liaison
office, but there's a . . . gap in coverage. Shouldn't be a big deal,
but I wanted to let you know."

"You left her with them? Under sedation?" Crucible
sounded awake now.

"Regs allow for it in extreme circumstances."

"They don't smile on it, though, Jan. What the hell happened?"

"It was just . . . better without me there. The Selfer was a
friend of one of the cops, and she got hurt. The press were
about to descend on me. I wasn't up to talking to them."

Silence on the other end, then a slow rumble across the
phone's speaker as Crucible rubbed his eyes. "You okay, Jan?"

"I'm fine, sir," Harlequin said. His lapse into formality told
both of them he was anything but. "I think I just frightened
them a little . . ." *The sheep,* he almost said.

"It's fine," Harlequin continued. "It'll be fine."

"Stand by," Crucible said. There was a click on the phone, and Harlequin held while he answered the other line.

Crucible clicked back in. "That was the liaison officer in Midtown. They've got her, it's fine. They'll document the gap in coverage, but whatever. I won't let it impact you."

"Thanks," Harlequin said. "Sorry to put you in that position."

"It's okay. I'm actually hopping on a plane tonight. You and I are meeting someone tomorrow. Rep from a big pharma company up there. Apparently they've got some product in development that they believe can help control the brain's emotional center, help us channel magic more effectively."

"Sir?" Harlequin was a year into his detail supporting the NYPD in their hunt for the rogue magic users known as the Houston Street Selfers. This seemed well outside the scope of those duties.

"Small corps. We don't have the bodies to spare. It needs to be a SOC rep. You're lucky it isn't just you. They want someone field grade on the job, so I'm coming up."

"It'll be good to see you."

"Nice break from the day-to-day. You go from beating up Selfers and hobnobbing with cops to brushing elbows with a corporate muckety-muck. We're meeting her at a wine bar."

"I don't even like wine."

He could hear Crucible's shrug over the phone line. "I'm sure they'll have beer. If they don't, you'll figure it out. Just make sure to stick your pinky out while you drink."

"What are we doing, exactly?"

"We meet her, get the lay of the land, make sure she's got the facility locked down, and be points of contact if anything goes south."

"Will anything go south?"

Crucible laughed. "Civilians with more money than sense developing experimental drugs that affect the emotional center of the brain to control magical conduction? Potential to be one of the most lucrative government contracts we've seen to date?

"What could possibly go wrong?"

CHAPTER III
OPERATIONAL PREPARATION
OF THE BATTLESPACE

On two separate occasions, Oscar Britton has shown himself to be the real agent, not just of Latent-Americans, but of the American people writ large. He has exposed the government as the corrupt and double-dealing entity it is and illustrated his own commitment to freedom and equality for all of us. We agree with Walsh's impeachment. We want a new president. But not Howard Porter.

—Recorded message distributed on the Internet from the Consortium of Selfer Organizations (CSO)

Five hours after seeing Scylla's picture on Crucible's phone, Lieutenant Colonel Jan Thorsson arced across the sky over Sandy Hook. His flight suit rippled, the visor on his helmet keeping his eyes clear of bugs. A magically heated envelope of air kept him warm in spite of his speed and altitude. That same magic drove him forward at a pace the helicopters to either side of him struggled to match.

The Hudson River gave out into the Lower Bay beneath him, sparkling in the rising sun. He could see Coast Guard response boats cordoning off the river mouth, herding freighters and yachts alike back out to sea.

Ahead lay Manhattan, echoing out of his past.

The Blackhawks on either side held what he was told would be his staff. He'd had no time to select them or even meet them before taking off from Washington. It wouldn't matter anyway.

Even behind the tinted visors on the door gunner's helmets, he could read the judgment, feel the disapproval coming off them in waves.

He'd busted Oscar Britton out of prison. *And killed eight Marines in the process.* The one thing the public didn't know about was the one thing he truly regretted. For the hundredth time, he replayed the event in his head. Stepping out of the cell, the Marines kneeling, raising their rifles, fingers tensed on the trigger.

He could have ducked back in the cell . . . and then what? Bolted the door? Waited for them to bring reinforcements? They would have stopped him. Britton would have remained in Quantico's brig.

And FOB Frontier would have fallen.

You traded eight lives for a division. You saved more people than you killed.

But the queasy feeling in his stomach still wracked him. He could still smell their charred flesh, still hear their screams. Eight men, doing their jobs.

He radioed his escort and indicated descent, then called the control tower at Fort Hamilton. The controller replied reluctantly, grunting approval. Harlequin sighed and began to circle down toward the baseball diamond that had been cleared as an impromptu airfield. The star-shaped stone walls of the old fort spun beneath him. Harlequin swallowed. The history and tradition of the army he loved was wrought there in stone, a reminder of what he had lost when he defied his president. He'd dreamed of touring this space at leisure someday. Maybe teaching at West Point, less than a hundred miles north of here.

But magic had changed everything.

Harlequin's boots touched down on the grass just a moment before the helo wheels beside him. He was here to command, and he would do it. They didn't have to like him, only respect and obey him. If he'd played the game the way they wanted, somewhere in the neighborhood of thirty thousand people would be dead, just so Walsh could get reelected.

Remember that. Remember that every time you think of . . . of what you did. Eight lives for thirty thousand.

A fire truck was parked beside two Humvees and a white sedan. A cluster of soldiers stood around the vehicles, arms folded. Their hard faces reminded him of the price of his choice and that he would never stop paying for it.

Harlequin could hear his staff piling out of the Blackhawks as the rotors spun down. He raised the visor on his flight helmet and delivered a crisp salute to the garrison commander, a bull-necked, mustachioed colonel whose name tape read HEWITT. Hewitt returned the salute reluctantly. The garrison command sergeant major stood beside him, her hair in a tidy bun knocked slightly askew by the dying helo rotor wash. Her name tape read KNUT.

Harlequin saw Knut's failure to salute for the challenge it was. It had to be dealt with immediately. He met her contemptuous stare for a moment before folding his arms. "Do we not salute officers on Tuesdays, Command Sergeant Major Knut?" he asked. "Or was there some change in protocol that I'm not privy to?"

Knut glanced askance at Colonel Hewitt, who nodded. "Salute the lieutenant colonel."

She turned and dragged a limp salute up to her temple, her eyes venomous.

"You've got your salute," Hewitt drawled. "I got the word you were coming, but nobody said you'd be putting down on my fort. What do you need?"

"That depends on what's going on here," Harlequin answered. "The president has appointed me incident commander, I'll need . . ."

"We both know why he did that. This is my AOR, and *I* should be running the show," Hewitt said, a fat purple vein beginning to throb in his forehead, "but people like your pretty face on TV so much that they forgot what you did."

They don't even know what I did.

"Colonel Hewitt," Harlequin said, "it isn't our job to set policy. It's our job to salute smartly and carry out the orders of our civilian superiors. That's the oath we all swore when we joined up."

"Yeah, that oath meant a whole lot to you when you broke Oscar fucking Britton out of jail."

I didn't break Oscar Britton out of jail for giggles. "Regardless," Harlequin went on, "your commander in chief has appointed me incident commander and sent me here to take charge of this . . . incident. This crisis is apparently magical in nature. Unlike you"—Harlequin let his eyes move from Hewitt's to Knut's—"I am Latent, with long experience in combat operations in the arcane domain. And you're right. The public-affairs aspect of this crisis can't be denied. The public wants to be assured that someone they trust is in charge of what is shaping up to be the first defense against an armed invasion of the homeland since 1812. For better or for worse, they trust me and have no idea who the hell you are."

He hated taking this hard line, but he'd dealt with dozens of Hewitts since he'd saved the FOB. Laying down the law early was the best way to secure cooperation.

"Whether or not those qualifications satisfy you is irrelevant. The president is satisfied, and last time I checked, he's in charge. So, my question to you is this: Are we going to sit here and argue about who is in charge, or are we going to get about the hard work of dealing with this crisis?"

With these last words, Harlequin pointed over Hewitt's shoulder, where the East River divided Manhattan from Brooklyn. Even at this distance, he could see smoke rising, hear the faint thuds of ordnance impacting.

Hewitt turned purple. "You disobeyed orders . . ."

Enough. Now it was no longer a matter of securing Hewitt's cooperation. Now it was about setting the record straight. "I disobeyed illegal orders given by a morally bankrupt commander in chief that would have resulted in the destruction of an entire division," Harlequin cut him off. "People, Colonel. That's who I joined the army to defend. And I will always put their needs first, before mine and, yes, before those of my superiors if they give orders that put those two positions at odds. You like orders? So do I. I'm particularly fond of the legal ones. The right thing now is to stop comparing dicks and deal with this crisis. If it's all right with you, sir, I'd like to get started."

The purple of Hewitt's face began to border on black. Knut started to speak, stopped herself. The cloud of anger around him coalesced, and Harlequin got ready to Bind his magic to fight, wondering if he'd finally gone too far, if they'd throw caution to the wind and attack him.

But this time, like every other time, the anger finally deflated in the face of authority. Hewitt's shoulders sagged. "Well, you're lucky that *I* obey orders. Come on," he said. "I'll show you the ops center."

Harlequin shook his head. "I appreciate it, sir, but I'm going to set up on scene. This . . . breach opened up outside the New York Stock Exchange, am I right?"

It took Hewitt a moment to swallow his anger enough to answer. He nodded.

"And you have it cordoned off?"

"So far," Hewitt said, "but it's touch-and-go. We've got it locked down along Houston Street all the way across the island. The enemy can't move north, but it's taking everything we have just to hold that line. We need help."

"I'm going to get you help. How far south have they gone?"

Hewitt turned to Knut, who shrugged. "Last report said Beaver Street, by the Bowling Green station, but only a few of them."

Harlequin nodded, pulling his smartphone from his trouser pocket and checking over a map of Manhattan's Financial District. "So . . . Battery Park is clear?"

"So far," Hewitt answered, "but I don't know for . . ."

Harlequin cut him off with a wave. "Respectfully, sir, I'll be setting up my incident command post there. I'm going to need to go in hot and secure it right now. Whatever you've got to spare will be greatly appreciated. You've got the best situational awareness of anyone here thus far, so I'll need you to turn this post over to your deputy and join me there."

Hewitt bridled, began to speak, but Harlequin was already turning, motioning his people back into their helos. "Or, you can stay here, sir," Harlequin added. "I'm trying to give you a role in this operation, but I'm in charge, and if you want out, you might be doing both of us a favor. I'm happy to pillage your resources using presidential authority with or without your consent."

He Bound the magic and rose into the air as the helos spun their rotors up. "But if you're willing to cut the crap and help me, I'd be glad to have someone who knows the lay of the land. Your call, sir."

The words were a gamble. The truth was that he desperately wanted Hewitt at his side. Harlequin hadn't been back to New

York City since he was assigned there years ago, and Hewitt's experience would be invaluable. But to win him, he'd first have to show him who was stronger. *Please, let that be enough.*

Harlequin gave a parting salute and rose into the sky, the two Blackhawks banking to join him, racing across the East River, the smoke and chaos of lower Manhattan growing clearer by the moment.

Governor's Island rushed by below, the abandoned buildings mostly cleared now, a scattering of rising I-beams hinting at the new structures to come. Harlequin jerked his thumb down and radioed to Captain Cormack, his aide for this operation, flying in the Blackhawk alongside him.

"That's our fallback," Harlequin said into the mic snaking along his chin, pointing to the island beneath him. He wanted to be closer to the fighting, but at least this was an option if they couldn't establish a foothold in the park.

"Roger that, sir," Cormack said. "Sorry about what happened down there. I understand why you did what you did, and . . ."

"Appreciated, but let's secure the chatter." It was encrypted end-to-end comms, so it was unlikely anyone else heard, but the last thing Harlequin needed right now was to be distracted by sympathy.

Get to the park, get it secured. Harlequin tried to focus on the immediate. His mind turned over avenues of approach, supply lines, how quickly they could get comms going. Anything other than the woman's face in that grainy cell phone video.

It's not the woman you knew. She's dead. There was only Scylla now.

He shook his head, letting the wind strip the question away.

They moved out over the blue-green of the Upper Bay, where the Hudson emptied into it around Manhattan's western coastline. The thick green of Battery Park stood in stark contrast to the haphazard gray grid of the buildings around it. Even from this height, Harlequin could see people thronging the edges of the park, fleeing the chaos to their north. Three white-hulled Coast Guard cutters were moored at South Ferry Terminal, with several smaller boats flashing silver and orange as they loaded refugees, shuttling them to safety in New Jersey. The highway to the Brooklyn Battery Tunnel was a parking lot. The flickering colors of police lights indicated that some effort to direct the traffic was underway, but every car in the Financial District was trying to exit the island at once, and the snarl was inevitable. In the middle of the working day, it was the busiest part of an already busy city.

There was no way they would be able to get them all out in time. Harlequin had conflicting reports, but he knew that, at a low estimate, scores were dead already. There would be hundreds if not thousands more in the hours to come. The faster he moved, the better.

"What's that?" Harlequin pointed to a gray circle amid the green, a low, brick structure rising out of it.

"Castle Clinton," Cormack answered in his earbud. "Old harbor fort from back in the day. It's a national park monument now. The Statue of Liberty ticket counter is in there."

Harlequin let his eyes sweep the park and surrounding buildings once more. For all the chaos of the refugee stream, there was no smoke, no explosions, no sign of any enemy.

So far.

He gestured at the old fort beneath them. "That'll be HQ. Set down and get it cleared. The rest of you, stay with me. I want to get a look at the fight."

He put on speed and flew out over the park as Cormack's Blackhawk peeled off and began to descend toward the castle. The other Blackhawk stayed with him, the door gunners watching warily as the wall of smoke rose to meet them.

They pushed out over the edge of the park and into stark reality.

Lower Manhattan had been sliced off by hastily erected cordons. Harlequin could just make out distant haphazard barricades assembled from parked police cruisers, National Guard Humvees, even stacks of tires and spare coils of razor wire. He put on speed, the blocks blurring beneath him. Closer up, he could see that police manned the barricades at each intersection, augmented by the sliver of national guardsmen who were in the city when the breach opened, choking off the major arteries north. An M1 Abrams tank had either fought its way through or been at one of the armories. It was drawn length-wise across Broadway, flipped on its side and burning brightly.

The roofs of the buildings all along the Bowery were clustered with snipers. Harlequin could see gun barrels pointing out of apartment windows where spotters and shooters had taken up position. Two Apache helicopter gunships circled impotently, holding fire as the civilians continued to stream beneath them, making toward the bridges and tunnels and the promise of a way off the island.

The ground just south of the barricades was invisible beneath a seething mass. Goblins surged over abandoned cars, threw themselves against the locked doors of apartment buildings. Many of the towering structures were on fire, and Harlequin could see a squadron of wolfriders come pouring out of a storefront, shaking shattered glass from their shoulders. One of the riders whooped, waving a spear, a dozen diamond tennis bracelets and wristwatches ringing the shaft. His mount had a dress in its mouth.

Not all the goblins were intent on raiding. A few were taking cover behind building corners, shooting arrows or throwing javelins at the barricades. Harlequin heard gunfire, saw muzzle flashes from a building window. There was fighting in the higher stories as the goblins sought to take the high ground overlooking the barricades.

It wasn't just goblins. Huge, snarling giants roamed the streets. They'd already pillaged the historic remnants of the old Dutch colony, waving black, hand-wrought streetlamps as clubs. A pack of the demon horses that roamed the Source stood outside an electronics shop, crooning crude imitations of the voices of the actors on the televisions in the store window. Small, ground-bound scaled creatures, looking like flightless wyverns, wandered the streets. A few of their flying cousins were in the air already, along with the giant eaglelike rocs he'd faced before. As he flew past, a spider as big as a sedan scurried up the side of a building, three people mummified in the silk dangling from its abdomen. Harlequin could feel the air thrumming with goblin sorcery.

He circled once, dipping lower, trying to get a count of the enemy. The goblins numbered in the thousands. There were at least a few hundred of the giants that he'd fought at FOB Frontier.

He flew south, then east. The Blackhawk trailed him as he lit out over New Street. Here, the numbers thickened. A few goblins pointed skyward and a shot or two from a stolen carbine cracked in his direction, their aim atrocious as usual. He spotted the white figures of sorcerers and readied himself to fend off a magical attack. But, for now, they were interested mostly in the barricades, where the defenders poured on fire, throwing the goblins back.

Harlequin saw a magical fireball shoot out from the attackers, slamming into a police cruiser piled with rubble-filled trash cans. Lightning answered back from one of the soldiers behind it, and he knew that the SOC's law-enforcement-support element was on the scene, the only magical forces ready to respond on such short notice. He'd worked SOC LE himself all those years ago. But even with arcane fire support, he could tell that the defenders were hard-pressed. The sheer volume of enemy fighters was staggering.

The Blackhawk jagged sideways in his peripheral vision, bringing its guns to bear over the scene below. "Hold your fire," he radioed. "We've got civilians down there." Here and there, he could see the corpses of traders and store clerks on the street, blood going tacky in their ties and aprons. He didn't see anyone moving, but in the fog of war, that didn't necessarily mean anything.

A huge black banner had been hung out the window of one of the buildings, at least ten stories up. FREE OSCAR BRITTON, it read. LATENT-AMERICANS ARE STILL AMERICANS. Harlequin had seen dozens of similar signs and posters all over the country since they'd saved FOB Frontier. The irony of it wasn't lost of him. *From public enemy number one to hero overnight. It's a mad world.*

Then Harlequin passed over Broad Street and saw just how mad it really was.

The city's financial hub was rent by a giant gate, bigger than anything Britton had ever opened, over fifty feet high and spanning the entire breadth of the street from the steps of Federal Hall to the offices on the opposite side. Its ragged edges pulsed green, bruised purple, rotten-looking. The air stank like a fresh corpse left out in the sun.

This area was mostly clear of goblins. Something far worse trooped through the gate, liquid black skin absorbing the fading light.

He'd fought less than ten *Gahe* as he'd flown air cover for the retreating force during the evacuation of FOB Frontier, and they'd been the toughest things he'd ever come up against.

Here were dozens, maybe scores.

All utterly impervious to bullets. Only magic could harm them.

He paused in midair, taking in the bobbing horned heads, the malevolent white smiles. The goblins kept a respectful distance as the *Gahe* fanned out, contenting themselves with looting the buildings and channeling their forces toward the barricades.

Harlequin noticed other creatures taking up positions around the stock exchange; giant rocs roosted in the eves, preening their sword-length feathers. A smallish-looking red dragon was curled around the base of George Washington's statue, Whispered on by a goblin sorcerer draped around its neck.

As he took in the gathering enemy below, he caught a flash of white. He focused, squinting, maintained his altitude. He told himself that he didn't want to go any lower for fear of coming in missile range of the gathering horde beneath him. But he knew it for the lie it was. The woman from the video was down there. His heart raced. He didn't want to see her, knew he had to.

There, the flash of white again. This time he made out a beautiful face, wise, dark eyes, a severe slash of black bobbed hair.

It's not Grace. It only looks like her.

She looked skyward, smiling. Harlequin had seen her reduce hundreds of men and women, dozens of helicopters and tanks, almost a mile of perimeter wall, to stinking slime. She'd used the same rotting magic that Harlequin could see at work on the edges of the rent between the planes.

Not Grace.

Scylla.

He pushed away the flood of memories that came rushing to the surface, clawing at him. She'd lived here once. They'd met mere blocks from this very spot. He'd told her he would help her. He'd failed.

That was a lifetime ago. Magic had different plans for both of them.

He thought briefly of taking her out now, dismissed it. She was surrounded by enemy, and who knew how many sorcerers were down there in addition to the *Gahe*. He could call in an air strike and condemn civilians for blocks to a fiery death.

He'd done his recon. Harlequin turned, motioning the helo to follow, and made for Battery Park, Scylla's face haunting him. He toggled radio channels until he raised Cormack. "You've got comms with Washington?"

"Yes, sir," Cormack said. "Satellite's a little spotty, but it'll hold."

"Great. Get a video teleconference going as high up the chain as you can. General Gatanas at a minimum, President Porter if you can raise him."

"Sir?"

"You heard me, Captain. Get it done. I'll be landing in a few minutes, and I want to go right into the call."

"I'll need to give them a reason, sir."

"Crisis. That's your reason. We're about to be outgunned. Tell them we're going to need help, and we're going to need it right fucking now."

CHAPTER IV
UNDERWAY

And now we hear that Oscar Britton has appeared at the Ngāpuhi Rūnanga, negotiating directly with the Māori. The American government has been unsurprisingly silent on Britton's whereabouts and actions, afraid to condemn such a public hero as a traitor and terrorist. Britton is clearly taking advantage of this, working to build a public movement in favor of the repeal of the McGauer-Linden Act. There are signs that he's gaining ground, particularly on the topic of Limbic Dampener. But I will bet you anything that the Porter administration has every spook working around the clock to find and stop him. If Britton suddenly goes silent, it won't be hard to guess what happened.

—Dick Schumann
News analyst, *Action6 News at Six*

Brigadier General Alan Bookbinder stood on the aluminum ramp and looked down at his cell phone. His home number was dialed in, his wife on the other end. All he had to do was push CALL, and he'd be speaking to Julie in moments. He twisted the simple gold band on his finger, staring at the phone. Touching it had become a habit over the long days away from his wife, and now it had become a ritual, his talisman against loneliness.

His thumb hovered over the button, his eyes hovered over his shoulder. The ramp led from the pier at Staten Island's Sector New York to the Coast Guard Cutter *Breakwater*. The black-hulled buoy tender sat low in the calm water, 225 feet of steel, his reward for the insubordination that had saved thousands and made him a folk hero. He'd helped Harlequin and

Oscar Britton save the division of people trapped in the Source, under siege on FOB Frontier, helped bring them safely back home. The surge of support had gone viral on the Internet, a groundswell that the government couldn't ignore.

They'd pardoned him. Promoted him. And put him out to pasture.

As the SOC's liaison officer to the Coast Guard, Bookbinder could do no harm to anyone and was still in the grip of military justice.

Just in case he had any other ideas that ran counter to orders.

The woman charged with keeping an eye on him waited at the bottom of the pier. She was slight, young, her uniform looking a size too big for her. Her dark hair was swept into a regulation bun beneath her patrol cap. He'd been her commanding officer at FOB Frontier, and like many of the "heroes" who'd survived the base's destruction, she'd been brevetted up a rank. Her name tape read RIPPLE, which was also her call sign. Her Hydromancer's lapel pin was askew on her uniform.

Ripple did her best to cast a steely eye at him, a no-nonsense look she hadn't mastered. Bookbinder felt his heart go out to her. The role of guard fit her as poorly as the uniform.

Ripple was there as more than a guard. She was there to keep an eye on Bookbinder's unique ability, which he had sworn to keep secret. Alan Bookbinder could siphon off magic and bind it into inanimate objects, or even people. Which was ostensibly why he was reporting to the *Breakwater*, to oversee the deployment of one of his "Bound Magical Energy Repositories," what he called "boomers," an oil drum brimming with a blend of Hydromantic and Aeromantic magic supposed to calm rough seas.

After saving FOB Frontier, he'd stepped through the gate outside Bethesda Naval Medical Center ready to be court-martialed. Instead, there'd been questions, tests, days and nights "for his own safety" in a blank, featureless room which felt suspiciously like a comfortable prison cell. When the cries for his release finally forced the government's hand, and he emerged blinking into the sunlight, he'd been allowed home for one night.

One.

The girls had flown into his arms, folding around his knees, the smell of their hair making his throat tighten. But Julie had hung back, one hand on the lintel, her face blank. She looked quickly away when he tried to meet her gaze, over his shoulder at his "protective security detail," setting up their posts in the living room. Ripple was among them. She'd been assigned that morning.

The girls remained attached to his legs for the entire afternoon, and it wasn't until they'd been put reluctantly to bed that he found himself alone in the bedroom with Julie, a guard outside the door.

She shrugged off his awkward embrace, looked at the floor. "There are a lot of people talking like you're a war criminal."

There were a lot of people calling him a hero, too, but not in the social circles of military wives where Julie spent her time.

She looked up at him. "Alan, what happened?"

He opened his mouth to answer, but nothing came out. How could he describe the adventure? The transformation? He'd left her a desk-bound bureaucrat and come home a battle-hardened war leader. That transformation enabled him to make the hardest decision of his life: defying the authority of his government in order to save tens of thousands of men and women.

The man standing across from Julie Bookbinder was not the man she'd married, and they'd both known that the moment he'd walked through the door.

He coughed, stammered. "Julie, I . . ."

The door opened, and the girls came running through. Ripple stood outside, shrugged, smiling. She looked scarcely older than his children. "They wouldn't sleep, sir. They insisted . . ."

Bookbinder was too happy to acquiesce to letting the girls sleep with them. After all, he was only home for the one night. Kelly and Sarah lay between them, Julie's silent form on her side, back to him.

As the girls snored, he reached out, traced a finger down Julie's spine. "I did what I had to do, bunny. I had no choice."

She stiffened, the pace of her breathing the only other indicator that she heard him.

"I did what I did to get back to you in one piece. If I'd left those people when I could have saved them . . . what kind of man would I be?"

Silence.

"Julie. The one thing that kept me going . . . it was so hard, and I was able to push on through dreaming about this moment. I kept thinking if I could just get back to you, if I could just hold on long enough to get back to you . . . then . . ."

"Then what, Alan?" she whispered.

"Then it would be okay."

"It's not okay. Nothing's okay."

He nodded in the darkness, biting back tears, unable to deny it. "It doesn't have to be okay. That's what 'for better or for worse' means. It means that loving you is enough. And I do love you, Julie. Even if you're angry with me. There's still us after all of this. There has to be."

Whether there had to be or not, she wouldn't answer for the rest of the night, her back a white wall to his face, looming over the sleep-tousled heads of his children.

A stranger.

Bookbinder put the cell phone back in his pocket undialed. The ache tore at him. He knew that leadership was about making tough decisions, but he'd never truly understood it until he'd had to choose between orders and what he knew was right. *That's the man you fell in love with. Right, Julie? It wasn't just about things being easy and comfortable. It wasn't just about being a high-ranking officer's wife?*

Was it?

He knew he should be angry. Angry at the government for forcing him into this position. Angry at Ripple for dogging his heels. Angry at Julie for turning cold, for not giving him the benefit of the doubt.

But all he could muster was fatigue. All he could manage to crave was his old life. He loved his wife and children, and he missed them. There was simply nothing else.

One more fight in a string of many. He had found a way to stave off the overwhelming odds facing FOB Frontier. He would find a way to reclaim his place in the army. He would find a way to make Julie understand why he had done what he had done. He would fix this. The phone weighed heavily in his pocket. He'd put off making this call too many times. He wasn't going to do it with a ship waiting for him to disembark. When he got back to shore, he'd grab a bench, wave everyone off, and talk for as long as it took. Ripple wouldn't like it, but he'd figure out a way to deal with her.

He sighed and headed down the gangway. Ripple fell in behind him. He felt the disciplined eddy of her magic and pushed back on his own, instinctively reaching out to tug at her current. "Must be good to be on the water," he said. Ripple had helped him create his first boomers, water-cleaning devices that helped him make the long trek across miles of hostile territory.

"You get sick of it after a while," she said. "Spend your life in Hydromancy, and after a while all you want to do is burn something."

Bookbinder smiled. "Back at the FOB, all you wanted to do was come with me on a mission."

Ripple looked around at the ship, the placid quay, the low buildings in the distance. Her mouth settled into a thin line. "Somehow, sir, this wasn't what I had in mind."

He laughed. "It's safer."

"I didn't join up to stay safe."

The *Breakwater*'s skipper had spared four sideboys, two to either side of the gangway, to salute him as the boatswain piped him aboard, calling out, "Now, Brigadier General Alan Bookbinder, United States Army, arriving." Bookbinder had been briefed to salute the flag flying from the ship's stern, but there were no officers visible to request permission to come aboard from, so he simply returned the salutes the sideboys offered, stepped onto the main deck, and stood awkwardly until the boatswain, a chief warrant officer whose name tape read RODRIGUEZ, came over to him.

She had a face like a granite block, hair cut efficiently short, black streaked with gray. Her hard muscle and leathery skin spoke of a life at sea. "Commander Bonhomme is waiting for you up on the bridge, sir," Rodriguez said. A breach of protocol and an insult, but Bookbinder had grown used to them.

Rodriguez led them into the superstructure, up a ladder, and down a narrow passageway. The *Breakwater*'s tight spaces made Bookbinder claustrophobic, the gentle rocking of the ship turning his knees watery. His appetite fled. Ripple took it in stride, also stumbling but not looking nearly as green.

He put out a hand against the bulkhead to steady himself, waving away Ripple's support. Rodriguez turned, regarding him doubtfully. "You okay, sir?"

"Fine," Bookbinder answered, straightening. "Just . . . not used to this is all." He felt his gorge rise and burped before he could stop himself.

Rodriguez's eyes narrowed, with disgust or sympathy, he couldn't tell. "*Breakwater*'s a stable platform, sir. It'll get a little worse out there, but not much. I'll ask the storekeeper if we've got a patch for you."

Bookbinder wasn't sure what a patch was, but he shook his head. "That won't be necessary."

Ripple glanced an apology at the boatswain, who shrugged. "Sure, sir." She led them up another ladder. The *Breakwater*'s bridge overlooked the bow, dominated by the massive buoy-hoisting crane, rising some sixty feet in the air. Sailors in blue uniforms bustled around it, stowing gear, making lines up, about the business of casting off from the pier and getting underway.

Commander Bonhomme stood in front of the console, beside a dour-looking lieutenant whose name tape read MARKS. Bonhomme was skinny, with tired blue eyes and a head of brown hair gone prematurely gray. Marks was young and robust with a weight lifter's frame. His brown eyes widened as they fell on Bookbinder. Not everyone looked on him as a traitor. Some treated him as a hero. It was better, but not by much.

Bonhomme held a radio in one hand. The other was braced against the console edge as he gestured out the window. "No! There, damn it!" he shouted, before realizing that he wasn't speaking into the radio. He thumbed it, and said, "Yes, there. Thank you." He turned and acknowledged Bookbinder with a nod.

Bonhomme had an unfortunate combination of a skinny frame and a potbelly. His uniform hung off him, rumpled and unwashed, but he moved with a veteran's efficiency. The stains on his uniform were engine oil, sea salt, and rust, his legs instinctively adjusting with the rocking of the ship. Rodriguez looked at him with respect.

"Welcome aboard, General, Captain," Bonhomme said, not sounding welcoming at all. "You'll have to forgive me for not greeting you at the gangway, but we're late getting underway as it is."

Bookbinder knew it was customary on ships to come to attention when a flag-grade officer like himself came onto the bridge. That, and Bonhomme's failure to greet him personally were carefully disguised as the carelessness of protocol shown by a veteran seaman, but Bookbinder knew Bonhomme was letting him know he was unwelcome on his ship with the petty, passive-aggressive slights that military protocol seemed to have been designed for.

The ship rolled, and Bookbinder stumbled again. He caught his reflection in the shined stainless steel of the console and marveled at the greenish tint of his cheeks. Bonhomme turned to one of his sailors. His voice was icy. "SK3? Can you get General Bookbinder a scopalamine patch? It'll take a few hours for it to kick in, sir, but . . ."

Bookbinder stopped the man with a wave. "I'm fine."

"Captain?" Bonhomme looked at Ripple.

"Thank you, sir. That's not necessary."

The sailor froze, and Bonhomme looked doubtful. "Sir, the chop will only get worse once we cast off . . ."

Bookbinder couldn't give the man any more excuses to disrespect him. "I'll manage. Where's the armed guard?"

Bonhomme, Marks, and Rodriguez all looked at one another. "Sir," Bonhomme stammered, "I . . ."

"Skipper, this trip will go a lot smoother if we dispense with the bullshit and be straight with one another. Captain Ripple is here for magical Suppression . . . aaand . . ." Bookbinder looked around, spotted a sailor behind him in body armor with a pistol holstered against his thigh. "Ah, there you are. I suppose having an armed and armored sailor on the bridge of a buoy tender is just SOP?"

Bonhomme broke eye contact, looked to Marks for help, then at his feet. Bookbinder felt the air of empowered hostility shift and nodded in satisfaction. "So, let's get it done. Let your command know I'm here and that you have me under guard, and we can get about our business."

"It's already taken care of, sir," Rodriguez said, a ghost of a smile appearing on her hard face.

"Good." Bookbinder smiled back.

Bonhomme didn't smile, but the look he gave Bookbinder lacked the hostility it held before. "Bosun, take us out," he said. Rodriguez nodded and began giving commands to the sailor at the helm.

Bookbinder came to stand alongside Bonhomme, looking out the windows over the deck. The engines sent vibrations up through their feet, as the *Breakwater* began to make way. The ship rolled as it cleared the dock and the current took it. Bookbinder's stomach rolled with it. He swallowed hard, loosening his knees and tried to let his feet move naturally with the deck, refusing to reach out a hand to steady himself. Black smoke belched from the ship's smokestack, wafting past the window.

Ripple rocked easily with the ship's motion, already used to the pitching deck beneath her boots. "How the hell do you do that?" Bookbinder asked.

She smiled. "Not that hard once you get used to it, sir. My dad used to let me sailing when I was a kid."

They shared the smile before Ripple remembered she was his minder and secured hers with an effort. Bookbinder grinned. *You know why I did what I did,* he almost said out loud. *You're just too damned young and insecure to go against the might of the US Army.*

The sailors on the deck rigged a black oil drum to the crane's hook. In a humorous nod to the *Breakwater*'s main purpose, the words LOVE ME TENDER were painted along the crane's giant boom. Bookbinder had spent two days Binding the magic of a half dozen SOC Aeromancers and Hydromancers, Ripple among them, into that drum, and he could feel the faintest touch of the magical current even from here.

"So, that's it, huh?" Bookbinder asked.

"Yes, sir," Bonhomme replied. "It's pretty calm here, but once we get out of the bay, we could get four-to-six-foot seas. Should be enough to test your . . . device."

"Boomer," Bookbinder said. "We call it a boomer."

"Yes, sir," Bonhomme said doubtfully. "Anyway, provided your tests don't take too long, we should be tied back up by sunset." *And then you can be on your way,* Bookbinder silently finished for him. "What exactly are we doing again, sir?"

Keeping me out of the public eye. Punishing me for disobeying the president. "Search me. You tell me how rough the seas are. We put that thing in the water. We wait a few minutes. Then you tell me how rough the seas are. I report back. Think you can handle that?"

Bonhomme looked affectionately over the crane. "She'll pull fifty thousand pounds with the auxiliary. I think she can handle one oil drum, sir."

"I'm sure she can."

"How's it work? You have to switch it on?"

"Don't worry about it," Bookbinder said. The SOC had been clear. The less people outside the program knew about his ability, the better. The truth was that there was no need for an on switch. The boomer held the spells, waiting for an occurrence that required their discharge. He remembered the short stubs of metal he'd Bound with Ripple's water-purification magic. They'd discharged their power when dropped in fouled water, longer-lasting and more effective than any chemical system he'd ever used.

There was nothing more to say, so Bookbinder stood quietly as the ship made way through the Lower Bay and out to sea, his nausea increasing with the chop.

The water seemed an unchanging blue-green expanse before him, until at last he saw the dull tan-green of Sandy Hook begin to crystallize out of the horizon off their starboard bow.

The bridge was silent as all turned their eyes expectantly southward, and the seas picked up, rocking the large ship less and less gently.

Bookbinder watched the horizon, trying to keep the line of sky in his field of vision, hoping it would ease the rising sickness. His stomach rolled worse than ever.

A dull thud sounded from behind them, echoing across the sky. Bookbinder turned, but his view was obscured by the instrument panels and charts that adorned the bridge's aft bulkhead. He could hear the crew shouting around the crane, rushing to the railings, craning their heads aft and holding their blue-and-white plastic hard hats to their heads. Bookbinder's current intensified with his heightened nerves, and he felt Ripple Drawing her own magic, ready to Suppress him. It was ridiculous. Bookbinder's magic could spike to the limit, and he would never go nova. His power was a parasite, only working off the magic of others.

Bonhomme knew better than to turn, and called instead into the radio. "Who's got the stern watch? What's going on?"

There was a pause; a brief burst of static. Then, "Sir, something big blew up . . . I can't tell . . . maybe the battery? Big column of smoke. Might be Brooklyn."

Bonhomme dropped the radio and pulled another handset down from a bank of them above his head. "Sector New York, Sector New York, this is Coast Guard Cutter *Breakwater*, over."

The response was hissing static. He tried again, his voice rising, edged with worry.

"Bosun"—Bonhomme turned to Rodriguez—"nothing on encrypted, can you . . ."

Rodriguez was already pulling down another handset. It crackled into life before she could depress the button. "Coast Guard Cutter *Breakwater*, Coast Guard Cutter *Breakwater*, this is New York Naval Militia Patrol Boat 21 . . ."

"Yes! Pete! Hi," Bonhomme said, snatching the handset from Rodriguez's hand. "What the hell is going on? We're seeing smoke. We heard an explosion."

The response was staticky, intermittent. ". . . talk to Sector?"

"No!" Bonhomme shouted into the radio. "I can't raise them. What's going on?"

". . . lot of folks talking at once right now. What've you got on board?"

"For what?"

"Armament." Pete's voice was also rising, breathless.

Bonhomme turned pale. "What the hell are you talking about? I can't discuss this in the clear on channel 16."

"Come on!" Pete yelled back.

Bonhomme stared at the handset. Bookbinder, despite his seasickness, was already feeling the familiar calm that began to settle over him in a crisis.

Bonhomme finally swept his arm over the sailors on the bridge and around the crane below it. None carried arms. If there were weapons mounts on the *Breakwater*, Bookbinder couldn't see them. "We're a buoy tender, Pete," Bonhomme said into the radio. "What do you think we've got?"

Silence.

Then the radio came alive again. "Get back to shore. Even law-enforcement gear will help."

Bonhomme dropped the radio and turned to Rodriguez. "Raise Sector any way you can. Try 21, 23, 83."

Rodriguez punched buttons on the radio console while Marks called commands to the helm, and the *Breakwater* began to come about, rolling harder as the waves took her on the beam.

"Sir," Rodriguez said as one of the radios began to repeat a message. "All vessels return to base. I say again, all vessels RTB." The encrypted radio lit up. "Coast Guard Cutter *Breakwater*, Coast Gu . . ." Bonhomme snatched up the radio. "*Breakwater*, Commander Bonhomme."

"Jeff, it's MAT4."

Bonhomme sighed. "What's up? The radios are going crazy."

"We need you back here right now. I've got gunner running an inventory, but what armaments are you carrying?"

Bonhomme stared at the radio. "Standard law-enforcement complement. Enough for two boarding teams."

"It'll have to do. Come on back as quickly as you can."

"Will you please tell me what's going on?"

A pause, then, "Manhattan has been . . . invaded. Have your guys ready to go the second you RTB. We're going to muster at Sector, then head up to the battery. Station's fleet is already on scene."

Bonhomme looked at Bookbinder. "Did he say invaded?"

Bookbinder's sense of calm deepened. He tried to will some of it into Bonhomme. "He did, skipper."

"What the hell does that mean?" Bonhomme looked at Marks. The younger man was also pale but continuing to give orders.

"It means we scrub the current mission," Bookbinder said, gesturing at the boomer still tied to the crane. "We get back to the pier and figure out what's going on."

He wanted to grab Bonhomme by the lapels and shake him, remind him that his people were watching, that his posture would determine theirs.

"Right. Right." Bonhomme turned to Marks, began to speak, realized the ship was already coming about. He stood, stammering.

"Skipper," Bookbinder said. "They did say to come ready to fight. You might want to turn out your boarding teams. Get them rigged up."

"Right," Bonhomme said again, looking at his hands. Focusing on a task seemed to return some of his presence of mind. He turned back to Rodriguez. "Bosun, keep scanning those channels. See if anyone out there is talking about whatever is going on. Ask if anyone has cell phone signal. Maybe there's something on the Internet."

He turned to the armed sailor behind Bookbinder. "ME1 Mattes, get both teams turned out and suited up."

Mattes said, "Aye aye, sir," but didn't move. He looked expectantly at Bookbinder.

"I'll be fine," Bookbinder said, before Bonhomme could respond. He gestured at Ripple. "She'll Suppress my magic. What am I going to do, jump off and swim? Go."

"Sir, I . . ." Mattes began.

"It's fine," Bonhomme said. "Get them turned out."

Mattes nodded and left. Bonhomme turned to Bookbinder while Rodriguez scanned the radio channels.

"Bad timing," he said lamely.

Bookbinder waved a hand. "It's fine. I'm more interested in finding out what the hell is going on." He worried at his wedding ring, twisting it until it became warm against his finger.

The radio chatter was confused. A couple of boaters were talking about an army in the Financial District, with some saying it was the Chinese, or the Iranians. Some said monsters were coming out of the sewers. Bookbinder frowned, wracking his brain. Did someone have a Portamancer? That was the only way he knew to get an entire army onto the southern end of Manhattan that quickly.

Was it Oscar Britton? Had the man decided to seek revenge against the government? Maybe free Latent-Americans by violence? As quickly as the thought rose, he dismissed it. *He'd never do that. Not the Britton who saved the FOB.*

The *Breakwater* began to pick up speed, the huge crane rising and falling as the bow cut through the waves. Bookbinder steadied himself against the rail in front of the console. The sickness faded to a thematic buzz in his belly that he could just tolerate. Marks raised a pair of binoculars and squinted into the distance.

He dropped them. "Sir, there's . . ." He looked down at the radar, back up.

But Bookbinder and Bonhomme could already see it. A curtain of air hung directly in their path. It shimmered, wavering like asphalt heated in the sun, as if the water had climbed vertically until it reached the height of a building. Its edges were made distinct by lines of green rot, wafting a necrotic stink that Bookbinder could smell even inside the bridge. Around it, the water frothed and churned. Bookbinder felt Ripple's magical tide spike hard. "Easy there, Captain," he said, smirking. "I wouldn't want to have to Suppress you."

Ripple blushed. "I'm fine, sir."

"All engines stop." Marks looked down at the sonar. "Sir, you'll want to see this."

Bonhomme pushed past Bookbinder and stared at the screen. "What the hell is that? School of fish?"

"Biggest school of fish I've ever seen," Rodriguez said, looking over, "and that's . . . that's a whale." Her finger tracked shaded blotches across the screen, moving steadily toward the city. As Bookbinder watched, the blotches paused, flickered, then began moving quickly toward what Bookbinder assumed was their position.

"That's not . . . normal," Bookbinder said, looking out the window over the buoy deck. The bow dropped as the ship slowed. The boiling patch of water around the shimmering square of air moved closer to them. Bookbinder thought he saw things breaking the surface . . . sharp and pointed. Spearheads?

"All engines! Back full!" Marks was shouting.

The *Breakwater*'s bow shuddered as it cut into the boiling water. The surface was seething now, light glinting off pointed shapes piercing the surface, as if an army swam beneath. A huge black shape, at least as big as the *Breakwater* itself, appeared alongside the ship. The sonar was a sheet of solid color surrounding the buoy tender.

"ME1!" Bonhomme shouted into the radio. "Get your teams on the buoy deck!"

A response crackled back, drowned by the yelling on the bridge.

The *Breakwater* ground to a stop, the hull echoing as if a thousand hands were drumming against it.

The water erupted.

Creatures flung themselves out of the waves, sticking to the *Breakwater*'s sides. They were small, skinny, with long, pointed ears and fingers, shaped like human children and scarcely bigger. Their pale skin dripped seawater, reflecting the sun. They were crusted with barnacles, seaweed clinging to their sparse hair. Tentacles sprouted randomly, wriggling between shoulder blades, protruding from under an armpit, writhing from the knuckles of webbed fingers. They clutched spears, knives, short hatchets that looked to be carved from bone or coral.

They paused, chattering to one another, then swarmed up the hull, just as Mattes's boarding teams appeared on the buoy deck, still tightening their helmet straps and adjusting the slings on their weapons.

The creatures came over the gunwales and down around the crane, scattering the unarmed sailors, who went scrambling back through the boarding teams, shouting. The creatures looked like the goblins Bookbinder knew from FOB Frontier, warped and twisted by the sea.

Bookbinder had lived and worked in the Source long enough to be unsurprised by the sight of monsters, but the crew of the *Breakwater* had no such advantage. The boarding teams stumbled backward, blinking. The sea goblins swarmed forward, grinning at the fear on the faces of the retreating sailors, brandishing their spears, brine trickling from their mouths, sun glinting off their pointed teeth, yellow, broken, and wickedly sharp.

CHAPTER V
HOLD WHAT YOU'VE GOT

We now have what the world is calling a second "Gate-Gate" scandal from the United States. This scandal confirms the revelation that America, in collusion with the Republic of India, has been operating in the alternate magical dimension known as "The Source." They have done so without respect to the security interests of this body, or the input of its members. This brazen colonialism is nothing more than what we've come to expect from these two powers. Which is why we have now assembled member nations from both ASEAN and the SCO to demand this body conduct a full investigation into the extent and the intention of this collusion, and take appropriate action to safeguard the interests of all member nations.

—Peter Tan
Singaporean ambassador to the United Nations
Speaking before the UN Security Council
in the wake of the "Second Gate-Gate Incident"

Harlequin watched the Chinooks circle overhead. The huge helicopters shed altitude, ground crews moving the T-shaped concrete barricade walls that hung from their undercarriages into place. They had mostly completed an impromptu wall around Battery Park, the gaps filled with sandbagged machine-gun positions. A navy Seabee unit directed another Chinook, lowering the top of a guard tower onto hastily constructed supports.

Harlequin could see a few of the enemy, less than a thousand feet away, still in numbers too small to mount an assault. But not for long.

"No!" he shouted into the radio handset, jerking to the side and forcing the RTO whose backpack it was connected to to stumble along behind him. "I need *all* your T-walls. I don't care if you don't have the fuel budget for this. I need you flying nonstop sorties. We need to keep this foothold, and that's not going to happen if we can't get a perimeter up. What part of 'from the president himself' don't you understand?"

A knot of civilians huddled by Castle Clinton's entrance, already outnumbering the soldiers inside the barricade wall four to one. Some were burned and bleeding, all looked ragged, exhausted, and thirsty. They needed water. They needed medical attention that his tiny force couldn't possibly provide. Most importantly, they needed to get the hell out of here.

Harlequin looked up as a thin-skinned Humvee drove in through a gap in the barricades and rolled to a stop in front of him. Hewitt stepped out of it, in battle gear, with Knut and two more soldiers.

Harlequin saluted. "Good to see you here, sir." *Unless you're going to break my balls. In that case, go fuck yourself.*

He looked back at the radio. The supply officer at the other end had taken his sudden distraction as an excuse to hang up.

Hewitt scowled but returned the salute. Knut didn't have to be reminded this time.

Hewitt gestured at the T-walls. "You haven't wasted any time."

"There's no time to waste. I'm being sucked dry by bureaucrats at Fort Dix. They sent the one helo flight"—he indicated the Chinooks—"but we need more if we're going to get this park walled off."

As each Chinook dropped off its T-wall, it landed long enough to take on a load of refugees before taking off back in the direction of New Jersey and safety, but it wasn't nearly enough.

"I've got more T-walls inbound from Hamilton and Wadsworth, too. I'm talking to the Coast Guard about making sure your back is covered." Hewitt indicated the water behind him. "There's some kind of problem there. They've got a ship underway that's not coming in. This"—he indicated a yellow New York City school bus that was even now unloading a platoon of soldiers—"is something, at least."

Harlequin met Hewitt's eyes. He knew how much this man must bridle at helping him. He'd make it as easy as he could. "Thanks, sir. I'm glad to have you with me. I'm going to need a New Yorker to help me understand the lay of the land."

Hewitt snorted. "I'm from Ohio. I was transferred here from Fort Bliss, Texas, a few months ago. I don't know New York, but I know it's my responsibility to protect it, no matter who the president puts in charge. So, let's get this straight. This is my ground, and I'm covering it. I've spent some time in the manuals since you came on scene, and there's definitely some wiggle room over jurisdiction. I'm not going to tug my forelock and step aside while some . . ." He swallowed, calmed himself with an effort. "While you take over. I'm here, and I have a voice in how this action is handled."

Harlequin considered arguing, decided to bite down on his pride. Hewitt was determined, and his rank was nothing to sneeze at. He'd played the military trump card, wasting your opponent's time. Countering him would require hours of his own spent poring over joint-service publications and incident-command-structure manuals. Any argument would have to be followed by an appeal up the chain, which would make him look weak and incompetent and underscore the lack of confidence the rest of the military had in him.

He shouted over to the soldiers piling off the bus. "Get that bus loaded up with refugees!" The civilians surged at his words, and his soldiers had to shove them back as they began picking the closest to load on the bus.

"Battery Tunnel is closed," Hewitt said.

"Then open it," Harlequin replied. "I don't have the supplies or the manpower I need to care for these people. We keep them here, and not only will they die, but they'll take us with them. Every one of them we can get out of here makes our chances that much better." *And these are the people we joined the Army to serve.* He left the thought unspoken, but Hewitt's expression showed he understood it as well as if it had been said aloud.

Harlequin wondered if he'd pushed the man too far, but the colonel nodded and barked a command to one of his soldiers, who jumped back into the Humvee and spoke into the radio as the bus, crammed with civilians, trundled off toward the tunnel entrance.

Harlequin turned back to Hewitt, relieved. "I've set up an ops center in the monument."

Hewitt and Knut fell in beside him as they made their way to the old fort. "So, you've done your recon. What's the SITREP?"

"There's some kind of . . . rent in the planar fabric, like a Portamantic gate."

"Like what you used in Gate-Gate," Hewitt said.

Harlequin ignored the barb. "It was Oscar Britton who used it, but yes. Except this one looks . . . rotted open. Or, it's being rotted bigger." Scylla, standing among the monsters, head craned up at him.

They moved past a bronze sculpture, a paean to the immigrants who had made this city great. Harlequin thought of the latest arrivals through the widening gate and shook his head at the irony.

"Rotted?" Hewitt's eyebrows arched as they entered the main gate. The wooden portcullis was wedged permanently open, but Harlequin had bulletproof police barricades with windowed tops dragged into place on either side, each manned by a solider. Inside, Cormack was hard at work setting up the video-teleconference system on a plastic folding table outside the Statue of Liberty ticket-sales desk, already looking forlorn and deserted. Soldiers bustled to and fro, carrying pallets of bottled water, crates of ammunition, radio equipment.

This old fort hadn't been occupied by real soldiers for over two hundred years. Suddenly, it was a military hub at the center of what could be the most important operation in the country's history. Harlequin felt the weight of that history on his shoulders for a moment. It made him tired.

"I've done some looking around myself," Hewitt said. "Most of these goblins are half our size and using bows and arrows. There are some bigger monsters in there, but they've got no real ordnance."

"There was a prisoner at FOB Frontier," Harlequin said as they took seats at the plastic table. "A Negramancer of considerable power . . ."

"Excuse me, a what?"

"A Witch, Colonel. A Probe with power over decay. When Oscar Britton ran, he let her out, and she nearly took half the

base down in the process. Her name was Scylla. Well, that
wasn't her real name, but all the prisoners we held there took
new names, and that was hers."

"So? What about her?"

"She's here, Colonel. She's leading this invasion."

"How do you know?" *I'd know her anywhere.*

"I saw her when I reconned the enemy position. I saw the gate,
I saw her using her magic to widen it. And that's not the only
thing I saw. The bulk of the attacking force are the same goblins
and giants that tried their luck with FOB Frontier the entire time
I was there. They're nothing you can't handle. FOB Frontier was
surrounded by them for ages and was able to fight them off. But
there's also a large contingent of *Gahe*."

Hewitt froze, his cheeks sagging. "You mean . . . the black
things . . . from the Apache reservation? How the hell did they
get here?"

Harlequin found himself grateful that there was at least one
aspect of this fight he wouldn't have to explain. "They're not
from the reservation, Colonel. We think they got there the
same way they're getting here . . . through some kind of tear
in the planar fabric. The issue is that we've only ever fought
them in ones or twos before. From what I saw, there are dozens, and more coming."

"They're worse than goblins." Hewitt made it a statement,
but Harlequin knew it for a question.

"They are," he said. "For many reasons, but the most important one is this. As far as I know, they're completely impervious to conventional ordnance. The only thing I've seen that can
hurt them is magic."

"We need the SOC," Hewitt said.

"We do," Harlequin said, "and I'm about to get them here."
He motioned to Cormack.

"How many?" Hewitt asked.

"All of them." Cormack typed on a ruggedized laptop computer, then gave a thumbs-up as the connection was passed to
a large flat-screen monitor that dominated the table's far end.

The VTC popped up, showing an office interior. The far
wall was dominated by the American flag crossed with a gold-
trimmed red banner showing three white stars. The same number of stars marked the shoulders of the man seated behind the

cherrywood desk. He had a craggy face, shadowed eyes, and a butcher block of a jaw. His buzz-cut hair had gone gray long ago. If it were any longer, the bald spot would be prominent. As it was, he looked more stone statue than human.

General Gatanas, Commandant of the Supernatural Operations Corps. That he hadn't been relieved of his command following the FOB Frontier debacle and Walsh's impeachment was a testament to Porter's commitment to the old order.

"Lieutenant Colonel Thorsson," Gatanas said. "I was expecting this call some time ago."

"I took an opportunity to recon the enemy infil point, sir. Frankly, I'm glad I did. This is a lot bigger than we thought it was. I saw . . ."

"Who's this?" Gatanas asked, gesturing at Hewitt.

"Colonel Hewitt, sir," Hewitt replied. "I'm the CO of Fort Hamilton in Brooklyn. This is my AOR."

Gatanas ignored him, looking back at Harlequin. "What's going on?"

Harlequin sighed internally. "The silver lining here is that we now know where Scylla is."

"In New York?"

"Leading the enemy, sir. The infil point is some kind of interplanar rent in the middle of Wall Street just outside the New York Stock Exchange between overflow offices and Federal Hall. It looks like she's using her Negramancy to expand the opening. When I did my overflight, it looked to be around fifty feet square, maybe larger. The attacking force is coming through there."

"I heard it was goblins and some of those giant birds."

"They look critically weak on air support right now, sir, but I've got a feeling they're remedying that as they speak. I've set up a command post on the southern tip of . . ."

"I saw goblins when I was at the FOB, Lieutenant Colonel. Even in numbers, they're weak, disorganized."

"I know sir, but . . ."

"And if you say they lack air support, why can't we just call in Apache squadrons from Dix? Doesn't the Air Force have fixed-wing strike assets at McGuire right next door?"

Harlequin took a deep breath and spoke slowly. "Sir, this is one of the most densely populated cities in the country. This

attack came without warning. While we've been able to evacuate a lot of civilians, there are plenty of people trapped in . . .'"

"The Breach Zone," Gatanas finished for him. "That's what
we're calling the operational environment."

"The Breach Zone. You don't want gunships raging in
there. And they won't help anyway, because Scylla has reached
some kind of understanding with the *Gahe*."

Gatanas leaned over the desk, cocking an eyebrow. "They're
there? How many?"

"Dozens? More? I saw them coming out of the . . . Breach,
sir. I doubt I'll be able to get eyes on the target again anytime
soon."

Gatanas steepled his fingers under his chin and closed his
eyes. "That's bad."

"Yes, sir, it is. So, you understand the urgency of this next
request. You know the *Gahe* are only vulnerable to magic. I
need the Corps' QRF scrambled. I need every asset you can
spare. We can't afford to have this breach spill its banks, sir. I
need the whole SOC, every man and woman."

Gatanas kept his eyes closed. "No."

It was a moment before Harlequin could speak. "Sir?"

"No. You can't have the SOC. I can give you . . . Fornax,
Carina, and Cephalus Covens."

Harlequin hammered his fist on the table. Both Cormack
and Hewitt jumped. "Respectfully, sir, are you kidding me?
Those are *training* Covens. I don't have time to babysit a bunch
of wet-behind-the-ears Novices! They'll do more harm than
good!"

Gatanas kept his eyes closed for a long time. At last, he
opened them, turned to his computer, and punched up an inset
screen that appeared in one corner of Harlequin's monitor.
"I'm patching something through now. Take a look."

The inset showed grainy camera footage piped in from a
helmet-mounted camera. The soldier wearing it was sighting
his carbine around a chunk of dusty rock, loosing three-round
bursts toward a low cinder-block wall. Men with long, black
hair in flannel shirts returned fire, until one of them leapt over
the wall, rocketing toward the soldier, lightning streaming
from his hands. Something huge and black shifted in the cam-

era's periphery, stutter-flashing past. Then the camera spun, and Harlequin heard screaming. Static.

"That looked like Mescalero," Harlequin said.

"It is," Gatanas replied. "This is a two-pronged attack. At approximately the same time your Breach opened up in Manhattan, a similar one boiled over on the reservation. At least, we're assuming that's what it is. Maybe the *Gahe* were hiding there all along. Same profile. Goblins, giants, more *Gahe* than we've ever seen in one place before. Add the Apache insurgency to that. The SOC is engaged there. It's a small corps, Lieutenant Colonel, as I'm sure you know."

"Sir, respectfully, what's the nearest town to the reservation? Ruidoso?" Harlequin asked. "That's got ten thousand people on a good day? We're in the middle of New York fucking City. If I don't get help, we're going to have a massacre on our hands the likes of which this country has never seen."

"You don't get it," Gatanas replied. "It's not Mescalero, or even Ruidoso. It's White Sands."

"White Sands?" Harlequin let all pretense of protocol drop. "Why should I give a fuck about White Sands?"

"Because it's the lion's share of our strategic stockpile. You're so focused on the new nuke that you forgot about the old ones."

Harlequin looked at Hewitt. The colonel was pale. "Our nuclear warheads," he said.

"We've been destroying them as fast as we can as part of the START V treaty. Most of what we've got left is secured at White Sands Missile Range, just a hop, skip, and a jump from the worst armed uprising this country has ever faced."

Harlequin couldn't think of what to say. "Is there a lot?"

"There's enough." Gatanas's voice was flat. "I'll send you those training Covens and as much conventional firepower as I can spare. You'll have to hold what you've got until we can get Mescalero put to bed."

Harlequin stood, began to respond, but Gatanas cut him off. "You're a soldier, Lieutenant Colonel. Do more with less. Find a way."

Harlequin sagged, sat. "Okay, sir."

"Okay," Gatanas said. He reached to toggle off the connection.

"Wait," Harlequin said, then remembered his manners. "Sir."

"What?" Gatanas frowned.

"I need some things."

"I already told you what I can . . ."

"With all due respect, sir, you're asking me to hold this ground against a foe only vulnerable to magic with almost no magical resources. More conventional troops aren't going to cut it. You want me to do this, I need some things. Four things, specifically."

Gatanas's frown turned ugly. "And those are?"

"I need FEMA here right now. The entire city should be evacuated."

"Now wait just a minute," Hewitt cut in. "The fighting is confined to . . ."

"Respectfully, sir," Harlequin said to him, "I don't have the time or resources to clear eight million people out of their homes and fight this enemy with one hand tied behind my back. Those barricades won't hold, and when the enemy breaks through . . ."

"Lieutenant Colonel Thorsson," Hewitt said through clenched teeth, "this is New York. I don't think you fully realize the kind of people who live here."

"Maybe not, but I realize the kind of people who are going to die here if we don't get this city evacuated."

"Gentlemen, enough," Gatanas cut in. "You'll get FEMA. I'm already getting as many SOF teams as I can beg, borrow, or steal into the city to get refugees out. They're going to be working on their own, but you might find them knocking on your door from time to time for resupply or to drop off civilians."

"Resupply? Sir, I don't have the . . ."

"What else?" Gatanas cut him off.

"I need General Bookbinder."

Gatanas looked uncertain. "The general is . . ."

"Sir, it would really help if we just dispensed with the illusion of secrecy. We both know what Bookbinder can do. If I can't have Sorcerers on the line here, then I need ordnance capable of harming the enemy. Magical ordnance."

Gatanas rubbed his eyes and sighed. "Yes, I figured that was coming. The general is . . . we're having some trouble raising him at the moment. As soon as we can get ahold of him, he'll be relieving you of command."

If Gatanas had meant the threat to Harlequin's authority to check him, it failed. "That's fine, sir, so long as he makes with the magic bullets. How long until he's inbound?"

"I have no idea. As soon as I know, you'll know."

Gatanas was clearly already at his wits' end. Pushing matters wouldn't get him the help he needed any faster. "Okay, next. I need Sarah Downer."

Gatanas suddenly looked awake. "What?"

"Sarah Downer. I need her out of detention, back in uniform, and standing next to me."

"You know damned well that isn't going to happen, Lieutenant Colonel. We're still questioning her. Her pretty face hasn't been on TV either, so Porter isn't under any kind of public pressure to play nice, which, I might remind you, is the only reason you're not in a cell next to her."

"No doubt, sir," Harlequin said, "but you're asking me to protect a city of over eight million people with no arcane support. Downer can take a couple sparking wires and make an elemental platoon. I need force multipliers, and apart from Bookbinder, she's the best one you've got."

Gatanas was quiet for a moment. "This is personal for you, Thorsson. You've been pushing for her release since we took her into custody."

"Downer is loyal, sir; she wants to serve."

"Which is no doubt how you feel about your own sorry ass."

"Your words, sir, not mine." *But absolutely true.* "I need her magic, and I need it right now."

Gatanas paused. "I'll see what I can do."

"One last thing," Harlequin said. "If this country doesn't have the magical resources to deal with this threat, then we need to reach out to partner nations who do. I need lines to the defense attachés for Canada and Mexico. This is a threat to them, too."

Gatanas rubbed his temples. "How is it that you can call all that 'just four things'?"

"Because that's what it is, sir. Four things, without which, I can promise this city will fall."

Gatanas shook his head. "What does she want, Thorsson?"

Harlequin tapped his finger against his chin, driving all thoughts of the woman he had known from his mind. Instead, he conjured the face of the monster who had slaughtered hundreds in the SOC liaison-office parking lot. "Revenge. And I don't just mean smacking the SOC in the face for what we did to her. I mean total revenge. Making all non-Latent society pay for what she perceives as some kind of genetic apartheid. I talked to her plenty when they first put her in 'the hole,' sir." *And plenty before that, too.* "She's convinced that she's the one to usher in a new age of Latents-on-top."

"Kind of what Oscar Britton wants."

"No, sir. Oscar Britton wants equal rights for Latent people. Scylla wants the apartheid she perceives to reverse. There's a difference."

"So why are the *Gahe* helping her? What do they want?"

"That, I don't know, sir. I only know that if they want it, then I don't, and violently."

"Okay, well I . . ."

Gatanas was cut off as a soldier ran breathlessly into the room behind Harlequin. His eyes widened as he saw who was on the screen, and he saluted halfway before realizing he was indoors. "Sorry, sir. I mean, to interrupt. Sorry. Master Sergeant Bilkes said I should . . ."

"It's fine, Specialist," Harlequin said. "What's the problem?"

"It's . . . It's the enemy commander, sir. She's outside the T-walls. She threw this up, said you'd know what it was." He handed Harlequin a chunk of broken street signpost, tied with a scrap of white bedsheet.

"What is that?" Gatanas leaned across his desk, squinting. "Hold it up to the screen? I can't see it."

It was a long time before Harlequin could answer.

"It's a flag of parley, sir," he said, holding it up. "You wanted to know what Scylla wants. I guess we're about to find out."

Scylla stood some distance away from the line of T-walls. A *Gahe* stood to either side of her, black bodies crouched, heads turning, scanning for threats.

He flew over the T-walls, gathering dark clouds around him, boiling with lightning. As soon as he cleared the perimeter, he lowered himself to just six feet above the ground. He

wanted the high vantage point, but if Scylla had some way to
Suppress him, he wasn't going to risk falling to his death.

The preparations were more than good battle sense. In a
moment he'd be face-to-face with this woman out of his past,
and that was not the time to lose focus. *The lightning is for
Scylla, not Grace. Remember that.*

"Isn't this dramatic?" Her voice carried over the distance.
"You and me, New York City. Just like old times."

She smiled, her confidence as smooth and enchanting as
the most talented politicians he'd known since he'd come to be
stationed inside the Beltway.

He breathed deeply in a failed attempt to slow his pounding heart. *Not Grace. Not Grace. Not Grace.*

"You come to surrender?" he asked, struggling to keep the
tremor out of his voice. "I should warn you that your list of
crimes makes it highly unlikely that any court in this country
will let you live."

She smiled wider. "I've been thinking about your court system. There're some changes I'll be making there. Thanks for
reminding me."

"What do you want, Scylla?" Saying the monster's name
felt good. *Don't call her Grace. That woman is dead.*

"To save your life, and the lives of whatever handful of
Latent people you have under your command. You're an idiot,
but it's an idiocy born of devotion to the institutions that raised
you. It takes a lot to break those chains. You turned down the
chance to come with me before, but . . . you know, since we
were close, I figured I'd give you another one."

"You're not making sense."

"I am the only one here making any sense."

She held up a pistol. Without taking her eyes off Harlequin,
she fired it into one of the *Gahe*. The creature didn't flinch, the
bullet vanishing into the dark surface of its body.

"You have a lot of these," Scylla mused, looking down at
the smoking gun. "Bigger ones, too. None of them will help,
you know that?"

"If you think that means I give up my position, you're wrong."

She shook her head, clucking her tongue. "That's suicide,
for you and your subordinates. And for what? So you can go

on doing the bidding of people who are terrified of you? We're the same, Jan. We both want to do good."

"You don't want to do good."

"We're the next rung on the evolutionary ladder, you and I. We are quite literally the same. It's foolish for us to fight."

"We're not the same. I'm an agent of the people of the United States of America, and you're a murdering criminal. Whatever happened between us died along with those people you killed. Now, tell your dogs to go back where they came from and surrender. I won't take it easy on you, but I'll be just. That's something."

"I think I'm done with your brand of justice, thank you very much," Scylla said. "If you're determined to remain a footrest for the humans, then I'll have to hold you to account along with them."

"Humans?" Harlequin asked. "You're a human."

"No, I'm not." Scylla's expression darkened. "I'm something else entirely. You could be, too, if you'd only let yourself see it. We're a new race to rule a new world. Your SOC and McGauer-Linden laws are just feeble flailings to stave that off. That flailing irritates me. I'm here to make it stop."

"New race, huh?" Harlequin gestured to the *Gahe*. "Is this what the new race looks like? Because you don't seem to fit in too well. And honestly? They're fucking ugly."

She exchanged glances with the *Gahe* she'd shot, back to Harlequin. "Looks can be deceiving. There's plenty to find ugly about humanity."

"And plenty to find beautiful, too," Harlequin said. "Are they equally devoted to this new order of yours? And what about all those goblins up on Wall Street? What did you have to promise to get them to help you?"

"And what were you promised, Jan? Are these humans you're so ready to die for rewarding your loyalty? Are they treating you like the hero you are?"

Harlequin swallowed. Faces flashed through his mind, the vein throbbing in Hewitt's forehead, Knut's curled lip.

"They're terrified of you, aren't they?" Scylla asked. "They curse you even as they beg you to save them. Why, Jan? I don't understand."

Because it's not about me. It never was, he thought. But all he said was, "You can't understand."

"Jan," she said, her voice low now, all anger gone from it, quivering ever so slightly. She sounded hurt. She sounded genuine. "Jan, please. Don't do this."

It's not her. Grace is gone. Harlequin looked down and shook his head.

Scylla sighed. The remnants of her smile faded. "Remember when I worked here?" she asked, sweeping her arm to encompass the now-silent Financial District. "Remember what I showed you?"

"I remember," Harlequin said. "It doesn't matter. You came up Latent. You came up Probe. You killed people."

The sardonic smirk returned. "And that is why they help me. The goblins, the mountain gods, all of them. They see you for what you are, and they know you will never stop until you control every action of everyone and everything that frightens you.

"They want the same thing I do. To be able to go to bed at night and never have to wake up worrying that you're out there, plotting to put us in chains again.

"We can't get that by negotiating with you. We can only get that by teaching you what those chains feel like. You'll have to wear them for a good, long while before you understand."

Her voice and posture stiffened. "Last chance. You can stand at my side, or you can crawl under my boot, but I'm done asking nicely.

"I've given you terms. Accept them, and let's be done with this."

Harlequin shook his head. "Your terms are refused. You're going to have one hell of a fight on your hands. I promise you this: When we beat you, and we will beat you, we're not going to throw you back in the hole. We're going to make damn sure that you can never hurt anyone else ever again."

"How pleasant to see we have precisely the same goals," she replied, "and yet another reason why it's foolish for us to oppose one another. I have a feeling that as this struggle wears on, you'll come to see the wisdom of my position. Please convey to your leadership that I'll be glad to receive any embassy from them under flag of parley should they wish to treat with me. They can find me there. Top floor." She pointed over her shoulder up Wall Street, where the Trump Building rose seventy stories over the Manhattan skyline.

"Nobody is coming to talk to you, Scylla. We're going to rout your army; and then we're going to put you to death."

"We've known one another a long time, Jan. I promised when you first took me that I would get free. I promised that I would turn that fucking gulag of yours to ashes. And I did, didn't I?"

Harlequin was silent.

"Didn't I?" she repeated.

"Yes."

"I also promised that I would make you pay. I always keep my promises, Harlequin.

"Always."

INTERLUDE II
SHEEPDOGS AND WOLVES

The problem was one of military authority. Title 10 of the US Code prevents the military from arresting or using deadly force against people not subject to the UCMJ. The navy uses the Coast Guard's legal authority to get around that when warships happen to come across drug smugglers at sea. The SOC Law-Enforcement Support Elements were the answer on the ground. The fact was that Selfers are really a police matter, right? American citizens breaking American laws. But when the bad guys have the kind of firepower that Selfers usually pack, well, even the best SWAT team in the world isn't going to cut it. You need muscle, and that's where we come in.

—Major Samuel Arneau
Judge Advocate General, US Supernatural Operations Corps

SIX YEARS EARLIER

Enoteca went silent as Harlequin and Crucible walked in. The Upper West Side winc bar was a staple for corporate executives, software tycoons, and the rest of New York City's power elite. They weren't used to seeing army officers in uniform.

Army Sorcerers were a bridge too far.

Harlequin was used to it by now. He'd been alternately reviled and admired by every non-Latent person he met, and he didn't prefer one reaction over the other. Both fetishized him. At the zoo, you stared in amazement at the lion. You waxed eloquent about its beauty, its lean, predator grace. But you sure as fuck weren't going to get in the cage with it. Thorsson met the shocked gazes evenly. He was not a human being to these people. Some thought him more, some less. It made him tired.

The silence began to abate into nervous chatter as the two officers took a seat by the window and looked over the menus.

"So, where's our contact?" Harlequin asked.

Crucible gestured at the crowd. "We're the standouts. She'll find us."

"It's a female?"

Crucible nodded, and they sat in moody silence, painfully conscious of the stares falling over them.

"We could take these off, I guess," Crucible said, tapping the SOC badge Velcroed on his sleeve. "Maybe they'd think we were National Guard."

Harlequin shook his head. "SOC is what we are. I'm not hiding that. I'll make captain soon, and then it's out of here. Less time around civilians, the better."

Crucible smiled, arching an eyebrow. "We swore to protect these civilians."

"We did," Harlequin agreed. "But that's not something they understand. We're sheepdogs."

Crucible's expression fell. "Jan, I got the same speech when I went through SAOLCC. It's crap."

Thorsson swept a hand over the crowd, men in thousand-dollar suits chatting amiably with women whose gym-lean figures were amply advertised by pencil skirts. "Sheep, Crucible. These are sheep."

Crucible frowned. "Don't drink the Kool-Aid, Jan. You don't have to believe everything they teach you."

Harlequin waved a hand. "It's the truth. They go about their lives blissfully ignorant of the danger that's all around them. At any moment, a Selfer could Manifest here, decide they want to practice desiccative Hydromancy on a city block. Then they're all dead, and all the money and power in the world can't change it.

"They're sheep, and there are *wolves* in the flock, Crucible. And they don't even know it."

"Wolves." Crucible sighed.

"Wolves," Harlequin agreed. "We keep those wolves at bay. And you know what the problem is with that?"

"That you keep talking?" Crucible asked.

"The problem," Harlequin went on, "is that sheepdogs and wolves look the same, smell the same. To a sheep, there's no difference."

"You need to secure that attitude," Crucible said. "You don't do the job because you expect to be thanked for it. It's not about you and never was. Neither of us asked to come up Latent, but we do the best with what we have. You distance yourself from these so-called sheep far enough, and you'll turn into a wolf yourself."

"I'm right, and you know it," Harlequin said. "And you don't have to worry. Because there is one critical difference between sheepdogs and wolves. One thing that keeps us on the good side of the dividing line."

"Our snazzy haircuts?"

"Regs. We obey the law. Selfers don't. That's the core. That's everything."

Crucible opened his mouth to argue when the waitress finally approached the table. She was young, with New York hipster beauty that hinted at artistic aspirations beyond the walls of the wine bar—cat's-eye glasses with leoprint frames, two-tone hair, an anchor tattooed on her tricep. "Hi, guys," she said. "Let me start by thanking you for your service to our country." Her voice wavered with excitement. Her eyes darted, looking away the moment Harlequin made eye contact.

Harlequin would have registered such nervousness as an indicator of guilt of some kind, but he felt no magical current from her, and everyone treated him with the same heady mixture of amazement and fear.

"It's our honor, ma'am," Harlequin answered. Crucible smiled mildly.

She grinned back, practically shaking, saying nothing.

Crucible broke the awkward silence. "So . . . maybe we could get a couple of beers here?"

"Oh, right!" she squeaked. "Sorry. Uh, we actually don't serve beer here. But we have some great wine selections."

Thorsson frowned. "I don't know a damned thing about wine."

"Oh, that's no problem. If you're . . . new to it, I can pick something out for you."

"That'd be great," Crucible said. "White for me."

Harlequin nodded agreement. The waitress nodded back and didn't move. The moment drew out.

"Sorry," she said. "It's just that I never met real Sorcerers before. You guys are SOC, huh? What are you doing here?"

"LE support, ma'am," Crucible said. "We help out your police department on arcane matters."

"So . . ." she said slowly, "you guys, you know, track down Selfers?"

Harlequin sighed inwardly. "When we have to, ma'am. It's not our favorite part of the job." That was public affairs talking. Harlequin liked taking down Selfers just fine.

"Still," she said. "That's really . . . scary, you know?"

"You get used to it," Harlequin said. The truth was, it *was* scary, but he'd found that was something you didn't really notice until afterward.

"So . . ." Her pierced tongue darted out to lick her lips as she glanced at his school lapel pin. "You're an . . . Aeromancer, right?"

Harlequin nodded. He appreciated the attention, her big brown eyes and pert breasts straining her tight T-shirt. Her sense of style spoke of a person who broke rules even though he knew she was conforming to her own special set, but opposites attracted, and the appearance alone was powerfully erotic.

But she wasn't talking to Thorsson the man. She was getting close to the canine in her midst, excited as she overrode her sheep instincts and sniffed at it. He was sick of it already.

"You can fly?" she asked.

Harlequin didn't answer, but Crucible was grinning like a fool. "Sure, he can. Just got off duty with a navy squadron in Florida, didn't you, Lieutenant?"

Harlequin glared at him.

"Wow," she said. "That is so amazing." She paused. When neither of them spoke, she pulled a scrap of paper from her skirt pocket. "Well, listen. I've always wanted to . . . you know . . . learn more about magic. Maybe we could hang out sometime. I'm sure you've got some awesome stories to tell." She set the scrap of paper down in front of Harlequin. Crucible looked down at his wedding ring, smiling fit to split his face.

"And if you're just out of Florida, I could show you around

New York a bit. I know a lot of people shy away from you, but I'm not like that." She looked up at Harlequin again, working hard to hold his eyes, failing miserably, looking so frightened that he half expected her to pass out.

"That's very kind of you, ma'am," Harlequin said, making no move to pick the paper up. A phone number and e-mail address were scrawled below a name—ALICIA.

"Okay!" she said, paused awkwardly, then walked away.

"Wow," Crucible said. "Somebody's getting laid."

Harlequin snorted. "No, thanks."

"Dude. I'm a happily married man, but if I was a swinging dick like you? Young, in shape, pretty blue eyes? I'd have gotten half the city pregnant by now. As your superior officer, I order you to go out with that girl."

"Hell, no. She's not interested in me. She just wants to tell her friends she fucked a Sorcerer."

"You're an idiot. Do you know how Sam and I fell in love?"

Harlequin shrugged. "At a monster truck rally?"

Crucible laughed. "Actually, that's not far from the truth. But, no. We got drunk in a bar and hooked up. I think I'd spoken a total of five words to her before we were making out. We woke up next to one another and freaked out, wondered what we'd gotten ourselves into."

"So . . . your point is that you're a man-whore."

"Yes. Wait, no. My point is that we just lived our lives and acted like human animals, and we kept waking up next to one another. We've been doing it for years now. And now we do it with our son in the next room. That's how life happens, Jan. It's not all regs. Sometimes, you have to let it unfold."

Harlequin frowned. "Magic changed that. You let stuff unfold, and people die."

Crucible shook his head. "You're an idiot."

Harlequin shrugged again as a drink was set down in front of him. It was a tall, mixed drink, the kind that was served in a giant martini glass. Big, fancy. Expensive. "Um . . . this doesn't look like wine . . ." he said, confused, "and he needs one, too."

Alicia looked unhappy. "It's for you. From the lady over there." She gestured to the far corner of the bar. A woman sat alone, in a black business suit that hugged a tight figure that rivaled Alicia's.

But that was where the resemblance ended. Where Alicia looked young and nervous, this woman was wise, confident. Her jet-black hair was cut in a short bob along her chin. Her dark eyes spoke of experience, command.

She quirked a smile at Harlequin, raised a glass that matched the one just set before him.

Alicia frowned and walked away, swishing her hips in a way she must have thought looked sensuous.

"Holy crap," Crucible said, ignoring the waitress. "Dude. I'm dead serious. If you don't go talk to this one, I really will bring you up on charges."

Harlequin nodded. His fatigue vanished. Her expression was fearless, looking at him with the naked anticipation of one person wanting to get to know another. After months of being treated like a zoo animal, that stirred him.

"What about our meeting?" Harlequin asked.

"I'll keep an eye out," Crucible said. "I'll come break you off when it's time. Speaking of which"—he tapped his watch—"if you're going to make any headway here, you better get moving. Go go go!"

Harlequin nodded, picked up the ridiculous drink. The woman watched him as he made his way over, giving him the uncomfortable sensation that she was looking through his uniform. He felt the heat of that look wash through his body and was amazed to feel his cheeks redden. He couldn't remember the last time a woman had made him blush.

He raised the drink, nearly spilling it on himself. "Much obliged, ma'am."

She snorted. "That's what they called my mother. I'm Grace."

"Grace." He tried the name out. It fit her. He struggled to find something to say, failed. "Thanks for the drink."

"You can thank me with some company," she said, patted the seat next to her.

He sat, her words propelling him as surely as if she'd steered him with an invisible hand. Again, he stumbled for words. Who was this woman? "I don't have a whole lot of time, I'm meeting someone in a moment. What can I do for you?" he finally said, his voice sounding stupid in his ears.

"You're pretty and you're in uniform. That's plenty," she

said. "That your boss over there?" She gestured to where Crucible was pointedly not looking in their direction.

"Yes, ma'am," Harlequin said. "He's going to give me hell about this later."

A charm glittered at her throat, a silver likeness of a six-headed dragon, crouched on twelve tentacle legs. She caught him staring, and he blushed again as he realized the charm nestled above the dark line of her cleavage, exposed enough to be enticing, not enough to be crude. Her skin was milk pale, a light tracery of blue veins visible below the surface, almost luminescent in the dim light of the bar's interior.

She smiled darkly. "Whatcha looking at?"

It was his turn to smile now. This was ridiculous. She was a human being who happened to be good-looking and slick and apparently not frightened of him. That was refreshing, but it was no reason to act like a teenager. He felt the current of his magic oscillating with his arousal and nervousness, and reined it in. "That's an interesting necklace."

Grace looked down at her breasts again. "Oh," she sounded disappointed. "That's Scylla. My sister has Charybdis. Mom said we were twin terrors."

"It's really cool." *I can't believe I just said that.*

"And here I was thinking you were checking out my rack."

"Maybe I was, a little." No matter how hard he tried to regain his composure, he kept talking like an idiot.

She smiled again. "Well, you know. I work out."

He laughed, the nervousness fading. He looked back up at her, met her eyes, held them.

"Can I ask you something?"

She cocked her head to the side, liquid black hair brushing her cheek. "Shoot."

"Why aren't you scared of me?"

She laughed. "Should I be?"

"Most people are."

"Because you're SOC?"

He nodded.

"Honey, I've seen the Night Dancers in Uganda. I've been to Mescalero. I practically financed Japan's first five Shukenja squadrons. Magic stopped impressing me a long time ago."

His eyes narrowed. That kind of civilian experience working with magic? "Who are you?"

She grinned, arched an eyebrow. "You can call your boss over now. We can chat here for a while, but the formal meeting should be at my office."

CHAPTER VI
MORE WITH LESS

We worked off the assumption that the Apache had a Porta-
mancer, and that was how the Gahe were getting onto the reser-
vation. We spent millions and years trying to track this
Portamancer down. We realize now that was more hope than
assumption, sir. Baker's "thin-spot" theory is correct. There are
intersections between the Home Plane and the Source, where the
planar fabric has worn thin. In such locales, the planes bleed
through into one another. In severe cases, entities can move
across.

—Lieutenant General Alexander Gatanas, Commandant
Supernatural Operations Corps
Briefing to the Joint Chiefs of Staff, Vice-Chairman for Intelligence

The boarding teams didn't stand a chance. They clumped
together outside the hatch into the ship's superstructure, gaping with disbelief. With the closed hatch behind them and the
ship's starboard rail to their left, they had nowhere to go but
into the enemy.

The goblins moved forward, grinning. One of them seized
the barrel of the boarding officer's rifle, yanked it. The man
cried out, carried forward by his rifle sling. The goblin barked
something, slammed a club into his head. His helmet skewed,
and blood sheeted down the side of his face.

One of the boarding team members shrugged off the stupor
of fear, raised his rifle with shaking hands, and fired. The round
whined off the crane's boom, three feet over the goblins' heads.

"Commander, get your men off that deck," Bookbinder said.

"What the fuck is going on?" shouted Bonhomme. He shouted the same question into the radio, not realizing that he hadn't depressed the button to talk, cursed. One of the goblins threw a spear. It arced across the intervening distance and buried itself in one of the sailor's shoulders. The teams began to move back through the hatch, trampling over one another, shouting.

The goblins swarmed the sides of the *Breakwater* until Bookbinder could barely see the ship's black hull.

More hauled themselves up onto the deck. One scaled the crane, its arm hooked around the throat of a dead sailor, hard hat trailing by its plastic chinstrap.

At long last, one of the sailors found his courage and turned to fight. His shotgun boomed, and some of goblins reeled back, peppered with shot, bleeding. Another sailor drew his pistol and let off a stream of undisciplined fire, most of his bullets thudding into the deck.

"Get them out of there!" Bookbinder shouted.

"What the fuck are we supposed to do?" Bonhomme pounded his hands on the console. "We're not equipped to fight a battle!"

Bookbinder shook his head and ran out to the passageway. Ripple grabbed his arm. "Sir," she began.

He shrugged her off. "No way. Now it's time for you to follow."

Then he was out the hatch and into the passageway. He threw himself down the ladder to his right, bumping his head painfully on the low ceiling. He saw stars, shook them off. The ship wasn't that big; he should be able to find the hatch where the boarding teams had come out. But when he got his bearings, he found himself alone in some kind of mechanical room with a huge winch in its center, lined with shelves of supplies and equipment. He blinked, looking for a way out.

Feet descended the ladder behind him. "Sir! It's this way!" said Rodriguez. He followed her back up the ladder, turned into a passageway he'd missed in his rush, and a few steps later heard the sounds of the struggle. The boarding teams had streamed back into the tight passageway, shouting, bleeding, falling over one another.

"Order!" he shouted. "I will have order, damn it!"

He shouldered his way through, some of the chaos abating. The petty officer who'd led them was hunched against the wall, clutching his bleeding head, rifle gone. Bookbinder reached down and unsnapped his pistol from its holster, dragging it out. The petty officer offered no resistance.

Two of the boarding team members found their feet, taking up positions on either side of the open hatch. One was reloading her pistol, the other firing his shotgun. The goblins withdrew to the cover of the crane's base. They winced as the shotgun boomed, but even Bookbinder knew it wouldn't be effective at this long range. They rose slowly, wiggling their ears as the terrified petty officer fired again, the gun kicking, smoking, and doing little else. The goblins chattered to one another, grouping to charge.

"Don't shoot me in the back, please," Bookbinder said as he stepped through the hatch. *What I wouldn't give for some magic right now.*

"Ripple, damn it!" he shouted. He felt for a magical current, came up empty. There was no time. He raised his pistol, took careful aim at the foremost goblin, and fired.

He'd never been much of a marksman, and the goblin charged as the bullet flew wide. Lucky for him, there were more rounds in the magazine, and they kicked off just as fast as he could pull the trigger.

The third bullet took it right in its swollen forehead, spattering a mixture of greenish blood and seawater, sending the creature spinning into its comrades.

Bookbinder didn't wait. He targeted another goblin, pulled the trigger, and moved on, targeting and firing, advancing a step with each shot. The goblins crouched, quailing under his disciplined fire, pulling back to the ship's prow.

Bang. Bang. Bang. Bookbinder felt himself fall into the familiar space that had become a second home for him after his many battles defending FOB Frontier, the old dance of move, shoot, and reload. His breathing slowed as his heart rate rose, the weird dichotomy between heightened alertness and greater calm.

Bang. Bang. Bang. Click. Click. Bookbinder's hand dropped instinctively to the magazine pouch at his belt.

And found nothing. His stomach clenched as he remembered he'd retrieved this pistol from another man's holster, forgotten to take his spare magazines.

The goblins lost no time. Three rushed out from behind the crane's base and charged him.

Bookbinder punched the first one in the face, the pistol barrel crunching into its skull and turning sideways, flaying open his knuckles on the sheet of barnacles that encrusted the creature's head. The thing reeled backward, thrusting out with its spear shaft as it struggled to maintain its footing. Bookbinder caught the shaft, wrestled for control of it.

Another goblin came at him from the side, swinging a long cleaver, face wriggling with a living beard of tentacles. Bookbinder jerked the spear shaft into the way to block the blow, then clubbed it in the face with his pistol. The goblin reeled backward, slammed into the port rail, went over the side.

By the time he turned to face the third goblin, it was on top of him, too close for him to do more than turn the spearhead into its gut, throwing out an elbow at its face. It slapped the spearhead down and reached for him, hands wrapped in some kind of salt-crusted skin, holding short, sharp blades to each fingertip.

The creature stiffened, green-brown skin turning gray. The amphibian-looking slime that coated it dried, then the tissue beneath. It peeled, wilted, the life-sustaining water that flowed through it puddling on the deck.

Ripple's magical current surged behind him.

Bang.

The goblin spun across the deck, half its face gone, salt water and slime pooling beneath it. Rodriguez stood behind him, a smoking pistol in her hand.

Bookbinder swung the spear shaft, the remaining goblin still clinging to it, its feet coming off the deck. Bookbinder released the shaft and hurled it into his fellows, pushing the crowd back against the base of the crane.

"Get off my ship!" he shouted.

Ripple moved up beside him, extended a hand. He felt her current Bind hard off the ship's side, lifting the water, the bow rising. Rodriguez stumbled, shouted at her. "What the hell are you doing?"

Then the bow slapped back down and a huge wave swamped the buoy deck. It coiled like a serpent's body, looping around the goblins, and leaving Bookbinder, Rodriguez, and Ripple bone-dry. The torrent swept the creatures up, slamming them into the crane boom with bone-jarring force, then shot skyward, throwing them into the air. They rained back down, some splashing into the water and some bouncing off the deck, leaving trails of brine and blood behind them.

The water flooded away, leaving the deck clear.

"Thanks," Bookbinder said, turning to Ripple. "That was some . . ."

The Hydromancer was collapsed beside the hatch, a javelin lodged in her chest. Blood soaked half her blouse, but she'd frozen the flesh around the wound, her hand clapped to the base of the weapon, the tide of her magic flowing erratically. "Fucker threw just before I got the wave going . . ." she said through gritted teeth. "I'm sorry, sir."

Her skin was waxy pale, sweat beading on her forehead.

"Jesus, don't apologize," he said, looking back at the buoy deck. The goblins were already swarming back aboard. A few started forward, took in Bookbinder's bleeding knuckles, Rodriguez's smoking pistol, held back. He'd bought them some time.

But not much.

"All right! Back in there and get that hatch secured!" he shouted. Rodriguez helped him to lift Ripple by her armpits and drag her, stumbling, back into the superstructure as the sailors sealed the hatch. Ripple moaned, apologizing over and over.

He pointed to the sailors with the shotgun and the pistol, leaning against the hatch, heads touching in their effort to look through the single porthole. "You've got it?"

They nodded, shaking off some of their fear and confusion. Two sailors were dealing with another's head wound. Another rushed to secure the watertight dogs on the hatch.

Bookbinder turned to Rodriguez. The boatswain looked pale but steady, biting down on the thousands of questions she must surely have. "Is there a sick bay? You got a doc on board?"

She shook her head. "We've got aid stations and defribs . . . but nothing that's going to help with . . ."

Ripple's magical current suddenly went faint. Her head lolled against Bookbinder's thigh.

"Come on, Captain!" Bookbinder gently slapped her face, shook her shoulders. Her hand fell away from the spear shaft, the frozen wound beginning to thaw, blood going tacky at the edges. Bookbinder shook her again, took her pulse.

Nothing.

Bookbinder laid her down, but the javelin's blade kept one shoulder elevated, making CPR impossible. Not that he remembered how to do it anyway. His mind was a jumble of fear and grief, shutting out the ratio of chest compressions to rescue breaths. Mattes shouldered him out of the way. "I've got it, sir!" The sailor eased Ripple's body down the javelin's shaft, getting her level. He squatted over her, drawing it out, then clapping his hands over her sternum, administering chest compressions. Ripple's ribs cracked under the pressure with an audible crunch.

"Get that hole plugged!" Mattes called to another sailor, as blood began to bubble out of the hole. Bookbinder looked at the position of the wound in horror as another sailor ripped off his blouse and began stuffing it in. There was no way her lung could still be whole and inflated beneath it.

Bookbinder murmured barely audible thanks. Already the hatch was thrumming with blows as the goblins beat their spear butts against it. He stared at Ripple. She was just a kid, and a brave one at that. Her face vanished, and it was his daughter Kelly lying there, her chest darkening as her life's blood slowly pumped out across it. His daughter's eyes staring sightlessly, her lips turning blue.

Oh, God. Kelly. I've got to get back to you.

There's no time for grief. If the goblins get in here, you'll lose the whole ship.

Bookbinder swallowed, forced himself to speak. "Can we seal off the superstructure?"

Rodriguez nodded. "This hatch and another on the port side. There's a central hatch to the winch room. We seal those, they can't get in from the bow."

"Do it," he said. Rodriguez nodded and began barking orders to the boarding team.

Bookbinder turned to the four remaining. "You hold." They nodded, frightened, but resolute.

He almost asked Mattes how it looked, then stopped himself.

There's nothing you can do here besides get in the way. If Mattes can save her, he will. Secure this ship, get to shore, and find out what the hell is going on.

"Hang tough," Bookbinder said. He turned to Rodriguez. "Bosun . . ."

"I've got it, sir. Go . . . help the skipper." Her eyes met his, rock steady.

That would have to do. He set off up the ladder back to the bridge.

Bonhomme was in the exact position Bookbinder had left him in, looking out the bridge windows over the buoy deck, watching the goblins regroup.

Bookbinder swallowed his frustration and tried to keep his voice even. "Commander, we've got the superstructure secure from the bow. The goblins are confined to the buoy deck. Now would be a good time to make an announcement to get the rest of the ship locked down in case they swarm aboard aft. Commander? Commander!"

Bonhomme turned, looked at him. His mouth worked silently. Bookbinder glanced at Marks, who nodded and picked up the radio.

"Commander." Bookbinder turned back to Bonhomme, keeping his voice low and soothing. "I will focus on making sure the ship is secure. I need you to get us turned around and back to shore."

Bonhomme continued to stare.

You fucker. Bookbinder's wedding ring felt heavy on his finger. *I am not going to lose my chance to fix things with my family because you can't get your shit together.*

Bookbinder took the radio from Marks, depressed the button and spoke, hearing his voice booming throughout the ship. "This is General Alan Bookbinder. I know what you're experiencing is . . . frightening . . . that's fine. The creatures you're fighting are goblins. I've fought them before. Don't underestimate them. They're as smart as you are. We're not letting them take this ship. You will hold the superstructure. There are a lot of them, but they are smaller and weaker than you. Your bosun and I just killed an even dozen or so without breaking a sweat, and we're old and fat. If you keep your composure, you can and you will beat them. Dig in and hang on. We're going to get home."

Bookbinder handed the radio back to Marks and took Bonhomme by the shoulders. "Commander, if we're going to get through this, you need to pull together. You've got people relying on you to show them the way."

Bonhomme blinked, and some of the color returned to his face. "Right. Right. Of course. It's just. We're a buoy tender. We're not equipped to fight . . . monsters."

"I know it," Bookbinder said, "but you don't have to fight them. All you have to do is keep them off the bridge and out of the engine room long enough to get us back to shore."

"Right," Bonhomme said again. He slowly turned back to the ship's console, started as gunfire erupted across the buoy deck.

Bookbinder spotted Rodriguez leading sailors through the hatch on the starboard side. They laid down a volley of disciplined fire, driving the goblins back until they hunched by the base of the giant crane. They cringed until the fire stopped, then came charging out, but Rodriguez had stationed two sailors with riot shotguns outside the hatch. They waited until the goblins were nearly on top of them before emptying shells into their massed ranks. A number of them fell, the rest either dove over the side or fled back to the relative cover of the crane. A few climbed up the boom and took aim at the bridge with bows and slings. The missiles pattered off the windows.

Bonhomme leapt back from the rattling glass and Bookbinder cursed inwardly. He opened his mouth to encourage Bonhomme again when Marks handed him the radio. "It's . . . it's for you, sir."

Bookbinder held up the radio and thumbed the button. "Bookbinder."

"General Bookbinder, sir! You're okay!" Bookbinder recognized the voice, but not the anxiety in it.

"Lieutenant Colonel Thorsson! You're the last person I expected to hear from! How the hell did you find me?"

"Gatanas said you were underway with the Coast Guard. I've been beating the hell out of this radio for the past hour."

"What's going on?"

"No time, sir. I need you onshore right now. Got a problem you're uniquely suited to solve. I'll explain everything once you're here. For now, just hang on. Help's coming."

"Onshore is . . . where the hell onshore?"

"Battery Park. Castle Clinton. We're right on the water. You can come straight to us."

Relief swamped him. Bonhomme visibly relaxed. "That's great to hear. We're under attack out here. Looks like . . . some goblin variant. They came through . . . it's like a gate, only . . ."

"I know," Thorsson answered, "we're dealing with the same thing here. It must extend out over the water. I'm sending navy support to pick you up right now; they're going to bring you to my position."

"We've got at least two casualties here," Bookbinder began, heedless of how Bonhomme blanched at the words. "One might be KIA, we need medevac."

"Just hang on," Thorsson replied. "We can't do anything until we get you clear."

"I see them, sir," Marks said, pointing over the horizon, where two ships were coming into view. The first was roughly the same size as the *Breakwater*, but sleeker, gray lines showing a prominent deck gun. Bookbinder could see men scrambling over her gun deck. Sunlight glittered off several light machine guns fixed to hardpoints on the railings. The other ship was double the size, bristling with armament.

Bookbinder began to breathe easy. These were warships. There wasn't a whole lot a pack of swimming goblins could do to them.

"Cavalry's here, Commander," he said to Bonhomme.

"Looks like it," Bonhomme said, clearly embarrassed. He began to give orders, and the *Breakwater*'s engines coughed into life as the buoy tender picked up speed, moving toward rescue.

A moment later, the radio crackled into life. "Coast Guard Cutter *Breakwater*, Coast Guard Cutter *Breakwater*, this is Littoral Combat Ship *Giffords*. Hold your current position. Stop all engines. We're going to try to clear some of the enemy here. We'll come to you."

Bonhomme gave the order as the *Giffords* opened up with her machine guns, and Bookbinder heard the familiar chatter of 7.62 rounds. The water off the *Breakwater*'s bow churned as the bullets tore into it. The goblins shrieked, flattening themselves against the crane. Their brethren in the water dove, but not before Bookbinder saw many of them cut to ribbons by the withering fire. Spears, hatchets, and knives bobbed in the froth. Small blooms of blood dotted the surface.

The hairs on Bookbinder's neck stood up as he felt a magical current eddying off the *Breakwater*'s starboard beam. The current felt charged, sizzling against his senses. Aeromancy.

He rushed to the starboard bridge window just as the water off the ship's bow began to bubble, something close to the surface channeling a torrent of electricity toward the approaching ships. Bookbinder hauled on the magical current, feeling it flow into his own body, blotting out his vision and buzzing in his ears. He doubled over, nearly overwhelmed by the force of the energy, then held out a hand and Bound the magic into the water where the goblin sorcerer swam.

His vision returned as the magic poured out of him, leaving only the steady flow of his own tide. The water sparked, flashing below the surface, runnels of steam wafting skyward, a lightning storm unfolding in the deep. Goblin bodies began to float to the surface, charred and smoking.

Bookbinder heard cracks from the navy ship, saw goblins behind the *Breakwater*'s crane spin and drop under sniper fire. He sucked in his breath at the risk. The skipper must be truly desperate to get him back if he was willing to chance hitting someone on the buoy tender.

The water around the *Breakwater* was a bobbing field of discarded weapons, shredded goblin bodies, and blossoms of brackish blood. The larger ship maintained position, while the *Giffords* held her fire, turned broadside, and began to the circle the *Breakwater*.

"Hold position until we're certain you're clear, then we'll come aboard," came the call over the radio. Bookbinder thought of Ripple and had to stop himself from yelling at them to hurry.

Bonhomme thanked them as Rodriguez came onto the bridge, sweating and bleeding and obviously relieved.

"Captain Ripple?" Bookbinder asked. "How's she holding up?"

Before Rodriguez could answer, Bookbinder felt the deck slide beneath him. At first he thought it might be the regular rolling of the ship, but the deck refused to right, the *Breakwater* leaning steadily to one side. Bookbinder flailed, grabbing Rodriguez's shoulder and bracing himself against one of the console rails.

Out the starboard window, he could see the water sloping, running down into itself, as if some vortex had opened beneath it. The *Giffords*'s bow slid downward, looking like she rode some bizarre aquatic roller coaster. She opened up with her small guns again, the deck gun spinning uselessly.

Bookbinder noticed the huge shape, the black blot below the water that Rodriguez had thought was a whale. It grew as it came closer to the surface, the black slowly resolving into gray-green, ridged and gnarled, some leviathan out of the Source. Its vast bulk crawled with living protrusions, swarming across the wrinkled skin, barnacle things, skittering as they waved frond tentacles. The thing tilted upward, bullet-shaped snout pointing toward the surface, spade-shaped tail trailing below, huge gill-like flaps flexing, drawing water. The rounds from the *Giffords*'s rail mounted guns rattled down around it, carving trails through the water, tiny puffs of blood wafting up where they impacted. The gill flaps pulsed, flexed as its mouth opened.

"Oh, Christ," Bookbinder breathed. "Everybody get down!"

The giant body spasmed, flexed. The huge mouth stretched wide. A sheet of bubbles issued forth, whipping the drifting blood into a froth, erupting through the surface. The *Breakwater* slewed drunkenly as the enormous wave arced up and out, sweeping forward at a speed breathtaking for something so large. By the time it reached the ships, it was a solid wall of water over twenty feet high.

It caught the *Giffords* straight on her bow, lifting her up in the air. The warship hung there, balanced on her stern, men tumbling into the water, until she finally corkscrewed sideways and flipped back onto the surface, shallow keel and twisting thrusters exposed to the sky. Beyond her, the larger ship spun in tight circles, looking suddenly like a giant bath toy, before heeling over on her side, her tall bridge smacking into the water with a thundering splash.

The wall of water raced past the overturned ships, looming above the *Breakwater*'s gunwales, its shadow racing across the buoy deck. Bookbinder could see corpses tumbling in the breaking foam, goblin and human, chunks of driftwood, knives, and spears, all sliding down the slick, gray-green surface.

And then it was upon them.

"Hold on to something!" Bonhomme shouted, as the wave curled in on itself, collapsing down toward them. Bookbinder looked at the wall of water and realized it wouldn't matter. He was no seaman, but even he knew the *Breakwater* couldn't hold against this.

Bookbinder felt a sudden pulse, a measured discharge of magical energy. He looked around wildly for the source, half-expecting to see Ripple standing on the bridge. But the magic was flowing from farther away. He narrowed his eyes, looking through the bridge window at the boomer, pocked with bullet holes and splashed with blood, but still tied to the crane. The magic flowed from it and the giant wave recoiled, split in half, suddenly going gentle around the bow. The fury of the rough water churned around them, but from the *Breakwater*'s beam to ten feet off her bow, the water went suddenly placid.

"Well, I'll be . . ." Bookbinder managed.

The vessel's aft had no such protection. The fury of the wave swatted it like a giant hand, spinning the huge ship on its centerline, the thrusters groaning beneath it. Bookbinder fell to the deck, the ship shaking, tortured metal rumbling. Papers flew around the small cabin. A clipboard bounced off his head. He could hear Bonhomme and Rodriguez crying out, wondered if the ship would hold together. Vertigo seized him, and he bit back nausea as the spinning slowly eased, stopped.

All was silent as the ship pitched, violently at first, then more gently, and finally stabilized. Bookbinder looked up, saw Bonhomme's horrified face. The commander slowly got to his feet. Bookbinder stood beside him and looked out over the buoy deck where the crew was already scrambling to look for damage. If the ship was taking on water, he couldn't tell. The console electronics had gone dark. The radios buzzed with static.

"What the hell happened?" Bonhomme asked.

"The boomer." Bookbinder pointed to the device, swinging gently from the end of the crane, its magic spent. He could still feel the current coming off it, but it was barely detectable. "Covered us from the bow, but not the stern. I guess that tells us its range." He smiled weakly. "I'll make a note."

Bonhomme didn't return the smile. Instead, he called into the radio, asking for a damage report. Silence greeted him. But the action was good, Bookbinder thought. At least the man was doing something without prompting, showing his crew some of what they needed to see. Rodriguez ran out of the hatch and stood in the ladder well, shouting down to the sailors below. Within a few minutes, shouts came back up to her. The hull was intact. They had power, the thrusters responded. Steering. But the radios were still down, as was the radar and sonar.

"Mast must have come down," she said.

"Well, that's good. We can still get out of here," Bookbinder managed. But Bonhomme's eyes were farther out, on the overturned hulls of the two navy ships. The larger one had already vanished beneath the surface. The *Giffords* still bobbed lightly, sinking slowly. All around them, he could see men thrashing in the water, interspersed with a goblin spear tip or arm, as the creatures regrouped and took them on. The goblins might be smaller, but they were in their element now, and the stricken sailors didn't stand a chance. Bookbinder couldn't make out a single life raft. They hadn't had time to deploy them.

Suddenly, Thorsson's words echoed in his ears. *Battery Park. Castle Clinton. We're right on the water. You can come straight to us.* That monster had capsized two warships.

It could drown a low-lying park at the water's edge.

They'd stumbled across the invasion's rearguard.

Bonhomme stared, and Bookbinder tapped his elbow. "Skipper, we should get over there, see if we can pick up any of the survivors."

Bonhomme gave no commands. His voice was only a whisper. Bookbinder knew what he was thinking. If two naval warships couldn't withstand the enemy, what chance did they have?

"We're on our own now, aren't we?" Bonhomme asked.

Bookbinder sighed. "Yes, skipper. I'm afraid we are."

CHAPTER VII
THE SYSTEM AND THE SYSTEM

Years of relentless pressure by the US government moved the Mexican authorities to push their Selfers underground, into the sewers. These "flushed" people, the "Limpiados," turned to the only force in the country with the resources to help them, the drug cartels. The result was a devil's bargain that enfranchised both parties beyond their wildest dreams. Years of declining central-government power saw the Limpiados rise on the tide of the cartels until they were a force in their own right. The sewers were no longer a refuge, they were a kingdom.

—Professor Osvaldo H. Soto
University of Michigan, Ann Arbor

Harlequin sat across from the two scouts, Special Forces operators just in from a reconnaissance run through the battlespace, drumming his fingers on the folding table.

Two days in command of the Breach Zone. Two days with only catnaps stolen in the corner of the bustling command post he'd made out of Castle Clinton. He'd gone longer on less, but that didn't mean he liked it. The creeping delirium eroded his focus when he needed to be at his best. He shook his head and gulped down the can of energy drink, willing the caffeine to do its work.

"I remember you guys," he said, setting the can back down. "You two escorted General Bookbinder to FOB Sarpakavu, right?"

The bigger SF operator was a grizzled sergeant first class whose resemblance to a desperado out of a Western was so strong it was almost comical. His name tape read SHARP. "We had that honor, sir. There were more of us when we started out. Specialist Archer and I were the two who made it." He chucked the elbow of the other SF operator, a short, thin sergeant with longish hair that clearly violated regs.

"I'm sorry," Harlequin said. "I remember the reports now. I should have . . ."

Sharp waved a hand. "We all do our jobs, sir. How are you holding up?"

Harlequin could control his expression and tone of voice, but not the bags under his eyes. "Tired."

Sharp nodded. "I can imagine. You should get some sleep, sir. You're no good to anyone if you're swaying on your feet."

There's nobody else who can handle this. I can't sleep until it's over. Harlequin stared at the empty can of energy drink, his fourth one that day. Or was it the fifth? He'd lost count. "I'll take it under advisement."

"Colonel Bookbinder here, sir?" Archer asked. "We'd like to say hi."

"General Bookbinder," Sharp corrected him.

"Right"—Archer grinned—"takes some getting used to."

Harlequin shook his head. "He's . . . he should be inbound. We need him."

Sharp nodded. "Yeah, I reckon his particular ability would help with the mountain gods."

"It is . . . sorely missed."

"Well, I hate to say this, sir, but I'd highly recommend you get him in here most riki-tik."

Harlequin suddenly felt wide-awake. "I do not need more bad news."

Sharp held up his smartphone and began thumbing through the photographs on the touch screen. "Well, then you might want to plug your ears and cover your eyes, sir."

Harlequin did the opposite. His eyes narrowed as he leaned in to examine the picture. "What the hell is that?"

"That's the Lower East Side, sir. Well, part of it. Along East Broadway," Archer said.

"No." Harlequin tapped the screen, trying to expand the picture. "What's that on the buildings?"

Sharp took the phone, magnified the picture, and handed it back. "Webs, sir. Those are spiderwebs."

The magnified picture showed a long stretch of a wide New
York City avenue, still clogged with abandoned cars. Apartment buildings hunched over restaurants and bodegas, many
with signs in Chinese. It looked like the Manhattan Harlequin
remembered from his tour of duty in New York, a hodgepodge
of mismatched buildings, beaux arts alongside ultramodern,
shoehorned in beside falling-apart.

All were draped in thick curtains of spider silk.

It hung from every building, sticky tendrils anchored to fire
escapes and car hoods. It drifted lazily in the wind over
awnings and fire hydrants, turning the street fuzzy, a vista seen
through a thin veil of cotton candy.

Thick black lumps dotted the webbing, meaty clots the size
of cars.

Harlequin knew what they were without squinting further.
Their spinnerets were blurs in the still frame of a photo. The
streets were deserted, but the webs were dotted with long, narrow cocoons of silk, each about the size and shape of a person.

Hundreds of them.

"Those are people . . ."

"We think so, sir," Sharp said. "We didn't investigate further."

"Why are you showing me this?"

"Because that's just one block. Rocs have set up the world's
biggest nest in City Hall Park's Fountain. We fought these . . .
burning things when we escorted Col . . . Sorry. Still getting
used to the promotion. When we escorted General Bookbinder
to FOB Sarpakavu. They live in ashes. They've taken over a
few blocks under the Williamsburg Bridge. Turned the whole
thing into a charcoal pit. We could barely get close enough to
sketch out the borders."

"Jesus. So we've got . . . monster ghettos. They're setting
up neighborhoods?"

Sharp nodded. "Except along the barricade line on Houston. That's where the fighting is."

"Okay. You've mapped all this out?"

"With notes on who's living where, sir."

"Outstanding. That'll help us match capabilities to missions
when we get it cleared. It's going to take a while to . . ."

"Sir," Archer interrupted him. "Respectfully, there's more."

Harlequin froze, mouth open.

"There are two . . . zones, sir. They're clear," Sharp said.

"Clear . . ."

"Clear, sir. Some signs of fighting, but they've held. No goblins, no demon horses. Not even *Gahe*."

It was a long time before Harlequin could speak. "Where?"

"One's in Tribeca. The other in Chinatown. They're just a few square blocks each, and separated by a couple of blocks that are completely overrun with . . . these snake things with two heads. Whatever they are, they are steering clear of both those patches. There are corpses around the edges. Mostly goblins, but others, too. Some of that . . . You know, the way stuff is frozen to hell and filthy when a mountain god bleeds on it? We saw some of that, too."

Harlequin swallowed. "Are there SOC units operating anywhere out there? I don't have any report of . . ."

"Neither do we, sir. We tried every frequency on the radio. No comms. If the SOC is working there, they're not answering."

"Selfers," Harlequin said. He struggled not to let the shock show. He'd been running to keep up since he'd arrived in New York, knocked left and right by the speed with which the battle evolved. And here a pack of Selfers had managed to do at least as well as a professional army. *They have magic. You don't. Not enough, anyway.*

"That's our guess, too, sir," Sharp agreed. "We figured maybe a gang. We were hoping you could check it out with the NYPD. They might have some answers."

Harlequin put his head in his hands. "Damn it. I've been trying to get an NYPD LNO in here. It's a little hard to get ahold of them just now."

Sharp nodded silently, but the message in his hard eyes was clear. Stop whining and figure out a way to get it done.

"All right, thanks, guys. Why don't you grab some water and some rack time and . . ."

Sharp and Archer were already standing, tightening the straps on their carbine slings, gathering up their helmets and packs. "If it's all right with you, sir, we're going to get back out there. Got a couple more items on the to-do list."

He tapped a thumb drive on the table. "Saved all our recon notes here. It's all in a map overlay you can load into your

GIS software. Has the MGRS coordinates of the bad guys in all the locations we talked about."

Harlequin blinked. "That's outstanding."

Sharp gave the faintest trace of a smile. "Archer's something of a comms geek, sir. Computer stuff, too."

"Just my luck."

"Yeah, well. It hasn't improved his aim."

Archer shook his head, headed for the door with a final nod to Harlequin. "Tell General Bookbinder that we asked after him, sir. If you wouldn't mind."

"Of course."

Sharp nodded. "A little tough to get in touch with us in the field now, sir. Comms are weird in spots. We'll be checking in every so often though. We've got a ton of tasking from Macdill we need to take care of, but if you had anything hot . . ."

"After I talk with the NYPD, I know I will."

"We'll be ready, sir."

"Thanks, both of you."

"It's our job, sir. Hope you can get some sleep." And with that, Sharp and Archer departed, leaving Harlequin with a thumb drive, a thousand questions, and a sinking feeling in his stomach.

Harlequin's contacts in the NYPD were stale, and in the chaos around the Breach, he wasn't sure of his ability to get through to them anyhow.

He radioed Cormack. "What's the ETA on our NYPD LNO?"

Cormack sounded harried. "No idea, sir. They were supposed to be here yesterday. I got a call this morning telling us to go through Fort Hamilton. I told them we needed our own."

"Good. I do not want to be slave to Hewitt's good graces. We need our own rep, and we need him now. I understand the NYPD is busy. We're all busy."

He always thought better in the air. He Drew his magic and lifted himself above the modular concrete perimeter.

Harlequin had no choice but to convey Scylla's offer of parley, and Gatanas had threatened to call in airstrikes from McGuire. Harlequin kept scanning the skies. Every scream and whistle was the sound of an approaching airplane engine.

But he had more pressing concerns. The enemy had finally pushed all the way south. The fighting raged from the barricades to the water now. The streets of lower Manhattan seethed with goblins dashing in and out of buildings, setting fire to storefronts. Here and there, rooftops blazed as the Army fought back, struggling to clear a safe zone where refugees could gather long enough for a helo flight to lift them out. Harlequin had given up trying to count the enemy after sunset on the first day. There were enough that he could never get them out with the force he had to hand. That was all he needed to know.

Goblins practically boiled around the T-walls surrounding the park, giants dotting the mass.

A small helo had dropped off a few of the Fornax Novices ahead of the rest of their class. One of them crouched on top of the barricade. She looked all of twenty years old, scrawny in her uniform. The training-Coven patch showed a belching furnace with the words FORNAX above it, and HELL HATH NO FURY! below. The Novice's name tape read BEAMER, and she didn't look furious at all.

A javelin burst out of the goblin horde below, and she skittered back onto the painter's ladder she'd used to climb up.

"You okay?" Harlequin called over to her.

Her eyes were frightened, but determined. "I've got it, sir."

"Okay. Just remember, you're here for the *Gahe*. Don't waste your efforts on anything else."

He felt for her current, pulsing and flaring with anxiety despite the Limbic Dampener running through her veins. She should be in a schoolhouse, not on a battlefield.

"Like right there," he pointed.

A *Gahe* swept through the throng, pushing a raging giant aside. The huge creature yelped and pulled back from its freezing touch. It flailed petulantly, but the mountain god was already gone, stutter-flashing toward the wall. It fetched up short, moving along the barricades laterally, looking for openings.

Harlequin sighed relief. Their short teleporting could move them quickly over open ground but not through solid objects. Otherwise, his tenuous hold on Battery Park would have fallen already.

"Novice Beamer," he said, "clear that scout off my perimeter."

Practice would make perfect. Might as well get her used to it.

She nodded, scrambling back up the ladder to the top of the barricade, in such a hurry that she overbalanced and Harlequin Drew his magic, ready to fly out to catch her if she pitched over the edge. She steadied herself, concentrated. He felt goose bumps rise as she Drew and Bound her current into a fireball that streaked out from her extended hands. Her aim was off, the ball lopsided and weak, but it slammed into the ground beside the *Gahe*, singeing it and sending several goblins shrieking, beating at their burning clothing. The *Gahe* shrieked as well, stutter-flashing backward, giving the barricade wall a more respectful distance.

We can hurt them, Harlequin reminded himself. *We can hurt them and that means we can hold.*

He smiled at Beamer, willing courage into her. "Well done. We'll make a Sorcerer of you yet." She smiled back, then craned her head skyward as churning rotors announced the arrival of two Chinook heavy helicopters.

Harlequin met the helos on the ground, where Hewitt and Knut were already talking to the crew chiefs. The first helo discharged a group just like the Novice up on the barricade wall; children in uniform. The rest of Gatanas's arcane complement, the training Covens Carina and Cephalus, scurried out, duffels on their shoulders, jostling one another as they tried to form up by squad in front of Colonel Hewitt, equally terrified of his scowl and his rank.

"At ease!" Harlequin shouted. "We don't have time for a muster. Once we take roll, I need everyone back in the air."

A chorus of salutes began, and Harlequin waved his arms. "I said 'at ease.' This is a no-cover, no-salute area."

Hewitt looked like he would argue, but he only stood with arms folded trying to look as if it were all his idea.

Harlequin turned to Knut. "Sergeant Major, could I ask you to take accountability, please?"

Knut reddened, gritted her teeth, and began calling out names, checking them off on a clipboard as the Novices responded.

"Everyone listen up!" Harlequin shouted. "You are going to turn around, get back on these helos, and from there on in,

Colonel Hewitt has the ball." He gestured to Hewitt, hoping the allocation of some authority would mollify him. "He's going to distribute you across the barricades that hold the northern edge of the enemy line. They are currently manned by a mix of National Guard, NYPD, and SOC LE support units. They have almost no arcane support and are in danger of being overrun. This is because we are facing the largest complement of *Gahe* we've ever seen. Everybody know what one of those is?"

The heads bobbed. Harlequin could see terror in many of the faces, passion and determination in a few. *They're eager at least.*

"You are going to make sure those barricades hold. There are millions of people in New York City. They are counting on *you* to give them the time they need to leave. The conventional forces can handle the goblins, rocs, and giants, but the *Gahe* are your problem. I know you haven't had a chance to complete your training, but you joined the SOC to help, and now is when that help is needed. Huah?"

"Huah, sir!" The response was uneven. A few voices broke.

"Everybody shot up with Dampener? There won't be any Suppression out there unless you're lucky enough to find one of the SOC operators. I can't have folks going nova on me now. Remember that skill beats will. Stay safe and controlled, but above all, hold your positions."

"Huah, sir!" Better, but still not what he'd like.

"All right." He turned back to Hewitt. "All yours, Colonel."

Hewitt nodded and began barking at them to get back in the helo. Harlequin accepted the clipboard from Knut. "All present and accounted for, sir."

"Thank you, Sergeant Major." Harlequin tried to let his tone reflect his gratitude. He couldn't afford another enemy. "I really appreciate you covering my six here."

If Knut was mollified, she gave no sign. She started to salute, stopped halfway, and jogged off to help Hewitt.

Harlequin turned to the other helo. The Chinook's cavernous interior was easily big enough to hold fifty men. Instead, it held three. The first was a solider kitted for war, carbine at the low ready. The second was a SOC Suppressor, arms folded, magical current steady and disciplined.

The third was Sarah Downer.

The young Elementalist's hair had grown long enough to be tied into a nub of a ponytail. The extra weight she'd carried when Harlequin had first brought her in was long gone. Her body was lean, taught, tensed. An operator's musculature. She was younger than Beamer, but she looked years older, already blossoming into a fierce beauty visible in spite of her evident exhaustion. She wore a one-piece orange prisoner's jumpsuit, her wrists zip-cuffed behind her, her head fitted with an antispitting hood, complete with collar and ball gag. Her eyes were icy slits.

"You've got to be fucking kidding me!" Harlequin shouted.

He stormed up the Chinook's ramp, easing the hood off her head. "Seriously? A hood? How's she supposed to spit on you when you've got her gagged? And why the hell is she gagged in the first place?"

The Suppressor shrugged. "SOP, sir. High-value detainee transfer." He produced a folded piece of paper from his cargo pant pocket. "I'll need you to sign the hand receipt for her, sir."

Harlequin yanked the paper out of the man's hand and stuffed it in his own pocket while he drew out his pocket knife and began to cut through her zip cuffs. "She's not property. She's a person."

"Still need that signed, sir," the Suppressor said.

"Nope," Harlequin said, "and if you don't like it, you can stay here. I can sure as hell use you."

The Suppressor paused, then shrugged again. "Suit yourself, sir," he said, then signaled to the crew chief as soon as Harlequin cleared the ramp with Downer. Harlequin felt her magical current spike briefly as the Suppression fell away. The rotors spun up, and the helo began to rise. Harlequin left Downer and flew up in front of the cockpit, blocking the helo's ascent. "Get the fuck back down! Land this thing right now!"

The pilot gestured to him to wave off. Harlequin didn't move. At last, the helo settled back down onto its landing gear, and Harlequin flew around to the open cargo bay where the soldier and Suppressor gaped at him. "Respectfully, sir," the Suppressor said, "don't make me Suppress y . . ."

"Shut the fuck up," Harlequin said. "You try to take off without loading this bird full of refugees, and I will have you shot down. Do you fucking understand me?"

The Suppressor gaped. "Sir, we're headed back to Virginia. We don't have anywhere to house and care for refugees!"

"Put 'em up on your damn couch! I don't give a fuck. Anywhere is safer than here!"

"Sir, I . . ."

"I'm giving you an order. Now, you hold position while my people load you up. I swear to God, I will not let you depart without a full hold."

The Suppressor threw up his hands and walked back toward the cockpit. Harlequin motioned to the soldiers tending the refugees, who began getting them up and over to the helo.

He returned to Downer, standing beside her while he watched the first refugees load into the helo and take seats on the Chinook's long benches. The rotors spun back up and blasted them with dust, but the helo stayed grounded.

Harlequin turned back to her cuffs. He sliced through them, Binding his magic to conjure winds that blew back the rotor wash spilling over them.

"I'm sorry about the cuffs," Harlequin said. *Poor kid must be terrified, confused. The Army has kicked her around, detained her. She must not know what to think.* "We'll get you cleaned up, some water. Maybe you can grab a . . ."

The cuffs came away, and Downer pivoted on the balls of her feet, slamming her fist into Harlequin's jaw. His head snapped to the side, the world spinning, his vision graying. When he found his bearings again, he was lying on the ground, Downer standing over him. She didn't look terrified, or confused. She looked furious.

"You want your ass-kicking standing up? Because I'm happy to give it to you lying down." She didn't look young at all. She looked ferocious. She looked beautiful.

Harlequin shook his head. *Poor kid, indeed.* He waved off a soldier who came running to help and slowly got to his feet, rubbing his jaw. "Actually, I was hoping you'd save the ass-kicking for the enemy. I need your help here."

"You . . ." She stuttered over the words. "You need. My. Help? Are you fucking serious?"

"Yes, Sarah. Completely. Utterly.

"Desperately," he finished. Her current spiked, and she

hauled it back in, far more disciplined than any of the Novices. He knew better than to use his own magic around her. Downer could turn any magical energy into a sentient elemental bound to her will.

She took a step, and Harlequin raised his hands. "Please don't hit me again."

"You deserve worse," she spit. "Where the hell am I?"

"New York City," Harlequin said. "Lower Manhattan specifically. It's being invaded."

"By who?"

"Remember Scylla?"

"She's here? How the hell did she get here?"

"She's figured out how to . . . rot through the fabric between the planes. And she's linked up with the *Gahe*."

Harlequin felt her anger spike with her magic. "I've been rotting in a cell for God knows how long! And for what? I did everything you asked me to! I worked for you! I fucking *killed* for you! This is how you pay me back?"

Harlequin couldn't deny the truth of her words. When Downer had first gone Selfer, he'd been the one who'd taken her down, spiriting her off to FOB Frontier, where her forbidden magic could be put to use in the SOC's secret Probe Coven. With most Probes, it took some convincing to get them to toe the company line, but Downer's youth made her impressionable, and her crush on him had been evident from the start.

He looked at the tension in her neck and shoulders. No crush now, that was certain.

A small group of soldiers rallied to him, standing in a wide circle, carbines ready. He waved them back.

They moved back a few more paces, watching warily.

He took a step, readying himself for another punch. "Sarah, that wasn't me. I never wanted that for you."

"The fuck you didn't! You stole my whole life!"

"That's bullshit, Sarah. You knew the law. You knew the consequences. Nobody stole your life. You fucking threw it away. If anything, I picked up the pieces and gave you something to work with. You didn't have to run. You could have turned yourself in."

"The fuck I could have! You know what they do to Probes!"

"Yes, Sarah, and now so do you. Is it really so bad?"

"Yes," she seethed, "it is. Living a lie, having your life forfeit to cover up your government's secrets, that's really so bad. Being a slave isn't a whole lot better than being dead."

She was right, and he knew it. But the system, broken as it was, was still far better than the chaos that was the alternative. He remembered Grace, the bubbling ruin of humanity she'd left behind her as she walked the path to Scylla.

A giant bellowed, as if to accent the point, the refugees huddling together as its howl of rage echoed across the barricade wall.

"Sarah," Harlequin said, "it's a fucked-up system and a fucked-up situation, but it's all we've got. People aren't frightened for no reason. You were destroying a school. You had to answer for that. You came around, but that doesn't change the fact that most Selfers out there haven't." *Grace hasn't.* "The Bloch Incident wasn't a joke. The Burning Man massacre wasn't a joke. People died, Sarah. *Lots* of people. That's what we're trying to stop. That's why we're so scared. Sometimes . . . sometimes, decent people get caught up in that. I don't like it, but I understand it."

He pointed at the top of the barricade, where another Fornax Novice flew clumsily, sheeting down lightning over the T-walls. He landed on top of a plastic water buffalo they'd rigged for gravity feed, doubled over, and vomited, shivering from fear. "That's all I've got to turn back this tide. I need you."

Downer was quiet. Harlequin was about to speak again when she finally said, "On the flight over here, I heard the crew talking. They don't like you very much."

Harlequin nodded. "They wouldn't. While you were locked up, I went . . . a little rogue myself, I guess."

"You? You're the one who always told me to get in the manual. Christ, I believed all that."

"It's still true, Sarah, but even I have my limits. The system's not perfect, but the ideals behind it are. They're what I swore to defend. When the system and the ideals are at odds, I know where my allegiance lies." His own words echoed back to him. The thought had plagued him since he'd defied his president and saved the FOB. *Who are you? What are you doing?* And here he stood, answering his own question.

Downer didn't notice. "Then why aren't you in jail?"

Harlequin thought of the irony of his situation and shrugged, amazed at how simple the answer was. "There's more than one system, Sarah. The public's got a system, too, and theirs covers a lot more people than the government's does. Our system, in the end, is made to serve theirs. What I did went public, and folks generally approve. I'm sure the president would like to see me right next to you in a cell, but he no longer has a choice."

Downer's eyes widened. "What did you do?"

"I'll tell you all about it. But, first, I need you to make me an army of elementals."

"I didn't agree to help you."

Harlequin shook his head. "There isn't time, Sarah." He pointed to the line of T-walls, the steady stream of rounds coming from the defenders, the amateur bursts of barely controlled magic from the Fornax Novices. "It's getting worse out there every second."

"So what if I don't . . . ." Downer was cut off by a shrieking rumble, the whining of jet turbines streaking overhead. Harlequin turned to see two low-flying aircraft shoot across the sky, gone so quickly he could almost believe he had imagined them if not for the contrails in their wake. An instant later he heard the low-throaty buzz of their 30mm cannons, the resounding echo of exploding glass and concrete.

He used his magic then, heedless of what Downer would do with it, raising himself high enough above the barricade wall to see the chaos the aircraft were unleashing below.

The line of Broadway was a slurry of tattered flesh and chewed concrete, fragments of goblins, giants, and rocs alike sprawling in the smoking wreckage. Here and there, Harlequin could make out other bodies. Civilians caught in the mess. He shuddered, wondering if the SOF teams still moving out there had been forewarned. Sharp, Archer.

A higher, fainter whine echoed above the cloud cover, and tracer fire showered down at a steep angle, sweeping the path the low-flying A-10s had just cleared. Somewhere overhead, one of the huge AC-130 Specter gunships was circling, lining up its massive cannon.

He knew where it was heading.

The A-10s circled back, banked sharply over Battery Park, and headed up toward Wall Street.

Harlequin toggled his commlink. "Cormack! Get me through to Gatanas right now! There are civilians down there!"

Cormack's response was grainy. "McGuire radioed in about thirty seconds ago, sir." *Making sure I had no time to object.* "They say the strike zone is clear."

"The strike zone is *not* clear, damn it!"

"They're going to take out the enemy HQ. They say she's in there, they've got solid intel."

Harlequin had been in the Army long enough to know exactly what "solid intel" meant. "Scylla's not an idiot! That's exactly what she wants! Get those airframes waved off!"

There was a pause. "I'll let them know, sir."

But it was too late. The stutter of the cannons sounded louder, the A-10s and the Specter directing the full fury of their fire at the soaring tower of the Trump Building. The huge structure vibrated, the green sheen of the bronze peak scintillating as it shed the corrosion built over decades. Chunks of concrete exploded from the surface. Flame blossomed across the building as gas jets blew, electrical infrastructure caught fire.

The A-10s banked out of the way of the Specter's cascade of fire, letting loose their Mavericks, the missiles flashing across the sky so quickly that they left glowing imprints in Harlequin's vision. The thundering explosion shook the landscape. Harlequin could see every living creature, soldier, goblin, giant, even *Gahe* crouch at the resounding boom. All around Wall Street, there was screaming as masonry collapsed on top of the living, a huge plume of dust arcing skyward.

And then the aircraft had cleared off, circling once back over the building and heading back toward their flight lines in New Jersey. The Specter probably still circled far above, keeping its eye on the target, radioing the battle-damage assessment back to mission control.

They would be satisfied, Harlequin thought. The spire smoked, the regal stonework already chewed to dust, rebar, and I-beams. The bronze finial was a patchwork of green and molten brown-black, flames rising from ragged holes that used to be windows.

As he watched, the spire and structure beneath it, ranging down some three stories, teetered to one side, the masonry beneath it collapsing. It hung over Wall Street for a brief moment, then tumbled over and down, bouncing off the building and crashing to the street. The cloud of dust billowed upward obscuring everything, save the Trump building's top, now headless and burning brightly.

Harlequin bit back a scream. He'd seen this before. *Just like her old building.*

He descended back to Downer in the eerie silence that followed.

"That's what happens, Sarah. If the enemy breaks out of here, that's what will happen everywhere."

"Why the hell did they do that?" she asked.

"They thought Scylla was in there."

"Was she?"

"Of course not. Scylla's many things, but stupid isn't one of them." He turned and headed into Castle Clinton, not waiting to see if Downer followed.

Cormack already had the VTC set up, with Gatanas shouting at him from the other end. Harlequin put his fists on the table. "Well done, sir. I'm not sure how many people you just killed, but I know one you didn't."

Gatanas didn't take the bait. "I see she's arrived," he said, looking past Harlequin's shoulder.

Harlequin turned to see Downer coming into the building behind him, her expression inscrutable.

"No more airstrikes," he said, turning back to Gatanas's image on the monitor. "I promise you that little exercise will be all over the Internet in approximately five minutes. It's not going to make my job any easier."

"It will if we just took out their command structure in one shot."

"But you didn't, sir. I already told you, Scylla *wanted* you to tear that building up. Why the hell do you think she chose the tallest and most visible landmark south of the barricades? Because she likes the view?"

Gatanas was silent.

"Scylla is trying to introduce a new order here, sir. She's smart enough to know that an army of monsters isn't going to do that. She needs propaganda victories like the one you just handed her. I need to drive her out of here without blowing up any more buildings."

"Are you done?" Gatanas asked.

"I'm just getting warmed up, sir. Downer is a great start, but I need more. How is it going with Canada and Mexico? Where's Bookbinder? When last I spoke to him, we had two warships inbound to intercept."

"Bookbinder is still inbound." Gatanas looked uncomfortable. "Mexico and Canada are deliberating. There's not a lot of goodwill toward the United States thanks to the stunt you pulled with FOB Frontier. A lot of countries are accusing us of colluding with India to take some kind of strategic advantage in the Source."

"That's bullshit. We didn't even know India had a FOB until our own was in danger of falling."

"Well, you reap what you sow, Lieutenant Colonel. I'm doing what I can from here." Gatanas did indeed look sleepless, his uniform rumpled, a day's growth of stubble on his face. *Life's rough all over.*

"We don't have time, sir. More enemy come out of that gate every minute. River's got them hemmed in on all sides, but the northern barricades are now held by two training Covens. They break through, and this entire island is toast. How's the evacuation coming?"

Gatanas was silent.

"Jesus, sir."

"The mayor gave the order. The people have other ideas. New York City practically functions like its own state. You have to realize how much money this place has, it's like the de facto capital of the country."

"So people keep telling me. Rich, important people die just as easily as everyone else in my experience. GAU-8's tend to do a pretty good job of that, actually." His reference to the A-10 cannons wasn't lost on Gatanas, who purpled again and stabbed a finger toward him.

"When this is over, you are going to learn a thing or two about how to be a team player."

"I'm sure I am, sir. Looking forward to it," Harlequin said.

"For now, I need you to get your ass up to the UN."

"The UN?"

Gatanas nodded. "And you don't have a whole lot of time either. They're in the process of winding down to a skeleton crew. Depending on how things evolve here, I'm not certain how much longer the Security Council will be able to convene in New York. China's lobbying pretty hard to have the body moved 'temporarily' to Beijing."

"Don't we have a . . . representative or something up there?"

"We do, but he's not Latent and he's not in the middle of the arcane fight, as you keep reminding me and every other conventional-element commander you come in contact with. As of fifteen minutes ago, the representatives from Mexico and Canada were still in the building. You're a public figure now, Thorsson. Get up there, tell them what's going on down here. Tell them what's at stake. Break them loose."

"How much time do I have?"

"Ambassador Hallert is expecting you. Go now."

"On it." Harlequin broke the connection and turned to Downer. "You're in or you're out. I'll make do either way."

She looked at him, arms folded, nodded. "Okay."

He exhaled, weakness flooding him. He steadied himself with a hand on the table, hoping she didn't notice. "Thank you. I promise when this is over, we'll find a way to make it right. What they did to you."

"A pardon," she said, "a full pardon. Some guarantee that I don't go back into a cell. I know I'm a Probe, but they're going to have to make an exception. And this is the last thing I do for you. For any of you. You make that happen."

"I will," he said.

She cocked an eyebrow. "Can you?"

"I have no idea, Sarah. But I broke Oscar Britton out of prison. You help me here, and I'll do whatever I have to do to make sure you never go in a cell again."

She was silent for a moment, then nodded.

He turned to Cormack. "Get her set up with some of the Fornax Novices. I need her to produce as many elementals as she possibly can."

Cormack frowned. "Sir, some of them may balk at working with a Probe."

"Then unbalk them," Harlequin said. He turned and headed out.

"Where are you going?" Downer asked.

"To get more help. Cormack will brief you up on the details, just get me as many elementals in the fight as you possibly can."

The NYPD will have to wait. He raced outside and launched himself skyward, Binding storm clouds around him, ensuring he had a ready supply of lightning to stave off any rocs that tried to intercept.

He put on speed, looking over his shoulder to see that Cormack had put a Kiowa aloft to escort him. There was a large cloud of rocs and wyverns circling the ruins of the Trump Building, but none seemed willing to risk tangling with Harlequin and his magic.

He kicked off, flying up Broadway, gaining altitude to get a better view of the barricade where the avenue ran into Houston Street. The fighting was thick there. Soldiers and police poured fire down the shattered street as goblins showed themselves, shouting and hurling javelins. A giant had pushed an old backhoe out into the road, and some of the creatures were using it as cover, slowly inching it forward, trying to get within bow range.

Here and there, a goblin sorcerer would add a burst of lightning or a flame strike to the mix, darting back into the buildings for cover. Harlequin could spot forward observers in the buildings to either side of the barricades, and the dull whistle and thump of mortar fire being called in wherever the sorcerers showed themselves. The goblins still adhered to their ridiculous custom of painting their sorcerers completely white, making them easy targets for snipers.

The *Gahe* worried him. Their short teleporting moved them to the barricade's edge in an instant, overturning cars to crush the defenders or snatching them from their cover and shredding them before their comrades' eyes. A few SOC LE support officers and the newly arrived Novices responded with bursts of Aeromantic lightning or ice storms, and here and there a Terramancer forced the earth beneath the cracked asphalt to rise, dragging the creatures down.

The defenders looked exhausted. The Novices were white-faced with terror. The *Gahe* ignored the bullets, taking one or two cops or soldiers with each sortie, until the magic drove them off.

There wasn't enough magic. If they kept this up, the barricades would give, and the enemy would break through into the rest of the city and everything beyond.

Once over the barricades, the city became oddly silent and calm. The streets were parking lots of vehicles attempting to escape, people filling the spaces around them. Many of them were moving south to get a better view of the fighting. Huge knots of media stood just to the north of each barricade, held back by lines of police desperately needed in the fight. Harlequin could make out groups of people carrying signs, chanting for reasons he could only guess. South of the barricades, flames, screaming, blood, and ash. North of them, it looked like a party.

Harlequin heard a low buzz and looked up to see a small blue helicopter sweeping past him. He could make out a woman seated in the open cabin, her feet on the skid, aiming a video camera at the chaos below.

Harlequin veered to intercept her. "Get the hell down!" he shouted. "No-fly zone!"

The helo ignored him, continuing south into the fighting. A group of three rocs spotted it and began winging their way toward it. Harlequin cursed and spun, extending his arm and unleashing a torrent of lightning that set one of the giant birds on fire. The other two banked and dove, sweeping underneath him. The escort Kiowa followed suit. Harlequin radioed to the pilot. "Keep them off the civilians! I can make my own way from here!"

This was at least the tenth civilian news helo that had violated the Breach Zone's airspace. Harlequin would have to rely on the Kiowa to do for those rocs. His own mission was far too pressing. He had to get help for those barricades.

He veered east over Grand Central Station, and moved toward a collection of tall silver buildings abutting the East River. He gained altitude, slowing as he approached the rooftop helipad.

It was ringed by flags from over a hundred nations, bright yellow letters painted in the landing circle: UN. The giant building was already under heavy guard, and Harlequin could see gun emplacements and Humvees surrounding the ground-level entrances.

Up here was no different. Men were already streaming out onto the roof, leveling guns at him, waving their arms. He radioed his intent to land on an open channel, and they calmed, stepping back as his boots touched down on the helipad.

His time on television paid dividends yet again. Recognition was flaring in the eyes of the security guards as they approached him, lowering their weapons. He identified himself anyway. "Lieutenant Colonel Thorsson, Supernatural Operations Corps. Breach Zone Incident Commander. I need to speak to Ambassador Hallert right away."

INTERLUDE III
NEW GAME, NEW RULES

I've served my country faithfully since I was nine years old. I hit puberty in Ladakh, graduated college via correspondence course in Tawang. I have never kissed a boy. I have never been to a ball game. I have long since forgotten my parents' faces. General Gatanas came out here on a tour once, met me personally, told me how grateful the country is for what I do, how many people sleep safe because of me. But, in the end, there's only this: I killed my brother when I Manifested. I didn't mean to, but I did. I have paid and paid and paid, and it just isn't enough.

—Suicide note found on the pillow of Captain Heatwave
Undisclosed location

SIX YEARS EARLIER

Grace's office was the archetype of the New York corporate landscape. Floor-to-ceiling windows left Harlequin feeling like he was floating in midair.

Crucible had been unable to wipe the grin off his face since it turned out the woman hitting on Harlequin was also the person they were there to meet. Harlequin still felt his cheeks burn at how easily he'd been taken, the sensation worsened by the fact that it hadn't diminished his attraction to her in the slightest.

The long meeting table was the quality version of what they used in the Pentagon, real wood instead of cheap plastic laminate. The sand-colored surface reflected the light streaming in from outside, bathing the room in a gentle glow that Harlequin was sure was by design. There was true wealth on display here, the kind that showed itself in a deliberate avoidance of ostentatious display. The room was simple, almost bare, but the little that was in it was perfect. The company logo was emblazoned tastefully on the table's corner: a smaller, stylized Scylla beside a Charybdis, a broad blue arrow pointing the safe passage between. Narrow black letters read, CHANNEL CORP beneath it.

Grace was joined by Noah Weiss, her Director of Research, a short, nervous-looking man who did the best impression of an anthropomorphized penguin that Harlequin had ever seen, complete with bald head, beak of a nose, and thick middle, all covered in a black-and-white suit that even got the color right.

Grace gave deference to Crucible's rank by addressing him, but her eyes kept straying to Harlequin, the smile never entirely leaving her face.

"Well," she said, her lips trembling slightly, "isn't this awkward?"

"Sorry, ma'am," Crucible said. "We're a small corps, and this is frequently the way the military gets things done. We're not entirely up to speed on the operation, but I assure you that we'll be able points of contact for you once we get everything smoothed out."

"Can you get us subjects?" Weiss said, leaning across the table. "I mean, I don't really see the need for any kind of liaison with the SOC, to be frank. We've got perfectly adequate security here, and . . ."

Grace placed a hand lightly on his cuff, and his voice stopped as quickly as if she'd stolen the air from his lungs.

"Mr. Weiss is merely enthusiastic to move forward with clinical trials. He understands, as we all do, that the military will be our largest customer," she said.

"If this stuff does what you say it does," Crucible said, "the SOC will be your only customer."

The smile vanished. "This compound offers unprecedented control over the brain's limbic system," she said. "The arcane applications are undeniable. But so are the antipsychotic applications, or what it could offer as an alternative to serotonin reuptake inhibitors. There is a universe of possible therapeutic effects."

"Ma'am, I . . ." Crucible began.

"We approached you," Grace cut him off, "out of good faith, and to continue Noah's line, in the hope that you would provide us with test subjects for clinical trials. Rats don't come up Latent, Major. We need to test this on humans. But allow me to remind you that we are a private corporation with the right to sell whatever we want to whomever we want. The SOC does not get to swoop in here and take possession of the product. You are dealing with a company with a lot of money and the kind of lawyers that kind of money can hire. Keep that in mind."

The major patted the air with his palms. "Take it easy, ma'am. Those kinds of calls get made way above my pay grade. We're here to be liaisons and to ensure security for the lab."

"Be liaisons?" Weiss asked. "What the hell does that even mean?"

"It means," Harlequin cut in, "that magic is serious business, and if you've got a drug that has a real chance of making an impact on how we use it, then the government has a vested interest. That means you work with us. Selfers don't like working with us, so they run. That's when they call people like me. By the time that happens, it's too late to be cooperative."

Grace's smile returned, along with her frank look. Weiss blanched and looked at his lap, sputtering. "There are contracting concerns . . ."

"Which will be handled by a government contracting officer," Crucible said. "Neither of us has that role. Can you help us to better understand what those are so we can convey that information more accurately to the folks who will eventually talk money with you?"

Weiss exchanged looks with Grace, who nodded, then punched a button. An invisible seam in the wood slid back, and a monitor rose out of the center of the table, propelled by silent motors. The windows darkened. Some kind of chemical tint, Harlequin guessed.

The monitor flashed into life, showing a series of ovals layered with colored blotches.

"What are we looking at?" Harlequin asked.

"These are brain scans of rhesus macaques from upstairs," Weiss said, gesturing to a set of ovals almost completely covered in bright red splashes of color. "They've been placed under a degree of emotional stress: brief separation from their mothers, having food displayed, then taken away. That kind of stimulus activates the limbic center in the brain," Weiss said. "You get emotional. The colors range from dark blue for low activity to bright red for high activity. As you can see, these brains are showing a tremendous amount of activity in the limbic system."

He addressed the next set of ovals on the other half of the monitor. The color overlays showed mostly blue, with some red flashes interspersed throughout. "That's after the application of the New Chemical Entity, what we're currently calling LL-14."

"So, it suppresses emotion," Harlequin said.

"Well, sort of," Weiss said. "Look at this."

He brought up a video showing one of the monkeys being placed into a cage with another. The upper-right corner of the screen showed one of the colored ovals, mostly dark. "This monkey is being introduced into the cage of a rival male. He's on a heavy dose of LL-14. The treated monkeys are a line we call 'lambda.' The other male is untreated, from our 'control' line."

The two monkeys stared at one another through the clear Plexiglas of the cage. The control monkey was intent, teeth bared. Every muscle was poised. The lambda monkey appeared calm, aware of its rival but not overly interested in it.

"They're going to fight," Crucible said.

"That's what happens in nature, yes," Weiss answered. "Watch."

The barrier was lifted, and the lambda monkey pushed into the cage. The control monkey was on it in an instant, flailing with its long arms, gnashing sharp teeth, shrieking. "Watch the brain activity," Weiss said, gesturing to the colored oval.

The lambda monkey hesitated for an instant. But only an instant. There was a brief and tiny flash of red on the very edge of the oval, then the center bloomed as if an artery had popped. The entire shape turned red as the lambda monkey answered blow for blow, clawing and biting its rival. It flung the control monkey into the back of the cage and fell on it, biting and clawing, as handlers wearing shoulder-length padded gloves and helmets reached into the cage and dragged it out, leaving the undrugged rival in a bloody heap.

The moment the danger was past, the lambda monkey went placid in the handler's arms, the colors vanishing from the brain imagery, going dark and placid as it had been before the fight began.

"Okay," Crucible said. "That's . . . so it's not emotional . . . until it is."

Grace laughed, but Weiss was deadly serious. "That's the point. That flash of activity you saw? On the edge of the brain? We keep seeing that just before the emotional center in the limbic triggers for monkeys on LL-14."

"What does it mean?" Harlequin asked.

"We're still figuring that out," Grace answered, "but we're fairly sure that was the brain's neocortex, where primates engage in logical decision-making. We've seen that activity on a consistent, repeatable basis. The animal *can* access its emotional center when it needs to, but we believe it's only on the basis of a rational decision, such as to defend oneself when under attack. No posturing, no bravado. Just action when it's required."

"Emotional when you need to be," Crucible breathed.

"To evoke magic when you need to and put it away when you're done," Harlequin added. "Holy shit, that's . . ."

Weiss raised his hands. "That's *preliminary*, is what that is. We need clinical trials. We need to try this on Latent people."

Harlequin exchanged a glance with Crucible. "You can't expect us to turn SOC personnel, even Rump Latents, into lab rats. We could certainly put out a call for volunteers, but I'm not even sure that the Joint Service Surgeon General would approve that. That's the kind of thing Congress would probably want to debate . . ."

Crucible's voice was steel. "Let me make some calls. We can probably have a subject available within the week."

Harlequin's jaw dropped. "Sir . . ."

Crucible's boot collided sharply with Harlequin's shin under the table. The motion wasn't totally obvious, but Grace and Weiss couldn't have failed to see the surprise on Harlequin's face.

Weiss looked shocked, but Grace smiled knowingly, her eyes dancing. Shame and fury boiled in Harlequin's gut, and he pushed back against his magical tide.

"Well, that's delightful," Grace said. "What else do you need from us?"

"That presentation," Crucible said, "along with any other evidentiary documents I can submit to my command. I'll also need a promise that not a word of this conversation leaves this room. I'll have nondisclosure agreements for you to sign by close of business today. Does anyone else know about this meeting?"

Grace and Weiss made eye contact, looked back at Crucible. "Our conference scheduler, the shareholder liaison officer, and another of my senior VPs," she said, "and none of them think it's anything more than an 'exploratory discussion.' We've kept the initial findings, the drug's efficacy, on lockdown."

"My team knows of the success of the research," Weiss added, "but not that we're talking to you."

"Okay," Crucible said. "We'll be having all of them sign NDAs, too. You'll tell them this meeting was unproductive. We're not interested."

"But . . ." Weiss began.

Grace silenced him with a look. "We can do that," she said. "When do we hear from you next?"

"Hopefully," Crucible replied, "tomorrow. If this shows as much promise to my command as it does to me, I think they're going to want to move very quickly indeed."

"I'm very much looking forward to that," she said.

"One more request," Crucible added. "Let me have the room alone with my colleague here for a few minutes."

Grace and Weiss nodded and stood. "We'll be upstairs in my office. Just have the receptionist buzz us when you're done. Let him know if you need water or crackers or anything. I'm really looking forward to seeing both of you"—she gave Harlequin a pointed glance—"later."

Then she was gone, Weiss trailing at her heels, their strained silence palpable until the conference-room doors closed behind them.

Crucible turned back to Harlequin, steepled his fingers.

"I'm really sorry about that, Jan. You tripped over some stuff that you're . . . not privy to yet."

Harlequin pushed back on his anger. "I gathered. What was all that?"

"We can give them a subject. The Selfer you took down last night."

Harlequin stared. "The . . . sir, we just captured her. What the hell are you talking about?"

"You know exactly what I'm talking about, Jan. Gatanas is going to flip when he sees this presentation. He's going to want this drug in our dispensaries yesterday. Can you imagine? Being able to guarantee control over your magical current? Accessing it whenever and however you wanted? No danger of going nova?"

As if to prove Crucible's point, Harlequin again pushed back on the surge of his magical tide, borne on the sudden feeling that he didn't know Crucible at all, coupled with the lingering embarrassment over being shut down in front of Grace.

"Jesus, Jan. What do you think we do with Selfers?" Crucible asked.

Harlequin's lips felt numb. "They go into Suppression at Quantico. In some cases, they're executed."

"Right." Crucible nodded. "All of them? Even the Probes? These people are legally dead, Jan. They have no rights. Understanding and controlling magic is the biggest priority on the national defense agenda. Do you think we're just going to let hordes of legally dead Latent people rot in prison? Or kill them? All of them?"

"I . . ." The room spun around him. Harlequin bit back on his tide and closed his eyes. "I . . . We don't catch that many . . . It's rare to come up Latent."

Crucible touched his shoulder gently. "And we don't . . . repurpose many. But sometimes, we do."

"Repurpose? Are you fucking kidding me?"

"What would you prefer, Jan? That woman is mentally unhinged. She almost killed an entire housing project full of people. She forced you to risk your safety to bring her in. She's here. She's available. We haven't even transferred her yet. Maybe this drug will help her."

"Maybe this drug will give her cancer, or brain damage, or bleeding ulcers."

Crucible rolled his eyes. "So, it's better for her to die by lethal injection. Or to rot away in the brig at Quantico on the taxpayers' dime for the rest of her life."

He sighed, leaned forward. "Look, Jan. All I'm saying is that we give her a chance to volunteer."

"You just said she was unhinged. How the hell can she volunteer?"

"Anyone ever tell you that you think too much?"

"I thought that's why they commissioned me. Sound judgment."

"This isn't sound judgment. It's a failure to see the world as it is. There are policies that exist that guide those of us above your rank and level of experience. The circumstances demand that you be exposed to them now. Before you're ready, apparently. Tough luck. The SOC makes those rules, and you carry them out, as you swore you would. Those rules say that Selfer belongs to us. They say that her fate is subject to commander's discretion in extreme cases. This is a call I'm going to let Gatanas make. And I need to know you're on board because I'm pretty damn sure what he's going to say as soon as he sees this.

"So, are we clear here?" Crucible asked. The hand had come away from Harlequin's shoulder, and his eyes were hard again. "You just gave me this big speech about the difference between us and Selfers, didn't you? What was that difference?"

Harlequin met his eyes and swallowed. "Regs. We follow the rules."

"Well, now you know what the rules say, Mister Sheepdog. Fucking follow them."

CHAPTER VIII
PARLEY

As children, we all struggle with an odd sense of nostalgia. We come to the edge of a lake, a copse in a larger wood. We feel . . . something. A sense of longing, a hint that there's something deeper behind the beauty, a thing we touch only in dreams, in bedtime stories. I've heard Christians refer to this as the heart's longing for a lost Garden of Eden. But now we know better. It is the current of the Source, moving through our plane, promising wonders just on the other side of the curtain, if only we can find a way to pull it aside.

—Margaret Torres
The Psychology of Magic

Swift leapt out the window.

He let himself fall for a moment before Binding his magic to the updrafts around him, the concentrated blast of air sending him bounding skyward, then dipping again, the bobbing flight of the swallow tattooed on his chest. He extended a hand, channeling a funnel of lightning above him, into the delta of winged-snake things. Their jeweled-looking feathers ignited, dart-shaped heads tossing. Their formation splintered apart, scattering them to plunge among the buildings.

Swift glanced over his shoulder. Betony stood at the window, hands braced on the pane. Her gray hair had come out of its jeweled clasp, tumbled across her shoulders. A non-Latent sympathizer, her apartment had been a haven to the shattered remnants of the Houston Street Gang since they'd first been splintered. Her endless wealth had fed them, bought clothing and medicine. He would not suffer harm to come to her. "Get inside and get down!" he shouted, then dove. At least twenty of the flying serpents swarmed over the few blocks they'd managed to keep clear. He'd have to pursue them one by one.

Below him, what was left of the gang joined the fight.

Guinevere had been a corporate mover before she'd come up Latent, easing into her early thirties in a bubble of soft wealth. Magic had made her a woman already one step ahead of him. She raced out of the building foyer, kicking off her fancy shoes, the skirt of her business suit riding up her thighs. He felt her tide coalesce, the moisture in the air below him crystallizing. A handful of the things suddenly dropped like stones, their bodies frozen solid.

"I've got it!" she shouted up to him. "Help Flicker!"

The Pyromancer stood on the top of the Terramantic wall they'd raised, spanning Hubert Street. Swift had first met him in a Manhattan subway tunnel when the Houston Street Gang had taken him in.

Little Bear was one of the gang's better Terramancers, so enamored of Big Bear that he took the diminutive of his name. Big Bear's death had devastated him, but it hadn't weakened his magic. He'd stretched the surface of the rock and asphalt wall into spikes at first, but had re-formed it glass smooth after the first wave of goblins used them to climb up.

Flicker's bald head shone with sweat, eyes closed, teeth gritted in concentration. The street before him smoked, burning in patches, dotted with the smoldering remains of the weird, talking-horse things that had made up the vanguard of this latest wave. Spur, the former NBA basketball player turned Selfer, hovered beside him, his magic Binding somewhere above them. As Swift watched, a gale howled across the building top, ripping the wooden water tower from its moorings, sending it bouncing down to shatter in an explosion of splinters. Swift, Spur, and Flicker cried out and ducked as the spray of shrapnel barely cleared their heads. When Swift opened his eyes, the street was clear, the burned patches smoking, corpses swirling, and the ash turning to slurry in the sudden flood.

"Nice one," Swift said, "not only did you almost blind us, but now we're without water."

Spur shot him a venomous look, and Swift immediately

regretted the words. None of the remnants of the gang had ever been to the SASS. They had no training beyond what life on the run had provided. Skill beats will, went the old SOC axiom. Swift was reminded of the truth of those words with each passing day.

The *Gahe* stayed halfway down the block, unimpressed by the exploding water tower or the Pyromancy that had preceded it.

"What the hell are they waiting for?" Swift asked.

"It can't be good," Spur said. "Come on, let's . . ." He gestured back toward Betony's building, indicating the winged snakes. Swift nodded, turned.

But the creatures had already resumed a smaller delta, were winging their way back over their heads and down the street toward the *Gahe*.

"You scared them off," Swift said to Guinevere.

The Hydromancer looked exhausted. Blood trickled from her temple. Her jacket had ripped at the shoulder. "No way," she panted. "They were all over me. Somebody called them off."

"Swift!" The shout echoed down the corridor of the street. He knew that voice. He shivered.

"Swift! I just want to talk!"

Guinevere look up, eyes widening. "Oh, my God," she breathed.

"I told you it was her," Swift said. "I'll go see what she wants."

He Bound his magic to fly up to the wall, found Guinevere's hand holding fast to his elbow. "What?" he asked, removing it gently. "You think she'll just go away?"

He let the wind carry him to the carthen catwalk. Spur and Flicker stared down the street.

The *Gahe* were closer now, stutter-flashing restlessly back and forth. Scylla stood between them. She'd traded the leather armor for a scavenged SWAT uniform, black trousers bloused into black boots, body armor still sporting the city's subdued coat of arms. Swift felt her current, so strong it battered his senses. His brief attempts at learning to Suppress had yielded mixed results. He knew that, even if he made the attempt, he lacked the strength to interdict her current. He'd seen what

Scylla could do. If she wanted him dead, he'd be dead. Swift
didn't believe in heaven, but it couldn't stop the tiny ember of
hope that he might see Shai again. He tried to muster some
steel in his voice. He'd spent a long night locked in the hole
with Scylla. He knew all too well how she could play on fear.
It was like heroin to her. "That's close enough. What do you
want?"

"You're angry about the attack. I'm sorry. This is a mixed
army of a hundred different races with hundreds of different
agendas. I have a lot less control over them than I like to admit."
The smug grin she'd always worn was absent. She looked tired.

"Why on God's green earth would you unleash that here?"
Swift asked.

"It's not God's earth, Swift, it's ours. And you know why I
brought them here. Armies aren't exactly easy to come by, and,
unfortunately, we're not going to be able to change things without one."

"We?"

"Well, sure. Why do you think I'm doing this?"

"You're doing this for us. You're obliterating the greatest
city in the country for us."

"Liberating, not obliterating, and yes. It's for all Selfers. I
can't believe I have to explain this to you. You were in the
SASS, hell, you were even in the hole with me . . ."

"And I'll never forget it . . ."

"Come on! I was in solitary confinement for years. They'd
stolen my company and my life, turned everything I'd built
over to a pack of scumbags who only cared about turning a
profit. Can you blame me for being a bit unpleasant?"

Guinevere had joined them on the parapet. "Grace," she
said.

"Don't call me that," Scylla snapped, "nobody calls me that
anymore." She shook her head, mastered herself. "You have
been running from the SOC for too long. This country will
never be safe for us until we take it back, and by force. Why
are they in charge, and you're shivering in this rubbish bin?
You're stronger than them, Swift. You always have been."

"What do you want from us?" Guinevere asked.

"Jenny." Grace beamed at her. "You remember. I wasn't
some greedy thug. I did good things with my money. I would

have done good things with Limbic Dampener if the whole operation hadn't been stolen from me. Tell them."

"It's true," Guinevere mumbled.

"You're on the wrong side, Swift," Scylla said. "Help me win this."

"We're not on any side, Scylla," Swift said. "We're on our own side."

"That's the wrong side," Scylla answered. "Divided, we fall. It's time we show the humans who's boss. When this is over, we'll build something beautiful, a place where Latent people can be free. But like all things worth having, we have to work for it. It's hard, bloody work, but it's so, so worth it."

"Speaking of humans," Swift said, "I don't see many with you, and by 'not many,' I mean 'none.'"

Scylla glanced at the *Gahe*. "They may not be humans, but they're people. We used to look at humans of different skin colors the same way, and we were wrong to. The *Gahe* love the Apache, Swift. They see them as their own children. You should see the jewelry the goblins have made for me. It's beautiful. They have a culture. They have goals and wants and a vision for the future, just like you and I. And that vision includes being free of threat from the SOC. They're people, Swift. Just like us, and every other Selfer out there. I want all the people under my banner. I'm about to put the word out to every Selfer in this country. I'd like you standing at my side when I do it."

"What's in it for us?"

"Freedom."

"That doesn't mean a whole lot. The SOC promises the same thing."

"You remember Limbic Dampener, don't you? I invented it."

"Bullshit."

"Well, to be fair, researchers working for me developed it, but it was still my project. That's why the SOC threw me in the hole, Swift. They wanted to give the whole operation to Entertech. That drug is the key to all of this. Freely distributed, it would change everything. People can't call us dangerous if all of us have our magic under control all the time. I remember enough about the development. With a lab and some support, I can get it moving again."

"I control my magic without Dampener. So do you."

"It's not about us, Swift. It's about the newly Manifested. It's about those who just don't have a knack for it."

She rolled her eyes at Swift's silence. "Fine. How about a place at the helm? How many of you are there?"

"Nice try."

"Whatever. However many of you there are will be part of the ruling council when we establish our new state. I can't say what will happen otherwise."

"Now, that sounds like a threat."

"It's a fact. You can't expect the people who bleed and die for the new order to have a whole lot of patience for those who sat on the sidelines."

"We'll take it under advisement. I don't rule here, Scylla. I have to talk this over with everyone."

"Two days. I'll come for your answer then. I'm only coming one more time."

"Okay. Think you can keep your pets out of here until then?"

She nodded. "One last thing. Oscar Britton wouldn't happen to be hiding in there, would he?"

Swift's blood went cold. He tried to keep his voice even. "Haven't spoken to him in forever."

"Well, if you ever do happen to speak to him, would you please pass on my offer? Britton has been pushing for the distribution of Dampener himself. He'll see reason."

Swift watched her go, the *Gahe* sliding along beside her, the goblins withdrawing into the alleys between the buildings. Within the space of a minute, the street was clear.

"We should keep watch," Spur said.

"No need," Swift said. "She'll keep her word."

"So, we're joining her?" Flicker asked.

"It's what we wanted, isn't it?" Spur asked. "She's got a real shot at undoing . . . this."

Swift felt a cold thrill work its way up his neck, pulsing painfully in his head. "You don't know her," he said. "She's fucking crazy."

"All revolutionary ideas sound crazy," Guinevere said. "Years later, when they're the law of the land, they don't sound crazy anymore. She built one of the most powerful companies in the country, Swift. You've got to be a little crazy to pull that off."

Swift shook his head. "No way."

"You don't speak for us," Flicker said. "You're not Big Bear."

"I never claimed to be. I'm just letting you know my limit. I'm not working with that woman. Not ever."

"So what do we do?" Spur asked. "She's going to come for us if we don't join up."

"She gave us two days. We take them. We discuss it," Swift said.

"And Oscar?" Guinevere asked. "Does he get a vote?"

Swift sighed. "Yeah," he said. "Him, too."

CHAPTER IX

DIPLOMACY

The Québécois "Loup-Garou" units boast some of the best Ter-
ramancers in the world. They anchor each squad, a Whispered
wolf never far away. These wolves are both the totems and mas-
cots of the Loup-Garou. The soldiers treat them like favored chil-
dren, eating, fighting, and sleeping beside them. If the Loup-Garou
have to starve to ensure their wolves eat, they gladly do so. When
the animals die, their masters wear their skins draped over their
shoulders, heads above their own helmets in ancient Roman fash-
ion. The words "Les nôtres" are stitched in gold thread along the
snout, French for "Our own."

—*Country Guide 207-66A: Sovereign Territory of Quebec*
Publication of the United States Marine Corps Intelligence Activity

The hallway was so thickly carpeted, it swallowed sound. The
walls were punctuated with white recessed paneling etched in
gold. Light fixtures dripped crystal beads, the compact fluo-
rescent bulbs shaped to mimic candles. The space had that air
of official sanctity that commanded silence. Harlequin's security detail stepped lightly, whispering to one another. He knew
the floors below were a maelstrom of activity, with some staffs
packing up to evacuate, others wheeling and dealing in the
midst of the chaos. Somewhere down there, his request through
Gatanas was probably languishing in a bureaucratic mire.

The climate was surreal, ostentatious decoration and office
politicking in the middle of an unfolding disaster. But that was
always the way for soldiers, forced to straddle worlds: one foot

on the battlefield, doing the dirty job they were paid to do, and another in an air-conditioned office with the officials who paid them to do it. He'd embraced that role a long time ago. It was the sheepdog's way.

Harlequin had expected a giant chamber with a semicircular table and a map of the world on the wall. Instead, he was led into a room furnished with a dark wooden desk and two leather-upholstered chairs. Two glasses of water stood on a silver tray. The contrast with the bloody, burning reality of the southern tip of the island stunned him.

"If you'll just take a seat, sir," one of the security men said, then left.

Harlequin paced instead, hands behind his back, thinking of the time they were losing while he lingered here. He looked down at his uniform, unchanged for two days now, covered with dirt, spent cordite, streaks of blood. He was ashamed of his appearance for a moment, but it was for the best. He was here to convince them that a desperate situation was unfolding just south of them. Desperate people were seldom clean.

The door opened, and a group of suits entered, five men and one woman, followed by two more of the armed security guards. One of them, a lean man with graying brown hair and dark eyes, led the bunch, smiling grimly, offering Harlequin a limp handshake. An American flag was pinned to his lapel.

"Ambassador Hallert," Harlequin said.

The man nodded. "Thank you for coming, Lieutenant Colonel." He turned to the man beside him, who had a shaggy mop of black hair and a beak of a nose. "May I present Marc-Antoine Desmarais. Monsieur Desmarais is the UN ambassador from Canada."

"Sir." Harlequin shook the man's hand, realizing that his own was streaked with filth. "Apologies, for that. I've just come from the fighting.

"I hope you'll pardon me," Harlequin said, "but would it be possible for me to have a word in private with Ambassador Hallert before we . . ."

"Your business here is with the council," said an Asian man in slightly accented English. "Given your nation's past history of making bilateral arrangements with other council members, it's critical that all conversations be held in full hearing of bloc representatives."

The last was addressed to Hallert. The ambassador didn't betray so much as the slightest discomfort, but Harlequin winced inwardly. *It's because of India. It's because we both had FOBs in the Source. They think we were working together, and they're mad as hell about it.*

"Ambassador Tan represents Singapore," Hallert said. "He currently holds the chairmanship of the council. I've already briefed the council on the situation, but they thought that you might be able to give a personal perspective on the matter."

Harlequin scanned the representatives before him. "The ambassador from Mexico . . ." he began.

"Is not here," Tan responded. He gestured to a stone-faced woman in a cream-colored suit. "Guatemala is speaking for the Latin American and Caribbean Bloc on this matter."

That couldn't be good. Harlequin swallowed, tried to find his center.

"It's bad," he began. "We have a major incursion from the Source into the southern tip of Manhattan. I have barricades holding the northern edge along Houston Street. They are hard-pressed, and I'm not sure how much longer they can maintain the perimet . . ."

Tan cut in. "I hear that you have an abundance of reinforcements from army bases in New Jersey and some as close as Brooklyn. Those barricades are well manned."

"That's partially true, sir, and it is helping, but that's not the root of the problem."

"And what is that?"

"Some of the enemy are impervious to conventional ordnance, sir. They are only susceptible to magic. We need arcane assistance on the ground to combat them. If they break through, I should remind you that it is only a five-hour drive to the Canadian border"—he addressed this last to Desmarais—"and only about a thirty-minute walk to this very building."

He turned to the Guatemalan ambassador. "And you are no doubt already aware that a similar incident is currently ongoing on the Mescalero Apache reservation in New Mexico. That's just over one hundred miles from the Mexican border, ma'am. This is absolutely Mexico's problem, and a problem for your entire bloc."

"And you are so certain that this enemy has designs beyond the borders of the United States?" Tan asked.

As if that's all that matters. Harlequin felt himself flush. Ambassador Hallert must have seen it, and he began to speak, but Harlequin mastered himself and cut him off.

"I know the woman who is leading this attack. I am the man who captured her when she first came up Latent. I knew her while we had her in custody. She will stop at nothing, absolutely nothing, to bring about what she perceives as a new and just social order: one in which Latent people rule all others. We know very little about the creatures she has solicited to help her, but we do know that they are killers and see themselves as gods among the Apache. I can't imagine they have positive intentions toward the rest of humanity, or that our idea of a border is going to mean all that much to them."

The Guatemalan representative looked at Tan, who turned back to Harlequin. "And how, exactly, are these forces gaining entry to this city and to the Mescalero reservation?"

Harlequin looked to Hallert and saw no help there. They both knew that Tan already knew the answer to his question.

"Through some kind of rent in the planar fabric, sir," Harlequin said. "We'd believed there were 'thin spots' in the past that the *Gahe* were using to access the Mescalero reservation, but only in ones and twos. It appears that the woman I mentioned to you earlier has found a way to use her Negramancy to widen the apertures. It's admitting the creatures at a greater rate than we're going to be able to handle."

Tan shook his head, turning to Hallert. "You sat on this council, not a year ago, trying to convince us of the wisdom of your McGauer-Linden Act. You have pressed for sanctions against Haiti for trafficking in Necromancy. My friend from Guatemala here has spent years lobbying for the *Dios de los Muertos* exception. The force the United States has put behind its prohibition efforts for your 'Probe' schools has been considerable. When we did discover there were . . . flaws in that presentation . . ."

Hallert broke in. "That's still under debate, Mr. Tan, and you must realize that the administration responsible for those violations has been impeached and resigned. Our current president . . ."

"You'll doubtless understand that there are some concerns about the representations surrounding the McGauer-Linden Act and your commitment to it moving forward," Tan said. "I do want to point out that the one Probe school this body is certain was employed by the US was Portamancy, and what Lieutenant Colonel Thorsson here is describing sounds very much like that."

"It is very much like that," Harlequin said, "but this isn't our doing."

Tan said nothing, meeting his eyes flatly. *Why should they believe us? Hell, I've got a Probe Elementalist inside my headquarters working illegal magic as we speak.*

"You are, no doubt, familiar with your nation's Cuban Missile Crisis, Lieutenant Colonel?" Tan asked.

Now it was Harlequin's turn to say nothing.

"Your country reacted with great . . . expediency in dealing with a strategic threat well inside its sphere of influence, in fact, on its very border."

Tan lowered his head, looking at Harlequin from under his furrowed brow. "The Source is on everyone's border, Lieutenant Colonel. And the threat proposed by the mightiest of your so-called prohibited magical schools is very strategic indeed."

Tan straightened, folded his arms. "The Asian Bloc of this body is currently undergoing an intensive examination of India's involvement in the Gate-Gate incident. Restoring this body's trust in the good faith and transparency of both of your nations is going to take some time. I've commissioned a fact-finding mission to your Breach Zone to ascertain the nature of the incursion. We're also sending a team to Mescalero. Until such time as the results of that commission are determined and analyzed, I cannot in good conscience concur with directing armed intervention on your nation's behalf, especially armed intervention with arcane units."

Harlequin's heart sank. He had known this was coming from the moment he'd first seen Tan's expression, but the reality of it hit home. "Sir, respectfully, whatever you may think of my government, please consider my people. We are facing an enemy in overwhelming numbers in the nerve center of our homeland. We need help, and we need it now. Without it, people are going to die. I would be delighted to stand for whatever atonement you think my nation should pay to make right for our failing to disclose our presence in the Source . . ."

". . . Lieutenant Colonel!" Hallert broke in. "That's not a commitment you can make! I'm sorry, sir . . ." he said to Tan, but Harlequin cut him off.

". . . but that's for later. The fight is right now. People are dying right now. By the time your commission gives its results and you reach a determination, it will be far too late."

He turned to the Guatemalan ambassador. "I need you to pass our request on to Mexico. We need their help in Mescalero if not in New York City." He turned to Desmarais. "Canada as well. Like it or not, this is your fight, too, or very soon will be if you don't get involved while we still have a chance of controlling it."

The Guatemalan ambassador looked from the floor to Ambassador Tan, refusing to meet Harlequin's eyes. Desmarais met his gaze steadily, then inclined his head to Hallert. "I will relay your request to my government and to the Western European and Other Nations Bloc."

Tan looked furious. "I think we've heard everything we need, Lieutenant Colonel. Thank you for your time."

Harlequin knew better than to press the matter. "Sir," he said stiffly.

Hallert escorted him back out into the hallway as the rest of the group exited by another door. "I would really have appreciated a chance to pregame that with you, sir," Harlequin said.

Hallert took his elbow. "You did fine, better than fine, in fact. You have to remember that things like this are usually already decided, and the real work is going on in the background."

"So you're saying I'm screwed."

"Quite the contrary," Hallert said. "Mexico is under a lot of pressure, but Mescalero is right on top of them, and we're their biggest trading partner no matter what pressure the LAC puts on them." He looked up at Harlequin's blank expression. "Sorry, the Latin America and Caribbean bloc. We can work on them."

Hallert's voice was placid, attentive, carrying that subtle undercurrent that made you feel like you were the only other person in the world. He wanted to trust that voice instinctively. It was the voice of government, of big institutions like the Army, of the structures that had been his home and career since the National Guard youth-challenge program he'd joined in high school. But he'd heard that voice before, and the memory sent a chill up his spine.

Former President Walsh sounded like that. So did Scylla.

"And Canada?" Harlequin asked.

"We've already got Canada. Desmarais assured me privately they're scrambling a support unit out of Quebec. Their *Loup-Garous*. Terramancy like you've never seen."

Harlequin felt an ember of hope in his chest, cautiously fanned it. The Québécois were famous for flouting the Geneva Convention Amendment's prohibition of Whispering. If there was any arcane fighting force that wouldn't balk at the stigma of Probe magic, it was them. But Hallert was a politician, and Harlequin had been learning a thing or two about them since Oscar Britton went rogue.

"Why would they help us if the Mexicans won't? Mescalero's a lot closer to Mexico than New York City is to Canada."

"I already said, don't count the Mexicans out. Besides, we've got a deal in the works to help them extract oil from the tar sands they've got up there. Promising nearly all of the Army Corps of Engineers Terramantic Support Element. It'd be an economic hit for us, but it'll help move them on the issue. The Chinese already do Terramantic engineering at home, and this will give us an excuse to get in that game."

He stopped, clapping Harlequin on the shoulder and smiling.

"What?" Harlequin asked, amazed.

"This is your doing, Lieutenant Colonel. I don't think you fully appreciate how your actions at FOB Frontier changed things. You changed the conversation. Things'll move slow, but they'll come, sure as the sun rises. Amazing. I know you don't get a lot of support for what you did, and I can't honestly say I don't have mixed feelings about it, but I wanted you to know that I, for one, am happy you're on the job here. There's a lot I've been wanting to accomplish that is only now becoming possible because of what you did."

"Because of what a lot of people did," Harlequin said, faces flashing through his mind. *Oscar Britton, Alan Bookbinder.*

Hallert shrugged. "Of course."

"You want to thank me for all that? Get me help, Ambassador. Convince them that it's in all of their interests to help."

"Sit tight," Hallert responded, clapping him on the shoulder again. "Convincing people is what I do."

CHAPTER X
DON'T GIVE UP THE SHIP

The real value in Probe magic is its power as a force multiplier. With the exception of Rending, pretty much every Probe school results in an increase in applicable battlefield assets or firepower. This is what makes the Shadow Coven program so incredibly important to our continued dominance in the arcane domain. That said, there are limits. A Portamancer employing GIMAC can only manipulate a single gate at a time. An Elementalist must Bind his or her magic to sustain the noncorporeal "body" of an elemental, greatly limiting the number that can be commanded at once. A Necromancer has it easier. Dead bodies already have cell cohesion, granting them the power to raise and command armies. But unlike elementals, zombies have no will and cannot act of their own accord. They are flesh automatons, requiring the Necromancer's constant attention and direction.

—Chief Warrant Officer-4 Albert Fitzsimmons
Inputs to quarterly report on the progress
of the Shadow Coven (C4U-Umbra) program

For the moment, the buoy deck was clear, while the aquatic goblins busied themselves with the sailors from the *Giffords*. Bookbinder watched their heads disappearing beneath the water as long as he could stand it, but the scene finally overwhelmed him, and he looked around the bridge on the pretext of assessing the damage.

The giant wave hadn't swamped the ship, but the *Breakwater* was listing badly to port, the ball and hook from the giant crane rocking threateningly over the bullet-riddled deck.

Bonhomme stood with his fists propped against the helm console, eyes locked on the carnage churning around the *Giffords*'s overturned hull. Rodriguez watched him, looking like she wanted to say something, but thinking better of it. Bonhomme finally said, "We can't go after them."

Bookbinder hated the words, couldn't deny the truth of them. "No, we can't."

What do we do? Bonhomme mouthed, jaw quivering.

"What's your recommendation, skipper?" Bookbinder asked.

Bonhomme shook his head. "We can't fight them."

"We've been fighting them," Bookbinder said, "winning, too."

"Maybe they want in on whatever's going down onshore," Rodriguez said. "We could head out to sea, stand off, and wait for help. We're oceangoing, sir."

"No way," Bookbinder said. "That thing swamped two warships. It'll flood the southern tip of the island just as easy. We can't let that happen." *Whatever is going on there, Harlequin needs my help. I should be there, damn it.* He bit down on the frustration.

"We don't have any stores laid in," Bonhomme said. "This was supposed to be a day cruise. I'm not even sure what the hull integrity looks like." He gestured to the obvious slope of the buoy deck. "I need a damage report, but I sincerely doubt the desalination unit is up and running right now. We've got wounded crew. This ship may not be stable. We need to get to shore."

Bookbinder knew this as well, but it didn't make him feel any better to hear it.

Screams reached him from the churning water around the *Giffords*. The goblins were taking their time only because they saw the *Breakwater* wounded and limping. There was no need for them to hurry.

"Once the navy knows their ships went down, they'll send helos. Maybe they can airlift us off," Rodriguez added, "drop depth charges on that thing."

"It's going to take time," Bonhomme said.

"Well," Bookbinder said, "let's make it easier on them and head inland. You've tried the radios ag . . . ."

"They're dead. Shore"—Bonhomme pointed past the *Giffords*—"is that way. I'm not sure what our engines will do right now."

You're not sure because you're standing here whining and not calling for a damage report! Bookbinder's mind shouted. Rodriguez spared him the need to say it. "I'll get an engine room SITREP, sir. See what casualties we have." She grabbed a phone receiver off the console before remembering the loss of comms and slamming it back into its cradle. She jogged out of the hatch, while Bonhomme turned around and punched the console.

"We've got to go back around that giant . . . thing . . . whatever it is in the water that let those monsters in."

"It's a gate," Bookbinder answered. "I have no idea how it got here, but that's what it is. It bridges our world and the Source." *If I name the thing, maybe it will frighten him less.*

"You were there," Bonhomme said.

Bookbinder nodded. "I was. It's not all that different from our world. If anything, it's simpler. There's no more reason to fear it than you would a desert. The worst thing we'll have to do is tangle with more of these water goblins, and we've already licked them once."

Bonhomme shook his head. "We won't last another round. We're not geared for warfighting. None of us have the training, we sure as hell don't have the equipment. You know who did? Those guys!" He stabbed a finger out the bridge window at the *Giffords*'s vanishing hull.

Bonhomme was shouting now, using anger to cope with fear. Bookbinder had seen it before. It never helped. "We're trained to pull buoys out of the water, tow broken-down yachts, and maybe arrest someone for having a nickel bag of weed. Christ, the most dangerous thing we've ever done was lay boom around a chemical spill."

Rodriguez stuck her head back in as Bonhomme built up steam, saw what was unfolding, and stepped back out into the passageway. Bookbinder excused himself and stepped out after her, catching her elbow. "Ripple . . ."

Rodriguez looked at the deck, shook her head, left.

Bookbinder's heart sank. Just a kid. The long line of what-ifs began to blossom in his head, already doing the blame dance that held himself responsible for each person under his command. He'd lost people before, his first on the journey to the Indian FOB in the Source. They were all volunteers, and they knew what they'd signed up for, but it never got any easier. Ripple was his minder, but she was also his subordinate and reminded him of the woman his own daughter might someday become.

He thought of the corpses of the Marines, smoking in the hallway behind him as he made his way to Oscar Britton's cell. *Harlequin bears those deaths,* he thought. *I'm responsible for enough without taking that on.* But he couldn't help turn the scenario over in his mind. Was there something he could have done to save them? *They were already dead when you stepped out into the hallway. They would have stopped you, killed you. Remember that.*

Bookbinder stepped back onto the bridge. Ripple was dead, and it wasn't going to be for nothing.

"The Coast Guard is still part of the military," Bookbinder said, "no matter what the mission is."

"Horseshit," Bonhomme said. "We're not ready to handle monsters from another dimension."

Bookbinder took a step back, giving the man his space. A smile slowly blossomed across his face. The more he tried to control it, the more it spread. After a moment, he shook his head and laughed.

Bonhomme blinked. "What . . . what's . . ."

The ship listed and the goblins churned in the water and Bookbinder laughed until he had to wipe his eyes. "Sorry about that."

Bonhomme's panic gave way to a hint of anger. That was something.

"I'm sorry," Bookbinder said again. "It's just that, this happened to me. I thought it was this big . . . cross to bear, like Job in the Bible. But I get it now."

"What the hell are you talking about?" Bonhomme asked.

"Do you know what I did before I became your branch LNO?"

"Only what I heard on the Internet. That you pissed off the government to save that FOB. That you're some kind of a folk hero."

Bookbinder laughed again. "Right. That's me, a fucking folk hero. No, skipper, I was a J1. I pushed paper. Before I came up Latent, I'd never pulled a trigger off a range. And then came

FOB Frontier. First I had to fight. Then I had to lead. I was suddenly responsible for thirty thousand men and women and a couple of billion dollars of equipment in the middle of a war zone. I kept shaking my fists at the sky, and crying, 'I wasn't trained for this! I'm the admin guy!' I compared my insides to other people's outsides. I kept thinking that the 11B types around me were spit out into the world steel-eyed and ready to kill.

"And now I'm standing here looking at you, salty as hell, running cutters for what? Ten years?"

Bonhomme's eyes narrowed. "Thirteen."

"Thirteen years." Bookbinder nodded. "Master of his element. I'm realizing that *everyone* has this experience. All of a sudden, you're in the hot seat, and you feel like a fucking fraud. Am I right?"

Bonhomme said nothing.

"Of course I'm right. But that's everyone. We're all frauds. We're all just pretending that we know what we're doing. The trick is to pretend so well that you convince yourself long enough to get through the rough spot.

"This is your crucible moment, only you can't see it because you're in it." He reached out and gently put his hands on Bonhomme's shoulders again. "But I can see it. Because I just went through it myself. And I can tell you, the guy who comes out on the other side isn't going to recognize the guy you are now. But that guy needs the guy you are now to pull the fuck together. You can do this. Believe me. I know."

Bonhomme stared.

"I was a paper-pusher, skipper, and I saved a division. You clean buoys for a living? Fine. You can save this ship."

He stepped back, folded his arms. "Now, skipper. I'm a landlubber. You're the cutterman. Tell me how we get out of here."

Bonhomme shook his head, looked at the deck. "Engines at full can do sixteen knots, depending on how bad they're damaged."

"Why are we . . . leaning over like this?"

"Listing," Bonhomme corrected him. "Could be a flooded compartment. Could be level problems with the ballast tanks. Could even be that a lot of gear slid around when we got hit.

Question is whether or not we're taking on water. I'll know as soon as Rodriguez gets the report from engineering."

Keep him talking. "Okay. So, what if the goblins come back?"

Bonhomme frowned. "I can put the rifles in the radar mast, they should be able to sight down the bow from there. I can put a rifle in each of the boat cranes to cover the stern. Keep the shotguns and pistols on the hatches into the superstructure."

Bonhomme was warming to the task. "We've got the Mark-79 flares, and those are practically incendiary bullets right there. The Mark-127's would probably start a nice fire if the bad guys are packed onto the deck . . ." He looked up at Bookbinder's blank expression. "They're illumination flares, burn hotter than hell. We use them to light up the water when we're searching for people."

"Right," Bookbinder said. "How many do we have?"

"Depends on how much water we've taken on and where, but either way, not enough."

They both went silent at that.

Bonhomme looked up suddenly, eyes widening. "OC!"

"Okaaaay," Bookbinder drawled.

"Sorry. Oleoresin Capsicum. Pepper spray. We use it on boardings."

"I know what pepper spray is. I don't think you're going to get away with handcuffing those goblins, skipper."

Bonhomme smiled. "You ever been exposed?"

Bookbinder shook his head. He'd been shot at, blown up, punched, kicked, and even stabbed, but nobody had ever sprayed him with OC.

Bonhomme's smile widened. "It's not what you're thinking, sir. It's like having your skin held to a hot frying pan for hours, while your eyes are filled with ground glass, and you suffocate."

"So? They just jump in the water."

"It doesn't wash off, sir. The only thing that helps is time, and while they're flailing, we're shooting."

Now it was Bookbinder's smile that widened. "I like the way you think. But I'm guessing you're going to have to get closer than you'd like to be able to blast them in the face with it."

"Well, they're aquatic, right? Like fish or frogs or whatever?"

Bookbinder shrugged. "Looked like it."

"That means membranous skin, gills. A puff of this stuff anywhere on their bodies should drive them fucking insane."

Bookbinder nodded. "Again, how much do we have?"

"Not nearly enough, but the canisters have a . . . thirty-foot range or so. Provided we're watching the wind, we can shower them with it."

"Area-effect weapon."

"It's crude, but I think it could work."

Bookbinder glanced over Bonhomme's shoulder and through the bridge windows. The *Giffords*'s overturned hull was streaked with blood where sailors had climbed up and been dragged back down. The aft lifted slightly higher out of the water, the giant bladed screws of the azipod thrusters sticking up in the air.

The water around the overturned vessel had stopped churning, the goblins having dealt with their prey and now turning toward the *Breakwater*. As Bookbinder watched, the first of them began to swim their way. The huge shape of the leviathan rotated slowly toward them.

"Skipper, I don't think we've got a whole lot of time here," Bookbinder said.

Marks and Rodriguez ran onto the bridge. "Number two motor is down," she rattled out breathlessly. "There's some flooding in the stores, and the bilges overflowed, but they're pumping it out. We're leveling the ballast tanks now." Even as she spoke, Bookbinder could feel the *Breakwater* trimming up beneath him, the giant crane boom pointing straighter into the air.

Marks glanced over at the console and tapped the radios. "That wave must have banged up the mast. VHF is down. No comms. The radar antennae are still spinning."

Bonhomme nodded. "Get us underway and back to Sector, fast as she can go." He turned to Bookbinder. "That won't be very fast, limping on one engine."

Marks nodded and shouted out into the passageway. A moment later, boots banged outside, and a helmsman ran onto the bridge, taking up position. Bookbinder felt the muscles in his back relax ever so slightly as the bridge regained the attitude of a command center. They were still in trouble, but at least now they had a chance.

"Skipper, you said you were going to put shooters in the radar mast?" Bookbinder asked.

"That's right, to cover the bow," Bonhomme said distractedly, busy conferring with Rodriguez and Marks.

"I'll go aloft with them if you don't mind."

Bonhomme looked up now. "What? Sir, I'm not sure if that's fitting given your rank."

"We both know that my rank was a political maneuver. You need all hands on deck, and I'm the one person on this vessel who has experience fighting goblins."

Bonhomme cocked an eyebrow. "On the water?"

"I've been in combat."

Bonhomme looked embarrassed, and Bookbinder added, "If they put a sorcerer aboard, I can deal with it. I'm no good to you sitting around here twiddling my thumbs."

Bonhomme lowered his voice. "Respectfully, sir, you've been a lot of good to me."

Bookbinder smiled uncomfortably. "Yes, well. Let me do some more."

Bonhomme nodded. "Marks'll go with you."

Bookbinder followed the young lieutenant through the maze of ship's passages, getting hopelessly lost yet again. Marks led him around a corner and into a tight space dominated by a thick, metal gear locker with the words PYRO stenciled on the white doors. The boarding teams had already opened it and were equipping themselves with armloads of foot-long metal cylinders. Marks handed Bookbinder a bright orange vest that looked like a deflated life jacket.

"Search-and-rescue vest," Marks said. "It's got your flares, among other things. I'll show you how to use it all once we get in position."

"Lieutenant"—Bookbinder stopped him with a hand on his elbow—"it'd help if I could have a rifle and armor, too. I'm in this fight, same as you."

Marks and the boarding team members exchanged a quick glance. "Of course, sir." The gear was pressed into Bookbinder's hands, along with a black utility belt. Bookbinder raced to don it all as he followed Marks back through the passageways, then out another hatch and into the air before mounting a ladder that led above the bridge. The radar mast stood before

them, looking thin and rickety, the mustard-colored metal
leaning dangerously to port despite the trimming up. Bookbinder swallowed, then followed Marks up.

The ship rolled, taking the horizon with it. Bookbinder's
gorge rose, and he clung to the rungs for dear life. Marks paused
above him. "Everything okay, sir?"

"Fine," Bookbinder said. "Just . . . fine."

Marks climbed up the rest of the way, and Bookbinder
finally joined him, cramming onto the tiny metal shelf underneath the ship's spinning radar antennae. The boomer had protected the ship from the worst of the giant wave, but much of
the radar mast had still been swept away. Jagged nubs of metal
marked where the VHF antennae used to stand. Bookbinder
clung to the railing for dear life, the world pitching around
him. Marks and the other sailors looked like they'd been born
on a pitching deck, not even bothering to hold on to anything.
Bookbinder felt as if they were a thousand feet off the water's
surface, the tiniest swell of the water making the metal beneath
his feet slip so dramatically that he could see himself tumbling
off it at any moment.

"You sure you're okay, sir?" Marks asked again.

"I said I'm fine," Bookbinder groused, knuckles still white
on the rail.

He glanced at the radar antennae behind him. "That bad
for us?"

Marks looked up the spinning antennae. "Hmm. Yeah.
We're not supposed to be this close for any extended period."

"So what happens?"

"Nothing. For a few years at any rate."

"Wait. What happens after a few years?" Bookbinder
asked, his vertigo and seasickness momentarily gone.

But Marks was already focusing on the water around the
ship's bow, churning white again as the goblins swarmed the
Breakwater's bow in earnest. Their suckered fingers found
purchase even as the giant ship shuddered, the hull groaning
a complaint against the thrusters roaring suddenly into life.
The engineers were driving the vessel to its limit, judging from
the sudden spray of water flying from the *Breakwater*'s stern
and shooting so high that Bookbinder could see it over the

smokestack behind him. Black smoke belched, and the *Breakwater* began to lumber forward.

Marks tapped a thin canister hanging from Bookbinder's belt. "That's your OC. Snap that orange safety tab off before you push the button." Marks licked his finger and held it up. "Wind's out of the east. Maybe five knots? Aim this way." He held his own canister off the platform's starboard edge. Bookbinder moved to join him, forcing his fingers to unclench from the railing and taking tiny, shuffling steps.

The lieutenant suppressed a smile. "You'll be okay, sir. Just take care, this stuff blows back in your face, and you are going to be out of the fight."

Bookbinder nodded as the first goblins swarmed up over the gunwales and perched on the buoy deck. "Hold your fire!" Marks called out. "Let's see how the pyro and the spray does before we go wasting bullets."

Short cracks from the boat-crane platforms behind them told Bookbinder that the other sailors weren't being so careful.

"Go with the flares first!" Marks said, pulling one of the metal cylinders out of the case one of the sailors had set on the platform. Bookbinder followed suit, popping the canister head off and seating it at the tube's bottom. He followed Marks as he pointed the tube at the massing goblins, then punched the base, driving the head in. His arm thrummed as the tube spit out a streaking missile. It shone sparking white even in the daylight, a gathered parachute failing to deploy at the steep angle, catching fire as it went, trailing smoke.

The goblins looked up as the flares streaked into them, eyes wide with hatred and surprise. They were packed densely on the deck, and while a few jumped back over the side, the majority threw up their hands as the flares struck and rolled, scattering burning fragments among them. A few of the creatures shouted, the flare shards and bits of shredded parachute smoldering against their wet skin.

The *Breakwater* was making way now, up to her limping top speed. One of the sailors reached into his vest pocket and brought out a pencil-sized flare launcher. Bookbinder watched as he screwed a flare into it, then aimed and fired into the churning mass of goblins on the buoy deck. Bookbinder copied

him. These flares were red and lacked parachutes, but the
pencil launcher kicked, and the flares sped off like gunshots,
at least one of them holing and dropping a goblin, every bit as
effective as a bullet.

The goblins flailed and fell over one another, crowding
around the crane, surging toward the superstructure. Two of
them held a thick piece of metal plating, probably scavenged
off the *Giffords*. They wedged it into the seam of the entry
hatch, grunting as they tried to find purchase to pry it open.

"Go with the OC!" Marks shouted. He held his canister as
far over the railing as he could without leaning, compensating
for the wind, and fired. The stream of liquid arced twenty feet
before the wind caught it and spread it out in a light cloud that
drifted toward the buoy deck. Bookbinder extended his arm
and pressed his own trigger along with the other sailors, adding to the blanket of spray. The high-vinegary smell of cayenne
pepper filled his nose, and he blinked, eyes watering painfully.
"Careful!" Marks called to him. "Don't breathe!"

Don't breathe? Bookbinder thought, closing his mouth.
How the hell am I supposed to not breathe?

The cloud was pushed gently by the easterly breeze, but
Marks had clearly used this weapon before and compensated
well. By the time the cloud of OC settled over the buoy deck,
it was near dead center.

The goblins paused, looking up at the strange mist drifting
over them. A few licked their lips. Some swatted at the cloud.

Their canisters empty, Bookbinder, Marks, and the sailors
unslung their rifles, took aim and waited.

The goblins crouched, blinking. A few who had jumped off
the buoy deck now climbed back aboard, their nostrils flaring
at the vapor. *It didn't work,* Bookbinder thought. *They're
immune somehow.* He looked down at his rifle, braced against
the rail. At FOB Frontier, they'd used carbines with extended
magazines, holding thirty rounds. These magazines looked
about half the size. Not nearly enough ammunition to last
against the numbers crowding the deck.

Then, as one body, the goblins howled.

Their skin began to bubble, going yellow, lumpen. One by
one, the creatures began to dance, tearing at their bodies, clawing at their faces. Within seconds, the entire buoy deck was

jumping, the goblins throwing themselves down, at one another, over the side. The scream was earsplitting. One goblin dropped to its knees, plunging its brine-covered claws into its own eyes, tearing them out of their sockets. Another hefted a small axe made from some ship's wreckage, and began to lay about among its own fellows, cutting them down as it wept thick, black tears.

A chorus of shrieking came over the smokestack as the same scene repeated on the ship's stern.

Bookbinder couldn't help but feel a small spot of pity for them. "Jesus," he whispered. "I guess Bonhomme was right about the mucus membranes."

Marks nodded along with him, equally horrified. "Guess so."

A few of the creatures plunged into the water, but only continued to thrash, beating themselves against the *Breakwater*'s sides. A light, oily sheen settled across the surface, broken apart by the ripples of squirming goblins and the forward momentum of the ship's hull. Bookbinder marveled as more and more of the goblins succumbed to flailing agony.

Many, but not all. As the mist began to clear, Bookbinder saw that more were unaffected or bulled through the pain, crying defiance as they threw themselves at the entry hatches. They pounded on them with spear butts and clubs, prised their fingers into the seams, worked the bit of metal they had wedged in, yanked on the wheel. Bookbinder imagined the sailors on the other side, struggling to keep the hatches shut. They couldn't hold forever.

"Shoot 'em now, sir?" one of the sailors asked.

It wouldn't matter. Despite the spray's work, the deck was still crowded with goblins. They could empty every round in every magazine and still not deal with them all. Once they gained the superstructure, it would be over.

He steadied his rifle and aimed into the press. *Make each shot count,* he thought. Every goblin down was one less they'd have to fight once those hatches gave way.

The throng was packed so thickly that it would be hard to miss, but he steadied himself anyway, controlling his breathing as he tensed his trigger finger.

"Where do we start?" asked one of the sailors.

"Just shoot until you're empty," Marks answered. Bookbinder set his teeth.

Then he felt something. A current, first a trickle, but growing stronger. His own current reached out toward it instinctively.

"Hold fire," he said.

"What?" Marks asked, but Bookbinder had closed his eyes, concentrating.

There was a splash off the ship's starboard beam and a creature burst out of the water. It was bigger than the goblins on the buoy deck, its surface sleek with patterned scales. A long, dorsal ridge ran from its head to its buttocks, translucent bone tips peeking above the stretched skin. Huge yellow eyes bugged from its wedge-shaped head. It trailed water, bursting through the remaining wisps of the OC cloud, gaining elevation, banking sharply to come back at them.

Bookbinder could see that it was a goblin, the features unmistakable in spite of whatever forces below the waves had twisted it into its present form. He could feel its Aeromancy, sharp and pungent. Maybe the damage done by the OC had forced the enemy to deploy their big guns, but it made no difference. Bookbinder could deal with Aeromancy, no matter what fishy package it came in.

Dark clouds boiled around the creature. The air hummed with electricity and Bookbinder smelled ozone over the chemical reek of the OC. Marks and his sailors crouched on the platform.

"Oh, shit." One of the sailors began to make for the ladder down to the bridge.

"Hang on," Bookbinder said, stepping to the railing. "I've got this."

The thing in the sky hissed and dove, the clouds gathering around it, pulsing, glowing at the edges. At last they unseamed, long tendrils of lightning arcing toward the radar mast. Marks shut his eyes. The sailors shouted and ducked.

Bookbinder reached out a hand. His own magic hungrily seized the Aeromancy, hauling it in until Bookbinder felt the double tide thrumming in his veins. He bit down, tasting blood in his mouth, grunting as he wrestled the sorcery under control.

The creature blinked, hissed again, flailed fins as the magic supporting its flight drained away.

Then it fell to the deck, thrashing among the goblins as they fought to clear away.

Bookbinder pointed, focused on the deck at the base of the crane, and Bound.

The doubled tide surged out of him, the torrent of electricity pouring into the deck, his magic tying the lightning into the ship's structure until the molecules shivered with it, sparking across the metal beams and carlins, rippling through the steel. Bookbinder sighed with relief as his body released the extra magic, his veins contracting.

The metal surface rippled, pulsed, came alive. The goblins shrieked, then danced a second time.

Blue lightning shot across the buoy deck, conducted by the water streaming off the creatures' skins, sizzling until it finally attenuated at the base of the superstructure. Ozone stink competed with the smell of cooked meat as the goblins shuddered and shook, smoking in a garden of dancing lightning. They fell away from the hatches, twitching. The combined stink of OC, seared flesh, and cooking brine billowed up from the still-shuddering corpses, writhing across the deck in a macabre waltz before flopping at the base of the crane or pitching over the side.

When he finally looked up, the buoy deck was still, layered with a light haze of drifting smoke. The stink was unholy. Marks gripped the railing and vomited. He sagged, wiping his mouth and shivering, looking up at Bookbinder. "Holy shit, sir."

Bookbinder nodded. "Sometimes, you win."

Marks's radio crackled into life, Rodriguez's voice sounded worried. "Are you seeing this, sir? Starboard quarter."

Marks craned his head. "Negative, smokestack's in the way. What's up?"

"Come to the bridge, sir. You can see from here. You might want to hurry."

Marks double-timed it back down the ladder, his sailors in tow. Bookbinder followed suit, shutting his eyes tight and trying to avoid looking down. He noticed the ship straightening as he went, which made the going easier, righting out the bad list to port faster than he expected.

By the time he hit the passageway outside the bridge hatch,

he realized it was too fast. The deck was starting to cant in the other direction.

Rodriguez and Bonhomme stood by the farthest starboard window, looking out over the water, eyes wide with concern.

"We've got a problem," Rodriguez said.

"Another problem," Bonhomme added.

"Let's call it a challenge," Bookbinder said as he reached the window and looked out. "What's up?"

But neither Bonhomme nor Rodriguez needed to answer. The dark bulk of the leviathan was closer to the surface now, its truck-sized tail waving gently under the water. Bookbinder could see a few goblins crawling over its surface, holding on to tangles of seaweed, and clumps of the limpetlike creatures clustering on its skin.

The water above it whirled, sucked down into the huge creature's opening maw. Bookbinder could see its shadow expanding as its sides ballooned, pregnant with seawater.

He could feel the *Breakwater* listing to starboard, leaning into the slope created by the inhalation. They'd been saved by the boomer last time, but its magic was expended now.

The *Breakwater*'s single engine moved them ahead at a snail's pace, the monster keeping up with them easily, pushing patches of mottled corpses, goblin and human, beneath it.

Bookbinder wracked his brain for a solution. *Go ahead, whine about how unfair it is. Maybe someone gives a damn.*

"We can't outrun it," Bookbinder said. "Maybe get farther away so the wave attenuates."

It was a statement, but Bonhomme answered anyway. "Those navy ships were at least a half nautical mile farther off, and you saw what it did to them.

"We can't outrun it. No way."

INTERLUDE IV
BUSINESS PROPOSITION

The question is one of resources. This "Source" as people are calling it, is the opposite of what we were led to believe. Not only can we survive there, but it's pristine. Here is a potential solution to our crisis in timber, in oil and natural gas deposits, without having to resort to Terramancy. Here is a place to jettison hazardous wastes the likes of which are unsafe to store anywhere else. Nuclear and chemical weapons stockpile disposal has been a thorn in the side of arms reduction advocates since the seventies. Sure, it's not our world. But with our own survival at stake, who the hell cares?

—Howard van Dalthrop
Appearing on WQXR radio while campaigning
for the congressional seat for Illinois' Sixth District

SIX YEARS EARLIER

Crucible left him at the building's entrance, heading back to the cramped liaison office they occupied in Midtown Manhattan, to contact Gatanas's staff for further instructions—the content of which they both already knew.

A breeze blew up the corridor created by the tall buildings, scattering leaves and trash strewn about the cobbled square. In the middle of it stood the statue of a bronze bull, snorting, hunched to charge. Harlequin stared at it and tried to collect his thoughts.

He didn't write the rules, and it wasn't his job to interpret them. He was a junior officer. His job was to carry out the intent of his chain of command, and, ultimately, their civilian masters. It felt wrong, but did that really matter? What he felt wasn't at issue here, only what he did.

He thought of his instructor's words. Before that night in the Bronx, they had seemed foolish, condescending. But they hadn't selected his teachers because they were stupid.

Regs. That was what made him a sheepdog. Without them, what was he?

"Well, hello, handsome," Grace's voice sounded behind him.

He whirled to find her standing there, ironic smile back in place, eyes dancing with humor, as if the whole exchange upstairs had never happened. She still stirred him, made his clothes feel tight. Maybe it was that very nonchalance. The world ticked by, and she didn't care. Whatever it was, it worked.

"Ma'am," he said, trying to bite back on his embarrassment.

"Oh, cut the crap." She kicked her toe against his. "You don't get to stare at my tits, then ma'am me because you didn't like the way a business meeting turned out."

"Grace," he corrected, smiling against his will.

"You do follow orders, don't you? That could work out really well for us. Where were you heading?"

He pulled his smartphone from his pocket and glanced at the screen. No messages. There were no calls to run. The truth was that he had no friends in the city other than Crucible. He could go to the gym, or go back to the office and answer e-mail. Or go home and watch TV.

Grace ducked her head and caught his eyes, standing just a hair closer to him than was appropriate. "That looks like nothing."

He laughed. "Yes, ma . . . Grace. Nothing."

"Well, it looks like we're going to be working together, so how about we take a walk?"

"Don't you have work to do?"

"Always. Endless. But this is the advantage of being the boss. It gets done when I say. Tonight, I say Weiss has to do it. I'm feeling like ice cream."

"Ice cream?"

"Dude. Come off it. I know you haul more Selfers off to prison before breakfast than most people do all day, but nobody, and I mean *nobody*, is above ice cream. Let's go."

"I don't know if that's a good idea. We're going to be working together on a project, and there are ethical concerns . . ."

She rolled her eyes. "Are you fucking kidding me? What the hell is the point of being CEO of a major corporation if you can't get ice cream with a hot boy once in a while? I'm not going to influence you. Well, not as regards to business, anyway."

Harlequin paused. Power had always been a heavy thing to him, pregnant with responsibility, bound by process. He tried to reconcile the playful smile and dancing eyes with the incredible wealth he knew she commanded. His eyes traveled up the enormous building behind her until he would have had to strain his neck to see the top. Hers. All of it, hers.

"So, your boss shut you down," she said. "That happens. I don't give a fuck about that. Lock it up and get over it. Let's have some ice cream and talk about other stuff."

He tensed, forced himself to relax. Once he'd accomplished that, the smile came easily. "Okay," he said.

She grinned. "Okay." She stepped over to him, linking her arm through his. "I've changed my mind. We'll grab gelato instead, then maybe I'll show you my other office."

He held fast as she steered him down the street, forcing her to pull closer, her hand sliding up over his biceps. "Who says you get to be in charge?"

"As you will doubtless learn, sonny boy," she said, "the one with the bigger dick is in charge"—she gave a tug, moving him a few steps—"and in any given scenario, that's me."

Ice cream turned into drinks. Drinks turned into walking, and that took up most of the night. She chatted with instant ease, as if he were an old friend. Harlequin had a tough time sorting through how she made him feel so easy with her, but he finally settled on the simple lack of fear or admiration. Women expressed interest, but whatever romance bloomed always did so in the shadow of his Latency. Grace couldn't care less. She liked his looks and his earnestness, it seemed. They walked close enough for the backs of their hands, their shoulders, to occasionally touch, leaning into one another unconsciously. It reminded Harlequin that sometimes two people just had chemistry. It didn't have to make sense.

They strolled up a bustling avenue, the noise and color surrounding them. New York was the most varied, diverse city

Harlequin had ever seen, but its frantic variety saturated the senses, blending together until one vista looked much like another.

"How much farther is it?" he asked.

"Another couple of blocks."

"I could just fly us there," he said. The truth was that he wasn't supposed to, would need to file a flight plan anyway, but he wanted to see how she'd react. He hadn't been with a woman since he Manifested who didn't ask him to take her up in the air by the third date. Most didn't make it past the first.

She snorted. "Sounds like a great way to get a mouthful of bugs. Besides, unless Aeromancy gives you super strength, your arms would just get tired."

He laughed. "I can use the wind to carry you. What do you weigh anyway? A buck ten soaking wet?"

She shook her head. "Wasted potential."

"I think I'm doing all right."

"That's the problem," she went on. "SOC is still government, and the government screws up everything it touches. You're flitting around like a miniature airplane and occasionally shooting lightning bolts? You're shutting down Selfers? Fly-schmy. You have the ability to summon and channel electricity, Christ, you could be a walking battery with the right technology. What about that?"

Harlequin frowned. "I'm not even sure it could be used that way."

"Yet," she said. "Who knows what you could do with the energy applications of magic if the SOC would allow for testing and development of supporting technology."

"We don't have time for that."

"Because you're busy enforcing the McGauer-Linden Act and running down Selfers. That's a problem you created. If there weren't a law prohibiting 'unauthorized' magic use, you wouldn't need to take them down."

"Taking down Selfers is what's likely to get you a subject for your clinical trials."

"If it weren't illegal for people to use magic privately, we could just put out a call for volunteers."

"Grace, you have the luxury of saying that. You haven't seen what I've seen. Without those laws, a lot of people would die."

"That's the thing," she said. "That's what's so tricky about these systems. You're *right*, of course, but that doesn't change the fact that you use being right to seize and hoard power. And when you concentrate that power in the hands of a few bureaucrats, they get stingy with it."

"Nobody appointed me Latent, Grace. I was faced with the same choice everyone who Manifests is. I'm not seizing power over anyone, I'm trying to help here." He was getting angry, and that made him want her even more. Conflict was an intimate act. With most people, he didn't feel comfortable enough to argue.

"I know you are," Grace said. "That's my point. You want to do good, you are doing good. But you're honestly going to look me in the eye and tell me that when you 'take down' a Selfer, when you kill them, or pound them into the pavement and lock them up, that there's not a power exchange there?" She gestured to the tall buildings around them, each small apartment worth at least as much as Harlequin would earn in his entire career. "I've been part of the elite of this city since my twenties. I know a thing or two about power and how it works. It's all business, babe. The government is just the biggest player on the block."

"That makes you better?" he asked her, his cheeks reddening. He felt the tide of his magic pulse. She'd touched a nerve.

"No way," she said, her voice suddenly serious. She sidled close, their hips brushing, and took his hand. Her touch was cool, and he felt his own heat fade as quickly as it had come. "It makes us the same. We're both trying to work our respective systems. Make some good come out of them." She squeezed his hand and let it drop, and he struggled not to reach out and take hers again.

She playfully called it her "satellite office," a giant, glass-walled space that overlooked Union Square.

"Is this where you bring all your boys?" he asked. The nervousness was a memory now, and Harlequin was able to appreciate her curves under her tight suit, the closeness of her, the slight citrus tang of her perfume. He could not remember the last time he'd been this turned on in his life. *Not since you came up Latent,* he thought. *Not since the world started treating you like a zoo animal.* He'd had liaisons. Sweaty, awkward fumblings with other SOC officers, reaching out to one another in desperate need, then quitting the bedroom with hesitant promises to call.

"When I want a man," Grace said, "I go get a man. I don't bring most of them here, but I figured you'd appreciate it."

"Why?"

She turned, bracing herself against her low desk, pulling her blouse taut across her flat abdomen. God, she was gorgeous. "Because I've got you pegged as a Boy Scout."

He cocked an eyebrow. "What's that supposed to mean?"

"Why do you do it?"

"What?"

"The SOC. The Army."

"I'm Latent. The law's pretty clear on what you have to do."

"Bullshit," she said. "You could have gone to the NIH. You could have joined the Marines. You could have run."

The very thought of going Selfer made his hackles rise, but there was something in her tone that made him think. From the moment they'd met, she'd wiped away his assumptions with an easy grace that matched her name. She left him exposed. He hadn't felt that way since he'd come up Latent. It was exhilarating.

He'd never thought of running, not for an instant. But it wasn't because he was afraid.

"I . . . wanted to do some good," he said slowly. "I wanted to help. I've always wanted that."

"See? Boy Scout." She grinned.

He frowned.

"Don't get your panties in a bunch," she said. "We're birds of a feather. I want to do some good, too. I think that's why we get along."

That wasn't the only reason. He felt the electricity sizzle between them.

She turned, gesturing at three computer monitors on the desk behind her. "I've had a very . . . rewarding career."

Harlequin looked around at the huge, well-appointed office, at her expensive suit, her gym-hard body and perfect makeup. He didn't doubt it.

"It's been rewarding enough that it pretty much runs itself at this point. Affords me time and energy to engage in my pet projects here." She clicked away at the computer, brought up pictures.

The first showed a dried-up field, probably once devoted to agriculture. Now it sprouted miniature solar panels like cross-hatched black cabbages. Rows and rows of them stretched off the screen. A smiling young woman was wrapped in an orange cloth that covered even her head, with three men standing around her. A white man stood beside her, kitted out with the kind of high-end military hardware that only the highest-priced mercenaries could afford.

"That's Ligoua," she said, "about twenty miles southeast of what politicians call the 'African Pole of Inaccessibility.' Supposedly, nobody can get there. It's a wilderness stuck in the Dark Ages. But Ligoua has electricity and those photovoltaics are generating enough to light the next three villages over. Best part?" She tapped the young woman's face. "Esther built them. And now she knows how to build more. We provided the training. Now we provide the supplies."

"Who's he?" Harlequin tapped the mercenary.

"That's Depaul. Of Executive Staffing Solutions. He keeps the Lord's Resistance Army from taking over the power plantation."

"He can't come cheap."

She smiled. "That operation costs me millions every year. It's worth every penny." She looked back up at him, their gazes locking again. "There's more if you want to see it. Microloan programs, wind farms. Sustainable livestock seminars."

He couldn't stand it any longer. He caught her wrist, pulled it up from the keyboard, stepped closer to her. She pulled back momentarily, but only from the sudden movement. She let him move in, kept her arm tense, surprisingly strong. He could smell her breath, the light hint of the alcohol she'd been drinking.

"Why are you showing me all this?"

She shrugged, her breath coming in close gasps now. Her hands found his biceps, squeezed. "You think you're the only one who gets treated like an outsider? You think in my line of work the stuff I do is popular? The people I run with like to make money, Jan. They're not big fans of bleeding-heart moves like these."

"So you're the Boy Scout," he husked, his hand moving to the small of her back, pulling her into him. The Scylla charm flashed, and now he let himself look down, unabashedly, glorying in the curve of her breasts, in the shadows pooling in the hollow of her throat. God, but it was so good to be close, really close to someone. He almost couldn't remember what it felt like. Maybe it was because he'd never truly known.

"Takes one to know one," she said, and nipped his lip. Harlequin was no Casanova, but he'd been with a few women in his life. None had moved like this, reaching, gasping, *participating*. Grace took ownership of her part in their union, from the conversation to the flirting, and now, at long last, to the touching.

She hooked an ankle around his, grabbed his ass, and tripped him over her. They fell onto the desk, knocking over one of the monitors. It toppled to the floor, the screen shattering. Harlequin winced at the expense. "Shut up," she said before he could say anything. "I'll get another one. We're busy."

And they were busy. For hours.

CHAPTER XI
BURDEN OF COMMAND

The actions of the United States and India are a breach of trust on a global scale. Not since the Iraq War has America's reputation sunk so low on the international stage. The Pope's statement yesterday, condemning the use of the secret base in the Source, joins a chorus of voices from formerly staunch friends and allies. We have stood with the United States for most of our collective histories, but I cannot ignore the sentiment of my people. They are furious, and frankly, so am I.

—Victoria II, by the Grace of God of
the United Kingdom of Great Britain and Northern Ireland
and of Her other Realms and Territories
Queen, Head of the Commonwealth, Defender of the Faith

Shouting broke Harlequin's concentration. He looked up from the report he'd been drafting for Gatanas and listened. There it was, louder now. He leapt out of his chair, made his way through the ready room, and out of the castle.

Harlequin dismissed the thought of running around the castle, Bound his magic, and summoned a gust of wind that hurled him into the air, launching him clear across the turrets and over to the far side. He Drew and Bound again, summoning an air cushion that slowed his fall until he landed roughly on his feet, still running forward. Crude, but simple and effective for a man in a hurry.

A crowd of soldiers had formed, shouting, swarming the row of tents facing the water where the Fornax Novices were setting up shop. Harlequin saw a couple of the trainee Sorcerers in the mix, could feel their currents pulsing wildly from anger.

"Order, damn it!" Harlequin shouted. "What the hell is going on here!?"

The fighting raged on, shouts drowning out his voice.

He raised his hand, Bound to the air just above the crowd's heads. A gray cloud formed, throbbed, pouring down a torrent of rain on the people below, rumbling thunder.

The belligerents shouted, covered their heads against the sheeting downpour, drew apart. Some of them noticed Harlequin and stood to attention, rendering shamefaced salutes.

He didn't return them. "Are you fucking kidding me? What the hell is going on here?"

He followed their eyes to a pair of soldiers. The first was Command Sergeant Major Knut, her uniform already soaked through. She ignored the rain, shaking a fist over the other soldier, lying on his back and rubbing at an eye already beginning to swell shut.

Harlequin recognized the beaten soldier as one of the Fornax Novices, a skinny Pyromancer with an Eastern European name that Harlequin had given up on pronouncing and had at last resorted to "Hey, you."

He reached the Novice in a few steps, hooked a hand under his armpit, and hauled him to his feet. "Are you okay?"

"I'm fine, sir," Unpronounceable said. "Just got a little carried away is all."

"Brawling!? In my fucking headquarters! In the middle of a holding action!? Are you out of your fucking mind?"

"Damn right he's out of his fucking mind, sir! He goddamn . . ."

"Stand down, Sergeant Major!" Harlequin cut her off. "Did you strike this man?"

"Sir, he . . ."

"It's a yes-or-no question, Sergeant Major," Harlequin said, eyes traveling over the woman's bloody knuckles, Unpronounceable's swollen eye.

"Sir, he could have used his magic to . . ."

"Yes. Or. No!?" Harlequin shouted. The rain stopped as the cloud over them dissipated.

"Yes, sir," Knut said.

Hewitt emerged from the crowd. He stopped long enough

to take in the scene, the bruise, Knut's shaking hand. "Damn it, Sergeant Major! You struck an officer!?"

Knut looked from Harlequin to Hewitt and back to the crowd, now so quiet you could hear a pin drop. None would meet her eyes. "Sir, you yourself said that . . ."

Hewitt cut her off, pointing to another soldier in the crowd with an MP tag on his sleeve. "Sergeant Feld, have Sergeant Major Knut taken under guard, subject to charges under article 90 of the UCMJ."

"Article 90!" Harlequin began, "Sir, I . . ."

"Lieutenant Colonel, please join me in the ready room right now. The rest of you, back to your duties. Let's go, people!"

The crowd responded to Hewitt's voice, dispersing, as Hewitt turned on his heel and stormed back toward the castle.

Harlequin turned back to Unpronounceable. "Do you know what the punishment is under Article 90 in time of war, Novice?"

Unpronounceable stared. "No, sir."

"It's death, Novice. During time of war, it's death. So, I need you to very carefully, calmly, and accurately tell me what the hell just happened."

"She . . . she was in my tent, sir. I came back to get stuff, and she was in there."

"Why was she in there? Was she stealing or something?"

The Novice started to answer. "Be very careful about what you say next," Harlequin said. "If you lie to me . . ."

"No, sir," Unpronounceable said. "I ordered her to leave, and she wouldn't."

"What? Why?"

"Fraternization, sir. Officers aren't supposed to bunk with enlisted. She had to go."

Anger brought Harlequin's magic roaring through him, and he took a moment to tamp it down. "So, what you're telling me is that this was *her* tent, and you tried to kick her out, is that right?"

Unpronounceable looked down, said nothing.

"You tried to displace the garrison commander's senior enlisted advisor in your gallant defense of the army's no-fraternization policy, Novice? Is that what you fucking did?"

"Sir, I . . ."

"Is it?"

"Yes, sir."

"Jesus leaping Christ. Have you ever heard the phrase term 'servant leadership,' Novice?"

"Yes, sir. They taught it in SAOLCC."

"Servant leadership means that you work for the people you lead. That's what good officers do. They don't eat until all their people have been fed. They don't stop working until the last of their people have gone home for the night. And they sure as hell don't hold out on their people when there's obvious over-crowding in the camp. Why didn't you at least come to me?"

"I would have, sir, but . . . she was yelling at me and I got pissed off and . . ."

"That's enough. Get your ass back on the wall and get to work. Whatever you do, do not get into it with anyone else. I'll come talk to you once I have the rest of this sorted out."

Unpronounceable nodded and stood to attention, rendering a crisp salute. Harlequin returned it and headed back to the castle, forming a game plan to mollify Hewitt. He hadn't seen any burn marks on Knut, which meant Unpronounceable at least had the sense not to use his magic. If he had, Harlequin wasn't sure he could have done anything for him.

Hewitt was waiting for him in the ready room, arms folded, leaning against a chair back and talking intently with Feld.

"Colonel," Harlequin said as he walked in, "I got the story from my Novice, and . . ."

"He tried to kick Sergeant Major Knut out of her hooch? That's what I'm hearing from the people who saw it go down."

"Yes, sir. That's what he said happened. Things got heated after that. I've spoken to Novice . . . to the Novice in question, and he understands I won't tolerate that kind of aristocratic behavior."

"That's good," Hewitt said, "but it doesn't change the fact that a Novice is a commissioned officer and Sergeant Major Knut struck him. Article 90 is clear. We need to convene a summary panel immediately."

Harlequin's jaw dropped. "You want to execute her?"

"She struck an officer in plain view of half the camp. I can-not allow that to stand."

"You're absolutely right. It can't be allowed to stand, but

fights happen, sir. My man was throwing his weight around, stupid JO stuff. He's new, inexperienced. He hasn't learned what being an officer means. He certainly hasn't learned that while he outranks a sergeant major, he sure as hell shouldn't be bossing one around. We all had moments like that when we first pinned on. I know I did, and it took a hard-ass sergeant or two to show me the ropes. Didn't that happen to you, too?"

"Of course, but it never involved said sergeant punching me in the face!"

"Looks like Knut knocked him on his ass and humiliated him in front of everyone. That alone is a hard lesson. We can discuss forfeiture of pay and confinement to base. We can demote her. Hell, we can put her out of the Army after all this is over. We don't need to *kill* her."

"We don't make that call!" Hewitt said. "The UCMJ clearly proscribes what constitutes a crime, and the penalty for that crime. You strike a commissioned officer in time of war, you receive summary judgment. That's not subject to interpretation."

My God, he sounds exactly like I did before FOB Frontier. Was I really that much of an ass?

Harlequin turned to Feld. "Sergeant, would you please excuse us?"

Feld looked askance at Hewitt, who dismissed him with a nod.

"This is a domestic disaster incident, not a declared war," Harlequin said. "I'm not even arguing the law with you. We are shorthanded in the middle of a conflict. I cannot afford to lose a competent NCO. She stays on until we win this thing and have a chance to do a postmortem."

Hewitt purpled. "Why am I not surprised? Clear orders, and you somehow find a way not to follow them. You don't tell me what to do with my own people!"

"Actually, sir, I do. I have struggled mightily not to invoke my authority as incident commander, but I'm doing it now. Convene your Article 90 panel, but any punishment that keeps Knut from working, including execution, is off the table."

"This will lead to a breakdown in good order, and . . ."

"No, sir. Executing her will devastate morale. It'll also exacerbate the hell out of the considerable divide that exists between regular Army and the SOC. People already treat us like dangerous zoo animals. Do you think that'll improve because we put someone to death for having the temerity to stand up for herself? I won't allow it."

Hewitt was silent, jaw tensed.

"Look, sir, I get it. I really do. But I need you to trust me on this," Harlequin said. "We're holding on by a thread here. The fact that this incident happened at all is a sign of how frayed everyone's nerves are. We need to do everything we can to put this to rest as fast as possible. I need you to back me on this."

Hewitt pursed his lips. "You're the incident commander. By order of the president himself."

"I'll use that authority if I have to," Harlequin said, "but I'd prefer you just be swayed by my argument."

"You seem to think this is my first rodeo, Lieutenant Colonel. You forget that I've been soldiering my entire life. I know a thing or two about how to lead people and what the consequences are when you fuck it up. You want to sway me with an argument? Make a better one."

He turned on his heel and stormed out of the room.

Harlequin let him go, content to let him have the last word. *He wouldn't have actually gone through with it. You didn't have to do that,* Harlequin thought. Then why had he confronted him?

Because there's a part of you who worries that he actually would. Because you see so much of the man you used to be standing there.

Would you have executed her?

He pictured himself, the man who'd chased down Oscar Britton, who'd thrown Scylla in the hole at FOB Frontier.

He turned away from that picture. He didn't like what he saw.

The room felt suddenly close around him, and he stepped outside into a camp bustling as if the incident had never happened, but he caught the sidelong stares, heard the muttering. The tension was palpable.

Better if he hid his face for a little while. He toggled his commlink and spoke into it. "Cormack."

"Sir," came the reply.

"I'm heading uptown to check on the barricades. Can you please make sure that . . . just make sure . . ."

"I'll let you know if anything happens with Sergeant Major Knut, sir."

Harlequin was silently grateful to the man for saving him the trouble of saying it. He launched into the air, letting the wind envelop him, closing his eyes and forgetting for a moment that anything else existed.

When he opened them again, Greenwich Street snaked beneath him, now clustered with goblins. They swarmed around the exit to the Brooklyn Battery Tunnel, where Hewitt had stationed a Stryker heavy machine gun letting out a steady stream of fire. A group of soldiers sheltered behind it, trading fire with the goblins, who took cover behind the wrecks of cars, throwing javelins and slinging stones. A few automatons of asphalt and dirt stalked the cracked surface of the road, soaking up rounds, advancing until one of the soldiers realized the danger and put a grenade through one of them. Harlequin couldn't see the Terramancer driving them, but knew it must be hiding nearby. He made a mental note to get a Sorcerer assigned to that position as soon as he could spare one. The tunnel was their main means to get refugees out and supplies in by ground. They had to keep it open. He sent a spray of lightning down into the goblin ranks and waved as a cheer drifted up to him from the defenders.

When he'd first set up in Battery Park, his only thought had been to ensure he had a presence close to the fight that was easily defensible and with a quick exit route should things go badly. He now realized that the position had an additional advantage. It kept a concentrated force in Scylla's backfield, a finger pointed at the Breach that kept her troops rolling in. So long as he held on there, she could never fully focus her attention on breaking out of the barricades to her north. He knew it was dumb luck, then smiled inwardly, calling it commander's instinct. *Is there really any difference?* He sent another blast of lightning into the goblins below and heard the tunnel defenders cheer again. The sound made commander's instinct seem more fitting.

Then he looked up.

The air cover had condensed. Rocs and wyverns swept

through the sky, getting the worst of it from two Blackhawk helicopters, hovering over the subway entrance in front of the barricade that straddled Varrick Street. The defenders had overturned two city buses, then stacked two more on top of them, forming a flying V that surrounded the enormous crane they'd used to drag the vehicles in place. Goblins swarmed the makeshift wall, climbing up over the buses' undercarriages, being handed up by giants. As quickly as they came up, they were gunned down. Harlequin could see the tops of the barricade manned by dozens of NYPD officers in riot and tactical gear, their numbers augmented by the sage gray-green camouflage of the National Guard.

Two *Gahe* slid through the throng, screening an advancing giant from the worst of the gunfire, until a figure in a black uniform rolled around the side of the crane and stretched out a hand, sending a torrent of flame shooting over them. The *Gahe* shrieked and withdrew, the goblins and giants falling back beside them as the Pyromancer made the cloud of fire dance, fed by whirling shreds of trash and corpses, and swept it across the barricade front.

Harlequin flew closer, pausing short of the Blackhawks. He gathered cloud cover, agitated the air molecules, expanding them rapidly, raising a thunderclap that shook the few unbroken windows in the buildings around them.

The heads below him looked up; dozens of the rocs and wyverns broke off from the Blackhawks, turning to face the new threat. He smiled and kicked off, floating backward and sideways, getting out of the Blackhawks' line of fire as the helos went broadside with the remaining stragglers, shredding them with columns of 20mm fire. The defenders on the barricade below cursed and slapped at their shoulders as the hot brass fell on them.

The Whispering Terramancer saw the futility of engaging an Aeromancer with helicopter gunships at his rear, and the rocs and wyverns scattered, winging away with a defiant scream.

Many of the defenders were cheering themselves hoarse. The wiser ones were silent, slumped over their guns, grabbing the few minutes of rest he had bought them. Harlequin flew down to alight on one of the overturned buses. A banner had been raised over it, torn and soiled. It was a repurposed base-ball pennant, stitched over with the NYPD and army logos. Beneath it, someone had scrawled BARRICADE 3. ROCK STEADY.

It was pathetic, slapdash, and torn, but it was a sign of morale, and that was good.

A haggard-looking National Guard captain jogged her way up the rubble to meet him, sketching a salute with a shaking arm. Relief blossomed on a face that clearly hadn't seen sleep in far too long.

"You command here?" Harlequin asked her.

She nodded. "For what it's worth, sir. I'm sharing command with the NYPD. They've got a sergeant here."

"A sergeant in charge of all this?"

She shrugged. "It's what they could spare. The rest of the city outside the Breach Zone has gone crazy. The looting in Queens alone has half the force tied up. Central Park is in the middle of the biggest smoke-out in national history. We're undermanned."

He shook his head. "I'm sorry, I'm . . ."

"I know who you are, sir," she cut him off. "I'd guess that anyone with Internet access in the past year knows who you are. For what it's worth, I get what you did and respect it."

He looked up at her, surprised. He scanned for her name tape, but it was covered by her body armor. Her eyes were old beyond the fatigue, and her nose had been broken more than once. It gave her that look of hard competence combined with empathy that he liked to see in soldiers.

"How are you holding up?"

She sighed, beckoned, and he followed down the pile of vehicles and out from behind a raised crane boom draping camouflage netting and providing inadequate shade to a medical triage area crowded with wounded. His eyes widened.

A wall of civilians thronged against metal police barricades, practically buckling from their combined weight. A mixed line of soldiers and police shored the barricades up, pushed the crowd back with batons and rifles held crosswise. A few of the police were in riot gear. Some of the soldiers were using ballistic shields borrowed from NYPD tactical units.

All were badly needed on the barricade behind them.

The crowd of civilians was a mixed bag. Some were reporters waving cameras and microphones. Others looked like anarchists and malcontents in their perennial black hoodies and jeans, bandannas covering their faces in anticipation of tear gas that was being used against the goblins to their south. Others looked like religious fanatics, holding icons high, eyes closed and hands raised in prayer.

"Holy shit," Harlequin said.

"Pretty much," the captain agreed. "Some of them think it's the Second Coming. Others think we're hiding some kind of experiment gone wrong and want to see the truth for themselves. Others have family and friends trapped in the Breach Zone and are demanding to go in after them. A few are property owners wanting to check on their buildings. It's like this at every barricade."

"They need to be evacuating," Harlequin said.

She nodded. "Yes, sir. I tried telling them that. You can't hear a bullhorn over all that shouting. I'm honestly tempted to just let them through. Give 'em a chance to see what's waiting for them south of the intersection."

She shook her head, smiled ruefully. "But I can't do that, can I?"

Harlequin sighed. "No, Captain. You can't."

"Well, we're expending roughly fifty percent of our manpower just keeping these people back. It can't go on like this. We need help."

"I'm getting it for you."

"Respectfully, sir?"

"Speak freely."

She met his eyes. "You're not getting it fast enough."

Harlequin's stomach turned over. "Help's coming. I promise." The words sounded lame in his own ears. "How're you handling the *Gahe*?"

She sighed. "We were doing okay at first, sir. The SOC LE support element was able to do for them, but they've been coming more often, and there are more of them. We're stretched pretty thin on that count, too. You know our regular ordnance just goes right through them." She shuddered.

"I know. Help's on the way in that department, too."

She nodded. "Yeah, Barricade One radioed that your Elementalist had arrived. They were able to repulse their attack with her help and she's working up elementals there to dispatch to us. Should be here shortly. Thanks for that, sir. I know trafficking in Probe magic is going to generate some blowback for you, but I also knew that after what you did for FOB Frontier, I knew you'd do anything to save soldiers. Huah."

Harlequin blinked. "What?"

"What, what, sir?"

Harlequin blinked again and swallowed. It wouldn't do this captain's morale any good to learn that he had no idea what she was talking about. "Nothing. Sorry. I'm as tired as you are. You said the Elementalist was over at Barricade One?"

"Yes, sir." She nodded. "Intersection of Houston and Broadway, just over . . ."

"I know where it is," he said. "I need you to dig in and hold on here. You make those fuckers pay for every inch of ground."

Her smile went grim, and she saluted again. "To the last bullet and the last man, sir. They won't get through while we draw breath."

Harlequin returned her salute and leapt back into the air, flying toward a tall building, its art deco water-tower housing crowded with snipers. A few toy-sized remote-controlled drones circled, relaying information on the enemy positions to the ground. A quick look down told Harlequin all he needed to know. The enemy were numerous, they were everywhere, and more were inbound.

A few of the snipers on the tower waved to him as he passed overhead and came into sight of Barricade One. Huge shipping containers had been flown in by helicopter or dragged by truck and overturned. One of the giant metal rectangles' doors hung open, the packed rubble inside spilling out.

Mortars were set up in a church's main steeple, raining fire down in front of the barricade, forcing the goblins to take cover. A few rocs and wyverns circled in the distance, but while they scattered as Harlequin approached, they were already keeping well back.

A moment later, Harlequin saw why.

Man-sized funnels of air, nearly invisible save for the dust whirling within them, hovered over the battlefield. The last time Harlequin had seen one, it had swept him off the high-school roof he was in charge of securing.

Air Elementals.

A moment later, Downer came into view. She appeared to be flying of her own accord, but as she came closer, he could see she was suspended in one of the whirling funnels, grinning.

Harlequin landed on the roof opposite the steeple, motioning for her to join him. She waved as her elemental brought her over, dropped her steadily on the rooftop, then spun off on its own mission.

"Just what the fuck do you think you're doing?" he asked.

"Saving your barricade," she replied, folding her arms across her chest, "or did you think they were going to handle the *Gahe* on their own?"

"I needed you to stay in Battery Park! I ordered you to . . ."

"Oh, I'm sorry. Am I still in the fucking Army? Or am I a contractor? Did my conditional pardon get reinstated when I wasn't looking? I'll have to admit, my current legal status and chain of command is rather confusing at the moment."

"Sarah, I do *not* have time for this! You get your ass back to Battery Park, or . . ."

"Or you'll what? Send me back to a cell? Did you think my elementals would just stay here without me?" She kicked the side of the crumbling water-tower housing beside her and raised her hand. The tumbling brick and mortar flowed out and re-formed into something approximating a hulking outline of a man. It took a step toward Harlequin, hunching its shoulders and sending a shower of desiccated concrete to the roof beneath it. "Did you honestly think I'd stand still for it? I am done being the government's bitch."

Harlequin thought about Suppressing her, decided against it. For all her bluster, she and her elementals were helping the fight, albeit at a different point than he'd expected. She was a serious force multiplier wherever she wound up, and the situation at Barricade Three had kindled a sick fear in his gut. *You should have put her here in the first place, and you know it. You're overwhelmed.*

Maybe. But he was still the incident commander, and he needed to be able to control his assets. Hewitt was enough of a problem as it was.

"Okay," he said, patting the air with his palms, "but you have to understand that magical resources are at a premium here. I need to be able to focus them were they're needed most."

"I'm a person, not a resource," she said, "and I am where I'm needed most. You think I'm blind? You've been running around like a chicken with your head cut off, and most of your staff thinks you're the Antichrist. While you were off partying at the UN, I figured I'd get the lay of the land. It's not lying so well up here. If I hadn't put elementals in the fight, we'd have lost this barricade before you showed up. There are a few *Gahe* making it down to Battery Park, but most of them are coming out of the gate and heading straight up here. They know the juiciest parts of the city are north, or, at least, Scylla does."

He smiled inwardly. *Not a little a girl anymore, that's for damn sure. And a natural head for strategy.* He burned at the thought of how the McGauer-Linden Act had forced them to this moment. Who knew the kind of officer she would have made if she'd only been given half a chance?

Harlequin looked over his shoulder at the battlefield before Barricade One. It was clear for now, the enemy withdrawn to the cover of nearby buildings or overturned cars. But he could see even from this distance that the street was rimed with a thick, glittering crust. It shimmered, tinted gray, like dirty snow. Evidence of the *Gahe*'s failure to break through the barricade. At least one of them had died in that space.

His mind screamed at him to fight her, to show some spine, to be a leader. But he couldn't argue with the facts. She'd put herself in the right place. She'd averted what could have been a catastrophe. All great leaders had one trait in common, they trusted their people.

He sighed. "You're right."

"I am." It began as a question, but she managed to make it a statement at the last moment.

"You are. I'm overwhelmed. You did it right. I should have had you here all along. Thanks."

She stammered before settling on, "You're welcome."

"I need three of you, Sarah. We can do for these goblins and whatever else all damn day, but the *Gahe* are going to get through. Help's just not coming fast enough. I keep thinking that if we can just hang on a little while longer, we'll get what we need to stop this."

She blinked, still stunned to find him agreeing with her.

"I don't suppose you can break off some of your elemental . . . cohort? Send them back to Battery Park?"

She shook her head. "Doesn't work that way."

"They . . . they need to stay close to you to keep alive?"

"No. They won't leave me."

"What do you mean?"

"They love me. They won't leave me. Well, not far and not for long, anyway. You have to remember that they're sentient. They can think for themselves."

Harlequin arched an eyebrow. "They love you. They tell you this?"

"No, but I can feel it. They know I made them. I'm . . . I'm their god." She looked down, embarrassed. *In all the years I knew her, I never once asked her what it was like.*

"When I first came up Latent, they were my friends, you know," she said. "It wasn't exactly something I could talk to people about, so I talked to them."

Harlequin tried not to let his remorse show. She'd been a target to him, then a tool. Never once had he stopped to consider anything else.

"Did they listen?" he asked.

She smiled. "They did. Much better than most people. More importantly, they understood."

"I'm sorry, Sarah," Harlequin surprised himself by saying, "for all of it. I'd take it back if I could."

Her eyes narrowed, some steel came into her voice. "I thought we were past the part where you talk down to me. I don't need your sorry. Never asked for it."

"I know, I'm saying it for me. To get it off my chest. I wish I had a dozen more like you."

"So you could win this fight."

"That, too, yeah."

Downer no longer sounded angry. "It's your own damn fault, you know. Who knows how many Latents might have helped if you hadn't forced them to choose between Selfer and SOC? Heck, some of them are probably in this city."

Harlequin's mouth went dry. There *were* Selfers in the city. And he knew where to find them.

It was one thing to employ a Probe who was already in government custody. It was another thing entirely to make common cause with Selfers. The thought made his stomach turn over for the third time in less than an hour.

But before he knew it, Harlequin had nodded to Downer and leapt into the sky, leaving her staring at his boot soles shrinking in the distance.

CHAPTER XII
FLUSHED PEOPLE

*The "Pangea Theory" posits that, perhaps prior to the First
Reawakening, in the ancient, even primeval past, the Source and
the Home Plane were united at a more fundamental level. The
division occurred later, owing to reasons lost to history. Radical
proponents believe that all life originated in the Source, and that
humanity itself (along with all Home Plane fauna) is a "lost
tribe" cut adrift, in search of its roots. "The Return" movement
espouses this position, putting them in line with the beliefs of the
goblin "Embracer" tribes.*

—Avery Whiting
"Into the Breach Zone"
Op-ed in the *New York Times*

Harlequin marveled at himself as he flew back to Battery Park.
He'd spent the best part of his early career working to bring
down the Houston Street Gang, and part of him burned to think
that remnants still existed. The thought of working with Selfers worked against something rooted deep in him, but Scylla's
army was obviously finding it easier to steer clear of them and
focus on the barricade. He should brief it up to Gatanas; maybe
the news would help move the man to send more arcane support. Harlequin thought of the tower of the Trump Building
slowly tumbling into the street as the A-10s completed their
run. No, better to stay mum on this for now. The last thing he
needed was to give Gatanas another excuse to bomb civilians.

He banked west, looking for the area Sharp had described.
With most of the fighting up at the barricade or around Battery

Park, the streets looked mostly empty, with only the occasional pack of demon horses or goblin patrols amid the smoke and wreckage. It was hard to tell which spot might be clear.

But as Harlequin flew over a small, horseshoe-shaped park off Canal Street, he could make out other barricades, tall shelves of earth and rubble, capped with slabs of broken concrete. They were seamless, drawn up out of the ground in one piece. He flew lower. The barricades looked empty, but they systematically blocked off two blocks square to the west of the park. Behind them, there was some damage, but not nearly as much.

He shed altitude, trying to feel for magical currents, but he didn't want to risk getting taken down, especially without an escort. What would a magical current tell him, anyway? The goblins had them, too.

He turned, flew due east, heading for Chinatown, following the wide expanse of Canal Street. The buildings grew tighter here, and he spotted the occasional Chinese sign, growing more and more frequent until it was the only language he saw. The neon still shed light in some places, but many more had been shattered, or had gone dark in blocks where the power was out.

As he closed on Walker, the contrast was stark. There were no barricades that he could see, but a rough line of corpses clearly delineated the borders of the clear zone. A bear-sized creature with bat wings and a disturbingly human face lay on its side, its purple guts strewn across its ribs as if some giant hand had reached in and ripped them out. Goblins were piled around it, many with their heads turned at odd angles, limbs ripped off. Harlequin felt his stomach turn as he made out what had probably once been a smallish dragon, until something had turned it inside out.

Rending. Offensive Physiomancy. What other weapon could do this? He shed altitude, circling above the line of dead, marveling at the lack of physical obstacles into the neighborhood. Even with a Render, it would be a tall order to keep the streets clear.

Yet they were clear. Just beyond the line of corpses, Harlequin could see working street signs, store windows intact. The streets were free of bodies; the only indicator that this block sat in the middle of the Breach Zone was the trash blowing across the streets, the smoke in the air.

Harlequin circled lower, radioed his position back to Battery Park, just in case. Where were the sentries? It didn't matter. This was a stupid, unnecessary risk. He could come back later in force and see for himself. He dipped low, spun around, and prepared to turn back south.

He stopped in midair, hovering. It was faint, but he could feel a magical current, rippling through the air . . . No. Two. Maybe more. If he could feel them, they could feel him.

There were Selfers here. Nothing he didn't already know.

He rose, turned, picked up speed toward the park, letting the feel of the magical currents fade behind him as distance ate the signal.

But one of them grew stronger, a rising in his senses with every foot he flew.

He was getting closer.

He slowed, shed altitude as fast as he could, denying an enemy the chance to Suppress him and drop him out of the sky. At last, he was level with the building entrances, head sawing wildly as he looked around for the source of the current, seeing only the blur of façades as the buildings raced past.

The current rose until it sang in his veins, tickled the back of his throat. He Drew his magic, feeling his neck dampen as storm clouds coalesced around him.

And then winked out. The foreign current crossed his own, stopping his flow and rolling the magic back. He strained, pushed against it, felt it hold fast. He flailed in the air, arms pinwheeling as he came down, his stomach catching the metal rod of an awning, folding his body in half, breath exploding from him. He scrabbled for purchase on the smooth plastic surface, struggling to suck in air, all hope of winning free from the Suppression gone.

He fell, shoulders and tailbone slamming into the sidewalk, head bouncing on the ground so hard his vision grayed. All sense of the magical current was lost. He felt three, then one, then none. He tried to Draw his magic, but he couldn't focus on his own flow through the ringing in his ears and the sudden pain blossoming behind his eyes.

His vision began to clear, and he heard shouting and the

slapping of bare feet on asphalt. Goblins. They were coming for him. He struggled to clear his head, got to his feet, blinking furiously. His vision was blurry, the pain in his skull blinding him. A high ringing in his ears began to give way to a loud buzz. He fumbled for his pistol, biting back vertigo.

He took a whooping swallow of air and swayed, but his legs held him, and he stumbled back a pace from the converging shapes. Small brown blobs, a white one at their rear. They snarled, shouted. He blinked again, his vision slowly resolving. Goblins, a white-painted sorcerer with them. One reached him, thrusting out a spear with a victorious yell.

Harlequin kicked it aside, finally managing his holster catch and dragging the pistol out, slamming the weapon into the goblin's face and sending it sprawling. Something sharp sliced past his arm. Another whistle of air past his ear. He raised the pistol and fired madly, not bothering to aim, unable to anyway, praying his rounds hit the sorcerer.

The goblins scattered, but sparks and spraying chips of brick and cement told him his shots had gone wide.

The goblin's current held his own fast. He was sure he could break free if he could only concentrate, but his lungs still burned from the lack of air, his lower ribs aching. The headache stabbed him less with each throbbing pulse, but the pain was still horrendous. He felt wet warmth on the back of his neck. Blood from his head, most likely.

He was certain he felt another current now. A second sorcerer. Even if he could break free, it wouldn't do him any good. *I can't believe this. I'm going to die out here just because I couldn't be bothered to move with a proper escort.*

Another goblin reached him, swinging an axe almost as big as it was. He ducked back, heels slipping off the curb, lost his balance, fell again, his head and vision clearing in exchange for a sharp pain shooting up his wrist as it took his full weight.

The goblin followed, swinging the axe around and up over its head for another strike. Harlequin kicked out, finding the creature's bony knee. It stumbled across him, lost its grip on the heavy axe, which went clattering to the ground. Harlequin seized its throat, squeezed, punched it in the face. Once. Twice. The creature went slack in his grip. He grabbed it by the shoulders and hauled it into the way of another spear thrust. The spearhead punched through the goblin's body, scoring Harlequin's cheek and spraying him with hot blood.

The goblin standing over him cursed, wrenching the spear, trying to pull it out of its comrade's back. Another three goblins appeared beside it. One raised a jagged-edged short sword. Another held a pistol. The gun looked comically large in the small creature's hands. The recoil would surely knock it on its ass.

But at this distance, it couldn't miss.

Harlequin yanked the goblin corpse to the side, pulling the spear from its comrade's hands, desperately trying to get it between him and the barrel of the gun. It was futile. Even a 9mm round would punch right through both the dead goblin and his head, and bury itself quite a ways into the street behind him.

Harlequin roared, hurling his tide against the Suppression as the goblin raised the pistol, dark tongue poking out of the corner of its mouth, finger tensing on the trigger.

Its head exploded.

It sank to its knees, the gun tumbling from limp hands. The other goblins looked up. Two of them suddenly contorted, arms twisting at unnatural angles, embracing themselves so fiercely their bones cracked. Blood fountained from their mouths, and they fell, their comrades running for their lives, spears clattering to the street.

Harlequin felt the Suppression drop away, his own tide racing back into him with such force that he fell back. He felt another tide, powerful and near, but the sorcerer made no move to Suppress him now.

He looked up, blinking the last of the cotton from his vision.

A man stood there, arms folded. Short, bull-necked, in jeans, work boots, and a button-down shirt hanging open, revealing his bare torso, dominated by a tattoo: the characters SUR3NO$ riding above the image of two crossed pistols. A yellow bandanna was tied around his head, and a necklace of thick wooden beads hung to his waist.

The bones of his face had been raised into sharp ridges, forming a stylized skull. His eyes sank in circles of dark pigment, lips in black half-moons that formed a grinning death's-head.

Harlequin didn't know the man, but he recognized the alterations. Only one gang used Physiomancy to bend their features like that.

"You a long way from the barricades, my son," he drawled, folding his arms.

"So are you." Harlequin struggled to get to his feet, wincing as his raw palm came in contact with the asphalt, and his strained wrist took his weight.

"Jesus, man. You is all fucked up." He came closer, extending a hand. Harlequin felt warmth tingle in his hand and wrist, watched as the wound spat out the gravel from the street, knitting together until his palm was covered with shiny, pink skin.

"Aw, man. I worked for years building up those calluses."

The man snorted, smiled. "I can fuck it back up again if you want."

"I'm good, thanks." He turned around. "I hit my head pretty bad. How's it look?"

The man grunted and warmth spread across Harlequin's skull, making his scalp burn. "You got a bald spot now."

"I'll live. Thanks again."

The man nodded, folded his arms. "You lost?"

"Came looking for you, actually," Harlequin said.

The man's smile vanished, his tide spiked. "The fuck why?"

"Easy, easy. I just . . . I need help."

"I helped you, man. Fixed your hand and your head."

Harlequin thought of the refugees, streaming in every hour. He thought of the help, from Mexico, from Canada, from his own country that was coming. Always coming. Never arriving.

"And I appreciate it. Maybe you could come help me some more. We don't have any Physiomancers at my camp."

The man jerked his chin at Harlequin's shoulder patch. "You SOC, man."

"I don't care about the Rending. I've already got one Probe in the fight."

"You think I'm stupid?"

"No stupid person could have kept this block clear. How are you managing it?"

"You ask a lot of questions. You keep sticking your nose around here, maybe you'll find out how we look out for our own."

"Don't try to push me around. If you were going to kill me,

you'd have done it already. We're clearly on the same side here. You don't want monsters on your block? Neither do I. We can help one another."

"Looks like you're the one needs help, Army man."

"How long do you think you're going to last once the monsters are done with us? Once they can focus their full attention on you? You don't want them here. Neither do I. You help us, maybe we can make an arrangement."

"I seen you on TV, right?"

"Right."

"You famous. You in charge here?" The skull ridges above the man's eyes rose slightly.

Careful. If they know you're in charge . . . Screw that. You want help? You have to take a chance. "I am. Tell your boss that I'd like to negotiate."

"What're you offering? What happens when this is over?"

Harlequin wasn't even sure he could convince the president to pardon Downer, and she was a known quantity. How the hell could he make promises to an international criminal gang?

The man shook his head at Harlequin's silence. "You fucking liar. Get off my block before I get sick of you."

"I'll do whatever I can. I'm the best shot you've got of getting the ear of the government."

"Wrong government, asshole. You know who we are?"

"You want to stop calling me names. I'm not stupid either. You don't spend this long in the SOC without hearing about the *Limpiados*."

"Then you know we've been living in a fucking sewer for years because of you motherfuckers."

"Bullshit. The *Zetas* run Mexico. You could walk in the daylight if you wanted to. You choose the sewers. I remember *El Perro*'s speech."

The skull face smiled. "Man. You been paying attention. That's good to hear."

"Help us. We've got all the bullets in the world, but they don't hurt the mountain gods. We need magic."

"Those bullets still hurt us. You fucking politicians are the biggest liars in the world. You think the NYPD hasn't made us the same offer? We saw what you did to Houston Street. Rending's illegal except when you're impersonating Big Bear. Or what you did to Oscar Britton? Fuck that, man. You're a bunch of snakes."

Harlequin winced internally. *Is he wrong?*

"You know Oscar Britton? Are you in touch with him?"

Skull-Face looked incredulous. "You kidding me? I ain't telling you shit."

Harlequin sighed. "Suit yourself. If you'd prefer the monsters, be my guest. If we lose, they win. That's not going to be good for you, for anyone human."

"You're asking me to choose monsters"—Skull-Face leaned in close—"or monsters. Go on home, Army man. Go on home and make more laws. Tell the *ratas* you work for that *Los Limpiados* say they can suck our dicks."

"Battery Park. You tell your boss that if he changes his mind, he can find me there. Ask for . . ."

"I know who you are, Harlequin. Go fly on home."

Harlequin swallowed his pride and rose into the air. "You know where to find me if you change your mind."

Skull-Face's laughter chased him all the way down Canal, ringing in his mind long after he'd left him behind.

INTERLUDE V
LUNCH

The Ponaturi have an uncommonly strong bond with a race of whalelike creatures they call Kan-Nay, whom they seem to both worship and herd. I say "whalelike" loosely. I saw humpback whales breaching off the coast of Nantucket. The Kanae are at least twice as large.

—Simon Truelove
A Sojourn Among the Mattab On Sorrah

SIX YEARS EARLIER

They spent the night entwined on the couch in her office, Grace softly snoring, Harlequin listening to the rhythm of her breathing, watching her face. As the sun began to fan pale light across the floor, Harlequin's smartphone vibrated with a text message. BRIEFING GATANAS. NEED YOU TO COVER THE SHOP. COME IN BY 0700.

Harlequin slowly disentangled himself from Grace's limbs and stood. She moaned, flopped over on her side. "You. Breakfast. Now."

"Sorry," he said. "I've got to go to work."

"Tell them I said you could take the day off."

"I'll pass it along." He bent to kiss her, tried to stand, but she pulled him back in, surprisingly strong.

So he kissed her again. And again.

By the time he finally got out of her office, he was rushing, his uniform sloppy, himself unshowered and unshaven. It was absolutely unlike him, and it felt fantastic.

Crucible was gone by the time he arrived, and the NYPD officers at the liaison office didn't say anything as he raced to the bathroom to clean himself up as best he could. Grace dominated his thoughts, but soon the day-to-day of his work stole them away, and he willingly gave himself up to the familiar rhythm. Special drugs and secret programs were exciting, but he much preferred helping the NYPD enforce the law. There were no hidden agendas there, no secrets. You ran, you paid. It was simple work. Sheepdog's work.

He stepped out of the liaison office in search of one of the food carts that lined the park outside the office. He spotted his favorite a few car lengths down from its regular spot. He was in luck. Instead of the usual line, there was only a single broad-shouldered man in a gray suit.

Harlequin made his way over, ignoring the stares and sudden stilling of conversations around him. After all his time on this assignment, it was so much background noise.

He moved his way around the man, trying to catch the cook's eye, but found the cart empty. The man in the suit turned to face him, smiling. Harlequin smiled back. The man was thickly built, with buzz-cut hair and smart sunglasses. Definitely former military, with the easy confident nature that Harlequin had come to note in real operators who had gone on to civilian service. The sunglasses obscured his eyes, but Harlequin could tell he was looking directly at him. He nodded and went back to looking for the cook.

But another man stood in the cart. His suit was black, but otherwise he could have been the twin of the man beside Harlequin. "Lieutenant Thorsson," the man in the cart said. "I'm Tom Hicks with Entertech. Nice to meet you."

Harlequin looked back to the man beside him, Drawing his magic and balling his fists. "What the hell is going on here?"

Hicks raised his hands and spread his fingers. "Easy, Lieutenant. We just want to talk."

"So you take over my favorite lunch spot? Why the hell couldn't you just call my desk?"

Hicks smiled. "We figured a busy guy like you would appreciate the change of pace. This is more dramatic, don't you think?"

"It sure is," Harlequin said, then jerked his head at the thickset man beside him. "If you just want to talk, I'm going to need you to call off your dog and make me a sandwich."

Hicks nodded to his companion. "I got it, John." The thickset man pulled his cell phone out of his pocket, waved it at Hicks, and walked off.

"Well, that's step one," Harlequin said. "Now, where's my sandwich?"

"Just a minute of your time, Lieutenant, promise."

"Okay," Harlequin said. "Clock is ticking."

"You know who we are . . ." Hicks said.

"Entertech? Of course. You're our main contractor. You guys are all over Quantico."

"Most of us are retired military. I was an O-5 in the army when I got out. Logistics."

"Am I supposed to be impressed?"

"You're supposed to feel a sense of kinship and trust."

"Sorry. I'm too damn hungry. Maybe if you got the cook back here?"

Hicks smiled at that. "We're your leading technical and manpower solutions provider. There are other Beltway bandits that build your tanks and planes, that staff your think tanks or develop your software. Magic is what we do."

"Wrong," Harlequin said. "Unless you've found a nifty new way to conceal your current, you're not Latent. Magic is what *I* do."

"I . . ." Hicks began.

Harlequin cut him off. "Enough. Get to the point."

"You're working with the Channel Corporation on an experimental drug, some kind of Limbic Dampener."

"I don't know what the hell you're talking about," Harlequin said. "I'm on a SOC LE support tour."

"You don't move as far in the field as we have without keeping your finger on the pulse of important business developments," Hicks said, spreading his hands.

"Well, then what do you need me for? Sounds like you're all over this."

"So, you are working with Channel."

"I'm not confirming or denying anything except that I'm hungry."

"Jesus." Hicks made a dramatic show of looking around under the counter. "There's got to be something here. Mustard . . . pickles . . . some . . . red-looking sauce. I have no idea what it is, but I'm pretty sure it's edible. If I give it to you, will you hear me out?"

"Let me see it," Harlequin said.

"Look, Grace Lyons made her fortune in finance. Why the hell is she suddenly dabbling in pharmaceuticals? Doesn't seem odd to you?"

Harlequin swept a hand over the food cart. "You want to talk to me to me about odd?"

"Channel has no experience with magic and, more importantly, no clue how to properly secure important developments in relation to it. You are taking a huge risk by working with them."

"I never said I was working with them. Where's that red sauce?"

Hicks went on without batting an eyelash. "We hope you're keeping an eye on Channel's lab security, Lieutenant. We hope you're reporting any violations up your chain with alacrity. We especially hope you're keeping a careful eye on Grace Lyons. If a problem were to be discovered in that program, we could step in and help out."

"Really? Would you not make sandwiches for them, too? Because right now, you're the worst fucking cook I've ever met."

"More importantly, I can't even begin to speculate on the damage it would do to your career if a security violation were discovered that you were remiss in reporting."

Harlequin felt his face flush with anger. "See, now it sounds like you're a lousy cook who's threatening me. That's two strikes. One more, and I might just have to climb in there and teach you some fucking manners."

Hicks shrugged. "Speaking of careers. Do you know what most SOC officers do when they retire? They come work for us, Lieutenant, usually at roughly double what they were making as a field- or flag-grade. It's a nice way to watch the sunset."

Harlequin snorted laughter. "Here's what happens now. I go call my boss and report this insanely unethical and illegal conversation. Entertech gets investigated and brought up on charges. You get fired and go to jail. That sound about right?"

Hicks's smile didn't falter. "Nobody has done anything unethical here, Lieutenant. We rented a truck and had a conversation. Both of those actions are protected by the First Amendment. Remember? The one you swore to defend?"

"Yeah, I remember it. So, here's my free speech. Go fuck yourself."

Hicks looked sad. "I'm sorry you see it that way. You're young. You don't know how things get done yet. I wish you had more time to learn before making a call like this."

Harlequin's blood went cold, his righteous anger abandoning him. He remembered his conversation with Crucible in the Channel meeting room just yesterday. *There are policies that exist that guide those of us above your rank and level of experience.*

"You haven't been very reasonable," Hicks said, "but, fortunately for you, I am many years in the Army and I saw a lot of JOs full of piss and vinegar just like you. Here's my card." He extended a business card between two fingers. "You change your mind, you give me a call."

Harlequin took it numbly. A dozen snappy retorts rose to mind, but he couldn't shake the sickening feeling that he was missing something.

He turned and headed back to his office, his appetite gone, sliding the card into his cargo pant pocket. He walked a few steps, stopped, turned back to the food truck. Hicks was gone, the truck shuttered and locked. He had no doubt it would open again shortly, with no indicator that anything had happened other than his memory of the conversation.

He shook his head. *Snap out of it.* It was one thing when Crucible, his supervisor and an authorized government agent, gave him lectures on policy. It was another when a contractor tried to push him around. He was not going to be intimidated.

He pulled his cell phone out of his pocket and raised it to call Crucible, only to find it ringing in his hand. It was Grace.

Excitement overcame trepidation and he had lifted the phone to his ear and answered before he knew what happened. "Grace . . ." he began.

"Get your ass back here," she cut him off. "Well, get your ass over here. I'm in my apartment. I never dismissed you."

He tried to chuckle, but the encounter with Hicks had stolen his mirth. It came out forced.

Grace was no fool. "What's wrong?"

"Nothing. I'm fine."

"You sound out of breath. Are you fucking someone else already?"

"What? No!"

"Relax, babe. I'm not the jealous type. Tell me what's wrong."

"I just . . . I got waylaid on my way to lunch."

"Sounds like it was one hell of a fight. You're practically panting."

"Are you meeting with Crucible today? I really need to talk to him."

"Why? Is something going on with the program? With the test subject?"

"Will you stop interrogating me?"

"Sure, just as soon as I get the answers I want. Did your command kill the project?"

"No, no. The Army is fine . . . can we please just . . ."

"Not the government then. Someone from the outside? A private entity?"

Harlequin stammered, his natural instinct against deceit warring with his instinct to take time and think the matter through.

Grace's voice went cold. "Entertech."

Harlequin's sudden silence was more damning than his words.

"It was Hicks, wasn't it? That fucker. Whatever he told you is shit. He's been dogging my heels ever since I founded Channel."

"You'd make one hell of an interrogator."

"And you'd make a lousy spy. You couldn't keep a secret if your life depended on it."

Embarrassment stilled Harlequin's tongue.

"Don't get your panties in a bunch," Grace said. "I'm not going to tell anyone. I should have warned you that Hicks'd come sniffing around."

"Grace, how did he know?"

"You think the government has the market cornered on spying? Corporations do it, too, Jan. We do it more, and we do it better. I'm sure Entertech has moles inside my organization. They made an offer to buy the project out of nowhere a few months back and were none too pleased when I refused to sell. It's not about making money for me, and never was. What did he say?"

"Not much. Just a lot of BS about how weird it was that you started a pharmaceutical company after doing finance for so long."

"My God, what a dick." Grace sounded furious.

"If you talk to Crucible, tell him I've been trying to reach him."

"Don't mention this to him."

"What? Why? He needs to know. Maybe he can help root these . . ."

"Trust me on this, Jan. He's a nice guy and all, but this is private stuff. I can't have the government getting involved. There's a lot at stake here."

"Like what?"

"Just . . . don't worry about it, Jan. Leave it, please. There's nothing Crucible can do anyway."

The phone started to beep, he held it briefly away from his ear to see who was calling.

"Grace, it's Crucible. Let me go, I have to talk to him."

"Don't tell him! I'm serious, Jan. This is a private concern of mine and the Channel corporation, and it's not to go any further than us."

"I have to go, Grace. I'll call you tonight."

Grace was yelling as he switched over to Crucible's call. "Sir."

"Sir?" Crucible laughed. "You okay?"

"Yeah, just . . ." Harlequin paused. He felt Hicks's card in his pocket, heard Grace yelling in his ear.

"Jan? What did you call me for? What's going on?" Crucible asked.

Harlequin's vision filled with Grace's sleeping form, tangled up in a blanket on her office couch, his arm wrapped around her slender shoulders.

"Jan?" Moonlight passing through the window, dusting her hair.

"Nothing, si . . ." Harlequin had said before he knew it. "It's nothing."

CHAPTER XIII
WHAT'S A TRAITOR?

Magic is possibly the most disruptive force in history. Governments exist because they meet the technological and security needs of their citizenry. They provide access to public transportation, critical utilities, a medical system. They provide police and firefighters, airports and roads. The simplest things: light, heat, healing, food, are all nearly impossible to obtain without working inside a government structure. But just one Sorcerer from each legal school can provide all of these things, and more besides. Why live under the yoke of a government if you don't have to?

—John "Little Bear" Inoa
Magic and God's Plan for Us All

The barricade walls around the park came into view and with them, the *Gahe*. Harlequin could see them just beyond the churning mix of goblins and giants, arms folded, stark, white-knife smiles shining from the unbroken black surface of their bodies. The shimmering pulses of air moved between them, their variant of speech.

Downer was right. He missed her elementals here, but if this position fell, they'd lose their foothold on the island and the ability to divide Scylla's forces. If the barricades fell, all of New York City would lie open to the enemy.

He radioed fire control. "Acc. Acc. Harlequin. Inbound from the north. Check your fire. I say again, check your fire."

The RTO sounded tired. "Roger that, sir. We were getting worried here. Colonel Hewitt has been looking for you."

"Put him through."

Hewitt's voice buzzed through the commlink, reluctant. "Well, you said you wanted to hear any big news directly. Come on down."

Harlequin was surprised to find himself irritated. He wanted to take some time to check on the wall, wanted to keep an eye on the gathering *Gahe* and the shaking Fornax Novices, wanted a minute to sit and think of a way to convince the *Limpiados* to help. He sighed. The truth was that he wanted to keep an eye on everything at once. He couldn't do that, and as much as he didn't want to share command with Hewitt, he needed him.

He switched channels back to the RTO. "The *Gahe* . . ."

"Roger that, sir. We've got eyes on."

"You buzz me the minute they move."

"Wilco, sir."

"Sergeant Major Knut . . . is . . ."

"She's fine, sir. She's in the motor pool. Nobody's touched her."

"Thanks, Harlequin out."

He floated over the wall and walked the rest of the way to Castle Clinton, giving himself the extra few minutes to gather his thoughts.

Hewitt met him in the ready room, his face worn, dark circles under his eyes. *Is that how I look? How we all look?*

As Hewitt's eyes widened, Harlequin realized that he looked a good deal worse.

"Jesus," Hewitt breathed. "What the hell happened to you?"

"I made a pit stop. Didn't work out so well."

"I thought you were checking out the barricades?"

"I was. That didn't work out so well either."

"You got ambushed."

Harlequin nodded. "Goblins. Selfer saved my life."

Hewitt scowled. "Great. One more fucking thing to deal with."

"One more opportunity to get the help we need. And the best kind of help. Looks like there's a cell of the *Limpiados* in Chinatown."

Hewitt's blank stare told Harlequin the man had no idea what he was talking about, and if he knew Hewitt at all, was far too proud to ask.

"I'm talking about the *Limpiados* branch of *Los Zetas*.

They're a branch of the Mexican Zeta drug cartel," Harlequin said. "They're a real political force in Mexico now, with hopes of having a voice in government. They've already got a few seats in the Chamber of Deputies. The Zetas have embraced Selfers for ages now, but they've put them underground to avoid public scrutiny. It's an open secret."

"There are a lot of them?" Hewitt asked.

"We don't know. That's something we've been trying to determine for a long time. They're not easy to pin down. They're called the flushed people because they live in the sewers. They're dug in worse than the Houston Street Gang ever was. And with the . . . entreprencurial spirit of Mexican law enforcement and the incredible power of the Zetas, getting a head count isn't exactly easy. Customs and Border Patrol drew heavily on their SOC liaisons in that fight, but since they legalized pot, things calmed down a whole lot."

"No, I mean here."

"I have no idea. I only saw the one, but if they're managing to keep four New York City blocks clear of the enemy, I'd guess there are more where he came from."

"We could call Dix, get an airstrike."

Harlequin swallowed his anger. "We're done with airstrikes. There are civilians all over this city. More importantly, we need their help. The man who found me was a Physiomancer. I'd be dead if he hadn't saved me. They're fighting Scylla, and that makes them a potential ally."

"But they're criminals . . ."

"So's Sarah Downer. You want me to send her back to jail?"

"This is different, and you know it. Downer's one of ours."

"We sure as hell didn't treat her that way."

"You can't do this . . ."

"We don't have a choice! Jesus, sir, do you not see what's unfolding around us? We don't have the magic to fight this fight. We're going to fucking lose. I'm not going to . . ."

"Wait. Just wait. Listen to the news I have for you first, then make a decision."

Harlequin felt hope surge in him, tried to keep the tremor from his voice.

"So, this news of yours is big?"

"Yup."

"Big, good? Please tell me it's big good."

Hewitt only pointed to the monitor, which was lighting up with black-and-white imagery. Harlequin could tell it was from an overhead satellite. Grainy gray waves flowed over black sheets dotted with white. Harlequin squinted. He'd seen images like this, and had never had trouble at least getting a basic read on it at a glance. He blinked, tried to shake off the exhaustion.

"So, what am I looking at?" he asked, part of him reluctant to admit he couldn't tell and part of him too tired to care.

"That"—Hewitt pointed to a dark patch—"is Franklin Mountain State Park."

Hewitt moved to a patch of light. Harlequin blinked again, and it came into focus. A city. "That's . . . this is Texas?"

Hewitt nodded. "That's Fort Bliss. Ever been there?"

"No. Hood. I did an LNO tour there once."

"Okay, well it rolls right up to the border, and Mexico is on the other side. Ciudad Juarez."

"And what's all that?" Harlequin swept his fingertips over a swath of dots and blotches spilling out from the city and into the countryside. Flashes of white and gray moved across the rocky line of the US-Mexican border. "Looks like troops."

"It is," Hewitt said. "Near as I can tell, it's the entire fucking Mexican Army."

Harlequin blinked again. "Outside of *Distrito Federal*? The cartels will take over the country."

"Something's got them more worried than the cartels, apparently."

Harlequin's heart leapt. "They're moving on Mescalero. They're going to help."

Hewitt shook his head. "I'm not an imagery expert, but I've worked with them. See those lines? Those tanks are digging in. Looks like the infantry are setting up scrapes. They're spread out, grenade sumps. DFPs."

Defensive fighting positions, the work of an army that had no intention of going anywhere.

"They're securing the border. Trying to make sure the conflict doesn't spill over."

Hewitt sighed. "Looks like it."

Harlequin bit his lip. "Ah, hell. I knew that would be the case anyway. I wasn't expecting them to get in the fight."

Harlequin sat in one of the metal folding chairs, closed his eyes, and breathed deeply. It was a fight to open them again. When he did, he found that Hewitt had set a supersized energy drink in front of him. The twenty-two-ounce can bore red lettering advertising EXTRA CAFFEINE! over its silver surface.

"Thanks," Harlequin said. "Not sure how much longer we can subsist on those. We need rack time."

"Rough on all of us," Hewitt said. "Anyway, there's some potentially good news."

"Does this good news have anything to do with us getting some sleep?"

Hewitt smiled. "Depends on how you look at it." He handed Harlequin a piece of paper. Harlequin cracked the seal on the energy drink, took a few swallows, and sat staring at the paper for a few moments before he realized that he wasn't reading it. He blinked, looked up at Hewitt.

"This is in French."

"Yup."

"And neither of us read French."

"Actually, I do, but there's translated text on the other side."

"Sir, respectfully? I am too fucking tired to turn this paper over."

Hewitt smiled again. "I think Canada couldn't make a move, but it looks like they pulled some strings with sovereign Quebec. I did my one attaché tour with them. They're pretty badass in the arcane theater."

"The . . . Winter Wolves, right?"

"*Loup-Garous.* You've never seen Terramancers like this."

"You mean Whisperers."

Hewitt shrugged. "You put Sarah Downer on Barricade One. I guess I've had to make my peace with that."

"She put herself there. That little girl is turning out to be a fucking force of nature."

"Well, either way, she's running around in front of every TV camera in the city, so I'm sure the world is getting an eyeful of Probe magic right about now."

"Any word from Gatanas on that?"

"Not yet."

"So, no airstrikes, right?"

Hewitt paused for a long time, his eyes rolled up to the ceiling. At last he nodded. When he finally spoke, his voice was halting. "I guess what I'm trying to say is that I think you did the right thing in putting her in the fight. They'd have broken through by now if it weren't for her elementals."

"They may still break through."

"Not if the *Loup-Garous* get every rat, spider, roach, and pigeon still left in the city crawling up the enemy's backfield. Your trip to the UN bore fruit. Requesting the help from Gatanas was a good call."

Harlequin blinked again. The caffeine, taurine, and sugar were already beginning to do their work.

"Who are you and what have you done with Colonel Hewitt?" he asked.

Hewitt laughed. "Yeah, well. You've made some stupid moves, too. I'm just getting the truth said and out. Don't make it harder than it already is."

Now it was Harlequin's turn to pause. "You still think I'm a traitor, sir?" he finally asked.

Hewitt sighed and slumped into the chair opposite Harlequin, thrusting his hands into his pockets. "I was pretty pissed off when I heard you were coming. I was excited to get in this fight, but I didn't want to work with you."

"Sucks pretty bad, huh? I don't even like working with me."

"Yeah, well. Working the Breach Zone has . . . given me some perspective.

"Look, everyone knows the facts of why you did what you did, that you broke Britton out to try to save the people on FOB Frontier. I think what pisses people off is that a lot of folks think there were other ways to get it done. And . . . people died in the process."

Harlequin rubbed his forehead. "I live with that every day. A lot more people would have died if I'd let those people stop me."

Hewitt looked at the ceiling. "That's what I tell myself. I also . . . what you did for Knut. You really looked out for her. She wasn't even one of yours, and you went to the mat for her. I guess, watching this thing here unfold, it's shown me that sometimes . . . events run away with you. You were academy?"

"ROTC." Harlequin held up his hand, spreading his fingers to show the lack of an academy ring.

"I did West Point. They talked a lot about hard calls there, about how when the chips were down, you'd have to make snap decisions and be held to account for your judgment later."

"ROTC was the same."

"Well, I guess the thing is that they *talked* a lot about it. Then, you get out into the field, and the hardest call you have to make is whether or not to write up an admin punishment for some dickhead specialist who got drunk and reported late. They don't talk about calls like this. Fate of millions of people in your hands. The regs pushing you up against the wall. No time to think about it.

"When you first said you were going to put Downer in the fight, I about freaked, but that barricade is holding thanks to her, maybe even the whole line. That's something. So, yeah, it kind of makes the *Loup-Garous* seem like small potatoes, especially when the only thing between us and the *Gahe* out there are these Novices zipping around the wall."

"You didn't answer my question," Harlequin said.

Hewitt met Harlequin's eyes. "You disobeyed orders. You freed a prisoner. Sure. You're a traitor. But I'm not so sure what that means anymore."

They were quiet for a long time after that. Harlequin finally broke the silence. "So, let me guess. You want me to wait for them."

"It's a safer bet than teaming up with Selfers."

"Not if they don't show up in time."

"Give them a day. We can hold for a day. If we don't have word by then . . ."

"Will they honestly be here in a day?"

"No ETA yet. They say there are some logistical concerns. A little more wrangling needs to happen higher up."

Harlequin tugged on his chin. "We can't count on that, sir. We have to assume they'll never get here. The SOC, too. I'm going to go to the other cleared zone."

"Jesus. Will you just wait? Just one day for chrissakes."

"We don't have time."

"They won't help us anyway. You said it didn't work out with the *Limpiados*."

Harlequin looked at his lap; he couldn't deny the truth of the man's words. "It's worth a try." His voice rang hollow.

Hewitt scowled. "We should talk to Gatanas. He could . . ."

"Gatanas will bomb the whole fucking city if he gets a whiff of Selfer gangs on the ground."

Hewitt nodded. "This is . . ."

"Sir, you agree with my call on Sergeant Major Knut?"

Hewitt nodded. "I do."

"Then please give me the benefit of the doubt here. This wi . . ."

He was cut off by Cormack on the radio. "Sir! You want to come out here right now."

"Once more unto the breach, my friend?" Harlequin asked.

"Or, we could go outside and see what the hell's going on."

Harlequin smiled. "That'll work."

Cormack intercepted them before they'd gone three steps, pointing toward the perimeter. "Novice Beamer is freaking out, sir. Up on the wall, swears something's coming."

"I'll cover for you," Hewitt said. "Go see what's up."

Harlequin nodded thanks and leapt into the air, following the direction of Cormack's finger to the top of the barricade, where the Novice hunched, elbows on her knees.

Before he'd gone three feet, he knew she wasn't mistaken. A powerful current whirled around them, growing stronger by the moment. Some magic was at work, and it was coming their way.

His boots touched down on the plywood catwalk, and he squatted alongside her. Her head was down, eyes closed. "Do you feel it, sir?" she asked without looking up.

"I feel it," he answered. "See anything?"

She shook her head, opened her eyes. The bags under them testified to the impact the endless hours on the wall were having on her. "Nothing. Quieter than ever."

Too quiet. Harlequin looked at the broken, looted buildings just beyond the park's perimeter. Nothing moved in them. The crowd of *Gahe* was gone.

He toggled the commlink and spoke into it. "Cormack, what's the situation on the west wall?"

"Normal, sir. Why?"

"By normal, you mean you still have contact with the enemy?"

"Yes, sir. They're taking a break, but they'll be at it again before you know it."

"Keep one Novice there and send everyone else to me. Pull a fire team as well. On the hop."

"Roger that, sir." Cormack sounded nervous, but knew better than to question Harlequin's motives.

Harlequin felt the undisciplined currents of two Novices long before he saw them, almost drowned out by the powerful tide coming toward them. Three soldiers jogged along behind, unslinging their guns as they approached the ladders up to the catwalk.

Two Novices. That was what Cormack could spare.

Harlequin swallowed his disappointment and extended a hand as they crested the ladder. He recognized them. A broad-shouldered Terramancer named Drake and Unpronounceable himself, the mouse over his eye swollen golf-ball-sized and turned an angry shade of purple. Both looked exhausted, but suddenly alert and nervous as they sensed the magical tide bearing down on them.

"What's going on, sir?" Unpronounceable asked.

"Not sure, but I want to be ready. You see what I see?" He pointed up Broadway.

"There's nothing there, sir," Drake said.

"Exactly. That seem normal to you?"

No one answered.

"All right, everyone stay here. I'm going to get some air cover and go . . ."

"Shh!" Unpronounceable brought his fingers to his lips, realized who he was talking to, then dropped his hand, shamefaced. "Sorry, sir. I hear something."

"It's fine." Harlequin's magical senses might be better honed, but he lacked the younger man's better hearing. "What do you hear?"

Unpronounceable held his hand up, eyes closed, listening so hard he looked like he might pull a muscle. He needn't have. After a moment, Harlequin could hear it, too.

A dull scratching riding over a squeaking, as if a thousand hands were being raked along as many chalkboards. It echoed along Broadway, the narrow confines of the street tunneling the sound straight toward them.

Harlequin squinted into the distance. Dust was rising down the avenue, billowing their way. The pulse of magic emanated from behind it.

"Is that Aeromancy?" Beamer asked.

"Not Aeromancy," Harlequin answered. This wasn't that sort of wind. Summoned wind tended to be clean, uniform. This looked haphazard, incidental.

The kind of dust kicked up by an army.

"Cormack!" he yelled into the commlink. "Get everyone to my position! Don't worry about guns. We need explosives. I need every bird with rockets in the air! Fuel lines! Get the fuel lines!"

"Fuel lines?" Cormack's voice came back. "For the motor pool?"

"Just do it!" Harlequin shouted as the first tiny shapes emerged from the dust and scampered down Broadway toward him.

Broadway was boiling, a torrent flowing from every manhole cover and alleyway.

Rats.

Rats in their aggregate millions. He had never known so many existed in all of New York. They flowed like a river down the avenue, a tide of brown, black, and gray fur dotted here and there by the occasional stray cat or dog.

Harlequin whirled on Drake, seized his shoulders. The big Novice stared out at the approaching horde. "Novice. Novice! Look at me!"

Drake looked, eyes pleading.

"Did you ever experiment with Whispering?"

"Sir, it's ille . . ."

"No time for that! I know most of you fuck around with it once or twice. Can you remember how to do it?"

"I . . . I don't think so, sir."

"Try anyway."

Cormack and Hewitt came racing out of the castle and stood at the base of the ladders. Harlequin could hear shouting, the sound of helo rotors spinning up. Two soldiers came running to the base of the wall, thick black hoses over their shoulders.

"Get those up here! I need them pumping down the other side!"

"They won't reach, sir," one of the soldiers said.

"So, move the damn trucks closer! Do it now!"

He turned back to the street as the ladders began to rattle, several soldiers mounting the top of the T-walls, claymore mines tucked under their arms. They froze at the sight of the oncoming tide, then got moving again at a look from Harlequin. He jumped into the air.

"Where are you going, sir?" Drake asked.

"Someone's Whispering them. I'm going to find out who."

He turned and flew out over the approaching mass. Above them, the noise was near deafening, a scrabbling, chittering cacophony. He let loose a gout of lightning, tearing a ragged gash in their ranks, but more of the rodents scrambled over the corpses of their fellows, the smoking patch refilled in moments. The rats picked up speed, the tide washing up against the store-fronts on either side of the avenue, sending ripples through the throng.

Harlequin heard sharp cracks as the claymores on the walls began to go off. More reports followed as soldiers reached the perimeter and began firing through the gaps and holes in the T-walls. Harlequin saw rats tossed in the air, cut in half, burned to a crisp.

There were always more. He could see Drake standing at the top of the wall, eyes shut, hands extended. A clump of rats in the middle of the throng had frozen, noses twitching in the air, bodies rigid, but their fellows flowed over them, driving on to the base of the wall.

Beamer and Unpronounceable let out blasts of flame, streaking down into the packed mass of vermin, sending up a shriek that hurt Harlequin's ears. The rats poured through the fire, a living ramp of furry bodies, rising higher and higher up the barricade walls.

Harlequin flew over the mass, dragging lightning as he went, tearing rents in the ocean of rats, gone as quickly as they were made. He focused on the current, desperately trying to locate it. He could hear screams behind him, both rodent and human, forced himself not to look. Their best hope to deal with this attack was to find the enemy Terramancer.

He sped out over the statue of the charging bull, Grace's old stomping ground. The statue was nearly covered in rats now, the lowered head dipping below the tide. The magical current grew fainter. The Terramancer, wherever he was, was closer to the park's perimeter.

Harlequin flew back toward the park, then stopped in mid-air, stomach sinking.

A small murder of crows had begun circling over the Bowling Green subway station, cawing loudly. As Harlequin watched, they were joined by hawks, pigeons, sparrows. The cloud of birds grew until it was a solid black mass, the chirping, cawing, and tweeting so loud that it nearly drowned out the gunfire.

A Kiowa had gotten airborne, its rocket pods already smoking as it fired into the mass of rats. Its miniguns tore into the cloud of birds, picking them off in ones and twos, barely making a dent in the growing cloud.

Harlequin shot back down Broadway. "Cormack! Get Downer down here!"

He couldn't hear any response over the sound of the animals beneath him. Clods of dirt were flying as the rats dug at the base of one T-wall, tunneling so fast the concrete barrier had already begun to sag outward. He Drew, Bound, and funneled lightning with all his strength into the diggers, furry bodies jerking and exploding like gunshots. The ground smoked, the T-wall sagging farther into the crater he'd created.

He shot over the wall. "Where the hell are my fuel lines!?"

The rats were an ocean outside the walls. Inside, they were a river, as more and more animals squeezed between the gaps in the T-wall segments. Soldiers and refugees alike were screaming, disappearing under the murine flow. Harlequin could hear the crunching and tearing of thousands of little mouths and claws on flesh. The creatures coursed up the legs of their enemies, biting the entire way, then moved on, leaving twitching corpses in their wake. The remains were horrifying, a patchwork field of tiny, leaking rents exposing hints of white bone.

He saw one of the fuel trucks, pulled up to the wall, black hose snaking out from the fuel tanks to disappear under the carpet of animals.

He heard the Kiowa's engine sputter, its guns go silent. He turned to see the helo spinning toward him, tail boom a whirling blade. Birds covered it, seething over the surface, a machine made of flapping wings and striking beaks. They dispersed as the spin became a tumble, and the Kiowa fell toward him.

Harlequin shunted his magic back instinctively. The lightning coiling around him winked out and he dropped like a stone.

He felt a brush of air as the helo shot past him, striking the ground and rolling into the motor pool, crunching against the Humvees, then exploding with a bang that forced Harlequin back out over the wall, squinting, his face showered with debris.

"The truck!" Harlequin shouted to Drake. "Move the damn truck!"

Drake nodded, turning from his failed Whispering. He focused, and a fist of earth lurched up from the ground beneath the fuel truck, launching the vehicle end over end, sending it crashing against the T-wall, toppling through. Harlequin could smell the pungent odor of gasoline as the fuel washed across the ground.

"No!" he shouted. He raised his hands, summoned a wind. It swept across the makeshift parapet, throwing the Novices and many of the soldiers off the plywood catwalk and clear of the blast area, sending them rolling on the ground below. He prayed they'd survive the fall. He turned and flew back up Broadway, getting only a few feet before hearing the sound that he dreaded.

A gunshot. An instant later, it was followed by a throaty boom so deep that Harlequin felt it before he heard it. His bones vibrated, a wall of heat slapping him out of the sky and sending him careening into a window. The glass gave, giving sharp-edged kisses along the way. He rolled, sliced and bleeding, along the floor of an office, slamming into a desk.

He shrugged off the pain, stood, limped to the window.

Broadway was a lake of fire.

The rats drowned in it, screaming out their lives as their bodies shriveled in the heat. Mad with pain, they shot out from the main body in ones and twos, fiery pseudopods streaming into sewer grates and open doorways.

One of the T-wall segments was down, leaving a hole in the barricade wall, a missing tooth that poured out burning rats.

The cloud of birds reconstituted, wheeled, dove back down into the encampment. Harlequin heard the roar of an antiaircraft gun, and a portion of the cloud dissolved in red mist, shredded by high-volume fire. The rounds were too big to catch them all, and Harlequin could hear screaming as he shook off the pain and flew out of the window, following the current. He had to fight against the urge to fly into the park, to lend his magic to the battle there, but the Terramancer had to be his priority.

The current grew stronger as he crossed the street. He could feel it eddying out from the low building in front of him, a stretch of offices looming over a ground-floor glass-fronted office displaying a scorched sign reading CITY OF NEW YORK— DEPARTMENT OF MOTOR VEHICLES.

With a roar, a Blackhawk shot free of the park, banking so steeply that Harlequin feared it would stall. It righted, miniguns firing at a smaller cloud of birds that detached from the main flock and pursued it, screeching as their numbers dwindled under the steady fire.

The Blackhawk won free of the park, only to be caught in the updraft from the fire, which sent it wobbling out over Broadway, birds lighting on the tail boom, swooping into the cabin. Harlequin could see soldiers inside stomping and swatting at them, but for every pigeon they killed and threw out the door, two more replaced them. The birds dove at the spinning rotors, seeking the engines. The whirling blades scythed through them, sending up clouds of blood and feathers, but more of the things kept coming.

Harlequin banked and flew toward the helo, extending a hand and summoning a gale that cut through the birds, scattering them, overwhelming their wings and sending them spinning through the air, hollow bones snapping.

The Blackhawk righted, and Harlequin flew alongside the open cabin door to see three soldiers crouching inside, eyes wide with terror.

"I need you to give me everything you . . ."

He felt a shift in the current beneath him, followed by a

deafening screech from inside the park. There was a rumbling patter, a thousand golf claps at once, and a torrent of birds raced up from the park, straight for him.

Harlequin shouted a warning and moved sharply away from the helo, funneling lightning into the cloud of flapping wings. The helo banked the other way, vanished behind a wall of avian forms. They swept after Harlequin, repeating the dance the rats had done below: his lightning ripping rents in the mass that filled in just as quickly.

And then they were upon him.

Harlequin wreathed himself in crackling electricity as the cloud of birds enveloped him, filling his ears with screeching, cawing, cooing. The stink was overpowering, the rancid odor of mattress ticking gone sour.

The first birds to reach him danced in the lightning, smoking and falling away, but their fellows came behind them in droves, damp feathers insulating against the shock and driving the burned corpses into him, weighing him down.

Harlequin closed his eyes as the first beak pecked at them, the first set of tiny claws fixed onto his flight suit. He summoned a wind, sent it sweeping through the cloud, but he couldn't see, and there were too many. The stink and screeching blotted out his senses. Talons dug at his scalp, feathers battered his lips, nostrils. He couldn't breathe. Was he sinking toward the ground?

Something sharp jabbed his eyebrow, dug lower, finding the soft indent where skull gave way to eyelid. It bored, pinching. He tried to raise his hand to swat it away, but his arm felt like it weighed a hundred pounds. He opened his mouth to scream, and it was instantly filled with feathers, cutting off his airway. A beak stabbed at the inside of his mouth.

He didn't think it possible for the screeching to get louder, but it did, then, suddenly, the pressure lifted. He flailed, shaking his arms loose, spitting out feathers and flying straight up, opening his eyes as he finally won free of the cloud.

Below him, they were dispersing. No. Being swept aside. He could see funnels of air, man-sized, becoming more distinct as they filled with the broken bodies of crows, jays, and starlings.

Elementals.

Downer hovered over Broadway, an air elemental wrapped around her. He shot her a thumbs-up, but she was concentrating on the ground as more funnels touched down, shredding what rats had managed to escape the fire.

That same fire now raged hungrily among the buildings closest to the park. He still felt the current from the DMV building, but it was reeling in as its owner abandoned Whispering and sought to escape the rising heat.

Harlequin made to dive toward it, but Downer's elementals beat him to the punch. They descended in a delta, whirling funnels of debris with just a hint of a human outline. They arrowed toward the burning building and split, one whipping around to the doors, the others moving for side windows. The fire parted, cooled instantly by the churning air of their tails.

Harlequin looked over his shoulder at Downer, suspended in the center of a larger elemental, eyes focused on the building below. The elemental's outline had coalesced, spinning thighs crossed beneath her, folded arms of churning air wrapped protectively around her. A discarded plastic bag twirled madly inside what looked like a cocked head.

It looked like a protective father, cradling his child, head lovingly laid across hers.

Harlequin was surprised by the sudden spike of envy in his gut. He beat back the emotion, locked his focus back on the fight, but not before the thought came to him unbidden. *She is always loved.* This pariah, cut off from everyone, only newly out of detention, had more than he did.

He caught the Blackhawk out of his peripheral vision, cursed himself, and shook off the thought. The helo was stable, but its rotors pitched drunkenly, the cabin shaking. The pilot was descending, struggling to find a safe spot to land amid the burning wreckage.

Harlequin bulled through the remaining birds, came alongside the cabin. Only one soldier remained. He crouched over the bloody remains of his comrade, his uniform shredded, exposed skin a field of bloody holes. The third soldier was gone. He turned to Harlequin, terror gone, simply exhausted.

Harlequin pointed at the DMV. "I need every rocket right there, right now!"

The soldier stared blankly at him. "Do it!" Harlequin shouted, and the man's paralysis abruptly broke. He lurched to his knees, crawling forward toward the cockpit.

Harlequin kicked off and raced toward Downer. "Move! Move!"

She looked up, saw his waving arm. The elemental shot skyward, taking her with it just as the rocket contrails streaked below him. Harlequin followed her up as explosion after explosion sounded beneath him.

He looked down in time to see the façade of the DMV collapse, the apartments above crumbling down around it, filling the street with rubble.

The Terramancer's current spiked, winked out.

The animal tide dispersed as quickly as it had come, receding like breakers from a rock, leaving the skeletons of Harlequin's people exposed to the sun, stripped nearly clean of flesh. The birds drifted apart with a final screech of confusion, a cloud dispersed by a strong breeze.

The Blackhawk touched down on a clear patch, killed the engines, let the rotors begin to spin down as the remaining crew abandoned it, fleeing the approaching fire.

Suddenly, all was silent save the gentle crackling of flames.

Harlequin let the summoned wind take his weight, drifted for a moment, closing his eyes and giving in to fatigue. But only for a moment. Screams from the park called him back to reality. He opened his eyes, turned to Downer.

"Thank . . ."

She cut him off with a wave, cupping one hand over the commlink in her ear. He felt her current focus, and the elemental around her began heading back north. "No time," she said. "Barricade One is getting hit hard."

"Of course," he said, but she was already gone.

More screams. He shook his head and dove back into the park's perimeter. Drake lay against one of the T-walls, cradling a shoulder he must have broken when Harlequin blew him clear of the exploding truck. "You okay?"

Drake looked up at him, tears streaming down his face. "I'm sorry, sir."

Harlequin crouched, the dying flames warming one side of his body. "What the hell are you sorry for?"

"I couldn't do it . . ." Drake said. "I tried, I really did. But I couldn't . . ." He sobbed.

"The Whispering? Hell, Novice, that was a long shot. Nobody could have expected that of you."

"I couldn't save them . . ."

"Beamer? Brezni . . . the other guy?"

Drake nodded, pointed. A few yards away, two corpses lay facedown. The bodies were so badly mauled that they could have been anyone. Harlequin stood, swallowed, tried to think of something to say. A better leader would comfort, inspire.

All he could see were the faces of those eight Marines. As deep as he dug, all he could find was hollow exhaustion. "You just sit tight," he said. "I'll get a medic for you."

Drake nodded, lowering his head between his knees, shoulders wracked with sobbing.

I know exactly how he feels. This will either make him or break him. He looked over his shoulder as he walked away. *And we won't know which for a while.*

He made for Castle Clinton, taking in the devastation. Corpses littered the ground, ragged patches ripped from them, clothing flapping open, showing excavations in flesh. Others were burned. The motor pool was destroyed, the vehicles still burning, piled atop the corpses of the refugees who'd sheltered close by.

Cormack leaned against one of the bulletproof barriers outside the entrance. A medic was taping a bandage in place, covering his left eye. His uniform was tattered, his exposed arm covered in scratches.

He came to attention and saluted. "Sir," he said, "we held."

Harlequin returned the salute, awed by the man's stoicism. "Outstanding, Captain. I never doubted you would."

Cormack seemed smaller as he dropped his arm, a tired man standing on a charnel-house floor.

"Your eye . . ." Harlequin began.

"Birds got it. Don't worry, sir. Not my dominant one."

Harlequin smiled at that. "What's the SITREP?"

"We'll try to get a body count, sir. I'm getting the breach in the perimeter sealed right now. Should take me a few minutes to get a crew together to put a replacement T-wall in place. Until then, I've detailed troops to keep it under guard."

"How bad is it?"

"Bad, sir. We lost a lot of people, and we didn't have many to begin with. I'd say . . . maybe forty percent? That's just a rough guess."

Harlequin blinked. Half a battalion to hold a postage-stamp piece of ground at the ass end of a war zone. "Where's Colonel Hewitt? We need to get more people here . . ."

But Cormack was already shaking his head. "I'm sorry, sir. We climbed on top of the barriers to get away from the rats. The birds came at us. I lost my eye hanging on. He . . . he fell off."

Cormack gestured to a boot sticking out from behind the opposite barrier. The tip had been chewed down to the steel toe. The top ended at a shiny white stretch of bone. Only scraps of meat remained to show what had once been a leg.

"Jesus."

"It's not pretty, sir. I know you two didn't get along, but . . ."

"We'd just worked it out," Harlequin said. "We were . . ."

There was nothing more to be said. "You've got a burial detail together?"

Cormack nodded. "I'll see what I can muster from Dix, and I'll get in touch with Hewitt's XO at Hamilton. We're going to need the command handoff done as quickly as possible to get supplies flowing again."

Harlequin covered his eyes with his hand. "Christ. They caught me flat-footed. I never thought they'd come at us that way. Why the hell didn't I think of that? So damned obvious."

"What difference would it have made, sir? How could you prep defenses against a hojillion rats and birds?"

Harlequin wracked his brain, but fatigue overpowered thought.

Cormack touched his earbud, looked up. "Gatanas is on the line. Sorry, sir. He wants to know what happened."

"I'll talk to him."

"Roger that," Cormack said, began limping away from the barriers toward the ruin of the motor pool. "I've got things locked down out here. We'll get the perimeter secured. Restore order. You focus on figuring out how to win this."

Without more arcane support, there is no winning this.

Harlequin walked into Castle Clinton, doing his best to shut out the cries of the wounded who'd been dragged inside, tended to by soldiers using what scraps of medical training they'd received in boot camp. A single trained medic moved among them, pointing, instructing, barking orders.

Harlequin slumped in the metal folding chair before the VTC monitor. Gatanas's eyes widened. "What the hell happened?"

"Whispering, sir. We just scraped by."

"A pack of animals?"

Harlequin was too tired to rouse anger. "A rather large pack, sir. Not sure what the exact casualty count is, but it'd be optimistic to call us at half strength."

"Can you hold?"

"We can damn well try, sir. I need more Sorcerers, I need more soldiers. I need General Bookbinder."

"It's all inbound, Lieutenant Colonel. You just need to hang on."

Harlequin didn't even bother trying to keep the incredulity off his face. "And the Québécois? Their famed *Loup-Garous*?"

Gatanas sighed. "You haven't seen the news."

"We don't exactly have a lot of time for TV lately, sir. I'm afraid my intel section's a little light."

Gatanas nodded. Leaned forward, tapped away at his keyboard. A small cutaway appeared in the lower-left-hand corner of Harlequin's screen.

A fat man with thick jowls and thinning hair stood behind a podium, purple-faced. He hammered the faux-wood surface with one meaty finger, his string tie flying. SENATOR DONALD LOVEWELL, the caption read, KENTUCKY.

". . . and now we are to be delivered by permitting foreign troops on American soil. And not just any body of foreign troops, no! *Probes*. We are to utterly ignore the tenets of the McGauer-Linden Act and make common cause with a nation whose own political status is a matter of some debate. We are to welcome the devil himself into our financial center? It is time to ask ourselves, are we a nation of laws? Will the president simply flout the rules made by the elected representatives of the people simply because he finds it expedient? As I am a servant of God almighty, I will not lie down for this. The people of Kentucky elected me to lead! And that means . . ."

"Shut it off, sir. I get the point."

Gatanas tapped a key and the screen inset disappeared.

"I assume this is all over the Internet?"

"It's gone viral. I think that's the term they use. Lovewell's getting a lot of support from a wide cross section of the population."

"Not from New Yorkers, I suspect."

"Kind of hard to poll them, just now."

"Any reaction from the Québécois?"

"They're citing . . . logistical concerns. They still say they're coming, but they fear they may be delayed."

"They're not coming."

"I wouldn't g . . ."

"Sir, please. I just lost half my unit. Is help inbound or isn't it?"

Gatanas was silent. Harlequin sighed and stood.

"There may be . . . significant delays in your relief. The Mescalero evolution is becoming . . . complicated."

"Understood, sir. Harlequin out."

"Now wait just a . . ."

Harlequin broke the connection and walked back outside, pausing to grab a bottle of water and a granola bar from the dwindling supply in stacked cardboard boxes along the entryway.

Cormack was deep in conversation with another solider. Over his shoulder, Harlequin could see a forklift moving another T-wall into place. Drake had stood, was running his hands over the seams and cracks in the concrete, his magic making the stone run fluid until it re-formed smooth and hard. That was good. Work was always good in the wake of a tragedy.

Harlequin was amazed by the resilience around him. Up to their ankles in gore, his people put their backs into their work, reconstituting the camp as if nothing had happened. They patched cracks, tended the wounded, passed out bottled water, MREs, and ammunition. They secured gaps in the perimeter and established new chains of command from the old ones holed by the deaths of their NCOs.

They worked as if nothing had happened.

But something had happened. And that something had left Harlequin's tiny force decimated.

There weren't enough of them. Not by a long shot.

And help wasn't coming.

INTERLUDE VI
OUR LITTLE SECRET

Mexico's attitude toward Latency is a study in conflict. It is a deeply religious, Catholic country, but also a country in love with mysticism and superstitious ritual. The Conquistadores were never able to fully eradicate the cultural roots that hearken back to shamanistic religion, and Mexican Catholicism is pregnant with iconography and pageantry not found to the north. Publicly, their attitude toward magic is one that will satisfy their northern neighbor. But privately, many Mexicans embrace their brujeria, which they feel is a gift from God himself.

—Professor Osvaldo H. Soto
University of Michigan, Ann Arbor

SIX YEARS EARLIER

Morelli Lopez stared into the middle distance. Her scorched dress had been replaced by a pair of ill-fitting cargo pants and a T-shirt that hung to her knees. Her long, tangled, black hair was streaked with gray. Her whole body seemed to droop, the extra weight dragging earthward. Harlequin found it hard to reconcile the demon who'd burned the housing project with the sad, fat, old lady who sat before him. Sergeant Ward and a SOC Suppressor, a bull-necked chief warrant officer called Rampart, stood behind her. The burned portion of Ward's moustache had been neatly trimmed away, leaving it lopsided.

Crucible knelt before her, tapping a clipboard. "We just need your signature, ma'am. Then we can get you out of here."

She stared over his shoulder, her mouth slightly open, saliva bubbling at the corners. "Ma'am?" Crucible asked again. Ward translated into Spanish.

She twitched, eyes coming into focus, grabbed the clipboard. "I speak English," she said. "I didn't want to do anything bad. I had the devil take me."

Crucible looked up at Harlequin, who in turn looked to Ward. Ward looked surprised. "I never heard her speak anything but Spanish before."

"The devil," she croaked again, dropping the clipboard.

"I got it," Crucible said, retrieving it and pressing it back into her hands, "but that doesn't change the fact that you need to be kept in custody. All we're promising here is more comfortable accommodations and a chance at some experimental therapies that may help you . . . get the devil out, let's say."

She looked up, eyes suddenly focused. "You can get the devil out?"

"Sure," Crucible said, gesturing at the clipboard, "in a manner of speaking. Sign it, and we can get started."

Harlequin stared at the back of Crucible's head, sickness churning in his stomach. This wasn't right. He looked at Ward, but the NYPD sergeant simply looked on. *He doesn't have the courage to challenge the SOC.*

"Sir," Harlequin said, "this isn't . . . she doesn't know what she's doing."

Her expression went hard at that, jowls quivering. "The fuck? I know what I'm doing." She shook the clipboard in his direction, brandished the pen at him.

Harlequin ignored her. "Sir, we should order a psychological . . ."

But she was already signing, pushing the pen so hard that he could hear the paper ripping beneath it. "Know what I'm fucking doing," she muttered. Crucible snatched the clipboard out of her hands the moment she was done.

"Thank you, ma'am," he said, then turned to Harlequin. "It's done, Jan."

"Sir . . ."

Crucible waved the clipboard in front of him, her signature half off the underline, illegible. "Leave it. It's done. We have authorization, and now we have consent. Let's do our jobs."

Harlequin was silent as they escorted her out of the room

and into an unmarked van and headed for the Channel building downtown, but the knot in his stomach wouldn't quit. He repeated Crucible's words in his head. *She's going to be helping, and the drug might even help her. This is all authorized by command. It's not my call. I have to follow orders.*

But he felt no better as they stepped out of the car and into the building's spartan lobby, her slippers padding across the reflective marble surface.

Grace and Weiss were there to greet them, along with two brawny security guards in matching gray shirts and cargo pants. Body armor was visible beneath their baggy jackets. Harlequin couldn't see pistols, but he guessed they were hidden in the smalls of their backs.

"Hello, Miss Lopez," Weiss said. "Welcome to Channel and thank you for volunteering."

"Huh?" Morelli asked, craning her head up to take in the building's atrium, blinking at the sunlight filtering in from the slanted windows. "You got plants up there." She pointed.

"Yes." Grace glanced at the hanging fronds arranged in the recesses of the ceiling. "Do you like them?"

"Why am I here?" Morelli asked, suddenly looking frightened.

"Because we're going to help you," Grace answered. "Because you're Latent."

"Latent? Latent! I'm not fucking Latent!" She tugged experimentally against Ward and Rampart, but they held her fast.

"You're Latent"—she pointed at Harlequin—"and you!" she added, pointing at Crucible. "I can feel it." She tugged an arm free from Rampart and pointed at him. "You, too."

Rampart smiled. "That, I am. You get used to it."

"And you." She pointed at Grace. "You, too."

Grace smiled nervously, her eyes flicking from Harlequin to Crucible. "No," she said haltingly. "No, I'm not."

"You are," Morelli said again. "You are. You need help."

The smile fled Grace's face, and her voice sounded tight as she moved toward the elevators. "Come on, let's take this downstairs."

Grace swiped a plastic card at an elevator that stood separate from the bank of six, a sheet of black in the stainless-steel surface of the wall. It opened to reveal a car large enough to house a truck. They walked Morelli inside.

"We'll take it from here," Crucible said to Ward. "Many thanks to you and the department for your help with this."

Ward hesitated, looked to Harlequin. After a moment, he released Morelli's elbow and stepped back. "Sure. So . . . You'll keep me posted?"

"To the extent we're able," Crucible said. "I'm sure I don't need to remind you of the nondisclosure agreement you signed when you agreed to work with us, Sergeant. It's super-important that you stick to that."

Ward tensed, still standing as the elevator doors shut, replacing his face with Harlequin's own, staring back at him from the stainless-steel surface.

The silence dragged on as the elevator descended, leaving Harlequin to contemplate his own reflection and Morelli's certainty that Grace was Latent. Crazy. Harlequin had slept with Grace, had been as close to her as another person could possibly be. If there'd even been a hint of a current in her, he'd have felt it.

Yet he still found himself reaching his current out to her, probing, feeling. Nothing. The ravings of a madwoman, nothing more.

"Where are we going?" Morelli asked, as the elevator began to descend. Nobody answered, and they rode in silence for what felt to Harlequin like an awfully long time. At last, the car shuddered to a stop, and the doors opened.

The room beyond was plain, a bench running along one white wall, a door beside it. A huge pane of one-way glass occupied the wall opposite. In the center of the room was a reclining chair, padded restraints attached to the armrests.

A bald young man with a beard and glasses stood beside the chair. He wore a white lab coat over his plaid work shirt and jeans. "Hello, Morelli," he smiled. "Thanks for coming! We're really excited to get started here. I'm Dan."

He turned on a monitor beside the chair, began unbundling electrical leads and wires that snaked over the chair's shoulder near the headrest. "You want some water?" he asked. "A soda or anything?"

Morelli only stared straight ahead, her jaw slack again, eyes unfocused. She placidly allowed herself to be steered to the chair and seated. Dan and Weiss began to fold the restraints over her arms. Harlequin could feel Morelli's erratic and powerful current pulsing against Rampart's, the only indicator that she was reacting to what was unfolding around her.

"She's not resisting," Harlequin pointed out. "We don't need that, surely."

"We don't know what we'll need," Crucible said.

"We're not going to need them in a minute," Weiss added, "but it can't hurt to be cautious." He caught Harlequin's glance, saw the disapproval there. "For her own safety," he added.

Once Morelli was strapped in, Grace gestured to the door beside the one-way glass. "Come along, gentlemen, let's allow Dan to do his work."

Harlequin didn't move. "I want to stay and observe."

Crucible looked at him. "Jan, come on. You'll just be in the way."

"Sir, respectfully, I took this woman in. I'm responsible for her."

"No harm is going to come to her, Lieutenant," Dan said. The friendly smile, beard, and casual clothing were disarming, but he swarmed over Morelli's head, connecting the electrical leads, tapping the monitor as colored images of her brain patterns began to flash across it. He placed a plastic case on the chair's armrest behind her elbow. "But I have no objection if you feel better staying." The only machine Harlequin recognized was an EKG, the steady, rapid pinging and white hills and valleys of the graph showing a level of anxiety not reflected on Morelli's near-catatonic face.

"Come on, Jan," Grace said. "Your man here"—she gestured to Rampart—"will keep her Suppressed. There's no need for you to be out on the floor."

"I'm staying," Harlequin said. "Unless it's an order?" he asked Crucible pointedly.

Crucible looked at Dan, who shrugged. "Fine," he said, then left through the door, followed by Grace and Rampart. The security guards seated themselves on the bench, arms folded.

Dan nodded at the one-way glass, then turned to the camera mounted to the ceiling. "Clinical trial. Initial dose of LL-14 administered to subject alpha."

He produced a syringe from the plastic case, filled with a light yellow fluid that looked disturbingly like urine. "Are you ready, Morelli? You might feel a little pinch."

She continued to stare into the distance, not responding. Dan waited a moment before wiping her wrist with an alcohol swab. "Little pinch," he muttered, and slid the needle in.

She showed no reaction beyond a slight wince. Her mouth closed. Dan finished depressing the plunger and stood back, putting a Band-Aid across her wrist. "Dose administered— 10 cc."

He dropped the empty syringe into a can marked with a biohazard sticker and crossed his hands in front of his thighs, watching the monitor intently.

"Now what?" Harlequin asked.

"Now we watch and wait," Dan answered. "Shouldn't take long."

It didn't.

Her heart rate began to slow, the EKG leveling out to a regular, steady chime. The rise and fall of her chest eased. The monitor behind her headrest showed the oval shape of her brain, the splotches of red slowly fading to purple, then to a deep blue.

But Harlequin felt an instant change in her magical current. The erratic pulsing, straining against the Suppression, slowly eased into an even droning.

She turned her head, focusing on the wall. She looked down at the restraints, pulled against them. "Why you got me in these?" she asked, her voice even.

"If I take them off," Dan asked, "what will you do?"

Morelli looked around the room, noting the guards, the single door, and the sealed elevator shaft. "This chair's fine," she answered. "Comfortable."

Dan nodded at the guards, who came closer as he undid the restraints. "How do you feel, Morelli?" he asked.

She rubbed at her wrists, sat up a bit. "I'm fine," she said. She blinked. "Am I going to get paid for this?"

Dan laughed. "You volunteered, but I promise you'll get fed and housed. How's that?"

She sank back into the chair. "That's good."

"Okay, Morelli. Now, we're going to do some things to put

stress on you. Show you a scary movie, maybe poke you a little bit. Are you okay with that?"

She shrugged. "Then I can eat?"

"Then you can eat."

"Okay. Can I have something now?"

"Sure." Dan motioned to one of the guards, who grabbed a pack of cookies from a small table and handed it to her. "Ready for the movie now?"

"Sure," she said. A screen descended from the ceiling before her. As the credits began to roll, she glanced at Harlequin, noticing him for the first time. "I remember you," she said. "You cracked my head."

"You cracked your own head," Harlequin responded. "You were burning down a building. Someone had to stop you."

Dan sucked in his breath slightly at this, watching the monitor intently. A brief flash of red in her limbic system sparked for an instant, only to be checked by another flash from her neocortex. He turned to Harlequin and twirled his wrist as if to say, *keep going.*

But, in the end, all Harlequin could manage was, "Are you okay?"

She shrugged, smiled. She nestled back into the chair, resting her elbows on the restraints and munching happily on a cookie as she looked up at the screen. The trembling violin music accompanying the credits told him it was most certainly a horror flick. "I'm fine," she said. "You don't look so good."

And then she focused, letting the images draw her in.

Grace shifted beneath him, the cool smoothness of her skin sending sparks through his body. She turned, moaned sleepily, opened her eyes first into slits, then wider as she realized Harlequin was awake and looking at her.

At last she frowned. "You realize that's creepy."

"I like looking at you; sue me."

"Silly boy. I'm the boss. I don't get my hands dirty. I have a legal team for that."

He snorted. "Do your worst. I'm on a lieutenant's salary, it's not like you'll get any money."

She shrugged and propped herself up on an elbow. The

satin sheet fell away to reveal one breast, the soft moonlight filtering through the blinds making her skin a gray-white alabaster surface. Perfectly inhuman.

"Meh," she said. "You'd just get revenge by having rain clouds follow me around all day."

He smiled, kissed her. "I don't use magic except as specifically authorized in the line of duty."

Now it was her turn to snort. "So . . . that whole fucking on the ceiling thing, and the thing you did with the lightning . . . what did you call it?"

"Electrolux." He laughed aloud.

"Right, Electrolux. That was in the line of duty?"

"Well, we're working together, right? It's good for the emerging contractual relationship."

She laughed again and nestled against him, gently kissing the top of his pectoral muscle where it met his collarbone. "Love this part," she said. Then she sat back, her face suddenly serious.

"What's wrong? You're not awake and staring at me because I'm some kind of vision."

"Actually," he said, "you are kind of hot."

She rolled her eyes. "Whatever. What's going on?"

"I keep thinking about Morelli," he said.

"I knew it," she said, looking down at the sheets.

"It's not right," he said. "She wasn't in a fit mental state to make the call to volunteer."

Grace propped herself up on her fists, anger flashing in her eyes. "Jan, she *ran*. She's legally dead. She's lucky she's not being strapped down to a gurney for lethal injection."

"What if that's what's actually happening? Just more slowly? What if the drug is slowly degrading her brain? What if she's getting cancer?"

"That's not happening, but even if it were, how is that different?"

"I have no problem with someone's facing justice, Grace. I do have a problem with their being used for medical experiments. Especially when it's . . . coerced. We're supposed to be the good guys here."

"You haven't been listening to Crucible," Grace said. "This

is justice. This *is* the law. Everything going on here is authorized."

Harlequin shook his head, reached for words.

She pushed herself out of bed, racing around the bedroom to find the clothing they'd hastily scattered in their eagerness to be with one another, sliding on her panties, grabbing her skirt.

He sat up, marveling at how sexy she was even when racing to get dressed. "I kind of liked you better without all that."

"Shut up," she said. "Get dressed."

He looked at the clock on the wall, the numbers displayed from a recessed projector in the ceiling, expensive and state-of-the-art, like everything she owned. "It's almost ten," he said. "Where are we going?"

"To the lab. We're going to pay Morelli a visit."

"What? Now?"

"Yes, now," she said, pulling on her blouse and buttoning it quickly.

"Grace. What are you . . ."

She spun on him, stabbing with a finger. "I am getting tired of the implication that we're using her as a lab rat. We have *helped* that woman. We have taken someone emotionally disturbed and given her some measure of control over her emotions. Not only is she not getting cancer, she's able to think straight for the first time in her life.

"You seem to have forgotten who I am, Jan. Yes, I've done well for myself. But that is incidental and always has been. It isn't why I do this. So, we're going to visit Morelli right now, and you're going to pay attention this time. This drug is the best chance the world has to put a lid on magic, to make it usable and controllable by everyone. And that's just one possible application. We're doing double duty, both saving someone's life and moving toward that goal. You need to know that, and I mean *really* know it. So, let's go."

He gaped at her sudden outrage. "Grace, it's late . . ."

Her hand flew to her face. When she pulled it away, Harlequin saw a bright trail of blood, slowly working its way from her nostril down to her upper lip. "Damn it."

"You're bleeding," he said.

She dabbed at her nose experimentally. "Oh, yeah. Let me get a tissue."

"Are you okay?"

"Sure. Happens a lot. Too much coke in my early days."

"Ha. Wait. Are you serious?"

"As a heart attack. You don't make it as a junior business analyst on Wall Street if you aren't doing blow with your colleagues. Don't worry, I quit a long time ago. This is the enduring wages of my sin. I'll be right back."

As she left, Harlequin sighed, slid out of the bed, and began fumbling on his pants. The ends didn't justify the means here, and he was right to be bothered by what was going on. But a part of him mourned the loss of the intimate moment, lying in bed with this amazing woman. If only he'd kept his mouth shut, he wouldn't be shrugging on his clothes to go down to the lab. As he buttoned his pants, he felt an urge, and followed Grace to the bathroom.

"Gang way," he said. "I'm willing to go outside in the middle of the night just to let you make a point, but I'll be damned if I'm not going to get to piss firs . . ."

Grace stood frozen, a syringe in her wrist. She quickly pulled it out, hiding it behind her back.

But not before he noticed two things.

First, the syringe was filled with a yellow liquid that looked disturbingly like urine. The white adhesive label had been peeled off, leaving the uneven residue of the backing.

Second, it had been faint, merely the whisper of an echo, but Harlequin had felt something. Anyone else would have dismissed it as a shiver, the games our nerves play with us when we stand up suddenly or twist our backs wrong.

But Harlequin had made his living for the past four years sniffing out rogue magic.

He knew a current when he felt one.

Before he knew what he was doing, he crossed the space between them, grabbed her wrist with one hand, and reached behind her back with the other. She twisted, tried to pull free, her head butting against his chest. She was strong, athletic, but he had at least fifty pounds on her and held her easily, his fingers digging into her palm and raking the syringe out of her hand.

He brought it around and stared at it while she swore at him. "Let me go!"

He did, feeling again for the current. It was gone. "What the fuck is this?" A tiny pool of the fluid remained in the bottom of the syringe. He glanced again at the label, carefully scratched off. It was possible he was mistaken, but this looked exactly like LL-14. 60 CCs. Six times the dose he'd watched Dan inject into Morelli.

"Is this . . ." He'd pay for it later, but for now he was ice-cold rational. The old mantra rose in his mind. *Easy now. Slow is smooth, smooth is fast.* "Is this LL-14?"

Grace opened her mouth, then closed it. She pulled away once more, then gave up.

"Jesus, Grace. You're Latent."

She gave no answer, only stared back toward the bedroom.

Betrayal. Hurt and rage swamped him. He felt his magical tide rise and fought it down. She'd played him for a fool on the night they'd met, and she hadn't stopped playing him since.

"Aren't you?" His voice rose.

"Are you going to kill me?" she asked. Her voice trembled. Grace the CEO, the power broker, the self-made millionaire was gone. This was the voice of a frightened girl.

Just as quickly as it came, the anger fled. In its place was a dull ache, grief for the relationship that now must change, compassion for this woman who must endure it. This beautiful, brilliant woman, who gave him the one safe space he'd ever known since magic had found him.

"No, Grace." His voice was thick. "I'm not going to kill you."

Hicks's voice filled his head, and he felt his knees weaken. *Grace Lyons made her fortune in finance. Why the hell is she suddenly dabbling in pharmaceuticals?*

"You weren't just looking to do good. You came up Latent and searched for a way to hide it. 10 ccs controls it, but 60 ccs makes it undetectable, is that how it works?"

"I *was* trying to do some good, Jan. Manifesting got me thinking about it. The SOC has made it impossible for people to even think about controlling Latency, and Channel's work was my answer to that."

He put his back to the wall and slid down to a sitting position, folding his arms over his knees. "Jesus. Antipsychotic. And I bought it like it was on sale. You fucking lied to me, Grace. You used me and lied to me."

"No, Jan. I didn't. Nothing has changed. Developing Limbic Dampener can still help you, help me, help anyone Latent. Look what it's done for Morelli already!"

"You're a Selfer."

"What does that even mean, Jan? I haven't hurt anyone. I am in complete control of my magic. Hell, you didn't even know I was Latent until ten seconds ago! I am producing a drug that will revolutionize the way you use magic, that will cure mental illness! I'm a productive, contributing, ethical member of society. If that's being a Selfer, then I'm proud to wear that label."

Harlequin sighed, trying to wrap his head around the realization. Failing. All he could concentrate on was the rapid pulse of his heart, each beat alternating thoughts. *Betrayed. Fool. Betrayed. Fool.*

"What would you prefer? That I'd turned myself in? That I'd given up all I'd built so your bosses could hand it over to Entertech? They are your prime magical contractor. Who do you think would develop the drug if not Channel?"

Harlequin shook his head. "And us, Grace? Keep your friends close and your enemies closer, right?"

She knelt in front of him, lifting his chin with a finger. If there was a lie in her eyes, he couldn't see it.

"Never," she whispered. "We're the same, Jan. Neither of us asked for this. Both of us made the tough choice, did what we had to do to keep going, to keep doing good."

"Bullshit," he said. "You could have self-reported. You could have joined up."

"Could I?" She pointed at the towel rack beside the basin. He felt her current now, rising up out of nowhere, tight, disciplined, as controlled as any SOC operator.

The towels began to shrivel, the cotton twisting, turning green, then purple, then black. A sulfur stink filled the room, tickling Harlequin's nose, burning in his throat.

"I never had a chance," Grace said, as the towels turned to black sludge, dripping off the rack to pool on the tile floor. "I never had a choice."

Harlequin could only nod. Because it was true.

Had the towels burned, things would be different, but the SOC didn't take Probes.

Thus always to wolves.

CHAPTER XIV
BIG FISH

Goblinkind is not united in the "Embracer" tribe belief that mankind needs to be brought back to the magical wellspring of its birth. The "Defender" tribes dub humanity as "keach," or "lost." To goblins raised in the Defender faith, humans actually died when they were cut off from the magical wellspring. The human incursion into the Source is nothing less than an invasion of the walking dead. We are zombies to them, and the exploitation of resources and destruction of their people is evidence of the consequences of our being allowed to exist here unchecked. Just as Embracers would give up their lives to save humans, Defenders fight just as hard to destroy us, with ejection from the Source being their ultimate goal. Unfortunately, Defender tribes outnumber Embracer tribes by roughly four to one.

—Simon Truelove
A Sojourn Among the Mattab On Sorrah

The slope off the *Breakwater*'s starboard side steepened, and Bonhomme ordered the bow around to port to keep the ship from heeling over dangerously far. The leviathan continued to match their pace, sides swelling as it pulled in more and more water. The goblins formed a frothing patch behind it, out of the line of fire, ready to pounce on the ship once the giant wave capsized it.

Bookbinder scanned the skies again for incoming helos, saw none. He thought of the *Giffords*'s sailors turning the white waters red. He closed his eyes and shuddered.

Think. There has to be a way out of this. Think. Panic clawed at his mind, clouding his thoughts. He couldn't afford that now. Bonhomme had found a way to use the equipment they had at hand in the last dustup with the goblins; maybe he could do it again now.

"So, we can't outrun it. Which means we have to fight it," Bookbinder said.

Bonhomme started to snort contempt at the idea, then his expression faded to thoughtfulness. "I'm wracking my brain here, sir. Don't see a way."

I don't either. "Well, that OC worked a miracle against the goblins. Flares were a smart idea, too."

"That thing is underwater, sir. There's no way to get the OC to it. We don't have a dive crew even if we had the time"—he looked doubtfully out the bridge window at the increasing grade of the slope—"which we don't."

"Can we shoot it? Maybe if we pour enough rifle rounds into it . . ."

Bonhomme glanced up at Rodriguez.

"That far down? That thing is huge. I don't think we'd be able to kill it quickly enough," the boatswain said.

"Not a lot of time here," Marks said, eyes growing wide.

"What we need," Bonhomme said, pounding a fist on the console, "are damned depth charges."

"Could we rig some of the pyro for that?" Bookbinder asked. "Some way we can waterproof it and chuck it over the side so it blows up down there?"

Rodriguez frowned. "I don't see how, sir. That stuff is all meant to go off in air. Get it wet, and it doesn't work."

The grade of the slope increased, and Marks turned to Bonhomme. "Sir, we've got to accept that we're about to be capsized. Let me get the crew as ready as we can. Let's get folks into PFDs and SAR vests and maybe put some rafts in the water, launch the small boats. Not sure it'll help, but it's something."

"Do it," Bonhomme said, and Marks raced out the hatch and down the ladder.

"We take the wave bow on," Bonhomme said. "If we angle it right, I guess there's a chance we can hold on better than the *Giffords* did. We're a different hull, broader and flatter." The look in his eyes showed he didn't believe it even as he gave the orders to the helmsman, and the bow began to swing around to face the creature.

"Maybe if we get right over it?" Rodriguez suggested.

"So it can blast us into the sky directly from below? That'd be worse," Bonhomme said.

The ship groaned as it came hard to starboard, heeling more deeply into the slope. Bookbinder was impressed with how agilely the buoy tender turned while simultaneously sickened by the steep grade sweeping past them. Out the bridge window, the wire-rope swung off the LOVE ME TENDER's boom, the huge crane groaning as its weight slewed to one side.

Bookbinder's eyes shot wide. "How much does that . . . thing on the end of the crane weigh?"

"What?" Bonhomme asked.

"The ball and hook thingie! The one that's holding the boomer?" Or what was left of the boomer. The oil drum was scorched black, splashed with blood and so full of bullet holes it looked more like a desiccated sponge than anything metal.

"The hook? I don't know. Depends on whether they've got the ball or the sheave block up there. I think it's the ball. It's more than half a ton. Maybe a ton."

"Is there any way we can drop it on that monster? Maybe tip the whole crane over the side? It's not a depth charge, but . . ."

"We can do it," Rodriguez said suddenly, her voice rising.

Bonhomme nodded. "We'll need to be right over the top of it, but if we drop the hoist brake or cut the wire-rope, the ball weighs enough to throw it down. If we extend the jib, it'll drop from sixty feet up. That'd give it some speed. Assuming that thing is as big as a blue whale? Should punch a hole in it. Jesus, that's a crazy idea."

"Well, the sane ones aren't doing us a whole lot of good right now," Bookbinder said.

"Point," Bonhomme said. "Bosun, get that boom extended as high as you possibly can, over the starboard side. Cut it as close as you can to the starboard rail, so the ball just misses us."

"We might be able to load a heavier . . ." Rodriguez began.

"No time for that," Bonhomme cut her off. "Just get it in position."

He turned to the helmsman and called out the commands that would bring the *Breakwater* directly over the leviathan. They had come fully about by now, the helmsman making slight adjustments as the monster grew larger before them. The bow dipped sickeningly far, the ship picking up speed as it slid down the slope.

Bonhomme gripped the console railing. "Shit," he whispered. "Shitshitshitshitshit."

A howl went up from the goblins as they realized the *Breakwater* was charging them. They rushed the ship, the water whipped to a froth around the leviathan's growing form.

Bookbinder heard splashes and saw one of the ship's small jet boats racing off the port bow, two of the precious rifles held by sailors on board. A small pseudopod of white water rippled out toward them, but the vast majority of the creatures swarmed back aboard for the third time, clambering up onto the buoy deck just as Rodriguez raced out of the hatch, making for the crane.

Bookbinder turned to Bonhomme. "Can you keep her on top of that thing?" Bonhomme kept his eye on the compass and continued calling commands to the helmsman, pausing only long enough to shout "Go!"

Bookbinder raced after Rodriguez, finding himself in the same passageway where he'd first stood with the boarding teams. The hatch stood open, Marks outside it, ushering sailors back inside as the first goblins appeared around the crane.

Bookbinder and Rodriguez charged out, waving at them. "Turn around! We've got to get to the crane!"

"What?" Marks asked.

"The crane!" Bookbinder shouted. "Get to the crane!"

Marks turned, leveling his pistol and firing twice into the packed group of goblins. They covered the buoy deck now, outnumbering the sailors at least ten to one, with more climbing aboard every moment.

"Well, shit," Rodriguez said.

"Yup," Bookbinder agreed.

"Charge of the Light Brigade, eh?" Marks asked.

"Something like that," Bookbinder replied.

"Can we do it?" Marks asked.

Bookbinder shrugged. "Only one way to find out."

He gave a yell and charged. Marks, Rodriguez, and the remaining sailors went with him. Guns boomed around him, the nonskid surface of the deck resounded beneath his boots.

He had time to draw his pistol and fire once before sailor and goblin collided and mixed, a writhing mass of blue, blaze orange, and sick sea green. Both sides let out a cry and Bookbinder found himself face-to-face with a thing out of a pirate's nightmare.

The goblin's face was distended into a long, lampreylike mouth, the round maw lined with three rows of triangular, sharp teeth. Its bald head trailed seaweed from a field of barnacle-like growths.

Bookbinder raised his pistol again, but the thing ducked low, catching him in the gut and driving him backward. The tube mouth snuffled at his chest, flexible lips working the teeth against his uniform. He shouted, trying to get a hold on it, hands scrabbling for purchase over the slick surface of its back. At last, he locked his hands over his own wrists and squeezed his arms together. The goblin gasped and he flexed, pressing forward against the monsters behind it. He felt the sharp prick of its small teeth punching through his uniform blouse and scoring the T-shirt beneath. He squeezed harder, and the gasp became a snarl, the bottom of its soft ribs bending under his grasp.

Bookbinder wasn't a strong man, but he was twice the size of a goblin. He shouted and squeezed with everything he had, crushing the goblin into its fellows for added leverage. The monster gave a wet wail as its ribs gave way. Bookbinder released it and kicked it, sending it to flop limply along the deck.

Rodriguez was at his side, hefting an empty shotgun barrel first, shouting incoherently as she laid about her. A goblin leapt over its comrade, reaching for Bookbinder with a saw-edged long knife before Rodriguez brought it down with a heavy stroke to its bulbous skull.

Behind the goblins, the crane hovered, tantalizingly close. The water had turned black to either side of the *Breakwater*'s bow, filled completely with the huge body of the leviathan.

A goblin grabbed Bookbinder's wrist, its fingers a series of sucker-tipped, waving tentacles. His arm burned as it pierced the skin. He turned to claw out its eyes, and found he couldn't find anything resembling a head. Its eyes were directly in the center of its torso, looking at him over a horned beak. He punched it. Punched it again and again. The grip on his wrist only grew stronger and more painful as it yanked his hand toward the beak.

Bookbinder saw Rodriguez's shotgun stock crash into one of the thing's limbs, but it didn't move.

"Gaaaah!" he screamed, yanking his hand away from the sharp-looking beak, tearing the skin against the sharp protrusions in the tentacles that held him fast. The bladed delta of the beak's tip hovered over his hand, his wrist . . .

A sharp crack sounded from over his shoulder and the thing spun away. The tentacles released his wrist, leaving a red, streaming patch that had once been occupied by his watch.

His finger smarted, bleeding from the knuckle. *My ring. I've lost my wedding ring.*

It was a token, a bauble, but grief swept over him, followed closely by rage. *Julie. I'm sorry. I should have taken better care of it.*

Bookbinder looked topside, where one of the bridge windows had either been busted out or opened. Bonhomme leaned through, a smoking rifle in his hands. He turned, taking aim at another goblin. If he was no longer bothering with the helm, that must mean they were right over the leviathan.

Now or never.

Bookbinder stepped on the goblin's corpse and launched himself into the air, landing across three more goblins, punching wildly. He heard a roar as the sailors followed suit. He felt something sharp slice into his face, his thigh. He shut his eyes tight, raw wrist screaming. His fist thumped against flesh once, twice, then banged painfully against metal.

He opened his eyes and found himself face-to-face with the crane operator's control-booth door. He yanked on the door handle and nearly yelled with relief as it swung open, sending him staggering back into Rodriguez, who was screaming, swinging the empty shotgun.

"Bosun!" Bookbinder shouted, grabbing her arm. "I can't work this! Get in there!"

He heaved, swinging her around him and into the open door as a goblin sank a bone club into his stomach, doubling him over. He slouched against the crane's side, winded, listening to the machine's motor roar into life. Marks was at his side, swinging his empty pistol, punching and kicking, buying him precious breathing room to recover. A moment later, the crane swung out over the *Breakwater*'s side, throwing Marks and Bookbinder back into the mass of goblins as another shot from the bridge sent one of the creatures spinning to the deck.

He turned back for Rodriguez, but nausea swamped him, and his vision grayed. Bookbinder had a vague sense of being dragged backward, the crane receding in the distance.

"Wait. We've got to get her out of there," he tried to say. Nothing came out.

With the sailors clear of the crane, Bonhomme opened up with the rifle in three-round bursts. The goblins hissed, cringing.

Bookbinder felt the shadow of the superstructure loom over him as they dragged him backward through the hatch. The nausea subsided, and he struggled to his feet, shrugging off the sailors. "I'm fine! I'm fine!"

But his voice was drowned out by a sudden metallic rasping. The crane's wire-rope began to race along the metal spool, spraying sparks and billowing gray smoke. The rasping became a scream as the heavy ball and hook dropped like a stone.

Goblins swarmed over the crane operator's booth, hammering at the plastic, smashing through with spears and clubs. One jerked back, gurgling, as Rodriguez grabbed a piece of the splintered plastic and drove it into its throat.

At last, the hook and ball splashed into the water and disappeared, the smoke from the wire-rope turning to steam as it abruptly cooled.

The goblins backed off, thrusting spear after spear into the operator's booth's opening. Bookbinder lurched forward, but Marks held him fast. "Don't, sir. There's nothing you can do now."

The goblins stabbed again and again, then turned, satisfied, moving toward the superstructure. Bookbinder strained to see Rodriguez in the operator's booth. He looked around at Marks and the remaining sailors, exhausted and bleeding. Any attempt to go back out there would be overwhelmed, leaving the superstructure open.

"Better get this hatch secured," Bookbinder said, his throat closing with grief.

He slumped as Marks and one of the sailors got the hatch shut and put the dogs in place just as the first goblins threw themselves against it, shouting and banging on the metal surface with spear butts and knives. Shots sounded from the bridge again as Bonhomme reloaded and opened fire.

They were silent for a moment before Marks sighed, "Come on, sir. Let's get up to the bridge and see what we can see."

He stationed one sailor on the hatch, all that could be spared now, and the two of them climbed the ladder, shivering from exhaustion and sadness. They reached the bridge to find Bonhomme pulling himself back inside the window, smoking rifle empty on the deck behind him.

The ship shuddered. The bow jerked suddenly, a huge wave materializing twenty feet past it and rolling slowly forward. The goblins cried out in a single voice. Bookbinder and Marks went to Bonhomme's side in time to see them pointing at the water, shaking with fury, leaping off the deck.

Then the stink hit them. Fetid, deep, and rotten, as if a century's worth of garbage left at the bottom of the ocean had bubbled skyward. "What the fu . . ." Marks began, then went silent.

All around the *Breakwater*'s bow, dark fluid rose to the surface, steaming the disgusting odor into the air. Chunks of something that Bookbinder couldn't identify floated in the midst of it. The dark liquid swirled, viscous and thick, breaking off into separate clouds, fed by funnels of the stuff from the leviathan's shape below.

A shape that was growing smaller as the creature sank, fins and tail thrashing.

"What would you call that?" Bonhomme asked.

"A direct hit," Bookbinder said. *You did it, Bosun.* He tracked the direction of the blooming liquid to the giant monster's front and knew Rodriguez hadn't died for nothing. "Right between the eyes."

CHAPTER XV
REUNION

With the death of their leviathan, the fight went out of the goblins. They made a few more halfhearted attempts as the *Breakwater* limped along on its single engine but seemed unwilling to stray far from the slowly spreading stain on the surface that marked the monster's final resting place. Bonhomme gave the weapons-free order and a few well-placed shots convinced them that they didn't want back on the buoy deck.

Bookbinder looked away as they retrieved Rodriguez from the ruined crane. His last sight had been of her face locked in a determined grimace, hell-bent on saving their lives. He wanted to remember her that way. The sailors seemed to be grateful to be left alone to tend to their own, and Bookbinder was content to leave them that way. *Thanks, Bosun,* he thought, making his way back to the bridge.

As Fort Wadsworth came into view, the dull thudding of rotors sounded, and Bookbinder made out two Blackhawk helicopters growing on the horizon. Their door gunners pumped a few short bursts of fire into the depths off the *Breakwater*'s starboard quarter, and the goblins finally gave up the fight altogether, the churning water finally going still. Bookbinder forced down the anger that rose at their appearance, but Marks gave it voice. "Better late than never."

The helos hovered over the ship. Bookbinder guessed they were trying to radio, but now had a good look at the damaged radar mast. They finally came as low as they could before tossing out a handheld radio wrapped in a poncho liner. Marks ran down to retrieve it, held it to his ear, and returned to the bridge with an arched eyebrow.

"It's for you," he said, handing the radio to Bookbinder.

Bookbinder took it. "General Bookbinder."

"General, this is Chief Warrant Officer Grieves from Incident Command Post Battery Park. I'm glad you're all right. We need to take you back to Manhattan."

"I'm fine, but we've got dead and wounded on board. This ship is in a bad way."

"Drop anchor where you are. We'll load up the whole crew and take them in. We can use the help."

"No way," Bonhomme said. "This is my ship. I'm not scuttling her, and I'm not abandoning her."

Bookbinder relayed this to the helo. Grieves's response was doubtful. "You sure you can make it? You look . . . beat up from here."

Bonhomme's eyes flashed. "It's not even a mile from the pier. I can get her in."

"Negative. No liftoff needed, they'll get in on their own power," Bookbinder translated. He turned to Bonhomme. "It's fine, skipper. You take your ship home."

"I'm sorry, I . . ."

Bookbinder couldn't bear to hear it. He remembered cowering before the bullying commander of FOB Frontier, Colonel Taylor, as the man's spit flew across the bridge of his nose. He hadn't been equal to the task, unable to stand up when he needed to.

Until, suddenly, he had.

Bonhomme's course was different, but too similar for Bookbinder to hold any grudge for his initial panic. He'd rallied. Bookbinder would have gone to pieces trying to hold FOB Frontier together if it hadn't been for Crucible, rock-steady at his side. *I guess we all have our Crucibles. I was Bonhomme's.*

"All right," Grieves said. "They can head in, but you need to come right now, sir."

Bookbinder hesitated a moment. A part of him rebelled against leaving the *Breakwater* after all they'd been through, but the real fight was on the island. Manhattan by helo was closer and faster than Staten Island on this limping ship.

He turned to Bonhomme and Marks. "Gentlemen."

Bonhomme stared, Marks inclined his head. "We'll get back, then we'll get in the fight."

"I've got a feeling that's where I'll be," Bookbinder said. "See you soon."

Bonhomme insisted on caring for his own, but the crew carefully wrapped Ripple's corpse in blankets, hoisting it up after Bookbinder. He stared at the rumpled cloth in the bottom of the helo cabin as they headed inland, the *Breakwater* slowly dwindling to a speck below them.

The two helicopters encountered no resistance as they covered the rest of the distance to Manhattan's southern tip, where one broke off to make for the northern barricades while the other descended slowly over Castle Clinton.

Bookbinder looked out of the open cabin. The park below was still burning in patches, strewn with rubble and fragments of smoking metal. Corpses were neatly stacked in a pile outnumbering the living. The survivors were near corpses themselves, filthy, ragged, and exhausted. Dead vermin were scattered everywhere, pigeons and rats mostly. Two soldiers were straining with entrenching tools, shoveling them into a pile that was already so high it threatened to topple over on them.

My God. What the hell happened here?

The Blackhawk touched down, and Bookbinder cradled Ripple's corpse in his arms. No sooner had he stepped out than the defenders began to load up the open cabin space with wounded and a few civilians. They moved mechanically, eyes hollow, paying no attention to the star on his uniform, too tired to notice or care.

Bookbinder laid Ripple gently on the ground, then tapped an airman on the shoulder. The man's rank had been lost when his sleeve burned away. The arm beneath was covered with bandages already stained yellow and red from the wound beneath.

The airman looked up at him, blinked. Then his eyes fell

across the star and he slowly dragged his hand up in a salute. "Sorry, General."

Bookbinder returned the salute, realized he was uncovered. He'd lost his patrol cap somewhere during the fighting on the *Breakwater*. Too tired to care, he waved the salute off. "I think we're past protocol for now, son. What's going on?"

The airman gestured toward the castle interior. "Colonel Thorsson can explain everything, sir. You bringing help?"

They look like they could use it.

"Sure, I am." The lie turned his stomach, but he couldn't bring himself to tell the truth. Not to this exhausted kid. "Help's on the way."

The airman nodded and stumbled off, shuffling like the walking dead.

Bookbinder made his way to the castle entrance. Two bulletproof barriers stood to either side, signs of a guard post that had once been set up here though it wasn't manned now.

Inside, soldiers worked in silence, triaging wounded, dispensing ammunition, all with the same hollow desperation Bookbinder had seen in the airman's eyes.

Lieutenant Colonel Thorsson leaned over a map sketched in charcoal pencil on butcher paper, talking in hushed tones with a young captain. Harlequin looked up as Bookbinder walked in, his expression igniting.

He reached Bookbinder in two strides and shook his hand hard enough to sprain his wrist. "Oh, thank God. Thank fucking God. It's so good to see you, sir."

Bookbinder gently pushed him back, nodded to the captain, who grinned despite a bloody bandage indicating the loss of an eye.

"Good to see you, too, Colonel. I would have come sooner, but we had goblin trouble out on the water."

"There's goblin trouble everywhere, sir. Our problem is the mountain gods. We need something that can hurt them."

"The SOC can hurt them."

"The SOC's pinned down, sir. Mescalero."

"Mescalero . . . ?" Bookbinder began.

"It's right on top of our nuclear arsenal at White Sands," the captain said. "We can't afford to lose control over that Breach."

Bookbinder shook his head. "Jesus."

"We were short on magical support to begin with. Working mostly off training Covens here, and few enough of them as it is. We just got hit again, and hard."

Bookbinder remembered the court of Ajathashatru the Fifth. The Naga Raja had kept him virtually imprisoned there in the hopes of using his power to imbue the naga arsenal with magic.

"Magic bullets. You need me to make magic bullets."

"Can you do that for us, sir? Our only other option is to reach out to some Selfer gangs in theater. I was just talking to Captain Cormack about doing that. With you here, we won't have to."

Bookbinder had always put his duty first, but he didn't have a star on his chest for no reason. If there was a time to use his rank, it was now. "First, I've got someone I need to bury."

"Respectfully, sir, we've got plenty of people to bury."

"Then let's do right by all of them. We can't fight standing knee-deep in our own dead." He took in Harlequin's shadowed eyes, his matted, bloody scalp. "Let's take a minute to lick our wounds. Then we can get back in the fight."

At Harlequin's request, Drake magicked a tomb for Hewitt's remains in the concrete foundation of the castle. There was little left to bury, but Harlequin had insisted. The Novice had even raised Hewitt's name in stone letters over the spot. "He fought like a lion to hold this ground," Harlequin said. "He shouldn't give it up now."

Drake also opened a hole big enough for a mass grave. The Novice seemed eager for the chance to do something, looked gratefully at Bookbinder when he'd given him the detail. He took him aside as the bodies were laid in the pit as gently as could be, which, given so many corpses and so few hands to do the work, wasn't very gentle at all.

"Listen, Novice. I've got someone . . . important to me." He pointed at Ripple's corpse, a tiny shape under the blanket. "I want you to take care of that one for me. Put her apart, deeper down. Do it right."

Drake's jaw set. His eyes focused, and Bookbinder knew he'd made the right call. "What'd she do, sir?"

"She saved my life," Bookbinder said. "I want a grave I can visit."

Drake nodded and set off. Bookbinder finally let himself return to Castle Clinton, where he slumped in a folding chair, sipping on bottled water. He let his head loll forward, eyes half-closing. His uniform was still striped with sweat and long ochre streaks that could have been older blood or might have been rust from the *Breakwater*. White patches bloomed across the fabric. *Salt.* He smiled inwardly. *I'm a real sailor now.*

He looked up. Harlequin had come into the room and sat down across from him, though he was too tired to notice when. He raised his head with an effort. Harlequin's eyes were half-shut, with bruised-looking half-moons beneath them. *When was the last time he slept?* Bookbinder wondered. *My God, that's what I look like, isn't it?*

"You okay?" Bookbinder asked.

Harlequin didn't bother to look up, reveling in the rest that came from simply allowing his neck to take the weight of his head. He half shrugged. "Picking 'em up and putting 'em down, sir."

Bookbinder floated on his fatigue, stared off into the middle distance.

"You know, Gatanas said I was supposed to surrender command to you once you arrived," Harlequin said.

Bookbinder snorted. "Hell, no. You've got things as well in hand as they can be."

Silence followed, then he laughed, a short bark.

"What?" Harlequin asked.

"It's just that, when we were at the FOB, the only thing I really wanted in life was to be a real dyed-in-the-wool commander. Now I'm doing it, and I can't think of anything I want less."

Harlequin nodded. "You got back with your family?"

"I'm in the doghouse with Julie," Bookbinder said. "Maybe if we win this thing and get medals from the president on TV, she'll get over it."

"In the doghouse?" Harlequin raised an eyebrow.

"She's . . . distant. I guess you're away from a person for a really long time, then when I got back, they wouldn't let me see her. Between the tests and the questioning, I never really came home. All that time, she's hearing from the news and the other officers' wives that I'm some kind of traitor. That can put cracks in a person."

"Or make her draw closer to you. That's what should happen."

Bookbinder shook his head. "We took up with one another in high school. She waited for me through academy, through every tour since. The Army was my life, same as yours. We've lived on or near a post since she was seventeen. All her friends are service. Everywhere we go. Everything we do. Did."

Harlequin's face was a mix of surprise and sympathy.

"Ah, never mind," Bookbinder said. "She'll come around."

He didn't know that, but somehow, saying it helped him believe it. "Once we beat this thing, that'll make everything right, right?"

Harlequin snorted. "Most definitely, sir."

"Don't get married."

"No danger of that."

"You got someone waiting for you?"

Harlequin was silent for a long time. "There was somebody. It didn't work out."

"Happens to all of us. You move on."

"I never did, I guess."

"You're a young man. Good-looking. You've been all over TV. I figured you'd have taken up with some vapid, music-video starlet. Hell, if things don't work out with Julie, I am most definitely sowing my oats again for a while."

Harlequin didn't answer, and Bookbinder realized with a start that his back had gone stiff and his expression blank.

"Ah, hell. I'm sorry. I didn't mean anything."

"It's all right, sir," Harlequin said. "It's just that we've got a lot of work to do."

"Of course. Let's get to it." They walked out of Castle Clinton and headed toward the barricade wall, saying no more of it, but Bookbinder's mind churned. *What happened to him?*

"I'm SOC, aren't I?" Bookbinder asked, trying to regain the friendly course of the conversation.

Harlequin arched an eyebrow, tapped one finger against the

SOC patch Velcroed to Bookbinder's sleeve, filthy and peeling off at one corner. "Says so right there."

"You guys all get call signs, don't you?"

Harlequin shrugged. "Sooner or later, yeah."

"What the hell am I? Chopped liver? Are you guys waiting for me to make O-8 before you give me mine?" Bookbinder looked down at his blank lapel. "I don't even have a school pin."

Harlequin broke out in a broad grin. "They don't have a name for your school, sir."

"How is this my fault? I'm pulling rank here. I'm a goddamn general. Fix this."

Harlequin smiled wider, then went thoughtful. He fished in a cargo pocket, then yanked off a bit of loose thread from his uniform. "With your permission, sir," he said, sticking the frayed string to a bare patch of Velcro where Bookbinder's rank had begun to peel off. "There's your pin, sir. I hereby christen you 'Binder.'"

Bookbinder looked down at the string. "What's this?"

"You know, like a rope. For binding things."

Bookbinder blinked.

"What?" Harlequin asked. "It fits. And it'll be easier for everyone to remember."

"Binder," Bookbinder said, trying out the name. He covered the BOOK in his name tape with a finger. "Binder. That works. I like it."

They had barely reconstituted the perimeter when the enemy came on again.

Harlequin, Bookbinder, and Cormack took up positions in one of the jury-rigged observation towers nestled up against the concrete barricades. The *Gahe* were bolder now, slivers of black mixed in with the field of brown and green that marked the giants and goblins. Small pockets formed around them as the goblins gave them a wide berth, pushed off by the cold.

Shooters in the towers kept the rocs off while the last Fornax Aeromancer hovered above the barricade wall, sending blasts of lightning out whenever the *Gahe* moved forward. One of two remaining Kiowas patrolled the perimeter, fireballs streaking out as the Pyromancer inside did his work. The *Gahe* kept their distance, stutter-flashing back from each flame strike, but where one fell back, another two came forward. The Aeromancer lighted on the barricade wall long enough to guzzle a bottle of water. She bent over, hands on her knees, panted. Two *Gahe* raced for the concrete barriers, flashing against them, long, thin fingers prying at the seams between the T-walls. Where their hands touched, the concrete rimed over with dirty frost. A shout from the soldiers, and the Aeromancer jumped into the sky again, showering them with lightning, driving them back, only to dive back herself as a wyvern swooped in and nipped at her before being chased away by bursts of fire from the towers.

"You weren't kidding," Bookbinder said.

Harlequin nodded. "You arrived just in time. I don't know how long we can keep this up. They're exhausted."

"Everybody's exhausted."

Harlequin shrugged. "You sure you can do this from here?"

Bookbinder nodded and waved at the helo as it made its next loop around the barricades. The Pyromancer shifted to the cabin's edge, boots on the skid.

"You sure you want me to do this, sir?" The Pyromancer's voice came over the radio.

"I want you to hurry the hell up about it," Harlequin said, reaching forward and sending a blast of lightning down at another *Gahe*.

Bookbinder watched as the young man pulsed fire along his arm, then pointed down at the tower. Harlequin tossed Bookbinder a magazine of 5.56mm rounds. Bookbinder caught it, rotated the magazine, pointed it out toward the enemy.

"What are you doing?" Harlequin asked.

"I'm about to Bind Fire Magic into a piece of metal just a couple of millimeters away from an explosive charge. If these puppies go off, I'd rather not be in the way. That okay with you?"

Harlequin smiled, and Bookbinder reached out with his current, feeling for the Pyromancer's as he Bound the magic and sent the flame roaring down to them. His current interlaced with the Fire Magic and drew it off, weak and halting. The Novice was frightened he would hurt them, holding back.

"Come on! Pick it up!" Bookbinder shouted up at the helo.

The Novice nodded, and the strength of the current rose, the flame jet thickening. He heard Harlequin curse and leap out of the tower, probably to drive off more of the *Gahe*, but ignored it, focusing on hauling the Pyromancer's magic in until the magic roared in his veins. He turned the current, funneling it into the tips of the bullets, sighing in relief as the doubled flow poured out of him.

The magazine grew hot, and he cursed, tossing it in the air and catching it again with his hand shielded by a dirty sleeve cuff. The heat was concentrated to one side of the magazine. That was good. It was the most precise Binding he'd done so far, the bullet tips containing the magic, keeping it clear from the powder behind.

"Get back in the fight!" he shouted to the Pyromancer. The young man saluted, and the helo spun away, as Harlequin alighted back on the tower platform. "Jesus. They're everywhere."

Cormack held a rifle out to Bookbinder, magazine well toward him. "That looks hot, sir. You better get it loaded."

Bookbinder rammed the magazine home and Cormack rested one elbow on the concrete of the barricade, where the tower abutted it, sighting down the rifle and keeping his hand well clear of the hot metal. "This is hot as hell, sir. Hope it doesn't foul the weapon."

"Just hope it works," Harlequin said.

"It will," Bookbinder said. "At least, it did with ice-bullets back in the Source."

"Here goes." Cormack sighted on one of the *Gahe* and fired. The muzzle flash extended, and the round streaked orange flame as it left the barrel. It took the mountain god in the chest, the liquid black surface suddenly glowing with an expanding ball of bright fire. The *Gahe* shrieked and flashed backward, black smoke billowing from the wound, the flames doused by the creature's freezing blood.

But it was still wounded, and badly. Its shrieks dropped to a whine. Freezing black smoke turned the ground hard, sending the goblins scattering.

Harlequin smiled. Cormack gave a brief shout of triumph. "That'll do it, sir. Let's get you to the ammo dump. We're going to need a lot of this stuff."

"All right," Bookbinder said. "You want to call that Pyromancer back in?"

Harlequin shook his head. "I didn't like the way that last transition went. Those things bleed cold, too, might limit the effectiveness of Pyromantic rounds.

"I'll come with you. Let's try it with lightning."

INTERLUDE VII
THUS ALWAYS TO WOLVES

People ask me, after I came up Latent, how I could still believe in God. Every time I look into the eyes of someone I know is walking around because of my magic, I think, how could I not?

—Captain Seraph
SOC liaison, Third Medical Battallion
United States Marine Corps

SIX YEARS EARLIER

"Do it," Harlequin said.

"What if I screw it up?" Grace asked. They stood in the center of her living room, dark-stained hardwood flooring covered with pools of slime and dustings of desiccated metal.

"You said you had it under control." Harlequin resisted the urge to scratch at the grease paint covering his chest. "Do you?"

"You know that I do. But . . . even people with control screw up sometimes."

"Control means real control. I can manipulate a single molecule in a single breath of air. You should be able to rot off this paint without touching my skin."

She sucked in her breath. "What if I hurt you?"

"Are we in this together or aren't we?"

She stared, chewed on her lip.

"We're sharing this risk, Grace. So let's share it."

"I've never hurt anyone with it. It's never slipped past me."

"Great. Then you won't hurt me. Now, enough of the jaw jacking. Let's get this done."

She stood another moment, still worrying her lower lip, arms folded across her chest. She looked so different out of the power suit. In her jeans and white tank top, she looked almost . . . normal. Sharing the secret only made him feel closer to her. No wonder she'd been so familiar, so at ease when they'd first met. She understood what it meant to be Latent.

Most people would have panicked. They would have run, or lashed out. Harmed others, gotten themselves killed.

But this was Grace.

The more he thought about the lengths she'd gone to to find a way, to not give up, to bend what most would see as a disaster into an opportunity, the more it impressed him. She was an amazing woman. Singular.

The kind he could spend his life with.

That was worth the risk.

"Do it," he repeated.

He felt Grace's current rise, coalesce out of nothing. The high concentration of Dampener gave her such complete control that the current was invisible until she called it. She should have the precision she needed.

Still, he couldn't keep from flinching as she Bound the magic to the thin layer of paint on his chest. He felt a tingling, gathered his own current, ready to Suppress hers if she began to harm him.

A moment later, the paint began to crinkle, peeling off in layers and crumbling to dry dust that settled on his boots. His chest hair went next, turning slick, then dripping down his stomach, the now-familiar smell of rot wafting into the room.

"Hey!" he said. "I was using those!"

She laughed, shunting the magic back. "Not too bad."

"Not bad at all," he agreed, "though you still need to tweak it a bit, spare my chest hair."

"That was on purpose. I like you smooth."

He laughed at that, his blood racing with the nearness of her. That they shared magic only intensified the feeling. He grabbed her around the waist, one hand cupping one tight buttock. "I bet you do."

He kissed her hard, and she jumped up, locking her legs around his hips and carrying him back a step.

At last they came up for air, and he floated for a moment before opening his eyes.

And saw another runnel of blood, dripping from her nose.
"Again?" he asked, putting her down.
"It happens a lot, I told you."
"Grace . . ."
"It's not the drug, Jan."
"How can you be sure?"
"Because Weiss is the foremost pharmaceutical mind in the
country, because my lab is staffed with the brightest bioengi-
neers that money can buy. Because they have an unlimited
budget for equipment and supplies. Because we have been testing this compound for years in a variety of doses, hosts, and
environments, and we have never, ever, ever seen nosebleeds
as a side effect. I know it makes you uncomfortable, but this
really is the function of too much blow in my misspent youth.
Just suck it up, okay?"

He opened his mouth to say more, but the alarm on her watch
chimed, warning her it was time to refresh her dose, and she
stooped to the compartment below her sink where she kept her
syringes. He watched as she pumped the Dampener into her wrist.

Morelli sprawled on one of the leather couches in the lab's
break room, playing a video game on a tablet computer. Harlequin and Grace walked past two of Channel's security guards
on the way in, but Rampart was nowhere to be seen. Dan stood
against the wall, arms folded, a smug smile on his bearded
face.

Morelli looked up and waved. She wore a comfortable-
looking sweatshirt and pants, the corporation's logo emblazoned across her chest. Her gray-streaked hair was clean and
drawn back into a ponytail. She looked heavier, better rested.
The couch was covered with a light dusting of crumbs, and a
small table was set with the remains of a meal. "You two are
up late," she said.

Harlequin felt her current from across the room. It lacked
the disciplined feeling of a trained SOC operator's, was nowhere
near Grace's, but it was firmly in control.

Harlequin stared in silence, in awe of the dramatic difference between the woman before him and the one he'd first
taken down.

"How are you doing?" Grace asked.

Morelli shrugged. "Pretty good, they're feeding me well."
She picked up a small dish of custard off the table and pointed
at it. Harlequin could feel her magic Drawing and resisted the
urge to Suppress her. The magical pulse felt erratic at first, but
after a moment it buttoned down, and a short blue cone of
flame stretched out from her fingertip. She smiled and waved
it back and forth across the bowl until the surface crystallized,
tinted a light golden brown.

She looked up at them, smiling. "Crème brûlée; I used to
be a hell of a cook."

Harlequin stared, glanced up at Grace long enough to see
that she was watching him rather than Morelli. "Where's Rampart?" he asked.

"He's here, sir," came the chief warrant officer's voice as he
came in behind them. "Sorry. I was in the latrine."

Harlequin turned, folding his arms over his chest. "Leaving her unsupervised?"

Rampart looked surprised. "Crucible authorized it days
ago, sir. She's got it locked down. I haven't had to Suppress her
since you brought her here."

Now it was Harlequin's turn to look surprised. He turned
back to Grace, whose look of anger had melted into smugness.

"Your control is that good, huh?" he asked Morelli.

"Not really," she said. "I've still got a ways to go, but Crucible says they're going to transfer me soon."

"To where?" Harlequin asked. The only thing he could
think of was Quantico, and to the best of his knowledge, they
didn't train Selfers there. He remembered Crucible's words.
*Understanding and controlling magic is one of the biggest pri-
orities on the national defense agenda. Do you think we're just
going to let hordes of legally dead Latent people rot in prison?
Or kill them?*

Obviously not.

*Maybe you can go to Crucible, talk to him about Grace.
Maybe she could be . . . repurposed.* The thought sent his
stomach into a nosedive. He wasn't sure how his boss would
react. And unless he was absolutely sure, the risk was just too
great.

Morelli shrugged. "Someplace nice, I'm sure. Watch this."

She Drew and Bound her magic, and a napkin beside the plate burst into flame. The orange peaks narrowed into a pencil-thin funnel, arcing upward and outward, scrolling through the air over the plate until they formed a crude cursive M. After a moment, the fuel was spent in a puff of smoke and a brief sprinkling of black ash. "Isn't that cool?" she asked. "I just figured it out yesterday."

"How are you feeling?" Grace asked.

"Great," Morelli said. "I even got to talk to my kids on video-chat." She tapped the tablet computer. "They think I'm in the hospital."

Grace coughed and clapped a hand to her face, taking a step backward. Dan came to her side. "Is everything all right?"

"Fine," Grace answered, pulling a tissue from her pocket. "Nosebleed. I get them all the time."

Dan's eyes narrowed, but he nodded. "Maybe go put some ice on it."

"Yeah, that's it," Grace said, heading for the exit.

Harlequin went to join her, then paused at the doorway.

"Can I ask you something, Morelli?" Harlequin asked. "Do you remember when we first met? In the Bronx? When I brought you . . . in?"

The smile faltered, and Harlequin felt her flow spike briefly, but only just. "I remember."

"What was going on then, Morelli? You knew what the law was, right? You knew you could call us when you came up Latent?"

Her forehead crinkled as she thought it over. Her current remained steady. "Yeah," she said slowly. "I knew that."

"Why didn't you call us? Did you think we wouldn't help you?"

"Nah," she said. "I knew you would. I knew you'd put me in the SOC or whatever."

"So, why didn't you call? Why'd you burn that building?"

She thought longer, her face going slack, the closest he'd seen to a return to how she'd looked when they'd first brought her in. At last, she jerked her shoulders up and smiled. "I was crazy," she said.

She tapped the fading bruise of the injection site on the inside of her arm. "I'm better now."

CHAPTER XVI
CALL TO ARMS

Forcing children into military service has been the hallmark of failed states around the world, and a tragedy that the UN and a slew of NGOs has worked tirelessly to combat. In the Ivory Coast, Uganda, Rwanda, Kurdistan, the cry of outrage is heard at each new report of children forced to go to war. Except in the United States. Here, Latent children are routinely indoctrinated into the SOC in the name of national security, and the voices of outrage are suddenly silent, quietly grateful that someone is dealing with the problem.

—Jill Vasconez
Human Rights Watch

Harlequin and Bookbinder double-timed it back to the ready room at Castle Clinton.

"Got a few cans of 7.62mm rounds under my desk," Harlequin said. "Let's start with those, then we can tour the ammo dumps after that."

"Why not?" Bookbinder asked, as they stepped into the ready room.

And froze.

The normally bustling room was completely still. The servicemen and women stood, eyes wide, gaping at screens that normally showed the park's perimeter, locations of supply dumps and troops, red triangles indicating where the enemy was attacking in the greatest force.

They now showed the news, an orange-and-blue banner reading—BREAKING: LIVE beneath it.

They were dominated by a single face. Dark, wise eyes

were surrounded by skin as pale as it was smooth. Jet-black hair ended at sharp points along the jawline. The full lips were set in a smile at one corner, as if the speaker were enjoying a private joke.

Scylla had abandoned her leather armor. Her skin tone was even, still creamy white, but showing well under the camera's scrutiny. Since Harlequin's appointment as Special Advisor to the Reawakening Commission, he'd been the SOC's public face, and that meant lots of time on television. He was no stranger to the tricks of the trade. He could tell a professional had been at work here.

Scylla wore a black suit, fashionable, reasonable, and probably looted from one of the upscale boutiques that her army had ransacked. A simple strand of pearls adorned her neck, matching studs in her ears. She looked presentable, professional.

Like a politician.

The sight evoked the Grace he had known—brilliant, hopeful, refusing to be locked down by the small minds around her. God, she was so beautiful. Looking at her made his stomach hurt. Harlequin could almost imagine that she was still Grace, that nothing had changed. That she should be reasoned with.

But then she spoke.

". . . greatest regret over the devastation wrought by the airborne attack against the Trump Building. It was an unnecessary loss of life that underscores the carelessness with which this nation's military has always handled its responsibilities."

In the lower-left-hand corner of the screen, a YouTube video clip ran on a constant loop, showing A-10s peeling off and the bronze finial atop the spire of the Trump Building slewing to one side, hanging for a moment, then finally crashing down in a cloud of sparks and smoke.

Scylla gestured to the clip. "Apparently we're not the only ones responsible for damage to this city. The free tribes of the Source do not fly attack aircraft.

"I'm not surprised, of course, and neither should you be. This administration has already shown itself to be interested in just one thing: perpetuating its own power. That's why we're here—because if we let the new president go on doing exactly what the old one did, and he will, then the next thing he'll conquer is the Source. The Native American tribes of the Home Plane have already experienced the American insatiable thirst for conquest, and that's why they're fighting, too, along with their indigenous brothers and sisters who have crossed into this plane to make sure that what happened to the Apache never happens to them."

The YouTube clip shifted to battle scenes from the Mescalero reservation. Giants and goblins surged around a core of *Gahe*, trading magical and conventional fire with barricades manned by uniformed soldiers. The magical fighting seemed to be more intense here, with bursts of lightning and flame lighting up the desert landscape. *That's because the SOC is there,* Harlequin thought. There were far less *Gahe* to be seen, but they were more than made up for by squads of Apache Selfers. Many of them were painted to mimic their mountain gods, skins pitch-black, horned and grinning masks over their faces. The non-Latent Apache moved with them, firing rifles, far more accurate and disciplined than any goblin.

"So, I'm speaking directly to the so-called Selfers of the United States. Is your experience really so different from what the Apache suffered when the West was supposedly won? Humans cannot stand one simple fact: that Latent people have a power over which humans have no control. The two Gate-Gate incidents have shown us something more, as did my time imprisoned at the now-no-longer-secret base in the Source: The government has no intention of making magic 'safe.' They have every intention of gaining control over it. They don't want to protect anyone; they want to empower themselves, and they want to do it on your backs.

"The SOC maintains control via a drug known as Limbic Dampener, which helps control the emotional center of the brain, which conducts magic. If this drug were freely distributed, all would have control over their magic, and there would be no need for the McGauer-Linden Act. But they will never distribute it. Because their contractor, Entertech, has made so much money off its production that they can afford to buy every politician on the Armed Services Committee.

"I know. I invented the drug. When I wouldn't sell it to the SOC, they threw me in a hole to rot. These are the people who rule you. They could end the crisis tomorrow, but money and power are too important to them."

Bookbinder shook his head, looking at Harlequin. "That bitch! Do you believe this cra . . ."

But Harlequin stared at the screen, biting back tears.

"It's true, sir," he said. "It's all true." *Oh, Grace. I lost you.*

"Your government would have you believe we are an invading army," Scylla went on. "What we are is an instrument of liberation. The United States of America ceased to be a free country the moment the McGauer-Linden Act was signed into law. Apartheid is apartheid, even when the class it seeks to oppress is a powerful one. To all the so-called Selfers watching, I say this: Against the might of the US military, you don't have a fighting chance. But banded together, we can throw down this traitorous regime and take our rightful place as free people, lords of our own bodies and minds. Together, we can be free at long last. Anyone watching the news this past week cannot fail to find us. You know where we are, and we welcome you. The so-called Breach Zone is just the beginning. It forms the kernel of a new society built on the ashes of the old. This country was founded on a fight for freedom. It was Thomas Jefferson who reminded us that 'The tree of Liberty needs to be watered from time to time with the blood of patriots and tyrants.' Now is the time to water. The time to sow comes after, and we will all reap the final reward together. Come, fight. And at long last, be free."

The screen flashed away from Scylla to split images of the action unfolding in both Mescalero and New York City. "This isn't what we want," her voice continued. "We have four demands. Once met, the fighting can cease, and there need be no more unnecessary bloodshed. The process of rebuilding can begin.

"First, the Mountain Gods of the Apache will be reunited with their children in a sovereign territory that encompasses all the land of the Mescalero, Fort McDowell, Jicarilla, San Carlos, Fort Apache, and Camp Verde reservations, as well as designated connecting corridors between them. There are other land disputes that will need to be arbitrated, but that can be ironed out after the immediate withdrawal of all armed human forces from these lands.

"Second, the five boroughs of New York City are declared a sovereign state safe for Latentkind. Magic-using persons from anywhere in the world will be welcome here, granted immediate citizenship. The Statue of Liberty will once again be a symbol of a place where the oppressed and harried can at last find rest, can build a new home where they are free to be what they truly are. In this land, our Arcania, magic will be recognized for the thing it is, a genetic evolutionary trait. We will build a new world, far better than the old, no longer prisoners of the limitations of technology and the fears of those who are chained to it.

"Third, the humans will recognize that the Source is a sovereign realm already inhabited by an indigenous people. This is not some backward land to be exploited for its positional advantage and natural resources. The so-called goblin tribes will send ambassadors to negotiate future exchanges and travel on both planes, but no human will ever set foot there again without first receiving explicit authorization from the tribe whose lands they enter. You did what you did to the indigenous population of this country a long time ago, when a technology gap gave you advantages they could not possibly counter. But now, thanks to magic, the playing field is level, and your heavy hand will no longer be tolerated.

"And last, you dissolve the Entertech Corporation, opening the stores of Limbic Dampener to all, free of charge. In the new state of Arcania, production will begin anew, and never again will Latent people Manifest out of control, fueling the profiteers' arguments that magic is dangerous, that we need the protection they provide for a generous fee."

The screen returned to Scylla, panning back to show her full body, the business suit rounded out by a shiny pair of black leather pumps. Harlequin bit down, but the sight of her still tore at him.

Two people stood beside her, also in suits though looking far less natural in them. One was a man with tattoos on his neck and face, scrawling script that Bookbinder couldn't read. He looked shoehorned into his clothing, thick neck resisting the trim collar of his expensive shirt. His hands were clasped in front of his belt buckle, smoldering gently, flames flickering up between the knuckles.

The other was a woman, her clothing invisible beneath a suit of armor, formed from overlapping plates of ice. It looked impressive, but Harlequin knew it was still ice. It would probably crack if she tried to move. Just the sort of useless drama that Selfers were known for.

Two goblins stood beside them, wearing beaded leather robes sewn with bronze discs. Their faces were covered with fields of white-painted dots. They looked noble, scrubbed clean, heads back and eyes haughty. There were no *Gahe* in the frame. He was sure that was deliberate.

"Make no mistake," Scylla said. "We will win this. This is what you have been waiting for all your Latent lives.

"Join us and fight for it."

The screen cut away to a news desk, where two analysts began discussing the clip while a cutaway at the top of the screen repeated it.

The room stood in silence.

"Every time I think we're digging out of the hole," Harlequin muttered, "we go right fucking back in it." He looked up at Bookbinder. "Those magic bullets aren't going to go nearly as far now. Ah, hell. I should have seen this coming."

Cormack shrugged. "It's not that bad. How many Selfers are there? And they're spread across the country and on the run mostly, right?"

Harlequin shook his head. "Have you ever heard of the Houston Street Selfer Gang?"

Cormack nodded. "Sure, everyone has. But you guys smashed them right before Gate-Gate round two."

"It took us years to get inside that organization," Harlequin said, "and the asset we used to take them down is long gone. They had steady funding streams and a network of tunnels underneath the city that the NYPD and the SOC combined couldn't take apart. They had safe houses aboveground, there's no shortage of sympathizers for Selfers on the run in this country, Captain. And now they're hunkered down in Tribeca, doing a better job than we are at keeping the *Gahe* out. The *Limpiados* are in Chinatown. I'll bet my right arm both are watching this news show right now. And there'll be others, from farther afield."

"This is New York, it's the capital of the world," Cormack said.

"I wish that were true," Harlequin answered, "but I've been in the Selfer-hunting business for a while now. There's the Haudenosaunee Nation in Buffalo. There's the Storm Lords in Charleston. There's the Bruja Bloods and the Suicide Girls in Maryland. And that's just the crews I know who are close to this city. You range farther afield, and you get more. In the past, we were able to keep more on top of them, but with the whole SOC siphoned off between Mescalero and here, that's probably not the case. It's only a five-hour flight from the West Coast to here, and even a lousy Aeromancer can match speeds with a jumbo jet."

Harlequin looked over at Bookbinder. Bookbinder remembered the stress test the SOC had given him at LSA Portcullis. He remembered being ripped from his family, remembered feeling his life adrift, powerless, at the whim of a bureaucracy who had no real interest in his welfare.

And he was one of the lucky ones, inside the system. *It's okay, sir,* Talon had said. *You reported yourself. It's fine.*

"She's a very charismatic woman," Bookbinder said. "She makes a compelling argument."

"She's also lying," Harlequin said, his voice thick. "I know Scylla. She's fucking crazy, and she's not interested in any free republic. She's interested in killing people."

"That won't matter," Bookbinder said.

"You tell me, sir. Think about it. If you were a Selfer on the run, with nowhere to go and no chance of amnesty, what would you do?"

Bookbinder frowned, thinking. Harlequin silently hoped he'd say something that would encourage them, knew he wouldn't. "I'd join her," Bookbinder said finally. "I'd join her and fucking kill you."

Harlequin nodded. "You're goddamn right you would. This is fourth-generation warfare at its finest. We're about to have a major insurgency on our hands. And these won't be tiny goblins or giants and rocs possessed of animal intelligence. These will be Latent *people*. Thinkers, planners, able to use guns and cast spells. They'll be as much of a problem as the *Gahe*, if not worse."

"So what can we do?" Bookbinder asked.

"We can fucking kill them," Cormack said. "We've held out

thus far. Now that we've got your . . . abilities, on our side, sir, we're going to do better."

"We can kill them," Bookbinder agreed, "but I guess it depends on how many come."

"All of them will come," Harlequin said. "I'd bet you the first ones are on their way now. And each and every one we kill will wind up on an Internet video feed that brings more. We're already at our limit. We can't fight our way out of every twist and turn. We need an advantage that sticks."

Bookbinder thought. "Can we offer them amnesty? Some kind of changed legal status?" He didn't look like he believed his own words.

Harlequin confirmed it out loud. "Our government has long since worn out its welcome with Selfers. They'll never trust us."

"So we're screwed," Bookbinder said.

"Maybe not. This is message warfare. We have to counter with a message of our own," Harlequin said. "We can't trust this to Gatanas and the idiots in DC. That will be the end before the beginning. We need to hit back right now, and we need to talk directly to them, Latent to Latent."

"Show them that they aren't the only ones with a dog in the fight," Bookbinder agreed. "This is about how people want to live with their magic. We live inside the system. They can, too."

"We'll have to offer them something," Harlequin mused.

"Why would they trust anything we offered them? We're wearing uniforms," Bookbinder said.

"Scylla is playing to be the spokesperson for the Selfer movement, to be their new hero. But they already have one.

"Any offer we present to them has to come from someone they trust more than her."

"Oscar Britton," Bookbinder said.

Harlequin smiled at the irony. "Oscar Britton.

"Again."

INTERLUDE VIII
TAKEDOWN

Why the military? The world has an interest in magic's being applied in a hundred more important causes. Hydromancers could single-handedly restore dwindling polar ice caps. Aeromancers could clear the smog in Beijing overnight. Terramancers could feed starving populations the world over. We have been handed the power to fix this world, and what do we do? We use it as a weapon.

—Loretta Kiwan
Council on Latent-American Rights

SIX YEARS EARLIER

Harlequin walked Grace back to her office on the building's top floor. She burned with excitement, practically skipping into the room. "It works, Jan. It really works. This is going to be amazing."

"Grace," Harlequin said.

"I mean, not just the magic, but her *mind*, Jan! She's a completely different person! I wish I'd thought to have a psycho-pathological assessment done before we got her so we could track the improvement. I was so focused on the magic . . ."

"Grace!"

She stopped in midsentence, hands clasped together in front of her skirt. Her face froze, the smile slowly fading.

Harlequin sighed. "You can't hide this forever."

She looked down. "I . . ."

"What's your plan, Grace? Do you honestly think you can go your entire life keeping something like this a secret?"

"I've done fine so far."

"So far. Do you plan to dose yourself on Limbic Dampener three times a day for the rest of your life? Sooner or later, you're going to slip up. You'll make a mistake, or someone will find out somehow. When that happens, you'll have no protection."

"Jan, this drug works . . ."

"So what? That doesn't change the law. It doesn't change what they'll do to you if they find out."

"What will they do, Jan? You saw what they did with Morelli. There's the law, and there's reality."

"Morelli's different. Pyromancy is a legal school."

"And that's it for Probes? They just kill us?"

"I don't know. I've never taken down a Probe before. You're the only thing rarer than coming up Latent in the first place."

She sat down in her office chair, webbing contouring to her slim back and buttocks, the individual threads ingeniously made to look like stainless steel.

"I just thought that . . . I thought that, if Latent people could demonstrate control. If we could show people that we're not a threat, then . . . maybe then the law will change."

Harlequin considered this. "Maybe," he said slowly, "but it'll take time, and during that time, you're . . . exposed."

"What do you suggest I do?"

"America has the most restrictive magic legislation outside of Saudi Arabia. You've got unlimited resources, Grace. Take a vacation. Go somewhere you can be safe. Run your project in Ligoua."

"And what about Channel? What about everything I've built here? I'm not letting Entertech take it!"

"Entertech's not taking anything. You don't need to be in New York to run Channel. You can do it over video teleconference. And with the project moving to a pilot phase, it's going to be as much in our hands as it is in yours."

She looked at her hands for a long time. Then she looked up, her eyes wide. "And us? Do you want to get rid of me so badly?"

His heart surged, tears pricked at the corners of his eyes as he knelt before the chair, taking her hands. "The opposite. I want to protect you."

"I can protect myself."

"From anything else in the world, yes. But not from us, Grace. Not from the SOC."

"You were with me for days, Jan. Intimately. Sleeping beside me. You never knew."

"Until I did. Life works like that. Sooner or later, things come out."

"I'll be more careful."

"And fill yourself up with that drug? What is it doing to you? What if it's hurting you?"

"It's not hurting me. I'm fine."

"What about the nosebleed?"

"What about it? I told you that was from mistakes I made when I was young and stupid."

"Bullshit. You haven't tested the effects of such large doses on yourself, have you? How the hell could you without letting everyone else at the company know you were on it?"

She didn't answer.

"Grace, just consider . . ." Harlequin's smartphone vibrated, and his hand shot into his cargo pocket instinctively. A text from Crucible flashed across the screen. MEET ME OUT FRONT OF CHANNEL. A little red flag indicated the message was sent with high importance.

"Crap, I'll be right back," he said, racing out the double doors, past the guard on duty. "The boss wants to talk to me."

He took the elevator down the thirty-nine floors, the ride so smooth and silent that he had to watch the digital readout to ensure he was moving. There was no doubting Grace's control, and the truth was that apart from a slipup, he would never have found out. But what if she had another slipup? What if she was stuck in an elevator and couldn't get to her supply of Dampener? What if she was in a meeting with Crucible that ran long?

The car slid to a stop at the lobby, and the stainless-steel doors slid open with a ringing of chimes.

He stepped out into the atrium, boots thumping on the marble floor. He swallowed his worry. He had time. There was no imminent danger of Grace's being discovered, no emergency. Slow is smooth, and smooth is fast. Think it through, come up with a plan. Maybe they could . . .

Harlequin froze midstride.

Crucible was entering the lobby from the front entrance, kitted out for war. Rampart came with him, along with another man in a bulky suit that poorly disguised the body armor he wore beneath. Harlequin recognized his buzz cut, his square chin, his arrogant aviator glasses.

Hicks.

"What's going . . ."

"Where's Grace?" Crucible cut him off.

"Grace? Why do you . . ."

"No time," Crucible said. "She's Latent, Jan. We're sealing the building off now."

Harlequin's stomach fell, ice made its way up his spine. He fell in beside Crucible, trailing him to the elevator, ignoring Hicks's smug expression. "That's . . . that can't be right."

"It is," Crucible said. He gestured to Hicks, who gave no indication of their past meeting. "This is Tom Hicks, one of our customer-relations officers at Entertech. He has some relationships with Channel employees, who brought it to his attention."

"Corporate spies?" Harlequin spit out the words.

"That's what the bad guys call us," Hicks answered, as they got into the elevator, "but I must admit I'm surprised to hear it coming from you." *How much does he know?* But neither Crucible's expression nor his tone held any accusation. Hicks stared at him suspiciously, but he didn't know the man well enough to tell if that was unusual for him or not.

"It's impossible, sir," Harlequin said, as the elevator climbed, his panic rising with it. "I would have known. We've been . . ."

"I know you're fucking her, Jan," Crucible said. "Christ, I practically ordered you to do it."

"Then let me go up there first and talk to her." *Maybe I can find some way to let her escape.* Ridiculous. Even without her magic, she was half his size and had no military training.

Crucible shook his head. "Between us four, I don't think we need to negotiate. We've got the jump on her, too."

"If she were Latent, I would have felt the current," Harlequin said.

"She's been funneling her own experimental drug," Hicks said. "Massively overdosing on the stuff. One of her researchers has noticed certain symptoms that are consistent with an overdose. It's slowly giving her brain damage."

"What, you mean . . ." *I almost said "the nosebleeds."* "What do you mean?"

"We also got a hit on her current," Hicks finished.

"A hit on her . . ." He turned to Crucible. "Does Entertech have . . ."

"Leave it, Jan," Crucible said, as the doors chimed, and they stepped out into the wide chamber outside the building's top floor, where Grace kept her office.

"But, sir. Latent contractors?"

Crucible spun on him while Rampart raised his submachine gun and sighted down the barrel. "Jan, I have already told you that there are aspects to how the SOC does business that you are not yet privy to. I promise you that after this is all over, I will have you read on to those programs where you have a specific need to know. Until then, I need you to do your job." He unsnapped his drop holster, pulled out the pistol, and pressed it into Harlequin's hands. "Now, get in the stack."

Like every other room in the Channel building, there was a minimum amount of furniture. The walls were covered in brass-rimmed panels of golden-colored expensive wood, the light sconces recessed and understated. The entire room spoke of impeccable taste, a deliberate attempt to underplay the height of opulence.

A desk stood outside the huge double doors that led into Grace's office. A man in an immaculate suit stood behind it, big as a linebacker. He was coming out from around his desk, one hand outstretched, the other reaching into the small of his back. "Gentlemen, you can't just . . ."

"Gun," Rampart said before his wrist cleared his jacket. His submachine gun barked, and the guard staggered backward. The body armor beneath his suit had stopped the first two rounds. The third punched a tiny hole in his throat. He went to his knees, clawing at his neck. A dull clatter on the floor told Harlequin that Rampart was right. He did indeed have a gun.

Harlequin went to the man's side as he collapsed, the gasping snaking out into a death rattle just as Rampart kicked open the doors and Crucible led the way in, shouting. "Get down! Get down right now!"

Harlequin leapt to his feet and followed behind in time to

see three other people dropping to their knees, hands raised. Grace must have called some kind of meeting once he'd left.

Grace, on the other hand, stood defiant behind her desk. "What the hell do you think you're doing?"

"I need you to show me your hands," Crucible said. "Rampart, get her Suppressed."

Rampart lowered his weapon and reached a hand out, his brow furrowing in concentration. "There's no current, sir."

"There's a current," Hicks answered. "You just can't feel it. We need to keep her under guard and wait until the dose wears off."

Her face went dark at the sight of Hicks. She pointed a shaking finger. "What is that doing in my building?"

"He's with us, Grace," Crucible said. "Now, let me see your hands."

She held them up, two middle fingers. "What crime have I committed that has you firing guns in my own fucking building? Is Larry hurt?" She leaned around the door, trying to see the guard. Harlequin stepped between her and the slowly spreading stain darkening the floor.

At last she noticed Harlequin. *I'm sorry,* he wanted to say. *This caught me by surprise.* He could see Hicks watching him from the corner of his eye. He couldn't even risk a hand gesture. Instead, he tried to pour those words into his eyes, hoping against hope the message would reach her.

If it did, he couldn't tell. The same feral anger she'd shown Hicks was still there, it dominated her face, never reaching above the bridge of her nose. Her eyes were narrowed, calculating.

"Sir?" Rampart said again. "There's no current."

"You heard your own Suppressor," Grace said. "Now, if you'd be so kind as to put your weapons down, I've committed no crime, and there is no evidence of magic here."

"What's that?" Hicks asked, pointing at the crumpled, red-spotted tissue on her desk.

"I have a nosebleed," Grace said. "Allergies."

"Sir," Hicks said to Crucible, "I promise you that if we just keep her under guard for a few hours, your man will be able to feel a current."

Harlequin felt a thin trickle of hope. He raised his pistol, tried to look stern. "I'll stay with her." *And then what the hell will you do?*

"We'll all stay with her," Crucible said, motioning to the three people at the back of the room. "You three, go."

They went, erupting into screams as they moved past the guard's still body.

"You killed him," Grace hissed.

"He pulled a gun on us," Crucible said. "Doesn't allow for a lot of room to maneuver. Now, if you'll just take a se . . ."

Harlequin knew she'd decided to chance it before she even moved.

Time slowed down. He lunged toward her, trying to tell her not to do it, that she had no chance against the four of them, that they'd find another way, but he already felt her current rise, saw Crucible's eyes widen as he felt it, too, a powerful eddy of magic materializing from out of nowhere.

She could have killed Crucible, could have left a thick, rotten smear where his body used to be. Instead, she went for his gun. It came apart in his hands, the receiver shriveling and dripping down his knuckles, the magazine falling out of the well, the follower spring jangling a crazy dance across the floor.

She kicked the desk hard, sending it spinning on its wheels across the floor, the corner connecting sharply with Rampart's crotch. The Suppressor grunted, sucked in his breath, doubled over.

Crucible hesitated, staring in shock at the stinking fragments that used to be his gun, settling in his hands. *He knows she's a Probe now. All bets are off.*

Hicks drew his pistol and aimed it at her. Harlequin shouted and sprang at him, catching him with his shoulder and carrying him to the ground as he fired, his shot going wild.

Grace's eyes darted like a frightened animal's. Her enemies blocked the only exit to the room.

So she spun to make a new one.

Harlequin felt her magic focus, and the room's back wall began to bubble. Rampart dropped to his knees, and Crucible finally shook his hands and gathered his own current as the expensive fabric wallpaper turned to slime, running down the crumbling wall. The massive iron girders behind it turned to dust, revealing the hallway beyond.

Grace was a talented Sorcerer, but she was no architect. Harlequin could see the wall was load-bearing even before the ceiling collapsed.

It bowed inward, screams sounding from above them, then Grace was staggering back, cinder blocks shivering with pops as loud as gunshots, showering them with masonry turned powder, not by magic now, but by the massive force of the building above them, suddenly without crucial support.

A chunk of something hard grazed Harlequin's head. He raced toward her, felt Crucible's hand grab his collar, yank him backward. The room shook. There was a sudden shattering of glass, and Harlequin caught something giant bounce off the building's exterior and plummet earthward. He shook off Crucible's grip, started toward Grace again, but suddenly the room had gone dark, his eyes stinging and his nose and mouth clogged with dust so thick he could hardly draw breath. He coughed violently, and at last Crucible threw himself over him as the rest of the ceiling came down, burying them all.

Laws, both civil and religious, are a veneer. They exist to impose a position on that majority of a population who has no hand in making them. Magic is haram in the Kingdom of Saudi Arabia. And yet a strange storm disperses a major protest no less than five times in a period of three months. Let's apply Occam's razor here. Is almighty God intervening on behalf of the king? Or is there an Aeromancer tucked away in the Mabahith building, telling himself he bears a heavy burden to keep his country safe? What do leaders do when their own laws bar them from greater heights of power? They break them.

—Walid al Ghamdi (alias)
ArabYouth Blog

Harlequin flew north again, this time up Hudson Street on the city's west side. The ruin below him was oddly quiet, but Harlequin knew that the majority of the enemy was drawn off and pressing the barricade hard to the north, confident that the Whispering had done its work.

Cormack's voice came across the commlink. "Sir, you left without an escort again. That didn't work out so well last time."

"You got a bird to spare?"

Cormack's silence was answer enough.

"We're getting calls from Barricade One. They're getting hit hard, sir."

"Downer will have to hold it for now. One more Aeromancer isn't going to make a difference."

"Are you headed back to the *Limpiado* enclave, sir? They're not going to . . ."

"The other clear zone. Hoping they might be more amenable."

"Sir, they're not likely to be members of your fan club."

"I'm not seeing a lot of other options right now. If I'm not back in an hour . . . well . . . tell Gatanas and work with General Bookbinder. Win this thing."

A pause, then, "Good luck, sir. Godspeed."

"Thanks, Harlequin out."

Harlequin felt the currents long before the cleared zone came into view. There were goblin corpses littered about the Terramantic barricades, the result of some failed push since the last time he'd been there. Otherwise, the streets looked the same—clean, peaceful, and empty.

Harlequin flew directly over the first barricade, then sped down as fast as he could. If they were going to Suppress him, let them do it on the ground. He hit the pavement and jogged a few steps, cupping his hands to his mouth. "Come out! Come out, damn it! I need your help!"

Silence. Wind blew garbage across the scarred leather of his boots. A door slammed somewhere.

"Come out!" he shouted. "It's just me! What can I do?"

The question hit home. "What can I do?" he asked again, softly.

He could feel the eyes on him, at least half a dozen magical currents reaching out, touching his own, pulling back. They knew he was here.

"Come out," he whispered.

Whispering in the shadows, some hushed argument, then a voice said, "Well, well. Looks like Christmas came early."

Harlequin recognized the voice.

A man stepped into the street. He was tall, thin. Ropy muscle bunched beneath a black leather vest. His mop of black hair had been long since shaved, but Harlequin recognized the scarred mess of a tattoo on his chest. It had once shown a swallow in flight.

Swift.

The Aeromancer looked exhausted. Swift had been a pot of simmering rage, leading a band of committed anti-SOC recalcitrants, refusing all attempts to retrain them. They'd called themselves the No-No Crew after their firm answer to the two pledges of allegiance the SOC required all SASS inmates to make before being released. Now his eyes were heavy with grief, his shoulders slumped. He leaned against the brick façade of a building and folded his arms across his chest. Harlequin's heart sank. There might be a Selfer in this world less likely to help him, but he couldn't think of one.

"Figured you'd show up sooner or later," Swift said.

"You did?" He shouldn't have been surprised to find him here. The Houston Street Gang had been splintered, but they hadn't caught every single one.

"Who else would they put in charge of this shit show?"

"I thought you were still in the Source with Oscar Britton."

"What's for me there? Scratching a living out of the earth with the goblins? No thanks. This is my home. This plane." His eyes flashed.

"Scylla feels the same way."

"She's not wrong. This was always your basic problem, Harlequin, you never understood that you're not the only person willing to die for something. We're not going to let the SOC run our lives."

"So you'll let Scylla do it?"

"You're the company man. You always saw the world that way. Good guys or bad guys. With us or against us. Doesn't work that way. We're not for Scylla, and we're not for the SOC."

"What are you for, then?"

"What you claim to be for: freedom. Real liberty. Not the bullshit you talk about in campaign speeches. Self-determination. Never understood why that was so complicated for you."

Harlequin felt the magical currents around him growing closer. Faces began to appear in the alleyways and windows. He recognized more than a few. Flicker, his head shaved as bald as Britton's, stylized red-and-orange flames sweeping across the surface. Spur, so tall that Harlequin had to tilt his head to see the former basketball player's face. Guinevere, still in her smart business suit, though it was covered in dust and smeared with blood.

He recognized each face from a targeting dossier, Selfers he'd spent his career hunting. He could feel the intensity of their currents, boosted by the anger kindled at the sight of their old enemy.

"You gotta be out of your mind coming here," Flicker said. "You got a death wish?"

Swift waved a hand, looking more tired than ever. "I had my chance to kill him. It won't bring Shai and Kadija back."

Harlequin could still remember lying on his back, Swift's twitching face behind the gun, ready to pull the trigger. *I am going to kill you,* Swift had repeated over and over again. *I am going to kill you.* That man, that fury, was long gone. "I didn't kill your girlfriend, Swift, I . . ."

"You were just doing your job." Swift sighed. "Collateral damage. It's always collateral damage, isn't it? Nobody is ever responsible." He waved in the direction of the ruins of the Trump Tower, spire smoking in the street, God knew how many corpses buried beneath.

Those eight Marines were just doing their job, too. Getting in the way of something important. Now they're dead just like Swift's girlfriend and baby. And you're alive. Funny how it always works out that way.

Harlequin's throat swelled. His shoulders slumped to match Swift's. *It's on you even when you're doing it for the greater good. You make the call, you own the consequences.* Harlequin tried to fight against the realization, to repeat his mantra: *Eight lives against thirty thousand.* But those numbers didn't add up to every Selfer he'd brought down, every innocent caught in the blast. He'd taken those lives. No one else.

"I'm sorry." Harlequin's voice was thick.

"That doesn't bring them back either," Swift said. "What do you want, Harlequin?"

Harlequin knew he should turn on his TV personality. Now was the time to deliver an oratory that would convince Swift of his need, of the need of everyone who would suffer if Scylla won the day. But he looked into Swift's eyes, saw deep grief instead of the fury that had once burned there. He'd hated the old Swift, but this new man was his making. Just like those Marines. Just like Scylla herself. His throat closed, his mind seized.

"What do you want?" Swift repeated.

"Don't you know?"

"We're not helping you."

"Damn right we're not," Flicker said.

"Shut up," Swift said to him, some of the old fire returning. Flicker tensed, but held his peace.

"You run the show now," Harlequin said. "Since Big Bear . . ." Another murder. The former leader of the Houston Street Gang had been captured, interrogated, and replaced with a Physiomancer talented enough to impersonate him.

"Don't try to flatter me," Swift said. "I'm not going to kill you, Harlequin, but I'll be damned if I'll save your bacon."

"It's Scylla out there, Swift. You know her. You know her game. What are you going to do if we lose? You want to live in a city ruled by *Gahe* and goblins? That's so much better than the way things are now?"

"Can't be worse."

"Yes, Swift. It can. Much worse."

"We're not the SOC; we can work out a deal with her."

"No, you can't."

"You don't know her."

Grace, curled beneath his arm, gently kissing his chest. "I know her better than you think."

"She used to talk about you. Back at Channel," Guinevere said. She'd worked with Grace, back before Scylla. A different time. A different life.

Harlequin shook his head. "Grace is dead. This is someone else."

Guinevere sighed. "Whatever gets you through the day. Is there no way to talk to her?"

"What can be said now? The death toll's even higher than it was when she ran. Half the city is laid waste. She owes for that."

"You owe for that," Swift said.

"I know," Harlequin said. "You think I don't know? Why do you think I'm trying to save this fucking city? For the landmarks?

"I tried with Grace . . . I . . . didn't know. I didn't know what she was."

"What is she?" Swift asked. "Is it really so crazy for her to try to overthrow the regime that's locked us down? The woman has a point, Harlequin. I'm not saying I like her style, but her message rings true."

"Whatever I've done," Harlequin said, "there are eight million people in this city. Help us. I'll work for a pardon. Downer's already helping. If you meet us halfway . . ."

"Sarah Downer's helping? You put a bomb in her chest, too?"

"She's helping because she wants a shot at amnesty."

"She honestly believes she'll get it?"

"She honestly will." *You can't promise that. You don't know what the president will say.* But he could feel the weight of Scylla's army at his back. If there was anything he could say to convince Swift to help him, he would say it. It was truth enough.

Swift turned, bent his head to Guinevere's, whispering.

He turned to face Harlequin. "Send her here. Let her tell me herself."

"She's pinned down in the fighting. We need her where she is."

Swift shook his head sadly. "I'm sure. Well, good luck with everything."

"Okay, okay. I'll ask her. And I need to talk to someone, too."

Swift spread his arms. "We're all here, Harlequin, at least all who survived the scouring after you killed Big Bear."

"You know who I'm talking about."

"Oscar Britton's not with us."

"Downer told us how you kept in touch before. Do you honestly expect me to believe you're not in touch with him now?"

Swift folded his arms and said nothing.

"Please," Harlequin said. "I know him. I know he'll help. Just ask him. Just tell him I asked. Let him know what's at stake."

"Send Downer," Swift said. "Alone. I don't want you looking over her shoulder while we talk. And she needs to come today."

"Please . . ."

"Enough," Swift said. "Get out of here."

Harlequin turned and launched skyward, speeding his way back to Battery Park. As he approached the perimeter, he radioed the access point, but no one answered. He guessed they hadn't had time to recover yet and tried Cormack.

"Sir?"

"Inbound. Check your fire to the northwest."

"Respectfully, sir? We don't have overwatch reconstituted yet. You're clear."

"Damn it."

"We're dancing as fast as we can, sir. How'd your . . . visit go?"

"It went."

"That doesn't sound promising."

Harlequin was silent.

Cormack finally transmitted again. "So, what do we do now, sir?"

Harlequin searched for words of inspiration, something to lift the man's spirits, give him hope to carry on the fight. But, once again, the exhaustion permitted only honesty.

"I don't know," he said, clearing the perimeter wall and circling over the broken remains of his tiny force.

"I don't know."

CHAPTER XVIII
EMBASSY

Sarah Downer felt the cushion of air lift her, spin around her, tickling her nose, her eyelashes. The air elemental was sentient, but that didn't make it smart. It loved her with the slavish devotion of the dog to its master, knowing in its soul that she was the thing that gave it life and that she could take it away in an instant.

She could feel it reaching along the current that connected them, seeking her will. She reached back, not understanding how the current conveyed her desires, only knowing that it did, the Binding transmitting the pictures in her head, the electrical signals she sent to her muscles, the emotions churning in her gut.

The elemental wavered, bent, descended.

Below her, the cleared blocks of Tribeca hove into view.

It was just as Harlequin had said, four square blocks, completely clear of the enemy, earthen barricades blocking the intersections, clearly the product of expert Terramancy. The elemental felt her trepidation, hesitated, whirled faster, the air pulling protectively around her.

The last time she'd seen the Houston Street Gang, she'd been shivering and feverish, vehemently denying her place at death's door. The fever stole most of the memories, but she knew she'd been betrayed, delivered to the SOC, tried to rejoin them only to begin the long nightmare of her incarceration.

Swift, she remembered. *Trust me, little girl,* he'd said. *You'll curb your enthusiasm fairly rapidly. Within a month, you'll be wishing these fuckers had shot you.* He was wrong then, but his words had proved prescient as she sat on the bench in her cell, waiting for the next "debriefing session" to begin.

She still remembered him standing over Harlequin, gun pointed at his face, his other hand pointing at her. Electricity leapt from his fingers, blue arcs rising across her vision, her hair standing on end, the smell of something burning. Then, agony and blessed darkness.

She'd remembered how Harlequin had looked to her then: square jaw, blond hair, those beautiful blue-gray eyes. A man who had mastered his magic, a man who owned the world he lived in.

It felt like a lifetime ago. The mooning of a stupid, little girl. She didn't trust Swift, but she sure as hell understood him now.

He stood in the street below, five others standing in a loose semicircle around him. The tall basketball player. The woman in the sharp suit. The Pyromancer who'd first found them in the subway tunnel. Swift looked much as she remembered, tall, lean, and pale, the mottled remains of the old tattoo smeared across his bare chest. But the similarity stopped at his eyes. They looked older, tired.

"Sarah," Swift said. "Good to see you."

The elemental set her down, moved between the two of them. It could feel her memories, Swift's lightning searing through her, the unconsciousness that followed. It spun faster, whipping the ground up between them. She dug into her current, sending her will down through it. In the early days, she'd barely been able to control her elementals. She shuddered at the memory of what they had done to her old school, but that was a long time ago, the same mooning girl who'd thought Harlequin was worth a damn.

That girl was gone. The elemental stayed put.

"Harlequin said you wanted to see me."

"No kind words for me?"

"There's no time for that. I'm needed at the barricades."

"All business, now. You've changed."

"So have you. Last time I saw you, you were straining at the lead."

"Yeah, well. That didn't get me very far. Slowed down a bit. Helps me to see more clearly."

"Seems to have worked out for you here. You going to throw in with us?"

"Well, I wanted to ask you about that."

"Me? Why me?"

"Because you were with us at the start. Because . . . you know him. He . . . talked about amnesty."

"Yeah, he's said he'll go to bat for me. Get me a pardon."

"Do you believe him?"

She nodded. "I believe he'll try. Harlequin's no liar."

"And what if he fails?"

"Then I'm hardly worse off than I was before. I'm not Suppressed and sitting in a cell."

"Yeah, but if they try to take you in again . . ."

Anger kindled in her belly. She raised a finger. "Last time, I gave myself up. I wanted back in. They want me this time, they'll have to come get me. And that's going to hurt."

Swift smiled. "I bet it will."

"Where's Oscar?"

"I don't know what you're talking about."

"Come off it, Swift. I'm not stupid. There's no way he sent you back here from the Source without a way to keep in touch. I'm not going to try to convince you to help save this city. If millions of lives at the mercy of someone like Scylla isn't enough, then you're too far gone for anyone to change your mind. Oscar will help us. I know he will. Let me talk to him."

Swift's smile faded. "It's not that simple. I don't want people to die . . ."

"So you're just going to dig in here and wait to get rolled over. Or you're going to rally to her flag? Help her hand this city to those . . . fucking things the Apache worship? Jesus, Swift. You haven't learned a thing."

"I've learned plenty," he said, "and you could use a bit of learning yourself if you think you can trust these people. You gave yourself up to them, and you just said they'd put you in a cell."

"I don't trust them," Downer said, "but Harlequin's right about one thing: Something good is broken, you fix it. You don't just chuck it out the window and put something worse in its place."

"I knew Grace," the woman in the suit said . . . Guinevere, she'd called herself. "She was one of most brilliant, decent people I ever met. I was in the room when they came for her. She invented that drug you use to help control your magic. She worked overtime to make this world better. I'm not so sure that's not what she's trying to do now."

"I didn't know her back then," Downer said, "but the woman now is a killer. The creatures that are with her are . . ." She turned to Swift. "You remember the schoolhouse in the SASS. You remember those videos. Tell her."

Swift stood with his arms crossed, said nothing.

"He remembers," Downer said. "We watched those things . . . they're nasty." She shuddered.

Swift turned to Guinevere. "What do you think?"

Guinevere shrugged. "We owe it to Oscar to let him make the call."

Swift sighed. "Yeah, I guess we do. It's your lucky day, Sarah. Come on."

He turned, stepped into a narrow alley between two buildings, his magic carrying him lightly over a pile of trash bags. He motioned for her to follow.

The tall buildings shut out the light, shrouding the alley in a thick gloom that cloaked all in gray. The rest of the gang made no move to follow. Downer hesitated.

"Come on," Swift said.

She was alone, with only a single elemental for protection, surrounded by six powerful Selfers. If he'd wanted to harm her, he'd have done it already.

She stepped over the trash bags and into the alley, her elemental hovering just above her head, the darkness thickening with each step. At last the gray began to yield to a light at the end of the alley, a flickering, static glow, like a television screen left on a test pattern.

Downer recognized the light instantly; that same light had been her constant companion through her time with Shadow Coven. It was a means of egress, it was a weapon.

A Portamantic gate.

Swift stood to one side, pressing his back against the alley wall and bowing slightly, gesturing to the door-sized portal hovering at the alley's end.

"His lordship will see you now."

Downer let her magic drop, the elemental dispersing back into the wind, closed her eyes, and stepped through.

The gate's light washed over her, offering no resistance. The only indicator that she had changed planes was the sudden sweetness to the air. She breathed deeply, filling her lungs with the wonderful scent of the Source.

"Sarah Downer, it's good to see you."

She opened her eyes, squinting against the Source's bright sun, bigger and closer than on the Home Plane. She stood on a broad plain of waving, saw-toothed grass, almost up to her knees. In the distance, she recognized the low, wooden palisade that marked the perimeter of Marty's village. Their tribal banner, a gnarled tree on blue cloth, fluttered from the gate towers.

Oscar Britton stood before her, unchanged since the day she'd last seen him.

His head was still shaved, huge frame covered in leather shirt and pants, beaded and fringed in goblin fashion. She'd known he would be here, but her heart still sped up at the sight of him. Like Swift, he'd fought her on her loyalty to the SOC, like Swift, events had proved him right.

Therese stood beside him, her hair hanging to her waist now, but otherwise exactly the same, save the leather dress she wore. Downer smiled. Therese had never been anything but kind to her.

Simon Truelove, she barely recognized. The Necromancer had filled out, stretching the same goblin leathers, intricate beadwork patterns covering almost every inch. His coke-bottle glasses were gone. The left side of his body was covered in the white chalk-paint goblin sorcerers wore, his hair sticky with the stuff. A battered notebook hung from a leather thong at his waist, and he carried a spear, an ornate thing with a painted head, more walking stick than weapon.

"Good to see you, too," she said, surprised herself by meaning it. There was more here than the hope of reinforcement, there was the pleasure of reuniting with old friends who'd weathered storms alongside her.

"You were right," Swift called through the gate before heading back out of the alley. "They locked her up."

Therese reached out, Binding her magic. "If there's an ATTD . . ."

"There isn't," Downer answered quickly. "Harlequin sent me here in good faith."

Britton nodded. "What does he want?"

"Help," Downer said. "We're losing."

"Don't," Therese said to Britton. "Once you're with them, they won't pass up the chance to take you."

"They're not here," Downer said. "All Harlequin's got is a bunch of training Covens. And General Bookbinder now. And me. It's not enough.

"He means it, Oscar. He's going to do what he can for me. If we beat Scylla here, then he might just have the ammunition he needs to help you, too."

"What did they do to you?" Britton asked.

Downer went quiet. "I talked, you know? I ran my mouth like you wouldn't believe, told them absolutely everything I could think of. I figured . . . I figured if I showed them I was loyal . . ."

"But the questions just kept coming," Britton said.

Downer nodded. "They kept me in a 'debriefing' room. Kept saying it was for my own protection. After a while, I started making shit up."

"I'm sorry, Sarah," Oscar said. "I should have dragged you through that gate, I should never have let you . . ."

Harlequin had used the same tone when she'd first got off the helicopter in Battery Park. "I'm not a fucking kid, Oscar. I make my own choices, good and bad. That was the choice I made. I can live with it."

Britton smiled. "You'd have made one hell of an officer."

"Yeah, well. That ship has sailed. I need to get back to the barricades. You helping us or not?"

Britton exchanged a glance with Therese. "Amnesty."

"It's what you want, isn't it? A chance to come back and campaign for Latent rights out in the open?"

Britton folded his arms across his chest, was silent.

"What happened to you?" Downer turned to Truelove.

"What do you mean?" Truelove asked, frowning.

"You look like half goblin sorcerer and half abandoned craft project."

Swift, Britton, and Therese laughed, and Truelove's frown deepened. "Nice," he said.

"Just like old times," Downer said. "I missed you, Simon. I really did."

Truelove softened. "I missed you, too."

"So, what's with the getup?"

"Marty's tribesmen took a liking to Simon's magic," Britton said. "They worship their ancestors here."

"And he makes them stand up and shake hands?" Downer asked.

"Something like that," Britton said. "It's won him a lot of status in the tribe."

"He's writing a book," Therese said, "the first real anthropology of Marty's people."

Downer stared at the book, at Truelove's painted body, realization slowly dawning on her. "Who's going to read it, Simon? You going to bring it back to the Home Plane and publish it there?"

"I've . . . I've made a place for myself here," Truelove said. "I'm not writing it for anyone else."

"So, I guess that means I shouldn't bother asking you to help."

Truelove said nothing, but shame and defiance warred across his face. "This isn't my fight," he said at last. "I did my time with the SOC."

"I never thought I'd see the day," Downer said.

"What?"

"Simon Truelove, a fucking coward. You're scared. Jesus,

Simon. I watched you stare down Fitzy. I was beside you when we took Chatto. I never thought I'd see the day when something could frighten you."

"Whatever," Truelove said. "You turned yourself into them, gave up everything you knew, and they locked you up for it. I'm not a coward, I'm just smarter than you. Here, I work my magic, study, and write. Nobody chases me. Nobody orders me around. I go to bed without worrying who's going to come get me while I sleep. The only thing the SOC ever gave me was near-death experience after near-death experience. Why the hell would I go back to that?"

"Because this isn't your home, Simon. Because you know Scylla. You know what she'll do if she wins. There are millions of people . . ."

"I've got people here, Sarah. People who respect me."

"These aren't *people*, Simon. These are goblins. I'm glad you get along with them, but that doesn't make you one of them. *Your* people are on the other side of that gate, and they need your help."

"I don't have to listen to this," Truelove said. Downer felt his current rise, and this time he did storm off, his narrow shoulders shaking as he made his way toward the village. Therese called his name, ran after him.

Downer turned back to Britton. "I'm not some stupid little girl who wants to be in the clubhouse anymore, Oscar. I don't know what you've seen of New York, but I'm here to tell you it's going from bad to worse. I need you to trust me, and I need you to take me seriously.

"Most of all, I need you to come with me. We need you in New York."

CHAPTER XIX
CRY FOR HELP

To New York, and a new world!

—Recorded message distributed on the Internet
from the Consortium of Selfer Organizations (CSO)

The first of them came that night.

Harlequin and Bookbinder stood on the parapet, watching the ground outside the barricades around the park, now mostly clear of *Gahe*. The sleek black creatures had taken some time to grow wary of Bookbinder's ensorcelled bullets, but they had learned at last, and hung back now, under cover of buildings in the distance.

"This is it," Harlequin said. "At least, I think this is as good as it's going to get. How are you holding up?"

Bookbinder's shadowed eyes were slitted, his lips cracked over mostly gray beard stubble. He scratched at one ear, an irritated patch had cropped up near the lobe, rubbed raw where he'd worried it. His nails were too long, filthy. The man desperately needed some rack time and a shower. They all did.

But Harlequin also knew that every single one of his ammo dumps contained at least a can of 5.56mm rounds crackling with electricity.

"I'm fine," Bookbinder said, smiling a rictus grin. "Ready to run a fucking marathon, actually." He took a pull on the small silver can in his hand. The energy drinks helped, but caffeine made them jumpy.

A round flew out of the darkness somewhere to their left, leaving a sizzling trail. It clipped the side of a building in the distance where a *Gahe* must have shown itself. Crackling blue electricity crawled along the brick surface before the round's magic was spent.

"You do good work," Harlequin mused.

"We do good work," Bookbinder said. "Without the payload, it's just a bullet."

"We need to start getting this stuff up north."

"I'd feel better if I knew what *Gahe* were where. I don't want to run our people out into those streets only to have them fall on us. We need to smoke them out of the buildings closest to the park."

"Could we try ensorcelling some mortar rounds? Maybe a couple of the Javelins? Or the rockets on the helos? How would the area effect work?"

Bookbinder paused, thinking. "Never tried it. I don't think the explosive effect would make a difference. Stands to reason that if I ensorcell a casing large enough to fragment, or the shrapnel inside a high-explosive round, that it would spread the magic that way. M67 grenades? I saw a case of those back in the ready room." He rubbed his forehead. "Jesus, I can't think straight."

Harlequin clapped his shoulder. "Maybe we should grab a few hours. We can't go out there half-drunk on fatigue."

Bookbinder shook his head. "I'll be okay, I just ne . . . ."

Both men froze as they felt a magical current prickle their senses, moving in quickly from the west. The remaining Fornax Novices were on the wall, but Harlequin knew the feel of their currents now. This was different. He turned to Bookbinder, but the general was already nodding to him. "Go."

Harlequin shot airborne, shouting into his radio. "We've got magic incoming, west wall . . . not sure of the dis . . . ."

He could already see the soldiers on the western perimeter, where a makeshift gate had been constructed from an enormous superdozer, its earthmoving blade bolted to a section of T-wall. The dozer had backed inward slightly to create a gap in the wall covered by soldiers, who were busy ushering in the latest stream of refugees. A few of them covered the opening, but most were busy helping the civilians in as quickly as possible, ushering them toward Castle Clinton and the makeshift camp beyond.

He scanned the crowd of twenty or so people, but they all looked uniformly bedraggled, exhausted, and filthy. Many were wrapped in fire blankets or sheets, heads down. None of them wore uniforms. The magical current intensified, emanating from among them.

Harlequin began shouting, waving at the soldiers to get the hell back. They looked up at him in surprise. The civilians joined suit, frightened eyes staring in shock as he sped toward them.

Save two.

They threw off silver fire blankets, one of them jumping airborne and unleashing a torrent of lightning that blew three of the soldiers off their feet, sending them tumbling in smoking heaps.

Harlequin reached the edge of Castle Clinton and both figures came clear under the klieg lights set up around the park. He hoped against hope to see the small, gnarled, white-painted figures of goblins, knew he wouldn't.

Both were humans, tall and lithe. The Aeromancer looked like a reject from a bondage film. Studded, black leather belts crossed his chest, his head hidden behind a mask with a zippered mouth. The other was female, broad-shouldered and stripped to the waist, heavy breasts sagging almost to her belt under a field of tattoos covering every inch of exposed skin.

Not goblins. Selfers. The first recruits answering Scylla's call.

The female stretched out a hand, and Castle Clinton's rear wall went abruptly soft, the stone flowing into itself, brick and mortar reverting to liquid and dust. Harlequin could hear shouts from inside, see the antennae arrays they relied on for communications droop and sink earthward. He dove as low as he dared, watching the patchy grass rise up to meet him before throwing his current forward to roll the Terramancer's back. His own magic, bound up in Suppression, no longer held him aloft, and he tumbled in the grass, rolling on his face and shoulders. He ducked into the roll, letting himself come up and into a kneeling position, ripping his pistol from its holster on his thigh. His head spun from the impact, but he gritted his teeth and leveled the gun at the Selfer Terramancer, who backpedaled, eyes wide.

Harlequin threw himself back, colliding with the softened

castle wall as a sizzling burst of lightning rent the ground beside him. The wall bowed inward, still standing, but only just. He raised the pistol again, fired at the Aeromancer, who danced aside, swooping around to get at him from behind. "West wall! West wall!" he shouted into his commlink.

He heard shouts as soldiers came running, heard the sharp cracks of carbines. The Aeromancer dove, extending a hand toward them. Harlequin could feel the hair on his arms rise, smell the ozone.

He swore, dropping the Terramancer's Suppression and Binding his own magic into a column of lightning that clipped the Selfer Aeromancer. He shouted, somersaulting in the air, coming around for another pass. Then he jerked sideways as a round caught him in the arm, yelping like a dog. He swooped low, arms outstretched to retrieve his comrade, but the soldiers were getting on their sights now, and well-placed shots drove him away.

The Terramancer, out from under Harlequin's Suppression, turned back to Castle Clinton's wall. Harlequin leapt out of the way, gathering his magic to interdict the Selfer's flow again.

But another flow raced past him, interweaving with the Terramancer's. The Selfer gaped as her magic was reeled in, then pushed back out, Binding to the ground around her feet. She sank to her waist, her tattooed body held fast by a mud pit of her own making.

Bookbinder appeared at Harlequin's side. "Got her," he panted, then pointed skyward.

Harlequin leapt airborne and flew after the remaining Selfer. The man ducked, dove, tried to loop up behind Harlequin, undisciplined bursts of lightning tearing rents in the ground, clipping the side of one of their few remaining Humvees. Like most Selfers, he was powerful but undisciplined. *Skill beats will,* the SOC mantra went. Harlequin stayed easily on his six, following him through clumsy loop after loop, dodging the bursts of poorly aimed lightning. He herded him carefully back over Castle Clinton, shedding altitude, firing his own lightning at a steep angle to force the Aeromancer higher.

At last, he alighted on the castle. The Selfer Aeromancer danced out over the barricade wall, looking over his shoulder one more time. He banked back over the park, one hand clutching his arm where the bullet had skimmed him.

Harlequin shook his head, reached out, and Suppressed the man's flow.

The Selfer shouted as his dive became a tumble. He pitched through the air, arms flailing, slamming into the harder part of Castle Clinton's wall with a sickening crunch.

Harlequin turned and flew back to the Terramancer. Three rounds had caught her in the chest, lifting her mostly up and out of the ground, turning her upper body at a disturbing angle from her lower. Her face had turned purple, tongue lolling out. She held a nickel-plated high-caliber revolver in one hand.

Bookbinder reached Harlequin's side. "She pulled a gun, started shooting. We returned fire. Damn it. Would have liked to question her."

"What would she tell you?" Harlequin shrugged. "She's from Mississippi. Or she's from upstate. Or Utah. Or maybe even the cleared zone in Tribeca. She saw Scylla's message and came to take her place in the founding of her new and glorious free country. These two are just the beginning. There'll be more, and they'll all have the same story."

Bookbinder nodded. "We'd better start screening any civilians from now on before taking them in. Make sure we have someone Latent get a read on them."

"Yes." He left unsaid the obvious fact, that they didn't have enough Latent resources to go around.

"We better radio up to the barricades, see if they're getting hit, too."

Harlequin nodded, his stomach sinking. Because, even without making that call, he knew what the answer would be.

Bookbinder shook his head. "We are well and truly fucked."

Harlequin realized he'd been fanning a tiny ember of hope for the past three days, guarding it against the winds of defeat that had been buffeting him since he'd arrived at Battery Park.

With Bookbinder's words, the ember died. "Yeah."

And then the gate opened, static light spilling over them both, stinging Harlequin's eyes until they watered, tracking dirty trails down his cheeks.

"It's fine, Oscar," Harlequin said to the shimmering surface. "No harm will come to you, I swear. We just want to talk."

The broad shoulders of Oscar Britton's silhouette were sharply outlined against the darkness of the Source at night. "If it's all the same to you, I think I'll hang out here for a minute."

Harlequin shrugged. "Suit yourself."

"Where's Sarah?" Britton asked.

"North of here on Houston Street. The barricades would have fallen without her help long ago, and they may still fall regardless."

"She's okay?"

"She's fine, Oscar. She's pissed off and angling for all kinds of concessions when this is over, but she's fine."

"Sir." Britton inclined his head to Bookbinder.

"Nice to see you." Bookbinder nodded back. Harlequin thought it an understatement. The last time he was this happy to see someone was when Sarah Downer had stepped off her helicopter and punched him in the jaw.

"Jesus, Oscar. Just come out here. It's stupid talking to you through that thing. It's making me dizzy," Harlequin said. "We need you. I'm not going to do anything to screw that up."

"You have my word on it, Oscar," Bookbinder added. "The word of a general." The words came out solemn, rang ridiculous. They all tried to keep a straight face, but a moment later they found themselves chuckling. The tension broke, and Britton stepped through, sticking close to the gate.

"A general, huh. I heard you were a big deal now," Britton said.

Bookbinder smiled. "Yeah. I have all these new responsibilities. Like . . . staying away from the media at all costs and . . . not seeing my family. Oh, and I almost forgot, making boomers for whoever tells me."

Britton turned and motioned at the gate. Therese Del Aqua emerged behind him, cautious, legs tensed to jump back in at a moment's notice.

"Ma'am," Cormack said, as he joined them. A small ring of soldiers gathered, pointing and whispering.

"This is . . ." Harlequin began.

"I watch the news, sir," Cormack said. "Nice to finally meet you. If you're wanting to do any healing, we've got a fairly endless supply of wounded here."

She nodded. "I'll always help with that"—she turned to Bookbinder—"especially for a general. Maybe you'll let me take a look at your eye first?"

Cormack nodded. "I'd be much obliged, ma'am."

"I've been seeing both of you in the press a lot," Britton said. "Figured you put Porter in a tough spot, being dissenters and public heroes at the same time."

"They put me out to pasture," Harlequin said. "They'd have been happy to leave me there if it hadn't been for the Breach."

"The right choice. Both of you," Britton said.

Harlequin paused. "Well, thanks. Anyway, I'm not sure if you've seen the news, but it seems one of your chickens has come home to roost on our doorstep here. It's Scylla."

Britton and Therese exchanged a meaningful look, and Britton swallowed. "I know."

"You helped start this, Oscar," Harlequin said, "now we need you to help finish it."

Britton's brows drew together. "You don't need to convince me of that. Not a night goes by that I don't remember what happened. I went after her as soon as I got free of the FOB. I even saw the team you sent to bring her in. Sarah told you, when you were interrogating her."

Harlequin looked uncomfortable. "I didn't interrogate her . . ."

Britton shook his head. "But you worked with the people who did."

"Oscar, it wasn't my call," Harlequin said. "I did everything I could to get her out. My star wasn't exactly on the rise at the time."

Britton had the bit in his teeth. "You people. You never fucking learn. This is why . . ."

"Easy!" Bookbinder interrupted. "You're talking to the guy who sprung you from prison. The man who defied the President of the United States, then came back to face him. The man who is currently dealing with a problem you created by letting that Witch go in the first place." *We both let her go, didn't we?* Harlequin thought. *Or at least it was close enough as makes no difference.*

"Sure," Therese said, "because it's one-sided like that. None of this has anything to do with your jacked-up system that created these conflicts. Without the McGauer-Linden Act, I would never have been at FOB Frontier, and neither would Scylla . . ."

"Enough," Harlequin cut in. "We do not have time for this crap! We have the same goal here. We all want to stop her. We get that done, then we argue the rest of it later. Congress made that damn law, Oscar. We wear uniforms. We do what we're told." *Not always. Not anymore.*

"What are they telling you to do this time?" Britton asked.

"To stand and fight. To wait for relief. But if we do that, we're going to lose. We don't have the magic to deal with the *Gahe*. Well, we did, before she put the all-call out to every Selfer in the country. They're starting to check in."

"And you need me to help fight them?" Britton asked. "You want me to work for you again? To run down American citizens? Forget it."

Harlequin was already shaking his head. "I know you too well to ask that of you, Oscar. I don't want your help fighting them. I want your help winning them. You're the only person in the country Selfers trust more than her. You're the only one who can convince them to fight for their country instead of against it."

Therese snorted. "You haven't exactly made them feel like this is their country."

"But it still is," Harlequin said, "and we both know that Scylla's vision for whatever would replace it is a hell of a lot worse than what's going on right now."

Britton shook his head. "Bullshit. You offer no proof of that. You can't just go to the Selfers of this country, whom you have been hounding and jailing and killing since the Great Reawakening, and ask them to help their oppressors because the alternative is worse. Scylla is offering something. She put money on the table. You have to do the same thing."

"I don't have the power to offer . . ." Harlequin began.

"Which is what government *always* says, and why nobody ever trusts it. It's not my job. I don't have the authority. I can't. Policy says. I don't write the laws. It all comes out to the same thing: No. Well, you don't have time to convene Congress and debate the issue on the floor. You need Selfers to help you now. That means you need to offer them something tangible and real." Britton gestured to Bookbinder. "Hell, you've got a flag officer here."

"One star," Bookbinder said.

Britton tensed, stabbed a finger at Bookbinder's chest. "That is *exactly* what I'm talking about. You want to duck the hard call, that's on you, but I will not help you convince Selfers to work against their own interest because you won't step up to the plate."

Harlequin sighed. "What are your demands?"

Britton exchanged another glance with Therese, then turned back to Harlequin. "They're not *my* demands. They're the demands of every Latent-American who has felt the SOC's bootheel on their neck. And you have to be behind them. I mean really behind them. You hedged your bets when we saved the FOB. You plugged right back into the system you bucked as soon as you realized that popular opinion would keep it from punishing you. Now, you have to be ready to break ranks for real. You have to be willing to put Porter in a chicken wing and hold him there. No matter what happens. You have to pick a side."

"You want us to side with Selfers," Bookbinder said.

"Selfer is a label the government sticks on Latent people who don't toe their line. They are Latent, just like you are. Scylla is offering them a community of self-rule. You offer them second-class digs at the feet of people who are terrified of them. You need to show them you are throwing in your lot with them. You need to do it on the air and in public."

Harlequin's stomach turned over. He met Bookbinder's eyes, saw the same doubt there. FOB Frontier had housed tens of thousands of men and women, most of whom had military training.

New York was a city of over eight million civilians.

Bookbinder looked down. "We did it once already."

"That was different, sir. We saved a military division from being overrun. This is trucking with Selfers. This unwinds the bedrock of the McGauer-Linden Act."

"Are Swift and the rest throwing in their lot with her?"

"He's no fan of Scylla," Britton said, "but he's no fan of yours, either."

"What have we got to lose?" Bookbinder asked. "Besides the city, I mean."

Harlequin sighed. "Okay," he said, "let's check in at the barricades, then we can bring it to Gatanas."

"Gatanas?" Britton's eyebrows rose. "He's not going to give you permission . . ."

"I won't ask for permission. I'll ask for forgiveness. Let's grab a helo and head up to Houston."

"Helo?" Britton opened a gate. "We don't need a helo."

Barricade One was already finished by the time Britton opened the gate from the quiet field in the Source.

They stepped out onto the building's roof and into the swirling chaos of the defenders' last gasp. Harlequin could feel the eddying of dozens of magical currents pulsing around him. Most rose from the street below, but a few reached him from above, flitting about the building. The snipers on the roof had scattered, some directing fire down into the street, most taking cover and firing panicked shots into the air.

He glanced skyward long enough to see two figures streak past, lightning blazing from their hands. They were moving too quickly, but he caught streaming long hair, jeans, and thick jackets. Definitely humans.

Below, the rock and gravel that packed the shipping containers flowed out of them, swirling and rising until a huge automaton stood, a hulking mass of asphalt, trash, and dirt. It lifted one of the now-empty shipping containers, tossing it aside like a toy. It smashed against the steps of the church, crashing through the dug-in positions of sandbags and piled tires, crushing the defenders behind them.

A hoarse cheer rose up from Scylla's army.

The *Gahe* surged, making for the gap in the barricade. The Terramancer who'd conjured the automaton appeared behind them, arms raised, two more men at his side, both pouring gouts of flame into the ranks of the defenders, pulling back as the *Gahe* pushed through.

The flames swept over the remains of the barricade, then suddenly swirled, sputtered, and re-formed as man-shaped things that settled among the *Gahe*, swinging and tackling.

Harlequin spotted Downer, kneeling at the building's edge, brow furrowed in concentration.

But for every *Gahe* who stopped to fight the elementals, another sprinted past it, racing through the gap and up Broadway. Screams reached Harlequin as the civilians behind the police lines splintered and fled, too slow by far. Horns sounded from the goblin ranks, and they followed the mountain gods through.

One of Downer's air elementals had carried her to the church's steeple, where she directed the flame-men below. The mortar positions went silent as the defenders mixed with the attackers and the hand-to-hand fighting began. Downer's elementals leapt among them, reducing them to howling smoke at the touch of their flaming fists, but they were extinguished by the *Gahe*'s freezing death throes, and more of them pushed past and into the city beyond.

The Terramancer's automaton reared above them, pounding with huge rock fists. It gripped a police mobile command center, lifted it two-handed, slammed it down into a knot of policemen and soldiers.

It was enough. The defenders turned and fled along Houston Street, firing blindly over their shoulders, leaving the way open.

"Jesus," Britton said. "I'll be back." He flashed open a gate and disappeared through it. A moment later, it reopened, and beaten police and soldiers came stumbling through, following as Britton pointed them to positions at the building's edge.

The defense coiled in upon itself, retracted, suddenly exposed at the flanks. Harlequin heard screams as the NYPD cops and National Guard soldiers suddenly found the enemy at their rear, in among them.

The rest went quickly. Harlequin watched in slack-jawed horror as the line of defense retracted east and west, a rubber band severed down the middle. Scylla's army pursued them, taking them down with spears and arrows in their backs, shouting insults and shaking fists.

In moments, Harlequin couldn't see a single uniform in the midst of the seething mass of enemy below.

To the last bullet and the last man, sir, the captain at Barricade Three had said, *they won't get through while we draw breath.*

True enough. There were precious few left breathing down there now.

Scylla's army took a moment to survey the field of victory, then followed the *Gahe* north, where New York lay before them like a sacrificial offering, defenseless.

Downer alighted on the roof beside Britton, stared frankly. She jerked her chin at Harlequin. "He promise you a pardon, too? I'm getting one once this is over."

She looked out over the ruin of the barricades. "Which I'm thinking might be sooner rather than later. Guess maybe he'll go back on his word now."

"I wouldn't worry about that," Britton said. "If there's any problem, I'll get us out of here."

"Enough," Harlequin said. "Let's get back to Battery Park."

"For what?" Bookbinder said. "They're through."

"Which means we have to find another way to stop them. It's time for us to get our own message out."

The reporter looked about twenty years old, with a scrubby beard and oversized eyeglasses. He bustled about, setting up a tiny camera on a tripod, hands trembling. He probably thought this scoop would make his career. Hell, it probably would.

There was no shortage of journalists risking their lives to document the story. Harlequin had plucked this guy off a tiny boat bobbing off the ferry terminal, taking advantage of the fact that all of the NYPD harbor and Coast Guard units had long since gone ashore to lend their guns at the barricades, or had their boats in either the Hudson or East River to harass the enemy from the water.

"So . . ." Harlequin said.

"Ben," the reporter said to Britton. "It's an honor to finally meet you, sir. I'm so incredibly psyched for this. I did a lot of the production for the second Gate-Gate coverage. Been a big fan of yours for a while."

"You said major networks," Harlequin said.

Ben rolled his eyes. "You're living in the Dark Ages. Nobody watches that crap anymore."

Harlequin felt his fists bunch. "The whole reason I gave you this story was because I need distribution. Now if you can't . . ."

The kid wasn't interested. "You want to reach the largest possible audience as quickly as possible? Or did you want to have the cachet of a major network and only be seen by a handful of geriatrics who are watching with one eye as they run off to work or put the kids to bed?"

Harlequin considered that.

"Have you ever heard of viral media?" Ben asked. "I just tweeted a link to my live feed," Ben went on. "I have over fifty thousand followers . . . no, wait. Make that over one hundred and fifty thousand. Go figure, folks like to see shots of your headquarters here. That link has been retweeted to a total of . . . uh . . . looks like almost two million nodes so far. That doesn't count online shares on other social-media sites. You've got to trust me on this. People are getting it. This is too big not to draw attention."

Harlequin and Bookbinder had donned fresh uniforms, cleaned themselves up as best they could. Clean-shaven, hair combed, they looked bizarre amid the bedraggled, filthy soldiers outside the ready room. Harlequin had stationed two guards to keep the room clear. The troops under his command would see the broadcast soon enough, and there would be a reckoning when they did. Therese had remained at the barricade with Downer. Her magic was needed everywhere, but there most of all.

"You ready?" he asked Bookbinder. "Once we do this, there's no turning back."

"We've already done it," Bookbinder said. Gatanas had cradled his head in his hands and nodded when Harlequin had given him the news. *You're relieved of command, Lieutenant Colonel. General Bookbinder has the ICP now.*

Very well, sir, Bookbinder had said. *My first command is to put Oscar Britton on the air. We're going to lose if we don't turn this tide. Barricade One broke less than an hour ago. There are enemy in the city north of the line. The Breach Zone is . . . breached. We need something, or it all comes apart.*

Gatanas had watched them for a long time, eyes tired. At last he shook his head. *Sounds like you've made your call.* He'd severed the connection.

Harlequin guessed that, secretly, Gatanas hoped they'd do it. He knew circumstances were desperate in New York and that this move had as much of a chance as any to halt Scylla's momentum. If it worked, Gatanas would take full credit for it. If it didn't, his hands were clean.

Harlequin looked over at Britton, dressed in a clean casual shirt and jeans. Clean was good, but the informality bothered him. "I can't convince you to put on a tie?" Harlequin asked. "We're surrounded by every store in the world. I'm sure we could . . . borrow you something Scylla's army hasn't managed to burn or shred yet."

"You're appealing to people who have been hounded by politicians for years," Britton said. "You want me to dress up like one?"

"Everyone is going to see this," Harlequin said. "Not just Selfers. We have to convince the whole country. The whole world."

Britton shook his head. "You're still trying to play their game. That's done." He nodded to Ben. "Let's go."

Ben nodded back, his voice trembling with excitement. "Live in five, four . . ." He mouthed the remaining countdown, flashing fingers until he reached zero. A red light shone from the camera's top as he started recording.

Harlequin's TV instincts kicked in and he straightened, put on the face he'd used on dozens of news shows since he'd been appointed Special Advisor to the Reawakening Commission: authoritative, serious. He was used to working in a professional studio, and the dirty, cluttered digs left much to be desired, but he knew from experience it would come across as authentic, and that would curry favor with the audience. As Britton began to speak, there was an explosion outside, and the building shook. He restrained the urge to rush out and see what had happened. This was too important. He had good people out there. They would hold.

"Most of you know who I am," Britton began, "but in case you don't, I'm Oscar Britton. I am the so-called Selfer fugitive who helped save FOB Frontier. There's a lot of people out there who have staunchly supported me, and I'm deeply humbled by that.

"And now I want to call on that support. Most of you also know that this country is experiencing the biggest threat to its existence since its founding. A powerful army of monsters is in our midst, and I won't lie to you, it's got a real shot of doing some serious damage.

"The leader of this army has put out a call to all Latent people to help her. From what I can see here in New York, some of you have already answered that call. That's a mistake.

"She talks a lot about freedom and being part of some master race of magical beings that rules over humanity. She's brought up the fact that she's Latent as if it gives her some kind of moral authority. She throws in some gripes about the government's treating her badly. Well, I'm Latent, too, and I've got as much of a beef with the government as anyone.

"Scylla has talked a lot about Latent people 'no longer being dogs for weaker beings.' I don't see non-Latent people as weaker than me. I don't even see them as being all that different. Science is just beginning to wrap its head around magic and how it works, but I already understand it well enough to know that there's something about my limbic system that allows me to channel it. That makes me powerful, but it doesn't mean I'm not human, and it sure as hell doesn't mean that this isn't my home.

"I know Scylla. I've watched her butcher hundreds of people. She's only interested in replacing the tyranny she rails against with one of her own. You'll see if you answer her call. You won't be fighting alongside other human Selfers. You'll form less than one percent of an army of monsters straight out of your worst nightmares. I've fought these so-called Mountain Gods, and they're not pretty, or nice, and they sure as hell don't care about the future of humanity. If they win this fight, do you think they'll simply say, 'Hey! Thanks for the help, we'll just go back to where we came from now!' They'll stay, and I don't want to find out what the world they'd build here looks like.

"Scylla's partially right. The government has done Latent people wrong, and it needs to change the laws. But we have to do it *right*. Blowing up the biggest city in the country isn't the way.

"It's slower and it's more complicated and it's frustrating as hell, but there's a *right* way to fix this. We need to amend the McGauer-Linden Act. I am standing here with Lieutenant Colonel Jan Thorsson and Brigadier General Alan Bookbinder of the Supernatural Operations Corps. Most of you know who they are, and that they were willing to defy their government rather than allow it to do wrong by you.

"Scylla has promised you a kingdom apart from humanity. That's bullshit. She is human, as are we all, and we don't need to live apart from anyone.

"Here's my counteroffer. Help us to beat her. The SOC promises to convene a special committee to review the McGauer-Linden Act with a mind toward allowing Latent persons who prove control over their abilities to live as free citizens: not in the SOC, not in the NIH monitoring program, not in the Marine Corps Suppression program. Their own magic at their own disposal. Private citizens, equal under the law."

There was, of course, no guarantee that the president would accede to these demands. No promise that a defeat of Scylla wouldn't instantly devolve into a civil war as Selfers demanded rights the government had never agreed to give them.

"We're with Scylla on this much: Limbic Dampener will be subsidized, mass-produced, and distributed. Control over magic will not be held hostage to the profits of the Entertech Corporation. All will have access, especially the newly Manifested.

"This process will be slow, there will be hurdles. It will be frustrating, but the alternative is what you see here and in Mescalero. I don't want to live in those ruins. That's why I'm for the slower road, the longer road, the *right* road.

"I'm here to fight against Scylla and what she stands for. I am Latent, and I'm human, like all of you. I am fighting for humanity, and I ask you to join me. After the victory here, we will start on the road toward freedom, equality, and peace for all of us. They called us Selfers because they thought we used magic only for ourselves. In New York, let's use our magic for others. Join me. Push back this threat. Save this city. Together, we'll forge a new world of magic with room for all."

Ben waited another moment before stopping the camera. They waited in silence as he opened a smartphone and began tapping away at the screen. "That's it," he said. "You're live."

"How can you be sure that . . ." Harlequin began, but the news channels on the monitors were already showing him and Bookbinder standing to either side of Oscar Britton with the words BREAKING NEWS scrolling beneath. On the major networks in an instant.

"Thank you," Harlequin said.

Ben shrugged. "Thank you. I truly hope you beat this thing, and I truly hope the government does right by its Latent citizens."

They'd promised Ben he could stay in the park and film, and he headed out of the ready room to start gathering footage. The three men stood in silence, thinking on the gravity of what they'd just done.

"Think it'll work?" Harlequin asked.

"Probably not," Britton answered. "I believed every word, and it still sounds like crap to me."

Harlequin shrugged. "They impeached Walsh. Hopefully, that was a step in the right direction."

"I think seeing you and General Bookbinder in the picture will help," Britton said. "A star carries a lot of authority."

Bookbinder snorted. "Porter might take to the airwaves any second and deny all of it."

"I don't think he will," Harlequin mused. "We're overwhelmed and losing ground here, and he knows it. He doesn't want a disaster on his hands any more than we do. He can't truck with Selfers or he publicly goes against his whole line. He'll wait to see if we're successful, make his call based on that."

"Gatanas didn't tell us no," Bookbinder said.

"An old mentor of mine once told me 'that which is not specifically prohibited is authorized.'" He wondered where Crucible was in this fight. The SOC was entirely on two fronts now, so if his old friend wasn't here in New York, then he was neck deep in Mescalero.

"So," Britton said slowly, "let's say this doesn't work, let's say that the Selfers stick with Scylla. What happens then?"

"Then?" Harlequin sighed. "Then they take New York. Then, we lose."

INTERLUDE IX
BEYOND THE PALE

Due to the critical security concerns surrounding the development of Limbic Dampener, the court has elected neither to liquidate Channel Corporation nor to solicit for proposals from the contracting community. As the government lacks the expertise in the federal workforce, we have selected the Entertech Corporation to take over where Channel left off after the unfortunate Manifestation and arrest of their CEO. Entertech has ably served the United States on arcane matters since its founding, and remains the only private entity in the country equipped to handle the unique technical, logistical, and security requirements of this crucial program.

—Cameron Williams
Attorney, Office of the Secretary of Defense

SIX YEARS EARLIER

Harlequin came to as Crucible dragged him upright, slapping drywall fragments from his shoulders. He blinked in the settling dust, staring in wonder at the pile of wood, wire, and metal that had formed a natural cave. He blinked again. Sunlight. The dust swirled out of what was now an open porch, spiraling as the breeze took it. The Channel building looked as if a bite had been taken out of its apex, left completely open to the sky.

"I've got her, sir," Rampart was saying, crawling out to join them. They'd been spared the worst of the debris. A huge chunk of masonry had crushed Grace's desk, followed by a double-thick sheet of drywall, serving as an impromptu lean-to, sheltering the four of them.

"You've got her?" Harlequin couldn't keep the relief out of his voice. "She's alive?" He felt for her current and found it, faint, but present, raced to the pile of debris covering her, digging frantically, heedless of his bare hands.

"Everybody okay?" Crucible shouted.

"He's not," Rampart said, kneeling beside Hicks and checking his vitals. "Breathing, but out cold."

"I've got her Suppression. Get him out of here and get him to an ambulance," Crucible said. "They shouldn't be in short supply."

Harlequin saw his point. He could hear the sirens echoing up to them already. He spared a glance down as he worked. Much of the building was scarred where the tumbling chunk of the building's canopy had struck it, windows shattered, walls torn out, offices left exposed to the gusting wind. Harlequin saw blood streaking the destruction and turned back to his digging. There would be innocent dead. He didn't want to think of what had happened on the busy street below when the piece of the building came crashing down.

He heard Rampart grunt as he lifted Hicks's unconscious body and carried him to the stairwell. Harlequin kept digging.

At last he found a pale arm. He grasped the wrist and felt a faint pulse. Relief flooded him, and he had lifted her hand halfway to his lips before he stopped himself. He went back to digging as Crucible joined him, finally exposing her torso, coated in dust, the jagged splinters of a shattered girder protruding from one arm. "She'll feel that when she wakes up," Crucible said. "She got the worst of it. Might be something broken farther down. Better not to move her."

Harlequin tried to sound neutral. "What'll happen to her?"

Crucible looked up at him. "What'll happen to all those people down in the street? Crushed under half a building because some fucking Probe couldn't be bothered to do the right thing?"

This is my fault. Every casualty down there is on my head.

Harlequin grappled with that guilt as his boss stood, emotions warring on his face. At last, he blinked hard, put his hands on his hips, and surveyed the damage. "What a fucking mess."

The wind whistled in Harlequin's ears, the bright sunlight revealing New York's cityscape in all its glory. At this height, with the dust clearing, it might have even been a beautiful view. Provided you didn't look down.

Crucible's voice was gentler as he looked back to Harlequin. "We're not going to kill her, Jan. There's a place we take Selfers, Probes especially. I guess it's time you saw it."

Harlequin barely heard him beyond what he needed to know, that Grace would live. He stared at her face, eyes closed, lips slightly parted, not so different from how she'd looked as she lay beside him on their last night together.

"Hicks told me some nasty bullshit, Jan," Crucible said. "Said you knew about her. Said you knew what she was hiding."

Harlequin's mouth went dry. "What are you going to do?"

"Told him I'd break his jaw if he spouted any more crap like that. Can't imagine this would have gone different if you tried to bring her down yourself. This is what Selfers do, they . . . break things."

Harlequin felt weak, whether from guilt or relief, he couldn't tell. Probably both. "Thank you."

"Love can make you do strange things," Crucible said. "Emotions are unreliable. That's why we stick to regs, Jan. I never liked that whole sheepdog bullshit you were spouting when we first came here, but it got me thinking. You were right about one thing. There's a difference between Selfer and Sorcerer, and it's a line that can't be left to the vagaries of human emotion. It has to be crystal clear. There's one thing, and you either get it or you don't."

Standing in the swirling dust of the collapsed building, hearing the tramping of boots heralding the approach of police, or SOC, or EMTs, staring down at Grace's face, Harlequin couldn't focus. "I'm sorry, sir. I don't remember."

"Really? You're the one who told me."

Harlequin shook his head.

"Regs, Jan. It's regs. We follow them, Selfers don't. That's the difference."

And it was.

Jan Thorsson stood in the wreckage, fingers holding Grace's

wrist, straining to catch her fluttering pulse, the screams and wailing sirens drifting up to him from the street, the short pops of sparking wires.

It was the sound of what happened when you thought you knew better than the people who wrote the rulebooks.

It was the sound of consequences.

CHAPTER XX
TRY THE BAD GUYS

When you weaponize magic, the ability to Draw and Bind is only one piece of the puzzle, maybe even the smallest piece. A helicopter pilot once told me that flying is like "driving, checking your e-mail, and dancing all at the same time." Mission-focused magic use is the same thing. Effective Pyromancers who don't know how to aim are about as useful as Aeromancers who don't know how to fly. Just because your daddy gives you a new Ferrari doesn't mean you automatically know how to drive it.

> —Chief Warrant Officer-4 Albert Fitzsimmons
> Inputs (stricken) to quarterly report on the progress
> of the Shadow Coven (C4-Umbra) program

With the barricades breached, Scylla turned her army north, and the pressure on Battery Park subsided.

Bookbinder worked around the clock, ensorcelling the ammunition arriving from Fort Dix and Hamilton, overseeing the soldiers who then packed it into helos that took to the sky to distribute it among the units desperately trying to corral the breakthrough.

Harlequin had been looking nervously to the south ever since he heard how Bookbinder had been delayed, until the news reported that the navy's Fourth Fleet had surrounded the Breach in the water. Anything coming out of it would do so under their guns.

"We have to do the same," Harlequin said to Bookbinder, as they rested inside Castle Clinton. "They think we're out of the fight. We need to get them looking at us again, threaten the

Breach. It's the one point through which Scylla receives supply. We put that at risk, and we force her to turn her attention to us."

"Outside the walls of this compound?" Bookbinder asked. "We won't last long."

"We've got Britton now. You helped us get an army on the hop last time, Oscar. Can't we do it again? What about your goblin buddies in the Source?"

Britton pursed his lips. "They're still getting back on their feet after saving our asses at FOB Frontier, and they only got into the fight after we'd disengaged. A raging battlefield with goblins fighting goblins? The friendly fire would be insane. Plus, we're fighting against other humans now. The Mattab On Sorrah have religious dictates that would have to be reconciled. It would be complicated. It would take time."

"We don't have time," Bookbinder said.

"Truelove"—Britton's brow wrinkled—"I doubt he'll help, but I can ask."

Harlequin's face lit. "We were wondering what happened to him."

Britton's expression set. "I can contact him, that's all. He's . . . not favorably inclined toward the SOC at the moment."

"Neither was Downer," Harlequin said. "Give me a chance to talk to him. We can offer him the same deal that we're offering . . ."

"Downer already talked to him. I think she . . . put some cracks in his defenses. I can work that angle."

Harlequin was about to respond when a sergeant came bursting into the room, out of breath. "Sir! There's an Aeromancer flying around out over the water. He keeps shouting that we shouldn't shoot him, and he wants to talk to you."

Harlequin rushed out of the exit, Bookbinder and Britton behind him. He raced past the guards and jumped airborne, rising up and over Castle Clinton, shading his eyes and looking south.

In the distance, a Blackhawk hovered, its guns broadside at a floating man, gesturing wildly at the crew. As Harlequin watched, the Aeromancer began to descend slowly toward the shoreline while the helo hovered behind him, keeping its minigun trained on his back. Soldiers crowded beneath him, guns aimed skyward.

As the man came into view, recognition bloomed in Harlequin's mind. He hung back, descended until he stood beside Britton and Bookbinder.

The Aeromancer saw him, of course. Harlequin felt the pulse in his current, saw the flicker of dark anger in his eyes, but he swallowed it and faced Britton squarely, breaking into a smile. Bookbinder recognized him as well and waved the soldiers back, though they only moved a few steps, guns trained on Swift. *They're going to have to get over this,* Harlequin thought. *Our only chance is to work with Selfers.*

"Howdy," Swift said.

"Took you long enough," Britton said. "I was worried about you."

"You worry too much," Swift said. "That was quite a speech you made. Any of it true?"

"Every word," Britton said.

"Yeah, I figured. You were always a pompous dick but never a liar. Might be why you've got so many die-hard fans in the Houston Street Gang."

Harlequin swallowed his excitement.

Swift's face went pensive. "I'm here because we know each other, and for all the help you've given us, but I still have to answer to the rest of them. Even after all that happened, some of the gang are still just barely off the fence. Luckily, they're outnumbered by your cheering section. You were the first to bring this thing public. After both gate-gates, when people watch TV, when they go on the Internet to debate Latent rights and the McGauer-Linden Act, it's your face they see. Hell, I know you. I was in a gulag with you. I've seen what a fuck-up you are firsthand, and I still get chills sometimes."

Britton looked embarrassed. "So, that's why you're here? Because I'm on TV? Hell, Harlequin's on TV all the time." Harlequin winced. *Don't draw attention to me. He hates me.*

Swift didn't even look at Harlequin. "Yeah, well. I'm not a fan, but the gang feels that his most recent appearances have gone a ways to balance all the crap he stood for before. You know, I'd still rather see the guy dead"—Swift raised his voice, making sure Harlequin could hear him—"but it's like I said. We make decisions as a group, and the decision is that the gang wants in. We want the new world you promised. We'll help you to get it. I was in the hole with Scylla. I remember what she's all about. I don't want to live with whatever she's got planned."

Britton grinned and clapped Swift's shoulder. "That's fantastic," he said, turning to Harlequin. "Is there an access point we can open to get them in here? Maybe we can have a helo . . ."

Swift cut him off. "You never were a good listener."

The Aeromancer finally turned to Harlequin. "We want all the way in. Not just to the fight. To the committee meeting. To the legislative process. When the law gets rewritten, we have our hands on the pen."

"We're out on a limb here," Bookbinder answered. "I can't speak for what the president or his staff are going to . . ."

"Well, we'll just go, then," Swift said. "You fucking people need to learn when your back is against a wall, and you can't negotiate anymore. I said that *I* know Scylla and *I've* seen what she's about. *I* won't join her. A few of us are of the same mind. But a lot of the others see her point. I'm sure when they hear that the president would rather take his time and dither over this, they'll know he's not for real. I thought you appreciated the precariousness of your position. I guess I was wrong."

"So you take Scylla's bootheel off our necks and replace it with yours?" Bookbinder asked.

"Goddamn right!" Swift said. "We've been putting up with yours on ours for years now! It's about time you got a fucking taste! If clinging to the trappings of your power is more important to you than winning this fight, then be my guest. But a nation 'of the people' actually has to be of the people, jackass. That means a place at the table."

The rage rose. Harlequin felt his magical current surge and his muscles bunch. *Is he wrong? He's here to help you! Why are you so angry?*

The anger suddenly competed with shame. *Because you're on the same side now. Because you're no different.*

Because now even you can't tell the difference between the sheepdog and the wolf.

"We're not trying to overthrow the government here. That's Scylla's game. We're just trying to force it to change. This is still America, Swift," Britton said. "That place at the table is for representatives designated by popular acclaim, not a power grab."

"Yeah, when it comes to Selfers, the Porter administration definitely has popular acclaim. Jesus, listen to yourself. What the hell do you think the SOC is but a giant power grab? It's the few Latents who have agreed to do the bidding of the people most terrified of them. All we're doing is trying to make sure our voices are heard."

Bookbinder opened his mouth to reply, but Harlequin could stand it no longer.

If Swift is your partner, then he's your partner.

"How many are you?" Harlequin cut Bookbinder off.

The anger in Swift's voice was unmistakable, but he answered. "Twenty, maybe twenty-five if I twist a few arms."

Harlequin looked at Bookbinder. "This whole argument won't matter anyway unless we win."

"Could it tip the balance?" Bookbinder finally asked.

"Maybe," Harlequin said. As if on cue, a series of booms sounded far to the north, followed by sizzling cracks of summoned lightning. The soft whisper of distant screams reached him.

Harlequin sighed, felt his shoulders slump. He was so damned tired. "Probably not."

"Maybe not," Swift said, "but we're one of the most well-known gangs outside of Mescalero. If we stand with you, chances are it could turn a few heads. Maybe turn a few coats, too."

Harlequin sagged, the exhaustion and the gravity of it finally sapping what little remained of his strength. They had come so far, and for what? He'd gotten Downer, gotten the training Covens, even gotten Bookbinder to produce magical ammunition. Now, at long last, Scylla played a trump card that he couldn't hope to beat, turning the government's own record of oppression against itself. Harlequin had faithfully served that system, and in doing so, maybe even helped to create the threat he was now called on to mitigate. And for what? He'd now gone on record calling on the state's greatest enemies to join him. What future did he have even if he did manage to win this? *Self-indulgent. Cowardly. It's not about you. You have people depending on you. Take care of them.*

"If you're bringing twenty Selfers to the fight"—Harlequin's voice sounded as if it came from a long distance away—"then we're going to need to turn a whole lot more coats. We need a serious contingent of magic-wielding troops. Quebec . . . All the good guys have been waved off by other good guys."

"Then we ask the bad guys," Swift said.

Harlequin looked up at him at that. *We already did that,* he thought. Better not to say it.

"You're already getting us." Swift was smiling now. "You need dyed-in-the-wool bad guys."

Harlequin began to take his meaning. "Who is worse than you?"

"In the eyes of the US? No one," Swift said. "But Mexico has its own prodigal sons."

"What are you talking about?" Harlequin was too tired to play guessing games, even if it did antagonize his potential ally. "You mean the *Limpiados*?"

"You know about them?" Swift asked.

"I . . . ran into them a day or two ago. They're not interested."

"They're not interested in *you*. They're damn well interested in Oscar Britton. I talked to them back when I first got here, tried to see if we could find a common interest. They weren't buying it then, but things have changed."

"Let me guess," Bookbinder said, "they'll want a place at the table, too. A voice in the new policy."

Swift shrugged again. "That's the only thing you have on offer, General. But yes, they want to curry favor with the American government for the same reason any Selfer would, so they can step out of the shadows. They may live in a sewer, but they're not stupid. If America's policy moves, Mexico's . . . heck, maybe the world's, will follow."

"So you're offering the assistance of a group of sewer-dwelling Selfers who work for the most notorious drug cartel in the world," Bookbinder concluded.

Swift nodded. "I'm offering you a chance to beat Scylla and save New York City. If you've got a better idea of where to get Latent troops, I'm all ears."

Bookbinder sighed. "Whatever I promise you now, the government can overrule. We can publicize the hell out of your involvement, show Selfers and the US military working together, I can put in all the good words I've got, but that's where it ends. This may finish up with everyone's head on the chopping block, win or lose."

"Seems to be something of an Internet media campaign, though," Britton said. "We've created a fact on the ground by making them public. Administration's had a tough time shaking that. Heck, not only are both of you still in uniform, you both got promoted."

"And put out to pasture," Bookbinder said.

Britton smirked. "I'm sorry, but you appear to be in charge of the most significant military engagement in the history of our nation. Wherever this so-called pasture is, I don't think you're in it."

Harlequin surprised himself by laughing. Some of the exhaustion fell away. "Okay, let's get the cameras back in here. We'll do another speech, this time with Swift in it. That is, if you're willing to make a public commitment?"

Swift nodded. "Two delegates. Myself and Guinevere. That or nothing. You insist on that when you get your meeting to reform the McGauer-Linden Act, and you hold the line if you don't get it. We bleed together. We negotiate together. You try to break us off at the critical moment, and you'll have a brand-new insurgency to deal with."

"Don't threaten me," Bookbinder said, "I've acted in good faith since I came up Latent. If I say we're honoring our commitments, then we're honoring them."

The crackling sounded again, the screams drifting from the north. Stuttering gunfire as the fight was joined in earnest.

"Fine," Harlequin said. "What are they going to do, fire me?"

Britton looked to Bookbinder, who nodded silently. "Okay. Get the cameras back in here, and let's go for round two."

INTERLUDE X
UNLEASHED

*When LL-14 was first developed, we were still figuring out the
artificial nanostructure we used for targeted delivery. We didn't
fully understand how the active ingredient was reacting with
the . . . DNA "box" we were putting it in. It turns out the combination was toxic. We fixed it eventually, mostly by keeping the
dosage low enough for the body to process over time. But in those
early days, and in high concentrations, LL-14 damaged the pre-
frontal cortex, impacting the subject's ability to interact socially,
to properly judge risk.*

—Noah Weiss
Senior VP for Research, Channel Corporation

SIX YEARS EARLIER

They took her to the infirmary at the liaison office in the same
unmarked van that had brought Morelli to Channel. The streets
were closed off, but the SOC placard Crucible placed on the
dashboard got them waved through.

The street was even more pristine than usual close to the
building, with the cops having cleared it of foot traffic. The
thick black smoke and stench of burning plastic told Harlequin
that conditions on the other side of the building were very different. Screams and wailing sirens overpowered him, the flashing colored lights setting off a splinter of a migraine behind
his right eye. Crucible placed their own spinning red light on
the dash, and that cleared the traffic on their route but only
made the headache worse.

Harlequin ignored the pain and focused on Grace, stretched across the center seat, the EMT kneeling beside her. Harlequin had almost wept with relief when he declared that she had no serious spinal injuries and could be moved safely, but they'd still strapped her down to a longboard, the cords holding her fast. With her pale skin, she looked like an action figure still in the box, cold and dead, and Harlequin reached out to feel her breath on the back of his hand to remind himself she was still alive.

"Don't even understand why the fuck I'm helping this bitch," the EMT groused.

"Because I told you to," Crucible said behind the wheel. "She's in SOC custody, and we take care of our prisoners."

"Who's taking care of the people she just flattened?" The EMT's lips trembled with rage.

"Your erstwhile colleagues," Crucible said. "You're needed here."

The EMT looked down at Grace, his lip curling. "I'm not helping this . . ."

Harlequin's hand locked around the EMT's throat, pushing him back until he rebounded off the far side of the van, the window vibrating. "If she dies, so do you." Harlequin's voice was a deep growl that sounded strange to his own ears.

The EMT struggled against his grip, desperately trying to cling to his anger, but fear won out rapidly, and he stopped fighting, eyes going wide.

"Jan!" Crucible shouted from the front seat. Slowly, Harlequin released the EMT's neck. The man shook his head, swore, and set about bandaging Grace's arm.

"Is anything broken?" Harlequin asked.

The EMT ignored him.

"Is anything broken!?" Harlequin yelled.

The EMT flinched but continued bandaging. "This arm, I'm pretty sure," he answered sullenly. "Her ankle's swollen, but it's just a sprain, I think. She might have a concussion. She's fine, man. She'll be okay." He spit out the last words.

Harlequin slumped against the seat, weak with relief. *She'll be okay.* Crucible put his foot down, the van picking up speed, weaving through traffic that was beginning to snarl as the news of the impact around the Channel building spread. Rampart fumbled on the radio, punching the scan button repeatedly.

Static, hiss, static, "word of an explosion in the financial . . ." music, static, "reports that a Selfer has killed several people in downtown . . ." He switched it off.

"Damn," Rampart said. "Word spreads fast."

Crucible nodded, the traffic finally thinning as they cleared Houston Street and headed north. "And doc's not going to be the only one in a surly mood. We need to get her out of here."

The EMT looked up as Crucible spoke, returned to his work at a glance from Harlequin.

The city was waiting for them as they pulled through the barbed-wire-topped chain-link fence that surrounded the SOC liaison office's motor pool. Two men in suits stood alongside a uniformed NYPD officer. Three bronze stars glinted from his shoulders. A crowd of officers stood behind them, arms folded, faces dark.

The crowd blocked the path to the brick building's rear entrance. Crucible pulled the van up short and turned to Harlequin. Before he could open his mouth, Harlequin said, "We're not giving her up, Rick."

"No," Crucible said. "We're not. But we've also got nowhere else to take her. We've got to get her into that building and keep her safe until we can get a team in here to escort her out. You ready?"

Harlequin nodded. The EMT backed away, moving to the rear of the van and fumbling with the doors. "Rampart," Crucible said. "You stay with her, keep her Suppressed, and *nobody* touches her."

"Got it, sir," Rampart said, drawing his pistol.

Crucible sighed and looked at his lap as the officer with the stars on his shoulders began to pound on the door. "Chief Alfano! Open the damn door!"

Crucible unlocked it as the EMT slid out the back doors of the van, leaving them open. Some of the cops raced around to them, but not before Rampart pulled them shut and slammed down the lock button.

Crucible opened the door just wide enough to slide through, closing it behind him. "Chief," he said. "That was fast."

"That's our prisoner." Alfano's Staten Island accent was a B-movie caricature. A vein throbbed in his forehead, disappearing beneath the brim of his hat. His small eyes were slits in his tan face. The cops pressed forward at his back, the heat of their anger so intense, Crucible imagined she could feel it from inside the van. They fanned out to either side of him, menacing, the line between police department and armed gang blurring.

"That's not what the law says, sir." Harlequin could hear the slightest tremor in Crucible's voice. "Selfers are under federal jurisdiction. We've got her, we'll stabilize her and get her to Quantico."

"I've got at least twenty dead downtown," Alfano raged. "That shifts jurisdictional lines."

"No," Crucible said, "it doesn't. Now get your people clear so I can bring her inside."

"You feds are like seagulls." Alfano's voice was a stage yell for the benefit of his mob of cops. "You fly in here, make a lot of noise, shit on everything, then fly away. Well, you're not going to do it this time. No hush-hush spook stuff. This is all over the news already. The people know, and they want justice. SOC's not in the justice business. That's for the police."

"And you're not in the lynch mob business, sir," Crucible yelled back. "We have jurisdiction over . . ."

"Fuck jurisdiction!" Alfano frothed at the mouth, and his mob of cops lost their patience, surging around him, reaching for Crucible and the doors to the van.

Harlequin slid the door open, Drawing his magic and rising over the crowd. He Bound hard to the air around him until it sizzled with electricity, thin tongues of lightning circling his body. A dark cloud formed from nothing, haloing him against a rising wind that sent the cops' hats flying, revealing Alfano's badly thinning pate.

Harlequin shimmered, a malevolent Tesla coil. "You're right," he said, sending a jolt of forked lightning to dig a furrow in the asphalt at Alfano's feet. "Fuck jurisdiction."

Anger can override reason, make a man brave. But reason is a persistent thing sometimes. Alfano's courage faded as quickly as the EMT's had. He stepped backward, mouth open, one arm stretched across the man beside him, his wrist waving back, back, back.

The crowd of police slowly parted, the path to the narrow

metal door clearing. Crucible raced into the van and silently helped Rampart wrestle the longboard out, moving as quickly as they could toward the door. The crowd of cops leaned in as they passed but moved away just as quickly as Harlequin descended, still wreathed in lightning. He landed in front of the door and reached for the handle.

Locked.

"Really, guys?" he asked the crowd. A quick burst of lightning blew the handle off. He kicked it open and held Alfano's gaze while Crucible and Rampart moved Grace inside.

"Anybody tries anything . . ." Harlequin said softly. The gray cloud thundered menacingly. He shut the door behind him and welded it shut with a short, focused burst of lightning. It wouldn't hold for long, but it was something. He followed Crucible and Rampart into the same ready room where Morelli had signed the papers. The station was deserted, eerily silent.

"Morelli," Harlequin said. "We need to secure her, too."

"Yes," Crucible grunted as he set the longboard down. "Yes, we do."

Grace had begun to moan, thrashing against the restraints. Harlequin felt her current pulse as she slowly became aware of the pain she was in. The Dampener must have been wearing off, her current came stronger with each passing minute. He knelt over her, nudging Crucible out of the way and undoing the restraints. It should be his face she saw first.

"Hey, babe," she said. "You look like shit."

He laughed, tears escaping before he could control them, kissed her forehead. She moved to push him away, winced at her wounded arm. She looked around, taking in Crucible, Rampart. "I guess I didn't get away."

"Grace Lyons," Crucible said. "Under the authority of the McGauer-Linden Act, I place you in military custody for unlawful magic use and practices proscribed under section 8.A.2."

He lifted his cell phone to his ear. "Now, keep it down so I can get us out of here before that mob gets over the scare your boyfriend gave them."

"Mob?" she asked.

"Some people got hurt," Harlequin said. "The wall you took down . . . it wrecked part of the building."

"How many?" she asked.

"I don't know . . . a lot."

Crucible was talking quickly into the phone, but his words were a background buzz as Harlequin focused on Grace.

"What happens to me now, Jan?" she asked. "That fucker Hicks gets my company? I go to jail? What happens to me?"

Harlequin dug for something reassuring to say, delving in his guts for an honest way to tell her everything would be all right. He came up empty. "I don't know."

"I'm a Probe," she said. "They're going to kill me, aren't they?"

"No . . . Grace. I don't know that."

"What do they do with Probes, Jan?" Her voice became shrill.

"I don't know!"

She propped herself up on her elbows, ignoring the agony the motion must have caused her. "Why the fuck don't you know? This is your job!"

He tried to ease her shoulders, gentle her back down. "I don't know!" he repeated. "I never . . . I'm not . . ."

She settled back down on the board, shut her eyes, gritted her teeth. "I'm fucking dead. They kill Probes, Jan. Everything I've built. The company. The drug. Entertech gets it all. Those fuckers."

Harlequin started as a rock slammed against the reinforced glass of the window. The shouts from outside the building were louder now, an angry chorus that spoke of a huge crowd. The NYPD had more discipline, no matter how pissed off they were. The location of the SOC LNO office was public knowledge, and it hadn't taken the enraged citizens of the city long to figure out where the perpetrator of the destruction downtown had been taken.

Crucible put his phone back in his pocket and moved to Harlequin's side. Through the crosshatching of the reinforced glass, Harlequin could see a huge crowd of civilians. Alfano's force had put aside their anger for now, were doing their best to keep them away, waving batons and shouting. But they lacked the helmets, shields, and training necessary for riot duty. As Harlequin watched, one of the cops was blindsided by a punch, sank to his knees. A man, purple-faced with rage, leapt over him before being clotheslined to the ground by another policeman.

"They're inbound," Crucible breathed. "It's going to take thirty minutes or so."

"We don't have that long," Harlequin said.

"No, we don't," Crucible agreed. "Let's go for the van."

"They're not going to let it through, sir," Rampart said.

"They'll move, or we drive over them," Crucible answered. "They're not getting her."

They bent and helped Grace to her feet. She cried out in pain, hopping on one leg, the opposite ankle swollen to grapefruit size, the skin mottled purple.

"Let's go." Crucible jerked his chin toward the door.

"Sir, I don't . . ." Rampart began.

"Now!" Crucible shouted.

Rampart ran to the door and opened it, scanning with his pistol as he led the way to the van. Grace hobbled along with them, her weight dragging on Harlequin's shoulder, hissing and wincing as each step jarred her wounded arm. Blood soaked through the bandage. Harlequin felt the warm moisture on his shoulder. "It's okay," he said. "We'll get you out of here."

"Why?" she asked. "So you can kill me yourself? Just leave me here. I'd rather have a public stoning than a private hanging."

"Shut up," Crucible said. "Hop faster."

The crowd was mostly concentrated on the building's front entrance. As the van drew closer, Harlequin dared to hope they might make it. The shouting grew slightly fainter as they moved away from the building. The steady patter of thrown rocks and bottles against the building's side increased.

"This is your fault," Grace said to Crucible. "Whoever died when that building came down. That's on you. If you'd just fucking leave Latent people alone, we wouldn't have situations like this. You left me no choice."

"There's always a choice," Crucible grunted. The van was steps away.

"They're here! They're here!" a voice shouted. Harlequin sawed his head to the right as an obese woman threw herself against the chain-link fence ringing the parking lot. It vibrated under her weight, adding a chiming protest to her shouting, calling to her comrades. "Comeoncomeoncomeoncomeon!"

A man joined her, then another, the fence bowed inward. Rampart pointed his weapon at them. "Get back! Get back right now!"

His trembling voice belied the empty threat of his gun. More bodies pressed against the fence. A screeching of metal reverberated along its length. A bottle arced through the air, shattered next to Rampart's feet.

"Come on!" Crucible said, as they cleared the remaining distance and hauled the van's back doors open.

Out of the corner of his eye, Harlequin could see dark blue flashes: Alfano's men lunging in the crowd, trying to haul the people back.

Failing miserably.

A gunshot. Then another. The hum of voices now so loud that Harlequin could no longer hear Crucible's shouted directions. He shoved Grace in the van, heedless of how it must hurt her. The crowd surged, the shouting rising until it drowned out all other noise. Crucible shouted silently, Grace screamed silently. Rampart pointed his gun in the air and fired it silently.

The fence gave a final groan of protest and collapsed silently.

Harlequin had never seen people move so fast. Before he could blink, Rampart had disappeared beneath a bellowing tide of humanity, a single protean creature composed of waving fists, pinched faces, and flailing legs. It spilled over him and flowed to the edge of the building before turning to face the van.

They'd never get the van started and moving in time. "We gotta go right now!" Harlequin shouted to Crucible, Binding his magic and going airborne. He hadn't carried two people in flight since training, but he'd figure it out. He grabbed Grace's ankle, began pulling her out of the van.

Something hit the side of Harlequin's head, sent him spinning, his vision going gray. He dropped to one knee, raised a hand to touch the wound, a harsh ringing rising in his ears. "Grace . . ." he mumbled, stumbling drunkenly to his feet. The horizon slid sideways, threatening to spill out of his vision and send him into blackness. He fought against vertigo, turned, got himself steady.

"Grace," he could hear his voice. The yelling had stopped.

Harlequin blinked as he recovered his wits and took in the eerie silence.

Crucible lay by the driver's side door, the fragments of a bottle littered around his head. Rampart lay crumpled against the far side of the fence, four people sprawled across him, staring in horror.

The crowd that had overrun the fence, the human tide, was gone. In its place was a slick muck blanketing the parking lot, spattered across the walls of the building, dripping from the fenders of the parked police cruisers. The stink of rot made Harlequin retch, leaning over the carpet of purple slime still dotted with shards of desiccated bone, twitching lumps of muscle.

People. Hundreds of people, in an instant.

Grace stood, ignoring the pain in her ankle, hand outstretched. She was smiling.

She turned to the flattened section of fence. A mixed crowd of police and civilians stood beyond, frozen in their fighting to stare openmouthed at the wet patch that had once been a horde of men and women. Alfano stood at their head, his uniform tattered, bronze stars long since torn from his shoulders.

"You wanted me," Grace said. "Here I am."

She raised a hand, and they doubled over as a single body, some screaming, some vomiting out a black porridge that had once been their insides. Alfano simply crumbled, drawing up into the fetal position as his skin blackened, sagged, then sloughed off him, running over the asphalt to join the egg-yolk ooze that had once been a crowd.

She turned to Harlequin, dusted her palms against one another. "Come on, lover. Let's go."

Her eyes were wide, almost fever bright. Her cheeks jerked upward in a coyote smile that showed too much teeth. Blood leaked from her nose, dripping off her lips to patter the ground between her feet.

What had happened at the Channel building had been an accident, the unintended collateral damage of a desperate woman trying to escape.

But this. This.

Harlequin shook his head slowly, Binding his tide across hers, rolling her magic back.

Her feral smile went ugly. "What the fuck are you doing?"

"What the fuck are you doing, Grace?" Harlequin asked.

"I am surviving, Jan. I am walking out of here and living my life to the potential it has always had. I have been doing good in the world, and I am going to keep doing it, whatever your stupid, narrow-minded laws say."

"Good?" Harlequin gestured to the mucal remnants of hundreds of people all around them. "How is this good?"

"That's on you and your fucking system," Grace snarled. "That's not my fault. You'd let me go, this would never have happened."

Ice ran up Harlequin's spine to the base of his skull. He shivered. "I'm not letting you go, Grace. Not now."

"Are you fucking kidding me? You want to live the rest of your life as a dog to a system that despises you? They'll keep you poor, Jan. They'll only let you do the things they say are authorized. Fuck them and their rules. Think of what we can do if we just let ourselves be what we are! They can't stop us, Jan. I see that now. We don't have to be scared anymore."

"I'm not kidding you, Grace. And I'm not letting you go. You have to . . ." He swallowed. "I'm sorry, but you have to pay for this."

All pretense of goodwill fled her face, her expression crunching into an animal snarl. She reached for him, took a step, sinking to one knee as her swollen ankle gave way. "They were here to kill me, Jan! I defended myself. How is that wrong?"

Harlequin only shook his head.

"You fucking government whore! Give me my magic back!"

"I'm sorry, Grace," Harlequin said, his voice breaking. "I'm so sorry."

She covered the rest of the distance on her knees, rose unsteadily to her feet. Her voice went smooth, her eyes little-girl wide. "I thought maybe you loved me."

Harlequin wasn't fooled, but it didn't stop the tears from coming as he answered her lie with truth. "I thought maybe I did, too."

"Fine." The little-girl voice went businesslike, and she leaned in for a good-bye kiss. "Do your job."

He knew what was coming and let it happen. He couldn't

shake the feeling that this was the last time he might touch her, and a part of him wanted that no matter the price. He cinched the first zip cuff in place as she leaned in, closing her eyes, then grunted as she brought her knee up into his crotch. He'd been ready, and turned aside, but her knee impacted the point of his hip, hitting a nerve cluster there, doubling him over sideways.

His current slipped from the pain, and she spun away from him, her arm jerking inside the plastic cuff, almost ripping from his grasp. But he held her fast, and she grunted as the plastic dug into her skin. He felt her current gather, surge, Bind. It was inexpert, poorly focused, but still far better than any Selfer he'd ever known. He reacted instinctively, launching his current at her, not even thinking to Suppress. She went rigid as a burst of electricity gripped her. She spun, dropped. Her suit smoked.

He knelt, checked her pulse. She moaned softly, stirring as he resumed the Suppression. "I'm sorry," he said, cradling her head in his lap. It was the truth.

But it didn't matter.

Harlequin had raised his right hand. He'd taken an oath. He was a sheepdog.

He hadn't been to church since he'd been assigned to the squadron in Florida; he'd felt nothing more than a vague sense of discomfort over the absence, like leaving a window open during a rainstorm. If God missed him, there'd been no sign. But now he couldn't help but feel the hand of something larger at work here. *You lost focus. You forgot why you do this. Something . . . someone had to remind you.* He looked down at her face, the beautiful contours of her mouth now creased in pain.

He'd forgotten the change magic had wrought in the world, forgotten what it could do. He'd forgotten why it was critical that the system keeping it in check be upheld.

He'd forgotten, and been reminded.

He would never forget again.

CHAPTER XXI
PUSH

The issue is, and always has been, one of funding. For a while, we were living in the age of counterterrorism. Then cyber threats were the new sexy. Now, it's all magic, all the time. The sheer volume of money, not just from government appropriations, but from private firms interested in "researching applications," is staggering. Think about the havoc unleashed in the financial sector when maritime shipping routes or agricultural yields are guaranteed due to weather control? Magic creates a lot of uncertainty, but it also eliminates it. We are only beginning to plumb the depths of the money involved here. And when sums this high are at play, the game can be very serious indeed.

—Robert Helm
Business analyst, Richmond Capital Investments

They came more quickly than expected.

The remains of the vehicle park became a de facto muster point for a small but growing group of Selfers. Harlequin marveled at their diversity. A woman with a shaved head in hiking gear. A man in the saffron robes of a Buddhist monk. Many wore tactical gear and surplus military uniforms. More than a few carried guns. They clustered around Britton, talking quietly, the look of reverence on their faces unmistakable. A few of them had already taken up positions on the walls, relieving the exhausted Novices, who joined the cluster of grumbling soldiers, keeping their distance, whispering to one another. Harlequin could tell they didn't like it, but it didn't stop them from accepting the relief, the chance to rest and eat. They knew they needed the help, wherever it came from.

Harlequin was painfully conscious of the mixed pulse of the magical currents. "We just need one of them to be secretly working for Scylla, and all hell is going to break loose."

Bookbinder sighed. "We don't exactly have time to run background investigations on them. If they move against us, we deal with it. What other choice do we have? We have to have faith in Swift and Britton."

Harlequin shook his head. "I am so sick and tired of taking the least awful of a host of terrible options."

"There are good options in war?"

Harlequin opened his mouth to respond, then froze, listening to a whirring thump, echoing between the buildings surrounding the park. "What's . . ."

"It's a helo," Bookbinder said.

Another moment's listening confirmed that it was. Harlequin's stomach clenched at the thought of one getting so close without his knowledge, but there was nothing to be done. Their comms array had been badly damaged in the attack, and it would be a while before they had radar again.

The Selfers surrounding Britton began to hear it, too. Swift rose into the air, hovering over his comrades' shoulders, head craned skyward.

"Don't worry," Bookbinder said. "I'm sure our antiair defenses will take care of it."

Harlequin snorted. "Let's just hope it's one of ours."

The helicopter finally cleared the buildings and banked into view. Harlequin's mouth went dry. "That's not one of ours."

It was an old Bell 210, a utility model, painted neither the deck gray nor camouflage patterns that would mark it for military service.

"Police?" Bookbinder asked hopefully.

"Those are blue," Harlequin said, and shot airborne, Swift following him up a moment later.

Harlequin Drew his magic frantically, readying a Binding on the air around the whirring rotors. If he put a bad enough storm cloud right on the blades, he might be able to . . .

And then he was dropping down, hand reaching out to Swift, waving him back. "Ease off!" he shouted. "Stand down!"

Swift shot him a questioning glance, lightning already balling around his fists.

Harlequin pointed to the side of the helo, a red swoop of a logo, the words below reading, ENTERTECH.

They followed it down, landing to either side as it touched down on a patch of cleared grass, opening the cabin door and pushing out a ramp, keeping the rotors spinning.

Two tough-looking men sat inside. They wore the kind of understated tactical clothing that could be mistaken for civilian shirts and trousers at a distance. Their weapons and body armor were professional grade.

A third man in Entertech coveralls was pushing a pallet onto the top of the ramp. He gave it a final shove and the ramp's small wheels slowly slid the pallet down until it came to a gentle stop, canted against the grass. The man kicked the end of the ramp out of the helo and moved to pull the cabin door shut.

Harlequin jogged the last few paces before the rotor wash began to drive him back. "What the fuck!" he shouted at the closing cabin door. "Wait!"

"General Gatanas sends his regards!" the man shouted back, then the helo was rising, banking hard out over the bay and into the distance.

Harlequin felt Swift's magic Drawing and turned to him. "Don't. We don't have time for that. Let them go."

Bookbinder had already reached the pallet, was detaching the bungee cords that anchored a tarpaulin over whatever was stacked on it. Harlequin went to his side, helped him until they had it unsecured. He met the general's eyes across the top, nodded.

They both pulled back the tarp in a single motion.

Revealing stack upon stack of syringes, each filled with yellow liquid.

Bookbinder's jaw dropped. "Do you know what this is?"

"Yes, sir. I do"—he looked up at the Selfers beginning to gather around them—"and I think I know what it's for."

"That's as much a green light as I think we're going to get," Britton said.

Much as he hated to admit it, Harlequin felt almost weak with relief. *He's with us. Gatanas is with us.*

Harlequin turned to Britton. "I'll get . . . your people orga-
nized and dosed. You said you would talk to Truelove. Now's
the time."

Britton nodded. "I'll be back."

Harlequin pointed to Swift. "It might help if you went with
him. You were with him in the village. He knew how much
you hated the SOC, and . . . well, how much you hate me. If he
sees you've agreed to help, it might move him."

"I don't hate you," Swift said. "I can't be bothered."

"Swift should come," Britton agreed, "but I need Downer
again."

"She's hard to spare," Harlequin said.

"Do it anyway," Britton said. "She's got his number. I've
never seen him actually get angry before Downer put him to
it. If there's anything that can tip him over the edge, it's her."

Harlequin exchanged nods with Bookbinder before turning
back to Britton. "Fine, but you've got to make it quick."

"One last thing," Britton said. "Got any sugar?"

Much of the fighting had moved north through the broken barricades, leaving the exit for the Battery Tunnel clear. The double maw gaped, surrounded by gun positions jutting out from
heaps of sandbags. Two precious Sorcerers had been drawn off
the SOC LE support team to guard the entrance, the only land
route leading off the island's southern tip.

Truelove emerged from it now, still in his goblin leathers,
still painted half-white. He looked tiny before the huge
expanse. He advanced a few more steps, small and alone, and
the darkness of the tunnel spat out the army behind him.

The dead had shambled along at his back for nearly two
hours, slowly making their way from Greenwood Cemetery,
across Brooklyn and under the bay. A cordon of soldiers
escorted Truelove, ostensibly to keep residents away from the
column, but precious little of that was needed. There were
nearly half a million dead under the ground in Greenwood,
and it looked to Harlequin like Truelove had raised them all.

They slumped out of the darkness, silent and steady, in various states of decay. Some stumbled along upright, their bodies fresh enough to be nearly whole, others dragged their

fragmented skeletons along by what remained of their fingers. They stank, but not as Harlequin had expected. There was no stench of rot. Rather, he smelled the rich, loamy scent of upturned earth mixed with the chemical reek of embalming fluid.

Cormack sat in an armored Humvee just outside the tunnel's mouth. Harlequin could see his face curdle at the sight of the Probe magic, but he nodded and turned the Humvee the wrong way down Morris Street. Truelove turned to follow, and his army of dead came behind him. Broadway had been cleared in the plaza around the statue of the charging bull, where he'd walked with Grace in search of ice cream. *It's going to end where it began.*

The troops were dug in all around the plaza, armed with as much of Bookbinder's ensorcelled ammunition as they could carry. The plaza was rimed in the gray slush that was the remains of slain *Gahe*. Goblin and giant corpses littered the ground. A knot of the enemy still clustered ahead of them, blocking their progress. Harlequin thought he could see a human or two in the mix, Selfers drawn to Scylla's banner, husbanding their energy as they waited to see what Harlequin's game was. One of them must have been a Terramancer, as an earthwork had been drawn up along the length of the street, the edges of the buildings to either side bleeding into it. A lone *Gahe* flashed before the wall, snarling. Goblins shouted insults from atop it, hurling javelins that fell short of the massing forces.

Truelove entered the plaza, and a hush fell across them. The troops drew back in revulsion, clustering to one side. The goblins went silent as well at the sight of the dead slowly marching in, rank after rank of the corpse tide spilling across the cobblestone street.

Harlequin turned to Britton and nodded. "That's it. They're staged. Now let's get our end moving." Britton opened a gate onto the Source, and they stepped through, then through another onto the rooftop above Barricade One, where Downer awaited them.

The fight raged in earnest as the enemy pushed back south, alerted to Harlequin's moving out from the park. The fighting below was mostly hand-to-hand. Here and there, a bullet exploded with magical force, but most of the ensorcelled rounds had been entrusted to snipers on the rooftops around the street, instructed to shoot only at *Gahe*.

Above them, rocs and wyverns circled, pulsing forward and pulling back from a formation of Blackhawks that turned miniguns on them whenever they threatened the top of the building, ensuring the defenders the high ground for now. An Aeromancer, one of the Fornax Novices, hovered between them. Harlequin couldn't see any enemy Selfers from his position, but he knew they were there, keeping hidden in the buildings, unleashing their magic when they had a chance. He could feel their currents whipping about the battlefield, saw one police officer fall to the ground, raking at his rapidly drying skin until it crumbled into dust, desiccated by some hidden Hydromancer.

Broadway north of the barricade now looked much like the Financial District: burning shops, corpses in the streets. The war-tourists had learned their hard lesson.

Harlequin turned to Swift. He sheltered with his group under a thick concrete shelf raised by one of his own Terramancers. He recognized a few of them, including the duo of Iseult and Guinevere. Guinevere had come up Latent after Harlequin had taken Scylla down, what felt like a lifetime ago. She glanced past him now, and he had to stop and close his eyes for a moment to clear the memories that came rushing to his mind. Coming up Latent had scattered them both. Scylla had gone to the Source, first to be convinced to help the SOC, and when that failed, and she proved more dangerous than they could have imagined, into solitary confinement. Guinevere had gone under the streets of the city, where Harlequin and she had met. And now she stood alongside him, ready to fight against her former colleague.

The bald, muscular Pyromancer known as Flicker stood beside them. Harlequin had actually hoped to see the Houston Street Gang's most notorious member, the Physiomancer Render, but he wasn't among the group that Britton had gated in. Render had a great deal of SOC blood on his hands, and it wasn't surprising for him to doubt any amnesty the government might promise, no matter what aid he provided. Render had been not much different from Swift, angry, unpredictable.

Rending was some of the worst Probe magic out there, but man would it come in handy in this fight.

All of their currents were steady, tight. Their hearts pumped blood charged with Limbic Dampener. If he closed his eyes, Harlequin could almost imagine he had a corps of hardened SOC operators alongside him rather than this band of Selfers. Skill beat will. The control would give them a badly needed edge.

"You ready?" Harlequin asked.

Swift nodded.

"And the flushed Selfers? Your contacts in the *Zetas*?"

"They'll be at the staging area. You got it fixed?" Swift asked Britton. Britton nodded back, tapping the side of his head. He reached into a mag pouch on his tac vest and tapped the photographs Swift had downloaded off the Internet last night, shadowy images of slime-skinned, rotting brick façades that made up the walls of the sewers under Mexico City. Swift assured them that their newest allies would be waiting there. For a moment, the reality of what he was engaging overwhelmed him, but he shook free of it.

"How do you know Scylla is there?" Britton asked him.

"She'll be there. That Breach is the key to her entire operation. Without it, she can't resupply. She's cut off in enemy territory. She'll show herself."

"And if she doesn't?"

Harlequin feigned a nonchalance he didn't feel. "Then she's just one more Probe Selfer we have to run down and bring to justice." He smiled. "Subject to the new laws we establish under the amended McGauer-Linden Act, of course."

Britton didn't look amused.

"Lighten up," Harlequin said. "We're leading a mixed force of police and military, who have almost no experience fighting together and who lack the power to harm half the enemy. We're outnumbered and outgunned. We're partnering up with known Selfer gangs and a sewer-dwelling element of the most notorious drug cartel in the world. Our goal is to secure a rent in the fabric of reality that we have no idea how to close. What could possibly go wrong?"

Britton smiled at that, and Harlequin grinned back. When he spelled it out, it sounded . . . easier, somehow, as if openly defining the parameters of the battle they faced took away its power to frighten him.

"Let's do this thing!" he shouted to Swift. The Aeromancer nodded and ran to the building's edge. Two members of the gang joined him, leaping skyward as the rest of them raced through one of Britton's gates. Harlequin recognized one of the Aeromancers at Swift's side as Spur, a former NBA basketball player who'd vanished after Manifesting a few years ago. Downer had reported he was with Houston Street when she was being questioned.

Harlequin watched the ground below as the gate flashed open again, the Houston Street Gang moving out around an overturned dump truck. With them came dozens of others, the patchwork ranks of the Latent who'd trusted Britton's word and answered the call. Harlequin saw their hopeful glances cast Britton's way, the uncomfortable distance between them and the uniformed service members around them. He felt their disciplined currents, brought under control by the Dampener, indistinguishable from the few SOC Novices and LE operators in the ranks. He shook his head in amazement as dozens of radios crackled into life, relaying his orders.

Britton opened a gate that spanned the street, and Harlequin's force moved behind it as the Fornax trainees moved to join the Houston Street Gang. The enemy charged forward as they retreated, eagerly taking the ground they yielded up. Downer's elementals, flame creatures evoked from the fires burning across the battlefield, threw themselves into their mass. They spread themselves across the line of the intersection, burning hot, doing their best to slow the enemy advance. The soldiers cursed as they fought the few sprinters who made it through.

Harlequin watched as Iseult turned and extended a hand toward a giant who pummeled the roof of an NYPD mobile command center, ignoring the light-caliber bullets the cops behind it were pouring into him. His eyes rolled up in his head and he began to dance, scratching himself madly. He collapsed, shaking, his skin first peeling like ancient bark and finally blowing away in the wind as all the water in his body misted the air above him, condensing into a tiny rain cloud that showered his desiccated corpse.

A *Gahe* moved smoothly around him, swiping at Flicker. The Selfer Pyromancer dove backward, shooting a burst of flame over the *Gahe*'s shoulder.

A sharp crack sounded from the steeple of Trinity Church and a round punched through the *Gahe*'s neck. The freezing black smoke billowed out of its holed throat, sending the Selfers scrambling as a burst of crackling electricity arced across its torso, burning fresh wounds with each lightning kiss. A sniper with one of Bookbinder's magic rounds. The monster fell forward, its freezing blood misting out around it, clearing the ground of human, goblin, and giant alike.

Shivering, Flicker moved behind the overturned dump truck, sweeping his arms over his head. The flames from the truck and the buses alike danced to the movement of his arms, swirling and funneling before jetting forward across the intersection, blasting down into the broad junction of the streets. One of the Fornax Pyromancers and a SOC LE officer added their flames to the burn. Harlequin could see the enemy clearing back, Scylla's Selfers moving up to counter the blast with summoned wind or water.

"Stack the burn," he called into the radio. "Go."

Mortars sounded from the steeple over the church, dull whistles followed by thumps as the incendiary rounds impacted in the intersection. The flames whooshed into the air, the roar of the fire loud as any artillery round. Downer's elementals moved into the center of the blast, shivering as they burned white-hot. The flames leapt higher, the defenders backing away from the intersection as the heat reached its peak, so intense that Harlequin could feel its edges from his vantage point, the square disappearing from view beneath a shimmering haze.

The enemy backed farther down Broadway. Harlequin could see water bubbling up out of manhole covers in the distance, as Scylla's Hydromancers tried to call up a flood to drown the flames.

Flicker and the other Pyromancers extended their arms and pointed south. The fire whirled, bent, and howled down the corridor made by the tall buildings. The enemy screamed and fled as Broadway became a burning tunnel. In one instant, there was a tide of goblins and giants, dotted with *Gahe* and enemy Selfers. The next, there was blackened rubble, carpeted with gently smoldering ash. The intersection was clear, a smoking wasteland. The fire had scoured the area so thoroughly that there was barely any odor, only a faint brimstone stink, blown on a gentle wind. The buildings to either side burned brightly, all the way south to the turning that would take them outside Federal Hall and to the Breach.

Harlequin knew it wouldn't last long, that the enemy was regrouping even now outside the rotting portal to the Source. But for the moment, the way was clear.

"Let's go!" he shouted, and leapt into the air.

On the ground, Guinevere and other Hydromancers swept their arms into the air, calling up a torrent of water that pulsed out of the sewer gratings and popped off manhole covers, streaming along the ground and raising a cloud of steam that the soldiers now advanced through at a quick trot, moving south down Broadway toward the Breach. With them came Swift and the Houston Street Gang, sloshing through the water that cooled the surface of the street even as the Pyromancers dialed their flames back, making it clear for the force to pass, moving into the mist and disappearing from sight.

Harlequin descended just above the cloud and joined Swift in summoning a wind that swept it aside, giving the defenders a clear view as they turned down Wall Street.

The shouts of encouragement slackened, then petered off into silence.

Heaps of enemy dead were slowly struggling to their feet. Many were charred beyond recognition, some burned so badly they lacked limbs to rise, their smoking remains shuffling and rolling along the pitted avenue to join the formation of more solid corpses behind them. Harlequin could hear the calls of sergeants, yelling at the police and guardsmen to hold their fire. A few rounds rang out regardless, harmlessly holing the ranks of dead moving forward to join Harlequin's troops. Truelove had wisely kept himself a couple of ranks back, but emerged now, grim-faced and sweating, the white-painted side of his body streaked with black trails of ash.

Harlequin's troops swallowed their revulsion, moving like a single organism to keep to Wall Street's north side, away from the horde of dead that now marched alongside them. Together, they turned onto Wall Street and moved east, the

Breach shimmering ahead of them, taller than Federal Hall, the edges still peeling, the fetid stink of decay overwhelming the smoke of the fires behind them.

Scylla's forces fell back to defend the portal. The street thronged with enemy so thick they spilled onto north- and south-running streets. The air was black with rocs, with more emerging from the Breach's upper edge, circling away as the Blackhawks opened up with their miniguns. Bursts of answering lightning and fire silenced the guns a moment later, and Harlequin saw enemy Selfers taking cover on the roofs above.

The tight confines of the buildings turned Wall Street into a shooting gallery. Both sides flattened themselves to the ground, crouched behind cover hastily raised by Terramancers, the street flowing up into makeshift barriers with slits for gun barrels. Bullets and blasts of magic roared down, a funnel of ordnance that made it impossible for anything to survive.

But Truelove's force was already dead.

The zombies shuffled forward, ignoring the torrent of fire, burning, freezing, soaking up ammunition until their bodies collapsed. Still they advanced. At last, the dead reached the enemy, began clawing their way into their ranks. The *Gahe* flashed among them, but the corpses ignored the cold of their touch. The goblins and giants clubbed and stabbed, but the corpses shrugged off the wounds, mutely striking back.

The dead fought, and the living came behind them, pushing deeper into the plaza.

SOC and Selfer, fighting side by side to defend the nation. History was unfolding before his eyes. The world was changing. *And you helped change it.* He thought of Scylla, in this same city, all those years ago.

His troops were a motley of different uniforms, police and military members from all branches. They were dotted with civilians, answering a call for help. They marshaled their magic to push the enemy back. A few of them fired guns, possibly not even Latent, New Yorkers taking advantage of the chaos to join the fight, indistinguishable from the Selfers beside them. When FOB Frontier had fallen, it had been on him to help save an army. Now an army saved him.

Wolves and sheep, saving the sheepdog's ass.

Not wolves. Not sheep.

People.

He dove toward the fight, saw a gate flash here and there as Britton brought more troops into the plaza, often behind Scylla's forces. Bookbinder was somewhere in the press, ensorcelling rounds as quickly as they were expended, keeping the troops in ammunition that could affect the *Gahe*. The enemy, taken from all sides, began to bunch around the Breach, forced back into it.

Harlequin's smile became a grin.

A cop ran out in front of the rest of the force, firing a shotgun at point-blank range. The shells were Bookbinder-specials, flashing gouts of flame as they sprayed into the enemy ranks. A *Gahe* twisted aside from him, bleeding freezing smoke where the massed shot peppered its side. A goblin covered its face, burning, falling back against its fellows.

Then the cop doubled over, dropping his weapon. His eyes rolled up in his head, turned black, then liquid, pouring down his face. He vomited, slick chunks of his innards sluicing down his chin. Behind him, a lane of Harlequin's forces five wide did the same, clutching their stomachs, dropping to the ground. Their weapons and gear bloomed rust, the plastic parts flaking paint and falling to pieces. Their clothing thinned with rot, then flapped away. Their skin followed, their flesh and bones. Within moments, a swath of Harlequin's troops had been reduced to purplish smears, man-shaped outlines that stank of sulfur, slowly soaking into the pitted cobblestones of Wall Street. The zombies among them didn't scream or writhe, they simply lost form, pooling into liquid and finally puddling on the street beneath them.

Scylla.

He'd known the fight for the Breach would bring her out. Harlequin frantically felt for her current. He needn't have bothered. She stood fearlessly at Federal Hall's peak, a hand pointing below, surrounded by *Gahe* and Selfers. Helos banked sharply toward her. She pointed at them without turning to look, and they spun earthward, rusting and cracking as they went, until they crashed into the packed troops below, their fuel rendered into inert chemicals.

The zombies collapsed as a single body, the magic that animated them cut off. Truelove must have gone down.

The advance ground to a halt.

"The roof! The roof! Hit the roof!" Harlequin shouted into his radio, descending toward Scylla. But the crackling that came back to him through his earbud told him what he already knew. The counterattack had thrown his troops into confusion. They scrambled for cover that would do them no good, the less-disciplined Selfers turning and running. The enemy could retreat into the open space on the other side of the Breach, but Harlequin's forces were hemmed in by the tight confines of the street. They jostled against one another as they tried to move back from the sudden new threat.

Selfers stood to either side of Scylla, one male and one female, both kitted out in tactical gear, body armor and helmets, pistols on their thighs. Harlequin recognized them from the video where Scylla had issued her demands. The man felt Harlequin's current and turned toward him just as the Aeromancer released a burst of lightning. The female dragged Scylla aside, Harlequin's blast burning a sizeable hole in the roof. The male cursed as the lightning burst burned his legs, but extended his hands even as he dropped to his knees.

Harlequin felt his magical current roll back. The momentum carried him forward a few feet before he dropped out of the sky.

He tried to pitch his weight forward, to connect with the much closer roof, but his arms and legs pinwheeled uselessly. The rotten sludge that had once been his troops raced toward him.

A shoulder collided sharply with his back. Harlequin spun in the air long enough to see Swift arcing away from him, chased by a razor-sharp shard of ice.

The momentum carried him forward, his own shoulder colliding with the roof. Pain rocked him, his breath escaped in a rush. He flopped to a stop, gasping, back and shoulders numb, magical tide still interdicted. He rolled onto his side, fumbling for his pistol, fiery pins and needles surging through his shoulder and arm as he fumbled the catch on the holster. His fingers were useless, dead things, unable to find purchase. His vision narrowed to a gray tunnel as he desperately sought to suck in air. Through that tunnel, he saw Scylla, struggling against the grip of her Selfer bodyguard, trying to drag her away from the roof's edge as rounds tore into the shingle and stone, sending splinters spraying.

Scylla's bodyguard threw them both flat as a funnel of lightning shot over their heads, engulfing a *Gahe* that stutter-flashed toward Harlequin, claws outstretched. The creature screamed, billowing icy black smoke. Harlequin pressed down hard on the holster catch, dragging the pistol out with numb hands, his body moving but the nerves not reporting, as if he were his own puppeteer, yanking dead limbs upward on invisible strings. He fired into the cloud of black smoke, toward where he thought the Selfer stood.

Out of the corner of his eye, he could see Swift dancing along the roof's edge, funneling lightning over it. Spur hovered beside him. A Blackhawk was turning broadside, the gunner reloading.

Swift, who blamed him for the death of his girlfriend and child, who'd sworn he'd kill him.

But he had saved him, and now fought to keep him alive.

Harlequin squeezed the trigger again, hearing the dry click as his pistol's bolt locked to the rear, the last round expended. The black smoke of the *Gahe*'s death throes settled, riming the shattered roof with gray ice.

Scylla shrugged off her protector and extended a hand. The helo shuddered as it came apart, the pilots slumping against the windscreen. The Selfer beside Scylla pointed at the dirty-looking gray ice patches that coated the roof. They rose into sharp gray shards, spraying out at Swift and Spur, sending the Aeromancers diving out of sight. Scylla walked back to the roof's edge, her current intensifying. Sick yelps echoed up from the street.

Harlequin's breath came in choked gasps, but at least it came. He leaned on his empty pistol, struggling to get his weight underneath him. A vise of agony stretched from his shoulder to his waist, cinching tighter every time he moved. His spare magazines were in his opposite leg pouch, pinned under the weight of his traitor body.

"You don't look so good," Scylla said, smiling. Harlequin looked up, trying to meet her eyes, to show her he wasn't afraid. A strong eddy of chill air told him that at least one *Gahe* stood behind him.

"Well, that's not entirely fair," she went on. "You're still a very attractive man, even with those cuts on your face. Even broken and twisted and crawling at my feet. Still attractive, physically, but broken losers lack a certain *je ne sais quois*, wouldn't you agree?"

"Fuck you," Harlequin tried to say. What burbled out sounded like an infant choking. He didn't mean it anyway.

"Nope, can't understand you," Scylla said. "Did you think your little hearts-and-minds campaign would work? Did you think you could pull a bait and switch with the Latent people of this country? You have no credibility, Harlequin. Your government has proved, time and time again, that it can't be trusted. A couple of idiots rally to your banner. After we've broken this little counterattack, do you think they'll stick around? You'll rob them, just like you robbed me. I'm not just winning this thing, I'm actually promising something real once I do."

She crouched, squatting down on strong thighs that strained the edges of her leather pants. Harlequin felt a bit stronger, some of the breath returning to his lungs, the feeling to his limbs. He was certain his shoulder was broken, some of his ribs, too, but he would live.

Until Scylla decided she was done with him. He levered himself up onto his elbow, crying out in pain as he darted his hand toward his spare magazine. Scylla rolled her eyes and gestured. The empty pistol crumbled to broken, pitted metal in his hand, dusting the roof beneath him. "I'll let you keep the bullets," she said. "Maybe if you throw them hard enough . . ." She laughed.

Harlequin smiled back at her though he knew the expression looked pained. "You can still surrender," he managed. "I can put in a word with the president. Ask him to go easy on you."

Scylla laughed again, eyes widening. "Yes, well. I don't think there's much of a call for that just now."

She nodded to her companions, and the two Selfers grabbed Harlequin's arms, roughly dragging him to the roof's battered edge, the street below coming into view.

They dropped him on his face, letting him see over the edge. The rotted paths Scylla had cut into Harlequin's force were covered over once again with goblins, giants, and *Gahe*.

His own people were retreating back down Wall Street's length in poor order, firing over their shoulders as they went. The Selfers from Houston Street were nowhere to be seen. The Breach stood open and unsecured, huge as ever, enemy pouring forth.

"And now they go all the way back to your barricade line," Scylla said, "and into the city beyond. I get New York, Harlequin. I mean, I get it again. I ruled it when we first met, in the fashion of humans, and now I'll rule it again for Latentkind. And I will bring it what you never could: justice.

"You do realize the irony here, right? If you'd just let me go, I'd be in Uganda right now, or Bhutan, or Gwalior, helping people. Hell, we both would have. And we would have been happy." Her voice went wistful.

She shook her head, chasing the thought away. "You reap what you sow."

She leaned in close, the smile vanishing, her eyes blazing. "Do you want to ask me to let you go? We could do a little role-playing of the time you took me in. I'll be you, and you be me." She put a boot down on his fingertips, grinding them into the rooftop. "Do it," she said, "tell me you love me. Ask me to let you go. Beg me."

"I do love you . . ." Harlequin coughed, struggled to get his breath, ribs throbbing. He got up on his elbows, grunting with the effort, feeling the bones in his sides grind against one another. "Grace . . ."

"Don't call me that!"

"Grace. You have a real chance here."

He felt the cold intensify on the back of his neck, beginning to burn his skin. He leaned into it, vision clearing. That was the thing about cold, it was a clarifying pain. Scylla waved to something over Harlequin's shoulder, and he felt the pain lessen as the *Gahe* behind him drew back. The male Selfer stood a few feet behind Scylla, Suppressing him. The female now moved back to the roof's edge, watching the street in satisfaction.

She smiled again. "You're offering me a chance?"

"Remember Swift from the No-No Crew?"

"Not too bright, that one. Too much anger, not enough focus."

"He's here, along with a lot of other Selfers. They're fighting with us, against you. They're fighting for the same freedom you're promising, only in this case it's real. We're going to change the laws, Scylla. We're not fighting on opposite sides anymore, we're just pushing for the same thing from different angles."

"I saw your videos, Harlequin. I know all this. Do you honestly think I'd take part in your new order?"

"Hell, no. You invaded New York City. You've killed thousands of people. You'll never be welcome on this earth again.

"But that's not the point. You got what you wanted, Grace. You changed the conversation. You wanted an America where Latent people aren't second-class citizens anymore. You're getting that, and you can get it without further bloodshed. Once this is over, we're going into negotiations. All you have to do is leave."

Scylla snorted. "I can't believe I'm actually hearing this."

"What is it you told me all those years ago? You wanted to do some good. You've done it. Things can never go back to the way they were. You've made your point. We've learned."

He leaned forward, gritting his teeth against the rasping of his battered ribs. "I've learned." He looked into her eyes, trying to see past the twitching madness in the dark pupils, digging for the Grace he'd known.

"You haven't learned a damned thing," she said. "I'm not interested in turning the fate of magic over to some corrupt debating society that will go back on its word the moment guns are no longer at its back. You've already proved you can't be trusted."

She stood, hands on her hips, nodded to the Selfers beside her. They lifted Harlequin to his feet, dragged him forward. "Do you remember that ridiculous speech you gave me when we first met? About sheepdogs and sheep and wolves? God, that was the dumbest thing I'd ever heard. Stereotypes like that are how stupid people break the world up into chunks small enough for them to comprehend. So, let me use small words that even you are likely to understand. Wolves don't negotiate with sheep, Harlequin. We hunt them. We kill them. We rule them."

She turned to the male Selfer. "Throw him off. Let him learn what it feels like to fall."

Harlequin wrenched against the Selfers' grip, but the pain of his broken bones was too much, and he finally sagged limp in their arms as the street appeared beneath him, thronging with goblins who surged down Wall Street after his own retreating force, feet sliding in the slick, purplish smears that had once been people.

He hooked his boots against a chunk of concrete. The female tried to pull him free, then cursed, punching him in the back. He screamed, and they flipped him around, dragging him the rest of the way.

Scylla watched him, no longer smiling.

A rectangle slid open behind her, washing the roof in television static. Harlequin heard the *Gahe* hiss in confusion; the Selfers turned to face the new threat.

The gate pulsed and spat out monsters.

They'd been men once. Years of living out of view of the sun had first been a curse, then a point of pride. Where their skins weren't naturally powder white, they'd used Physiomancy to bleach them. Tattoos scrawled across their bare chests and thighs, riding on ridges raised by the same magic. Most were groupings of letters and numbers, codes that made no sense to Harlequin in his battered state. There were images, too: the head of a weeping Christ, crown of thorns ablaze.

SUR3NO$, above two crossed pistols.

The Physiomantic artistry chilled him. The Sculptor had specialized in retooling himself as a perfect imitation of another human. These Selfers used Physiomancy to cast their humanity aside. They raced out of the gate, their features a patchwork of images out of nightmare and legend. One woman's skin had been reworked into a snake-scale pattern, her eyes lengthened at the corners to resemble a stylized Egyptian deity. One of the men had sprouted horns, dorsal ridges marching evenly down his back. Some of them had fangs. Others, claws that could rival the *Gahe*. All were the product of expert Physiomancy, the changes permanent, their flesh molded to make them something new.

Their currents hit Harlequin like a tide. Not all of them were Latent, but many were, and those were strong. The non-Latent carried carbines: tricked-out military-grade hardware probably smuggled across the US border. The unarmed howled battle cries, flashing gang signs, forearms and fists together, thumbs out in a crude facsimile of devil's horns.

Scylla's bodyguards dropped Harlequin, his back banging agonizingly against the rooftop, shoulders and head dangling off into empty space. He scrabbled with his hands, enough feeling returning to report the pain of his skinned palms and fingertips, and dragged himself back onto the roof. Scylla whirled, hesitated. The Houston Street Selfers, she knew. The *Limpiados* were something else entirely.

One of the *Limpiados*, a tall man with taller horns, unrolled a forked tongue that hung halfway down his chest. He extended a bleached hand and pointed at the female Selfer standing above Harlequin. The woman shrieked as her arm detached from her body, trailing muscle and sinew, and flew across to grip the male by the throat, flinging him off the roof. What should have been screams were only choked gurgles as he met the fate he'd intended for Harlequin.

The *Gahe* shot forward, shrugging off the bullets the *Limpiados* pumped into it. It snatched one of them up, sinking its teeth into his shoulder before he clapped a hand to its side engulfed in flame, sending up a familiar plume of freezing black smoke. The *Gahe* fell back, its companions retreating with it as another *Limpiado* unleashed a cone of sizzling electricity after them.

Harlequin felt his magic flood black into him. He summoned a wind, which gently lifted him upright, buoying his broken ribs and steadying his damaged shoulder. The pain was enormous but bearable. He teetered for a moment on the roof's edge before he called on the wind to blow him a step forward, long enough to see another gate flash open on the street below, soldiers moving out, renewing their attack on the Breach.

Scylla's face compressed into an animal snarl. Harlequin could feel her tide rushing out, ripping into the ranks of the *Limpiados* on the roof. A few of them had already collapsed into pools of stinking sludge, many more had fallen to their knees, clutching their stomachs as they succumbed to rot. But a few rose under the torrent, gritting their teeth. The long-tongued Selfer stood behind them, Physiomancy repairing their bodies as fast as Scylla's sought to break them down.

Harlequin felt his arms prickle and burn as they were spat-

tered with freezing droplets and turned to see the remaining
Gahe falling back off the roof, magical lightning engulfing
them from above as Swift returned to the fight.

Harlequin settled himself on his feet and let the magical
wind go. His body protested the weight, but he managed to
hold himself upright. Scylla caught him out of the corner of
her eye and turned, abandoning the *Limpiados* to focus her
magic on him.

Harlequin caught her eyes and her magical current, held
both. Scylla was strong. He could feel the rage in her magical
tide, his teeth grinding together as he sought to contain it.
There was no trace of the woman who'd called him a Boy
Scout, smiling sardonically as she pinched his ass while they
walked in Central Park. These eyes were hard, remorseless.
They no longer wanted to do good.

The eyes of a wolf.

Harlequin remembered lying at Swift's feet, his eyes cross-
ing as he stared down the barrel of the pistol in the Aeromancer's hand. *Do you like me now? I'm a fucking product of your
goddamned system.*

As was Scylla. As was this whole conflict. The chickens of
a failed policy coming home to roost.

"I'm sorry, Grace," Harlequin whispered through his clenched
teeth, knowing she couldn't hear him. "This is my fault."

But that didn't change what she'd done. What he had to do.

Since he'd saved the FOB, he'd been drummed out of the
only institution he'd ever called home, come up against the ire
of the Hewitts of the world. It had drained him, a fight within
a fight, counterpunched by the relentless pace of the events
unfolding in New York. Exhaustion flooded him. He had nothing left. He'd poured too much of himself into this struggle;
he'd fought too hard and too long.

Too hard and too long to lose.

Harlequin screamed as he punched his current through
Scylla's, wrapped the tendrils of his own magic around hers,
and interdicted it. Her jaw went slack as she felt the Suppression take hold.

The roof went silent as Scylla backed away, the *Limpiados*
crowding forward. Swift landed in front of them and waved
them back as Harlequin advanced on her.

His lips felt numb, his mouth too tired to form words, but he dug deep again and found a way. "Grace Lyons. Get on your knees and put your hands behind your head. I place you in military custody for unlawful magic use and practices proscribed under section 8.A.2."

The hard eyes shot left and right. She was still a wolf, but a panicked one. Her hips and thighs tensed, poised to break and run, but there was nowhere to go. Below her, crackling gunshots were followed by sizzling pops as Harlequin's troops used Bookbinder's magical ammunition to push the enemy back into the Breach.

Regs said to bring her in alive. *Fuck regs*. Regs created this mess in the first place.

But there was still justice.

And something more, the wrenching in his gut that reminded him that, despite all she'd done, he loved this woman, couldn't bear to see her die. Even now, even after everything.

A low growl started in her throat, rising to her jaw to erupt into a bass scream. Her eyes narrowed to slits, cords standing out on her neck, her fingers hooked. Harlequin's eyes widened as he saw tears stream down her face. The scream gradually shifted to sobs, then to words.

"Why, damn it? Fucking why? Why would you help them? They're the fucking sheep! You hated them, and you were right to! They're beneath you."

"You're wrong," Harlequin said. "I was wrong. They are me, and I'm them.

"That's the thing you never understood. You think a couple of differences, even big differences, makes us another species?"

He swept his hand in a wide arc, taking in the *Limpiados* and Swift on the roof, the soldiers and police officers below. Selfer and soldier, Latent and non-Latent, surging around her, fighting to get the Breach secured. "So, we're different. That's what it means to be human. A couple of folks, even a lot of folks, hurting you doesn't change that. It doesn't make them sheep. It never did."

He took a step toward her, ignoring the burning in his fingers as they followed the familiar course, pulling out a pair of zip cuffs, the kind he'd never ceased to carry in his cargo pocket. "Get on your knees. Hands behind your head."

Helo rotors beat the sky above, and he heard ropes slap the roof behind him, followed by the whirring of reinforced leather palms against braided nylon as soldiers fast-roped down. Scylla crouched farther away, eyes flicking back and forth, desperately seeking a way out.

She looked back to Harlequin, her composure returning. The corner of her mouth quirked, and she stood, looking as if her capture had been part of the plan all along.

"You'll reap what you sow," she said. "They won't negotiate, and they won't amend anything. They'll bicker and lie and put their boots right back on your neck. The only way to ever get them to treat you fairly is to crush them. Nothing you've done here changes that. You may move from the fields to the house, but you're still a slave."

Harlequin looked over the fighting in the street below, saw one of the Fornax Coven Novices standing alongside a Selfer in a billowing red dress, pouring their flames together to ignite a crescent of ground around one corner of the Breach, the *Gahe* drawing back inside the portal as the flames rose.

I'm sorry, he thought. *Oh, Grace. I'm so sorry.* But, "We'll see," was what he said. "We'll both see. The difference is that I'll be at the negotiating table, and you'll be locked up and awaiting judgment."

Scylla laughed aloud at that, tossing her head. Her careless look was belied by the surge in her current, struggling to break through the Suppression. Struggling and failing. "Silly boy," she said, "nobody can judge me."

And then she threw up her hands, pushed off with her heels, arced her back as gracefully as a diver, and leapt backward off the roof.

Harlequin cursed and raced forward, dropping the Suppression to get himself airborne, following her passage. But he was injured, slow. The wet slap of her body against the pavement below had sounded before he'd cleared the edge, offering him enough of a glance to make him turn away in horror.

Currents swirled around him, coming from Swift, the Selfers, and the Sorcerers fighting on the street below. But he knew Scylla's, had come over the years to be able to recognize it like the smell of his father's pipe smoke.

It was gone.

A gate flashed open beside him, bringing Britton, Book-binder, and Downer onto the roof. They came up short at the stunned looks of the assembled people there. Looked around, back to Harlequin.

"What happened?" Bookbinder asked.

"Where is she?" Britton added.

"She's gone," Harlequin said, trying to keep the sadness from his voice. "It's over."

"No." Swift didn't sound sad at all. "It's just getting started."

EPILOGUE
HORSE TRADING

Sudden, explosive change never sticks around. It's the slow, thematic shifts that last.

—Professor Barabara Quinn
Political Science Department, New York University

Oscar Britton looked ridiculous in a suit.

Uncomfortable for starters. The shirt collar was too tight, his bull neck spilling over the sides, muscle looking more like fat. With his bald head and lantern jaw, Britton looked like some kind of mob enforcer hauled in for a criminal trial. It didn't help that his tie was skewed off to one side, and he kept making it worse by tugging at the collar, trying to get himself some much-needed air.

Harlequin had never imagined the man could ever look so . . . official. *We've come a long way, friend. Haven't we?*

The breakout room in the basement of the US Capitol was well guarded, both inside and out. Armed police lined the curving walls of the chamber in their dress uniforms, but the tailored jackets didn't hide the bulky body armor beneath. The shining, patent-leather holsters held guns with operational loads, unsnapped and ready to go.

Not that it would help if it came to a fight. Half the people in the room were Latent.

The delegations had broken out informally, sitting together out of interest, familiarity, and common goals around the circular table. Harlequin sat beside Bookbinder, both in their class-A uniforms. Sarah Downer sat beside them in a cream-colored suit. She wore simple pearl studs that matched her necklace, combining with her serious expression to make her look a lot older than she was.

Britton sat beside Therese. She wore a suit as well but looked much more natural in it than Downer. Swift and Guinevere, the two promised delegates from the Houston Street Gang, sat with them. Their suits were hipper but still respectful of the official proceedings.

A small group of staffers surrounded the Mexican ambassador, Arturo Suchicital, whose cologne was so thick that Harlequin could smell it from across the wide table. Beside Suchicital sat another man, head shaved, faint scars on his scalp and ears where Physiomancy had leveled protrusions and closed up holes. His suit matched the ambassador's, but he'd deliberately kept a small tattoo of some numbered code below his left eye, a reminder to the assembled that while he was officially part of the Mexican delegation, he spoke for the *Limpiados* and their masters in the Zeta cartel. Harlequin could feel his current, strong and controlled, and wondered what school he was. Bookbinder would know.

Beside Harlequin and Bookbinder sat Senator William Bainbridge. He was a clone of Walsh and Porter both: fit, older, perfectly coiffed and upright, a look of benevolent gravity etched on his face. A small plaque had been placed in front of him, the only one on the table. CHAIR, it read. MCGAUER-LINDEN ACT WORKING GROUP.

Bainbridge, Harlequin noted, was not Latent. Nor were any of his staff, a small army of lawyers, policy wonks, and analysts who took up the rest of the chamber, dwarfing the other delegations by a factor of ten.

Behind him, flat-screen monitors reeled off the video feeds from dozens of cameras stationed around the room, playing back to a global audience glued to their screens as the future of magical legislation in America was hammered out on live television.

Bainbridge wanted the session closed, but Britton insisted it be televised live and threatened to go directly to the public if that wish wasn't granted. Bainbridge acted reluctant, but in the end had acquiesced. *That's because he knows it plays to his advantage,* Harlequin thought. *We may have beaten back*

Scylla, but that doesn't mean that people are any less terrified of us.

One of the screens behind Bainbridge showed the ongoing rehabilitation of Lower Manhattan, and another showed the fighting in Mescalero, where the tide had begun to turn once the *Limpiados* had turned their attention to the battlefield closer to their border, along with a growing body of Selfers assured that this particular meeting was, finally, really going to happen.

In New York, at least, the smoke had cleared, the battle over. The Breach was still open, surrounded by so much dug-in firepower that it could be turned into a burning cauldron at a moment's notice.

And the Selfers were still there. In public, for all to see.

Harlequin could feel the tension in the room and imagined it magnified tenfold outside it. The people of the United States could be no more comfortable if some strange army had come to encamp in their collective backyard. What would they do next?

That depended largely on the outcome of these proceedings.

Harlequin looked to Bookbinder and smiled, then across at Britton. The big man nodded back at him, smiling thinly. Their countrymen crowded around them, terrified, wielding authority they couldn't be sure of, facing a power they didn't understand, couldn't control. The lawyers and policy makers, the senior military officers, all looked grave and attentive, bringing the power of the state to bear before the unblinking eye of the television cameras.

But Harlequin pierced that veil now. He saw the fear beneath. *You're not going to hurt us, are you?* was the message written on each face. This must have been how Scylla saw the world.

But just because he could understand her perspective didn't mean he shared it. He wasn't going to hurt them. Because he was part of them. That was the thing about war, wasn't it? In the end, someone has to be willing to overlook past wrongs, inequalities. In the end, war had to serve peace, to drive forward toward an end state that worked better for everyone.

Otherwise, what were they fighting for?

Britton didn't trust Bainbridge and his lackeys. Harlequin didn't either, frankly.

But that didn't mean that they couldn't bring about the new order that Scylla had so violently sought.

Harlequin straightened as Bainbridge brought his gavel down and the proceedings began. A room of men and women, Latent and non-Latent, soldier and civilian. Harlequin could feel the fear and tension, could see the agendas boiling below the surface.

But the conversation had started. The issue was on the table, that Latent people were still people. That genie couldn't be put back in the bottle, no matter what happened.

He turned to listen as Bainbridge read the invocation, and he felt something stir in him that he hadn't realized had been absent across these long days since he'd arrived in New York City.

Hope.

APPENDIX

MAGIC IN THE SHADOW OPS UNIVERSE

The Great Reawakening brought magic back into the world, granting people extraordinary powers. Unfortunately, it didn't also grant an instruction manual, and most of those who "came up Latent" with magical abilities were unable to control them. This culminated in the Bloch Incident, where uncontrolled magic use resulted in the destruction of the Lincoln Memorial and the deaths of thirty-four people. In an effort to prevent future catastrophes, the McGauer-Linden Act created the Reawakening Commission of the US Congress, which designated five "authorized" schools of magic and five "prohibited" schools, otherwise known as "Probe" schools. Certain practices within authorized schools were also prohibited.

AUTHORIZED (LEGAL) SCHOOLS

PYROMANCY

Commonly called "Fire Magic," Pyromancy allows the Sorcerer to manipulate flame. Pyromancers can boost and direct existing fires, even start them with a glance. Pyromancers can cast fireballs or cause firestorms. They are primarily employed as fire support for assaults but also assist with clearing vegetation or sanitizing contaminated areas.

> *People talk about the cleansing properties of fire, like it's something you'd use to clean your shower. That's bullshit. Fire's not a cleanser. Fire is an answer. The question is, who is going to triumph in this struggle? How will this all turn out?*

> —Lieutenant "Ash Trail" (call sign), SOC Liaison Officer (LNO)/
> Pyromantic Assault Team Leader, 1st Armored Division

HYDROMANCY

Commonly called "Water Magic," Hydromancy allows the Sorcerer to manipulate water. Hydromancers can raise or lower water levels, divert the course of existing waterways, and cause moisture in the air to condense into rain. Hydromancers can create and dissolve ice, and employ "desiccative" Hydromancy, which drains a target of water, fatally if necessary. Hydromancers are frequently employed in logistical support roles due to their ability to provide abundant clean water. They also serve as breachers in assault teams due to their ability to freeze and shatter doors and walls. Hydromancers clear swamps, assist troops with fording rivers, and frequently work with Aeromancers to control weather in support of maritime maneuvers.

> *Remember how everyone used to make fun of Aquaman? The superhero with the lamest power. Well, you just met the real-life Aquaman. You're not fucking laughing now, are you?*
>
> —Major "Storm Surge" (call sign), Executive Officer (XO)
> SOC "Breach and Clear" Program—Tactical Procedures School

TERRAMANCY

Commonly called "Earth Magic," Terramancy permits the manipulation of earth and associated flora. Terramancers are sometimes referred to as "Druids." Terramancers can raise roads out of swamps, create buildings out of mountains, and spur plant growth to feed an army. While Terramancy permits the Sorcerer to communicate with fauna, the practice is strictly prohibited. Terramancers are commonly employed as military engineers, assisting with the movement, feeding, and housing of troops. Combat Terramancers frequently use suddenly shifting landscapes to destroy armored columns or to turn vegetation against enemy troops using it for cover.

> *Gran had a favorite apple tree in the backyard. It was old when I was a kid, and dead by the time I was six. She saved a couple of dried-out seeds as a memento. Called them "heirlooms." I kept them in a cigar box until I came up Latent, then I took 'em on my first tour. Good thing, too. We were cut off for two weeks, hiding out before they could extract us. I opened up the ground and built us a nice hidey-hole down there, and we lived mostly off Gran's heirloom apples until the QRF got us out. The guys said I saved us. But it was Gran, wasn't it, really?*

> —Lieutenant "Harvest" (call sign), SOC Liaison Officer (LNO)
> 10th Special Forces Group, US Army

AEROMANCY

Commonly called "Air Magic," Aeromancy allows the Sorcerer to manipulate air. Aeromancers can heat or cool air and cause it to retain or discharge moisture or to gust at terrific speeds. Aeromancers can also agitate particles of air to release electrical charges. Aeromancers can fly, though they are actually manipulating air currents to lift their bodies. They are frequently employed as forward observers and in reconnaissance roles, as well as for close air support. Aeromancers often work in conjuction with Hydromancers in weather-control operations.

> *The irony is that everyone thought the future of aviation was drones. Unmanned aerial vehicles. But magic turned that on its head. You got the opposite. I'm an unvehicled aerial man.*

> —Captain "Sparrow" (call sign), SOC Liaison Officer (LNO)
> 1st Special Operations Wing

PHYSIOMANCY

Physiomancers are commonly known as "Healers," and Physiomancy is sometimes called "Body Magic." Physiomancers are able to manipulate living flesh. Under the McGauer-Linden Act, Physiomancy may only be applied to heal living things. All other uses, including wounding or deliberate alterations of the body for practical or cosmetic purposes, are strictly prohibited. Physiomancers are employed exclusively in a medical capacity.

I know it hurts. I have to get the bullet out. I can only do that by getting your body to push it up through your thigh. I have to knit the flesh and close the blood vessels as we go, make sure you don't bleed out. That takes pretty much all of my concentration. I can't worry about the nerves at the same time. They're everywhere and they're complicated as hell. You're just going to have to suck it up. Look at me. Look at me, damn it! You're going to live. Now just bite on this and hold the fuck on.

—Captain "Second Chance" (call sign), SOC Liaison Officer (LNO)
Tactical EMS Support Detachment Alpha
1st Marine Expeditionary Unit

PROHIBITED, A.K.A. "PROBE," SCHOOLS AND PRACTICES

NECROMANCY

Necromancy permits the manipulation of dead flesh. Most Necromancers use this power to reanimate corpses. The results of this work are commonly known as "zombies" and function as magical automatons, able to perform simple tasks (such as moving and attacking) at the direction of the Sorcerer. Because zombies are structurally coherent on their own, Necromancers can focus their magic entirely on command and control functions, permitting a single Necromancer to command a vast army of the risen dead.

> *Hello, Carlos. You remember my wife, Maria, don't you? You should, you killed her. That's made us both rather upset. But, since she's the dead one, I figured I'd let her do the honors of ripping your head off. After twenty years of marriage, I've learned to let her have her way.*
>
> —Witness transcript following the decapitation of drug kingpin Carlos Mendoza Brooklyn South Task Force, NYPD

NEGRAMANCY

Negramancy is commonly known as "Black Magic," or "Witch-craft," and its practitioners are frequently referred to as "Witches" or "Warlocks." This rather dramatic nomenclature covers the simple manipulation of decay. Negramancers employ their magic to vastly accelerate the process of decomposition, causing complex structures, such as a building, an airplane, or even a human body, to break down to their component elements nearly instantly.

> *Feeling sick? Me, too. The difference is, I'll feel better once I don't have to look at your ugly face anymore.*
>
> —Supposed statement of the Warlock known as "Ghoulish"
> prior to his murder of the Bulgarian ambassador

PORTAMANCY

Portamancy, also known as "Gate Magic," is the rarest of all magical schools, with fewer than five Portamancers documented since the Great Reawakening, though more have been rumored. Portamancers are able to manipulate the fabric between dimensions, opening portals between them and permitting transit. Gate Magic can be employed to "summon" living creatures from either side to the Portamancer's defense. The gates themselves have micron-thin edges able to cut through any material instantly.

> *Israel does not now possess nor have we ever possessed weaponized fissile material or fully assembled nuclear weapons of any kind. The accusations that we are hiding such devices in some alternate magical dimension is the stuff of fairy stories and shows that the Iranian delegation is not serious regarding these negotiations.*
>
> —Gili Chayad
> Israeli ambassador to the United Nations

SENTIENT ELEMENTAL CONJURATION

Sometimes known as "Elementalists," Sorcerers in this school of magic can manipulate various forms of energy to create sentient (self-aware) elementals. Elementals serve the Sorcerer's interests but do not require direct control, as zombies do. Elementals must be conjured from kinetically active sources, such as burning fire, sparking electricity, or blowing wind.

You want to kill me? Get it over with. I know what I did, and I'm not sorry. Would you blame a mother for killing to protect her children? Because that's what they are. I brought them into this world, and I love them with a ferocity that only creators can have for their created.

—Alison Berger
Statement during the sentencing phase of a closed hearing

OFFENSIVE PHYSIOMANCY
(PROHIBITED PRACTICE)

Physiomancers may defy the law and turn their magic to the
wounding or killing of living things. Such magic is commonly
called "Rending" and its practitioners "Renders." Rending
reverses the Physiomantic application, severing blood vessels
and muscle, changing bones into blades that turn against the
flesh they once supported. A Rending death is inevitably painful and bloody. The public outcry against this practice is
understandable.

> *The only thing he said to me was: "Your bullet is fine, but my
> magic's a crime? Dead is dead, you fucking hypocrite." That's
> all he said, I swear.*
>
> —Sworn statement from captured US Marine
> after rescue from the Houston Street Selfer Gang

WHISPERING (PROHIBITED PRACTICE)

While manipulation of plant life is authorized, Terramancers are forbidden to use their magic to communicate with and command fauna. Those who do so are treated as Selfers, though rumors abound of secret pardons and leniency, owing mostly to the incredible utility of Whispered wildlife as scouts, intelligence sources, and even food in desperate times.

Yes, sir, that wolf is wearing your skivvies. No, sir, I have no idea how he got them on.

—Old SOC joke "General Adams's Druid"

GLOSSARY OF MILITARY TERMS, ACRONYMS, AND SLANG

This novel deals largely with the United States military. As anyone familiar with the military knows, it has a vocabulary of acronyms, slang, and equipment references large enough to constitute its own language. Some readers may be familiar with it. For those who are not, I provide the following glossary, expanded from the version that appeared in *Shadow Ops: Fortress Frontier*. As some of the action in *Shadow Ops: Breach Zone* takes place on board a ship, I have included some basic nautical terminology as well. Many of these terms are fictional. Many are not.

11B—11 Bravo. The Military Operational Specialty code for the infantry.

225—Colloquial term for a 225-foot-long Seagoing Buoy Tender of the United States Coast Guard.

A-10 WARTHOG—A heavily armed fixed-wing, ground-attack aircraft.

ABRAMS—A Main Battle Tank.

ANG—Air National Guard.

AOR—Area of Responsibility.

APACHE—An attack helicopter, also known as a helicopter gunship.

APB—All Points Bulletin. A broadcast alerting law-enforcement personnel to be on the lookout for a particular individual.

APC—Armored Personnel Carrier.

ARTICLE 15—The article in the US Code of Military Justice that provides for administrative/nonjudicial punishment of troops.

ASEAN—The Association of Southeast Asian Nations. A geopolitical/economic organization of Southeast Asian countries.

ATTD—Asset Tracking/Termination Device. A beacon/bomb that can be placed inside a person to track their movements and, if necessary, to kill them.

AWOL—Absent Without Leave.

BEAM—The width of a vessel at its widest point. Colloquially used to indicate the side of a ship.

BINDING—The act of utilizing Drawn magic in the making of a spell.

BINGO-FUEL—A term indicating that an aircraft has insufficient fuel reserves to accomplish its mission.

BLACKHAWK—A utility/transport helicopter.

BMER—Bound Magical Energy Repository. Also known as a "boomer," a BMER is any object, inanimate or otherwise, into which magic is bound. BMERs normally dispense the effects of the magic bound into them.

BOATSWAIN—An officer or petty officer in charge of a ship's maintenance, deck force, topside gear, ship's movement, and other ship's operations that are not under the jurisdiction of engineering, operations or weapons officers, or petty officers.

BREVET—A field promotion, granted as an honor before retirement or under extreme circumstances when required senior personnel have been killed in action.

BRIDGE—The part of a ship from which it is controlled.

BUOY TENDER—A type of vessel used to maintain and replace navigational buoys.

BUTTER-BAR—A second lieutenant in land- or air-based service, or an ensign in maritime service. The lowest commissioned officer rank in the United States military.

CAC—Common Access Card. A government identification card used across all five branches of the US military.

CARBINE—A shortened, lighter version of the traditional assault rifle used by infantry. It is better suited for tight spaces common in urban operations.

CHINOOK—A large, double-rotor transport/cargo helicopter. Larger than a Blackhawk.

CO—Commanding Officer.

COMMS—Communications.

COMMS-DARK—A situation in which communications are either forbidden or impossible.

CORPSMAN—A medic in the US Navy.

COVEN—Replaces a squad for organizational purposes when magic-using soldiers are concerned. A conventional squad contains four to ten soldiers led by a staff sergeant. A Coven contains four to five SOC Sorcerers, led by a captain. Training Covens are led by a warrant officer.

CSH—Combat Support Hospital. Pronounced "cash." A field hospital, successor to the MASH units of TV fame.

CUTTER—Any ship sixty-five feet in length or longer in the service of the United States Coast Guard.

DANGER CLOSE—Indirect Fire impacting within two hundred meters of the intended target.

DFAC—Dining Facility.

DFP—Defensive Fighting Position.

DRAWING—The act of summoning raw magic in preparation for Binding it into a spell.

DRUID—Selfer slang for a Terramancer.

ELEMENTALIST—A person practicing the prohibited school of Sentient Elemental Conjuration. This is the act of imbuing Elementals with self-awareness. This is different from automatons—Elementals with no thought, who are entirely dependent on the sorcerer for command and control.

FEMA—Federal Emergency Management Agency.

FLAG GRADE/FLAG OFFICER—Generals in the land and air services, and admirals in the maritime services.

FOB—Forward Operating Base.

FORCE RECON—The US Marine Corps special operations component. While primarily focused on deep reconnaissance, it has direct-action platoons. These platoons form the basis for the US Marine Corps Special Operations Command or MARSOC.

FULL BIRD—A full colonel in the land and air services, or captain in the maritime services (O-6). The term refers to the silver eagles worn as a symbol of the rank, and distinguishes the wearer from a lieutenant colonel (or "light colonel" O-5), who is designated by a silver oak leaf.

GANGWAY—A ramp between a ship and land to let people get off or on the ship.

GIMAC—Gate-Integrated Modern Army Combatives—MAC integrated with Portamancy. Also known as "gate-fu." See MAC definition below.

GIS—Geographic Information System.

GO DYNAMIC—Command given to assault a target without regard to stealth.

GO NOVA—When a magic user is overwhelmed by the current of their own magical power. This results in a painful death similar to burning. A person who has "gone nova" is sometimes referred to as a "magic sink."

HEALER—A Physiomancer. They are sometimes also referred to as "Manglers" or "Renders" in deference to their ability to damage flesh as well as repair it. Offensive Physiomancy is prohibited under the Geneva Convention's magical amendment. Offensive use of Physiomancy is also known as "Rending."

HELM—A ship's steering mechanism.

HELO—Helicopter.

HOOCH—Living quarters. Can also be used as a verb. "You'll hooch here."

HOT—Under fire. Usually refers to an arrival under fire. A "hot LZ" would be landing an aircraft under fire. Also refers to a state of military readiness where personnel are prepared for immediate action.

INDIG—Indigenous.

INDIRECT FIRE—Sometimes shortened to simply "Indirect." An attack, either magical or conventional, aimed without relying on direct line of sight to the target. This usually refers to artillery, rocket, or mortar fire, but also Pyromantic flame strikes and Aeromantic lightning attacks.

JAG—Judge Advocate General. The legal branch of any of the United States armed services.

JO—Junior Officer. Also known as a Company Grade Officer.

KIA—Killed in Action.

KIOWA—A light reconnaissance helicopter.

KLICK—A kilometer or kilometers per hour.

LATENT—Any individual who possesses magical ability, detected or otherwise.

LATENT GRENADE—An auto-suppressed or "Stifled" Latency. A person who possesses magical ability, is not a Rump Latent, but for reasons unknown, will not Manifest their powers.

LE—Law Enforcement.

LIMBIC DAMPENER—A drug that suppresses limbic function, enabling recipients to better cope with emotions. Incredibly expensive and strictly controlled, it is used primarily by the SOC as a means to grant greater control over the use of magic conducted by the human limbic system.

LITTLE BIRD—A small helicopter usually used to insert/extract commandos.

LOGS—Logistics.

LSA—Logistical Staging Area.

LZ—Landing Zone.

MAC—Modern Army Combatives. A martial art unique to the United States Army, based on Brazilian Jujitsu.

MANIFEST—The act of realizing one's Latency and displaying magical ability. Latent people Manifest at various times in their lives—some at birth, some on their deathbed, and at all times in between. Nobody knows why it occurs when it does.

MARK 19—A crew-served, fully automatic grenade launcher.

ME1—Maritime Enforcement Specialist 1st Class.

MGRS—Military Grid Reference System.

MINIGUN—A crew-served multibarrel machine gun with a high rate of fire, employing Gatling-style rotating barrels and an external power source.

MOST RIKI-TIK—To do something very quickly.

MP—Military Police.

MRE—Meal Ready to Eat. A self-contained field ration for use where food facilities are not available.

MWR—Morale, Welfare, and Recreation center.

NCO—Noncommissioned Officer.

NIH—National Institutes of Health. Among many other services, NIH runs a Monitoring/Suppression program for those Latents who refuse to join the military but don't want to become Selfers. Participants are monitored continuously and have virtually no privacy. Most are treated as social pariahs.

NODS—Night Observation Devices.

NONCOM—A Noncommissioned Officer; sergeants in the air and land services and petty officers in the maritime services.

NON RATE—Enlisted personnel in maritime services below the rank of E-4 (E-3s are sometimes rated). A non rate achieves a rate when he/she has graduated from "A-School" and can demonstrate certifiable skill in a particular field. At that point, the non rate becomes a petty officer.

NORMALS—Selfer slang for those who are not Latent. The term is respectful. The term "human" is sometimes substituted in derogatory fashion.

NOVICE—SOC Sorcerers still in training, before they graduate SAOLCC.

OC—Officers' Club.

OC—Oleoresin Capsicum, also known as "Pepper Spray." A nonlethal agent used primarily in policing, riot control, and personal defense.

O&I—Operations and Intelligence. This usually refers to a meeting/briefing held once or more times daily to update commanders on past actions and prepare them for the day's work.

ON MY SIX—Directly behind the speaker.

OPSEC—Operations Security.

OUTSIDE THE WIRE—Area beyond the secure perimeter of a military facility.

PFC—Private First Class. A junior enlisted rank. E-3 in the United States Army and E-2 in the United States Marine Corps.

PFD—Personal Flotation Device, also known as a Life Jacket.

POAC—Pentagon Officers Athletic Club.

PROBES—Short for "prohibited." Those Latents who Manifest in a school of prohibited magic such as Negramancy, Portamancy, Necromancy, or Sentient Elemental Conjuration.

PX—Post Exchange. A store selling a variety of goods located on a military facility.

QRF—Quick Reaction Force.

R&R—Rest and Relaxation.

READING—Slang for the military practice of using Rump Latents to "read" the currents of other Latent individuals in an effort to discover their magic-using status.

RENDING—Offensive use of Physiomantic magic. See Healer definition above.

ROE—Rules of Engagement. The conditions under which members of the military and law-enforcement communities are permitted to employ deadly force.

RTB—Return to Base.

RTO—Radio Telephone Operator. A military member who specializes in the use and maintenance of radio equipment.

RUMP LATENT—A person who Manifests magical ability that is too slight to be of any real use. Such a person can only use magic to a very slight degree but can feel the magical tide in another person. Rump Latents are not commissioned as full SOC officers but make up a small percentage of the enlisted and warrant-officer support in the corps.

SAOLCC—Sorcerer's Apprentice/Officer Leadership Combined Course. Basic training for SOC Sorcerers. This rigorous training regimen teaches Latent soldiers the basics of magic use/control while simultaneously preparing them for their duties as officers in the US Army.

SAR—Search and Rescue.

SASS—Suitability Assessment Section.

SAW—Squad Automatic Weapon. A light machine gun, capable of being carried and used as a rifle but heavier and with a greater magazine capacity. It is frequently equipped with a bipod enabling it to be used in a fixed position as a crew-served, belt-fed support weapon.

SCHOOL—A particular kind of magic, usually associated with a mutable element (earth, air, fire, water, flesh, etc.). Latent individuals only Manifest in one school.

SCO—Shanghai Cooperative Organization. A mutual security organization consisting of several Asian and Eastern European nations.

SEABEE—Colloquial pronunciation of "CB"—construction battalions of the United States Navy.

SELFERS—Latent individuals who elect to flee authority and use their magical abilities unsupervised. Selfers are usually tracked down and killed.

SF/SOF—Special Forces/Special Operations Forces.

SINCGARS—Single Channel Ground and Airborne Radio System. A networked radio system that handles secure voice and data communications.

SITREP—Situation Report.

SK3—Storekeeper third class.

SOC—Supernatural Operations Corps. Not to be confused with Special Operations Command (or SOCOM, under whose auspices the Supernatural Operations Corps falls). The SOC is the corps of the US Army responsible for all magical use. The SOC is a joint corps, which means it handles magic use for all US armed services to include the Air Force, Navy, and Coast Guard (though the Army is the executive agent). The Marine Corps does not participate in the SOC and runs its own Suppression Lances.

SOP—Standard Operating Procedure.

SORCERER—A SOC magical operator—an officer of the SOC who employs magic as his primary military specialty.

STANDOFF ARMOR—A type of vehicle armor designed to protect against rocket-propelled-grenade (RPG) attacks.

START—Strategic Arms Reduction Treaty.

STRYKER—An armored combat land vehicle.

SUPERSTRUCTURE—The part of a ship above the main deck.

SUPPRESSION—The act of using one's own magical current to block that of another. This is typically a one-to-one ratio. The strength of a Suppressor's Latency must exceed that of the individual he is seeking to Suppress.

SUPPRESSION LANCE—A US Marine Corps unit that employs a Suppressing officer to block the magical abilities of the riflemen in the unit.

TAR BABY—SOC Slang for elemental automatons. See Elementalist definition above.

TOC—Tactical Operations Center.

T-WALL—A modular, portable section of rebar-reinforced concrete barricade. Shaped like an upside-down T. Usually six feet wide and twelve feet tall.

UCMJ—Uniform Code of Military Justice.

USTRANSCOM—United States Transportation Command is one of ten unified commands of the United States Department of Defense. The mission of USTRANSCOM is to provide air, land, and sea transportation for the Department of Defense, both in time of peace and time of war.

VTC—Video Teleconference.

WHISPERING—Terramantic magic used to control the actions of animals. This is prohibited by the US Code. SOC Terramancers are not permitted to Whisper.

WIA—Wounded in Action.

WITCH—Selfer slang for a Negramancer. Male Negramancers are sometimes called Warlocks.

XO—Executive Officer.